MICHAEL WILLS was born on th
the Priory Boys School and Cari
a teacher at St Peter's College, Salt
at a secondary school in Kent for

After re-training to become
Language he worked in Sweden foi .... years. During this period
he wrote several English language teaching books. His teaching
career has included time working in rural Sweden, a sojourn that
first sparked his now enduring interest in Scandinavian history and
culture – an interest that after many years of research, both academic
and in the field, led him to write *Finn's Fate* and the sequel novel,
Three Kings – One Throne.

His boyhood interest in Georgian military history was re-
kindled by a visit to The Rifles Berkshire and Wiltshire Museum in
Salisbury, and subsequently developed by time spent doing research
in Quebec and New York State.

Today, Michael works part-time as Ombudsman for English
UK, the national association of English language providers. Though
a lot of his spare time is spent with grandchildren, he also has a wide
range of interests including researching for future books, writing,
playing the guitar, carpentry and electronics. He spends at least two
months a year sailing his boat which is currently in Scandinavia.

You can find out more and stay up-to-date by visiting his
website: www.michaelwills.eu

THE
WESSEX
TURNCOAT

MICHAEL E WILLS

SilverWood

Published in 2014 by the author
using SilverWood Books Empowered Publishing ®
2019 edition independently published

SilverWood Books Ltd
www.silverwoodbooks.co.uk

ISBN 9781081152284 (KDP paperback)

British Library Cataloguing in Publication Data
A CIP catalogue record for this book is available from the British Library

Printed on responsibly sourced paper

Acknowledgements

I have never served in the armed forces, so to write a book with significant military content, and that in the 18th Century, was a challenge. I started my learning journey at The Rifles Berkshire and Wiltshire Museum in Salisbury and I am very grateful to the Archivist, Chris Bacon, for introducing me to the story of the 62nd Regiment of Foot. I owe a great debt of gratitude to Allan Jones, re-enactor of the 23rd Regiment, Royal Welch Fusiliers (UK), for guiding me in matters relating to military life in the 18th Century. Allan has an encyclopaedic knowledge of the British Army of the period, which he willingly shared with me.

It was a surprise to me to see the extent to which the British Regiments, which fought in the American War of Independence, are re-enacted today in the USA. I was extremely fortunate to have Eric Schnitzer as my guide when studying the part played in this war by the 62nd Regiment. Not only is Eric an enthusiastic re-enactor of the 62nd Regiment, but he is also the Historian at Saratoga National Historical Park, where I was fortunate to see an impressive re-enactment of the Battle of Freeman's Farm.

It was an embarrassment to me to have to use the period term for Native Americans in the story, for they were then called 'savages'. I was lucky enough to have John Fadden, Curator of the Six Nations Indian Museum in Ochiota, New York State, to help me to understand the way in which the Native Americans lived and fought. He also showed me graphically how these people were systematically exploited by the French, the British and the Americans.

On technical matters relating to hearing, I had as my guide an audiological scientist, my brother, Roger Wills MSc.

If, in spite of the excellent advice given me by the above consultants, there are historical discrepancies in my story, the fault is entirely mine.

Finally, I owe a debt of gratitude to my wife Barbro, for accompanying me on a journey through fields and forests, up mountains and across rivers and lakes to retrace the path of a doomed army.

Michael Wills
Salisbury
March 2014

Preface

In September 2012 while on a short holiday in New York, I wandered across Central Park to see the John Lennon Memorial and then crossed Park West to visit the New York Historical Society. In the palatial society building I was accosted by a very elderly guide, presumably a volunteer. He offered to show me around. It is not in my nature to be guided as I prefer to discover for myself; however, to humour this gentleman I accepted. To him I am eternally grateful for opening my eyes to a period of history and British involvement in it, about which I was embarrassingly ignorant.

Recalling my school days, and subsequent study, I can see why I knew little about the American War of Independence: we are seldom taught about our failures and defeats. The overweening confidence of a king and country was shattered by a vain, if in most cases gallant, attempt to subdue the desire for self-determination of a people three thousand miles away.

Wars are usually started by politicians and fought by armies. In my story I have deliberately neglected the role of politicians; I have only mentioned generals when the narrative absolutely depended on it. For I wished to tell the tale of how men, often with very simple backgrounds and frequently with very dubious or even criminal pasts, were melded into fighting forces of robotic efficiency. How millers, tailors, weavers, farmers, fishermen and criminals were plucked from their hamlets and towns in Britain, relentlessly trained and then ferried thousands of miles to fight and often die in an American wilderness for an unwinnable cause.

Some of the military, naval and other terms of the period of the book may be unfamiliar to readers. There is a list of words and phrases in the Endnotes.

Michael Wills

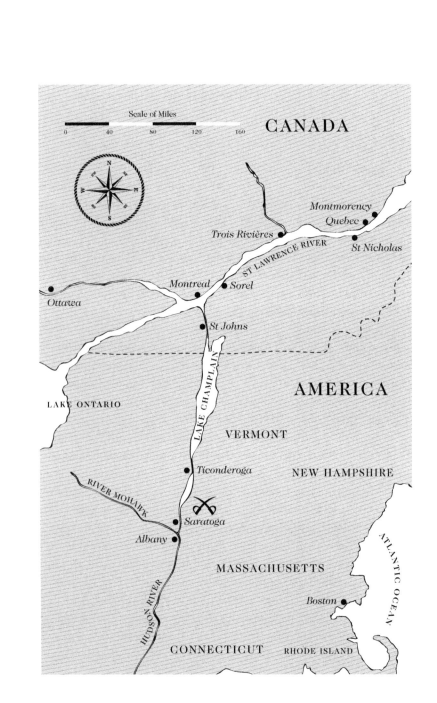

Chapter 1

The blacksmith's young apprentice had prepared all the tools in anticipation of the arrival of the mare and now had a few moments to dream as he waited behind the bellows. He was excited; this evening the dull, but secure routine of life on the estate was to be punctuated by the annual feast. And the village girls would be there. If he was lucky he might get one of them to kiss him when they played games behind the barns.

His reverie was broken by the clatter of heavy hooves outside on the cobbled yard. The burly figure with rolled-up sleeves standing in front of the forge, Thomas Sykes, his master, watched while the cart horse was brought into the hot, dusty building. The dust was a mixture of everything to do with their trade, mainly dried mud, soot and ash. The smith stood with his arms crossed, observing the way the animal walked. He could tell, even without checking, that the horse had a loose shoe.

In a thick Hampshire dialect he commanded, "Bring her round with her arse near the anvil." For it was the horse's rear left hoof which was to be the focus of his attention, and he wanted that to be closest to his hearth and anvil. He watched as the big animal was turned round by the farmhand and noticed with satisfaction that the horse's tail had been plaited and tied up. A swish of the beast's tail would not only sting anyone in its way, but also cover them with filth which consisted not only of mud.

"She's neat and tidy, Jed."

"She is that, Tom. She's going to a new master tomorrow."

The smith strode forward, his thick leather apron flapping on his legs. The apron was in two parts, having been made with a split up the middle. This allowed him to work on a hoof held between his legs, while the flaps of the apron protected his breeches, one part on each side.

He stroked the fetlock of the huge animal and then encouraged the powerful beast to relax while Jed kept the animal's head still by holding its halter, and speaking calming words to it. The farrier then quickly turned and positioned himself with his back to the powerful bulging thighs of the horse and seized the rear hoof. He assumed a half crouching position with it held firmly between his legs and pushed the horse's long white hair sock to one side. He then pulled a scraper from a pouch hanging on his belt and cleaned the mud and grit from inside and around the loose shoe. All horses were prone to throw a shoe, but draught horses working in mud and on uneven ground were more prone than most.

The apprentice craned forward to watch what his master was doing and then quietly crept nearer to get a better view. He was keen to learn, for up to now, even after three years of his apprenticeship, he had only been allowed to shoe donkeys and one or two of the less valuable cobs.

When Tom was satisfied with his work he placed the scraper back into his pouch and selected a nipper from the row of tools adjacent to the anvil and within his reach. He used this to withdraw some nails and cut off others until the worn horse shoe clattered to the stone floor.

"Seven and a half inch, Bill. One with the scotches on the heels," bellowed the farrier.

His labourer, Bill, selected a metal shoe from the hangers on the wall. The scotches were protruding metal lumps on the back of the shoe, which helped the horse to grip when walking over cobbles and on rough ground. There were horse and donkey shoes of every size and description hanging inverted on wooden rods protruding from the planks on the wall. All of them had been made in the smithy and were waiting for future use.

Bill handed the shoe to the farrier who held it close to the hoof between his legs, just to confirm that his judgment of the size was correct.

"He'll do," he said, handing the shoe back. "Move out the way, Aaron, you're taking my light."

The fair-haired apprentice scampered back to his original position, knowing that his services would soon be required, and grabbed the long wooden handle which protruded at shoulder height from the overhead bellows. He waited for the order. Bill used a tong with a long handle to place the shoe in the fire on the hearth and then shouted, "Let him blow, Aaron."

The boy started pumping, feeding the fire with a blast of air which brought it to life. Sparks jumped like shooting stars from the red charcoal and crackled as they flew.

Meanwhile, Tom had taken a cutting gouge from his pouch and beat it with a hammer around the profile of the horse shoe, to remove the overgrown hoof. Had he not had his back to the animal's hind quarters he would have seen the massive upper leg muscles rippling with nervousness. But the horse did not move. The smith then trimmed the surface of the hoof, slicing curls off it which left white trails on the previously muddy brown surface. When he was satisfied with his carving, he put away the sharp knife and took a rough rasp from several protruding from a wooden box nearby.

This was too much for the beast! The sound and feel of the file on its hoof, the noise of the squeaky bellows and the roar of the fire compounded to panic the horse. It made an effort to move forwards, and the smith dropped the hoof and swiftly jumped sideways to avoid a kick or a stamp. But the farmhand held his grip on the bit and whispered more words of comfort. After a minute or so the horse was calmed and the smith resumed his position.

Soon the smithy was ringing to the sound of the red-hot horse shoe being beaten on the anvil as it was smoothed off and straightened before being placed hot on the trimmed hoof. The blue smoke from the burning hoof drifted on the air and worried the horse, causing it to shrug its leg, but this time the farrier held his grip, calmly taking the shoe away and slicing a little more of the hoof before placing the shoe back and nailing it in place. Finally, after rasping around the finished shoe, he let the horse's hoof to the ground.

The distraction of watching the shoeing of the mare had temporarily held Aaron's keen attention, but with the job done he remembered why he was excited. He quickly did his task of cleaning and clearing the tools and then sidled up to his master. The man turned round, clapped his apprentice on the shoulder and said, "You be wanting to go to harvest-home, won't you lad?"

"Yes sir, if we be finished."

"Take him with ye, Jed. I'll be up later for a draught of ale."

Aaron joined his father, Jed, and walked beside him as he led the horse out of the blacksmith's yard and up the track to the farm. Farmhand and blacksmith's apprentice walked side by side. Aaron was a strapping boy who was already taller than his father. One of the main reasons the smith had indentured the boy was that even three years ago he had showed early promise of inheriting his father's broad shoulders and barrel chest. Physical strength was a prerequisite of the blacksmith's trade.

"I don't know why you wanted to become a blacksmith instead of doing the same work as your father, and your grandfather, and even his father if it comes to that."

Aaron had had this conversation many times before and he knew how quickly the topic could lead to an argument. He was painfully aware that it was only his mother's insistence that had badgered his father into relenting and accepting that his son would not become a farmhand. He tried to avert further discussion by saying, "You'll see, Pa, one day when you are too old to work, I'll have my own smithy and I will be able to support you and Ma."

"Ha, I won't believe that afore it's a fact."

"Soon, I'll be working with the big horses."

"Perhaps, but I don't know how you can stand being indoors all day in that heat. And you've got four more years' apprenticeship to serve."

"But I enjoy it."

"That's as maybe."

Aaron could have repeated what he had heard his mother shout at his father in the kitchen of their home three years ago, while he was trying to sleep in the bedroom he shared with his brother and sisters: "Do you want your children and theirs to share the misery and poverty and danger of being a farmhand? Your eldest son has a chance to make something of himself – something better than you are." But Aaron could also remember the sound of the slap and the scream when his father took retribution. The boy was still unaware that when Jed had suddenly agreed to the apprenticeship that the reason for doing so was penance to his wife for striking her, something he had never done before and had never repeated. Aaron had lain awake long into the night full of anger, considering what he should do to support his mother. But such vague intentions that he had formed to confront his father were dissipated when, next morning, his mother woke him early to announce that his father had agreed to let him become a blacksmith. However, since then, fearing for her son's welfare, his mother always advised him that the safest thing to do when he wanted to argue with his father or indeed anyone else, was to bite his bottom lip; that way nothing would be uttered. Though he would not have recognised it himself, despite the fact that he would soon be eighteen, he was still, by dint of motherly protection and living in an isolated village community, very much a boy.

Aaron kicked at a piece of flint lying on the chalk track to vent his frustration, bit his lip and wondered why his father would not show pride in what he was doing instead of pouring scorn. In silence, father and son hurried along as fast as the steady plod of the horse would permit, for they wanted to be present when the last of the corn sheaves were loaded on the haywain and the traditional procession from the top field, the biggest and best on the Squire's estate, wended its way to the farmyard, following the cart. The last load of harvest symbolically marked the success of the year's labour in the fields, the bounty of nature and the assurance of survival through the coming winter. The latter was never a foregone conclusion; hunger stalked the countryside in the years of poor harvests, but this year the weather had been kind and there was much to celebrate. In the farmyard there would be a barrel of ale to be drunk by the revelers, to the accompaniment of the village musicians.

When they reached the open gate to the top field, Jed said, "Aaron, take the horse down to the yard and then come on up to the field."

The boy resentfully took the leading rein and did as instructed without protest, realising that he would now be delayed and might miss the final act of the harvesting. He set off down the hill to the farm buildings in the hollow, while Jed went through the gate and headed for the cart in the middle of the field. The haywain almost resembled a ship in shape. It was curved with a high front and back and a relatively low centre. Two shire horses were in the shafts of the cart, both of them with nose bags on. The bags contained a mixture of hay and barley which kept the horses from getting impatient while the cart stood still. A procession of helpers were bringing the corn sheaves to the wagon. Earlier, when the other fields were harvested, the work had been done by the farmhands and temporary harvest workers, many of them women. By tradition this, the last day of the harvest, was a time for all those villagers who were capable to lend a hand. And it was not only the strength of tradition which attracted them. Tonight was one of the rare occasions when the Squire dispensed his largess. There would be a festive reward to the workers with victuals of a range and in a quantity such as most of them saw but once a year. The Squire's cook had been baking bread, making pies (savoury and sweet), stuffing sausages and roasting beef for several days in preparation for the feast. Thus, those carrying the sheaves to the cart were not only the brawny white-shirted farmhands in black breeches, but a whole array of people including old women wearing their widow's black garb, bonnetted mothers in long dresses with small children scampering by their sides, and the boys and girls of the village of varying ages. Some of the latter could hardly lift a sheaf of corn, but were doing their best to drag their burden, often losing most of it.

The corn stood in stooks. It had been cut underripe to minimise the loss by scattering the ears of corn and was tied up by 'bandsters' into sheaves. These were built into stooks which were thatched and then left in the field to ripen further. On this fine early September evening it was the job of the harvesters to break up the stooks and load the sheaves onto the haywain. The willing helpers queued, waiting to pass their loads up to a farmhand standing on the cart. He was clearly being overwhelmed by the enthusiasm of the helpers as he tried to lay the sheaves neatly across the vehicle. Jed clambered up to help him.

"About time too, Jed. Where've ye been?" said the man.

"Never ye mind, Jake, I'm here now."

The pile on the wagon got higher and higher and soon the helpers had to use pitchforks to lift their loads up to the farmhands.

As Aaron made his way back up the hill and the haywain came into sight, he immediately saw that something was wrong — the procession was no more. Instead, the motley crowd of helpers were gathered in a large knot around the cart. The boy started to jog towards the throng. When he arrived in front of the haywain some of the jostling crowd of people recognised him and a gap opened for the son to get a view of the subject of the crowd's attention. He was horrified to see that his father was sitting against one wheel of the cart with a scarlet stain spreading the length of his shirt arm and down his left chest. The farm worker looked pale and was wincing as he clutched his left arm with his right hand.

"Pa, what happened?" screamed the frightened boy, pushing his way forward and crouching down beside the injured man.

"There be more blood than pain, lad. Don't worry yourself."

Aaron looked up to Jake who was staring down helplessly at Jed.

"It were an accident, lad. There was that much commotion and folk pushing up sheaves on their pitchforks. I think Jed must have slipped and fallen on one of them."

Aaron looked back at his father. "Do it hurt, Pa?"

"It be just a wound through the flesh, Aaron, but bad enough."

Aaron looked round and shouted at two youths who were peering at the victim, "Come with me, we got to go down and get the handcart to fetch him down to the farm."

The three of them ran off down the hill. When they reached the yard Aaron wrenched open the door of a shed and went inside. Voices called after him, "What is it, lad? What be going on?" The other two boys shouted hurried answers to the women who were laying out the food for the celebration.

The three of them dragged the heavy handcart up the slope to the top field. When they arrived at the scene of the accident, Jed was helped to his feet and willing hands lifted him first to sit on the edge of the handcart and then eased him onto his back. One of the women lifted his head, while another pushed a bundle of straw under as a pillow.

News of the accident had spread, so by the time the handcart arrived, preparations had been made by the women to treat the injured man. His wife Ann had been called and she had just arrived with a baby in her arms and three other children of descending ages trailing behind her, the oldest hanging on to her skirts and the other two trying to keep up. A cot had been made up in the barn and water was being heated to wash the wound. When Ann saw her bloodied husband she gasped with alarm, but did not scream, for she was well used to living with the expectation that injury could befall those toiling in the harsh environment of a farm.

Jedidiah Mew had married well; his handsome looks and fine physique had proved irresistible to the daughter of the baker in a nearby village. She had married below her station. It was her stubbornness and tenacity which had eventually worn her parents down and forced them to accept the match: marriage to a mere farmhand. These were the same two traits of personality which had helped her to cope with the weaknesses in the character of the man of her choice. For although he could be loving, sometimes too much so, and he was a very hard worker, he had difficulty in accepting that his wife was better schooled than him and had a mind of her own. She handed her baby girl, who was also called Ann, to one of the other women and followed the handcart into the barn.

The size of the farmyard reflected the wealth of the Squire. His big house was on a slight hillock well away from the yard to escape the bucolic smells, but close enough for him to be able to survey work being carried out there. Apart from the stables, the cowshed and other outbuildings, there were two large barns. One of them was already full of ricks, with the corn from the other fields awaiting threshing and the hay harvest. The corn from the top field was to go into the other barn, part of which was occupied by Jed and his carers. The food and drink for the evening had been placed on trestles in the yard itself. Adjacent to the yard was a small cottage, the residence of the farm manager, Mr Newman. He too had a good view of the yard and it was not long before he noticed that something was amiss. He strode out of the front door of his cottage with the tails of his jacket flapping and then stopped to ask one of the crowd what had happened. He surveyed the gaggle of helpers and onlookers at the barn door and then walked across to the door. The crowd parted respectfully and he peered inside.

"Master Aaron, come here if you please," shouted Mr Newman.

Aaron turned from watching the ministrations to his father and immediately stepped outside to where the manager was standing.

"Did your father get the draught mare's shoe done?"

"Yes, sir, she be in the stall now."

"Good. But now I am perplexed, for Jed was to take the mare to Salisbury tomorrow. The deal has been agreed. The Wilton estate manager has arranged to pick her up in the city."

Aaron had never been further than the next village. It was on Oak Apple day the previous year, but he knew which road led to Salisbury. He was mindful that his father would have his wages docked while he was unable to work, and his family needed every penny he earned. If he himself missed a day at the smithy he would lose only three pence and a farthing, part of his apprentice's pay. His father's loss would be much greater, his weekly pay being nine shillings.

"I can do it, sir. I am good with horses, for it's my work at the smithy. And I know the way to Salisbury."

Mr Newman scratched his beard and peered at the muck on the ground around his leather boots, pondering Aaron's offer. The farm would be short-handed if he sent another of his men; they were needed for the threshing, and in any case none of them had the wit to find the buyer in the big city. He had heard folk speak highly of Jed's boy. The horse was as good as gold and shouldn't be a problem for him.

"Can you count?"

"Yes, sir."

"Sign your name?"

"Yes, sir."

"Show me."

The farm manager gave the boy his walking stick and indicated that he should use the tip of it to scratch his signature in the mud. The lad carefully drew the stick around the necessary curves to make two letter a's and then continued with the other letters to scribe 'Aaron Mew'.

"It's ten miles to Salisbury. The horse is not to be rushed – she must look her best, not in a sweat. When you reach Downton, which is about halfway, take her down to the White Horse Inn – there is a horse trough outside the inn. Give her a good drink. If the trough is empty take her down to the river. There is a track along the side of the river which, if you follow it, joins up with the Salisbury road again a bit further on. Can you remember that, lad?"

"Yes, sir. I wouldn't forget to water her, don't be worried about that, sir."

"When you get to the village of Harnham, just outside Salisbury, you must pay the road toll for you and the mare."

There was a pause while Aaron tried to take in all the information. He was desperate to carry out this task; he would save money for the family and he hoped that his father would be proud of him for that, but also because the prospect was hugely exciting. He did not want to ask questions as he was afraid that doing so might undermine the farm manager's confidence in him. But this was a shock. He had to ask a question.

"Where must I pay, and how?"

"The toll is at Harnham on the second bridge. Don't worry, I'll give you six pennies for the horse and you to pass and you will need two pence to pass alone on the way home. How much is that all in total, boy?"

Without hesitation, Aaron said, "Eight pennies, sir."

The manager was taken aback by the swiftness of the boy's reply and asked, "Who taught you sums?"

"My Ma, sir."

"Has she taught you to read?"

"Not much, sir."

"Why did she teach you sums, but not to read?"

"She says that a blacksmith needs to be able to do sums, but he don't need no book learning."

"What about reading the Bible?"

"Ma says that I should know the important bits by heart."

Mr Newman had warmed to the boy and grinned. He thought for a moment and then said, "You'll find the bridges easy to cross. They were widened last year."

"How am I to return, sir?"

"Walk, of course. If you leave the stable at seven, after her feed, you will be in Salisbury by midday."

"Where am I to take her, sir?"

"Mr Briggs, the Wilton estate manager, will be at the Red Lion and Cross Keys Inn from midday. The inn is in Milford Street. It is easy to find, just follow the Cathedral Close wall until you come to the White Hart Inn and then keep going in the same direction. After a while you reach Milford Street."

The boy was feeling less confident about the enterprise now, but in bluff said, "Leave it to me, sir. I will see that the horse is delivered safely."

"Ah, I almost forgot. Leave the horse with the inn hostler and ask for Mr Briggs inside the inn. He will pay you twelve pounds for the horse. Do you have somewhere safe to put it on the journey home?"

Aaron hesitated – twelve pounds! He had never seen such a sum in his life.

"Well, do you?"

"Er, er, yes, sir. I can borrow my mother's neck pouch." He was referring to a cord around his mother's neck on which was a leather pouch, though none could see it as it hung deep between her milk-filled breasts.

"Right. Now, Mr Briggs will give you the money in the inn. You should count it and then give him a receipt which I will write for you."

"I, I, um, I can't read long words, sir."

"You don't need to. All you need to do is write your name at the bottom of the page when you are sure the money is correct and give the paper to Mr Briggs. Come to the farm at six o'clock or so. Take a head collar for the mare from the stable, catch her in the field and bring her in to the stalls. Give her a good grooming and a feed. I will come to give you the paper at about seven o'clock. Is that alright?"

"Yes, sir, thank you, sir."

"Now, you had better go to see your father and explain to him that you will do his task for him."

Aaron nodded, suddenly remembering that his injured father was inside the barn. He went inside to break the news to him.

Jed was sitting up on the cot. Blood-soaked rags, which once must have been his shirt, were on the floor at the end of the bed. His left arm was bandaged and bound by a strip of cloth to his body to take the weight of the arm off his shoulder. In his right hand he held a wooden tankard. It was clear that he was not going to let the injury get in the way of his right to a share of the free ale. The cot was surrounded by his wife, children and others who were curious to see the victim of the accident.

Aaron pushed his way through the crowd. "Father! Father! I'm going to Salisbury tomorrow."

"How so, son?"

Aaron recounted his conversation with the manager. As he did so he became the subject of people's attention, in place of his father. There were many exclamations of surprise and envious comments, for only two of those present had been to Salisbury and not one of them had ever seen twelve pounds.

"Mother, can I borrow your money pouch for the safe keeping of the money?"

His mother hesitated and then said, "I'll make ye another one this evening, for I need this one." She was aware that Jed would be paid his wages the next day. On Saturdays she met him at the farm to make sure that most of his money was put into her own private secure place where she would notice if anyone tried to take it, and she could see that the money was spent wisely. In the early years of their marriage, too much of Jed's cash never got further than the Baker's Arms on his way home on Saturday evenings. Even though she would have to collect his wages on Saturday, as he would be unable to, she still wanted to stow the money in a safe place.

Soon, there was the sound of the cart horses' hooves as the haywain came through the gates of the yard with the babble of excited children's voices as the young harvesters hurried to keep up with it. The wagon stopped outside of the barn and the traces were taken off the horses. They were led off to the stables and the heavily laden cart was then dragged and pushed through the wide open door of the barn by a crowd of volunteers.

It was time for the festivities to start. The village fiddle player began playing and like bees round a honeypot the crowd swarmed so that the food tables could no longer be seen.

At first the accident did not stop Aaron enjoying the evening's festivities. He was soon lured away to join the horseplay of the village lads of a similar age to his, all the while hoping that some of the girls would join them for gentler games, but with his father incapacitated it was not long before Mrs Mew insisted that he help her with the feeding of the children. The age range of her family was unusual, but the cause of it was altogether too common, for after Aaron's birth she had had a series of miscarriages and had also lost four infants in the first days of their lives. Thus it was that when eventually Aaron had a little brother, Matthew, who was nine years younger than him, the bigger lad doted on him. From the time Matthew could walk, his big brother tried to share his pleasures with him, be it birds nesting, netting sparrows for the table, snaring rabbits or many of the other normal country pursuits. When the little sisters came along, the first one, Elizabeth, three years later, Aaron was much less inclined to try to occupy them with his interests, simply because they were girls and they should be doing other things. His relationship with his sisters was also much conditioned by the fact that the frequent calls which his mother made on his leisure time to help with the girls, were often a cause of resentment.

Despite his injury, Jed vehemently refused to be taken home at the same time as his wife when she decided that it was time for her younger children to be put to bed. So it was arranged that later in the evening Jed would be wheeled back to their cottage by his work mates. Aaron volunteered to help with this, but despite his protestations, Ann was adamant that he had to leave the party with her as she needed his help. In fact, she was well used to coping with the children on her own, but secretly she wanted to defer the time when he got a taste for the beer, for she feared that he might go the way of his father. She was a God-fearing woman and through attempting to shield her eldest son from the evils of the world, she hoped to ensure that he grew up in her mould and not that of his father.

Chapter 2

Aaron woke at first light, knowing that dawn at this season of the year was around half past five. He was immediately consumed by excitement when he remembered what the day was to bring. He cautiously got out of bed. The reason he had to move very carefully was that his four-year-old sister, Mary, slept in the same bed beside him and his brother had a pillow at the far end of the same bed and slept with his feet towards Aaron. The big brother knew that if he woke either of them they would wake the other children and he would be delayed by them running around the house and getting in the way of him doing his chores.

He recovered his clothes, which were in a neat pile on the chest of drawers, and took them with him so that he could dress in the kitchen where there was no risk of disturbing the rest of the family. As eldest son, many years ago he was allocated tasks which had to be accomplished before he set off for work. He disliked his job of cleaning out the ashes and lighting the cooking stove. Sometimes it would light first time, other times it would take several tries and he would be late with the other chores. Today he was lucky and as the flames spread in the ancient stove, he made several trips to the wood shed and brought enough logs into the kitchen for the fire to be kept going all day in his absence. He then picked up the cudgel which his father kept in the kitchen in case they had unwelcome visitors during the night, and walked round the back of the building to open the hen house. Several times foxes, and one time a weasel, had got trapped in the chicken pen when trying to find their way into the hen house. He always took the cudgel in case he came across one of the four-legged thieves, for he had been told that they could be dangerous, but on the rare occasions when he had seen them they disappeared quickly, being much more frightened of him than he was of them. He let the chickens into the coop and fed them. Finally, he drew two pails of water from the well in the garden – one for cooking and one for the family ablutions. When he brought the last pail in he found his mother in the kitchen.

"Morning, Ma."

"Morning, Aaron, you excited?"

"Some, I can't deny."

"Well, I am, and I'm not going."

After cutting several thick slices of bread and wrapping them in a cloth together with a wedge of cheese, she placed the package into Aaron's leather shoulder bag, together with three apples. Then she opened a drawer in the kitchen table and took out a leather pouch on a cord – the pouch which she had been sewing until after midnight when her husband had been carried in. She had been charitable enough to consider that his state was as much to do with the physical pain he was suffering from his wound as it was from the free ale provided by his employer. At least the injury had stopped him from bothering her as he often did when he was the worse for the drink. She had five children, one of them still at the breast, she did not want more.

Aaron placed the last bucket on the kitchen floor and then sat down to wait for his bowl of porridge.

"Mother, have you ever been to Salisbury?"

"No, nor would I want to. Can't be healthy for those folk living cheek by jowl in the city."

"I wish I had listened more careful like to the directions I was given. I got me doubts now."

"Well, you'll be seeing the manager this morning, ask him to make it clearer for you."

"I can't do that, he'll have doubts about me."

"Better he has doubts than you get lost with a girt great horse."

The woman laughed heartily and Aaron understood that there was no point in pursuing the matter. She carried the saucepan to his place at the table and scooped some porridge into his bowl with a wooden spoon, then replaced the saucepan on a cool part of the cooking range and moved back to where her son sat.

"Now, I put plenty of cheese in your bag. Be sure to save some to eat on the way home, it's a long road." In a lowered tone she added, "Here, I want you to have a few pennies to spend in the city."

She looked round to assure herself that neither the other children nor her husband were coming into the room and drew up the cord around her neck. She untied the string which held the pouch closed and delved into the bag with her fingers. She counted out six pennies onto the table, took the newly made pouch from Aaron's bag and put the money inside.

"Now, perhaps you can buy something for yourself or the little ones."

Aaron was aware of the importance of every penny in this household.

"Mother, you shouldn't have. You can't afford it."

"That's true enough, but I want ye to have something to spend. They say there's street traders and stalls all over the city."

Aaron did not protest further as he had already decided that he would buy something for his mother. He put the pouch inside his shirt and the cord over his head. As he ate his porridge he could hear the children in the bedroom beginning to stir. He unhooked his jacket from the back of the kitchen door, picked up his bag and made to leave. Then he stopped and said, "I'll just go and say goodbye to them and Pa. It will be a while before I see them again."

"There's no point in going in to see your father, he's dead to the world. I'll tell him later that you said goodbye."

After a short time he reappeared in the kitchen towing Matthew, who was in his nightshirt and was refusing to let go of Aaron.

"Say goodbye to your brother, dear, he'll be back soon."

"But he's going such a long way, Ma. He might not come back!"

"Don't be silly, love. Now let go of Aaron and come to the window with me so that we can wave goodbye."

The little boy reluctantly released his grip. Aaron bent down to give him a hug and then hastily made his way to the door before his brother seized him again.

"Be careful, son, God bless you. Come safely home. It is such a long journey, please be careful."

"Mother, I am only going ten miles, don't fuss. I will be home long before dark."

"You make sure you are."

With that, he opened the kitchen door and set off for the farm. The low sun cast Aaron's shadow far ahead of him as he walked the track to the farm. The trail was deserted save for groups of rabbits feeding in the verges. They darted into the hedgerow, startled at his approach. He opened the gate to the farmyard and noted with some disappointment that all trace of the previous evening's activities had been cleared and cleaned. He had hoped that there might be some leftovers to complement the breakfast he had just had. He walked across the yard to the stables. The two cart horses which had been taken in the previous evening heard him coming and one of them neighed with excitement in anticipation of food. The other stalls were empty as the rest of the horses were out in the paddocks. Aaron ignored the cart horses and unhooked a head collar and a leading rein from the row of tack on the wall. He hung the bag with his food by one of the stalls and went out. When he reached the paddock which the mare shared with several other horses he saw them lift their heads from their grazing and look at him inquisitively. Several started walking towards him as he approached. He climbed over the gate and called to the mare; she joined the others and plodded slowly towards him.

"Come on girl, easy now," said Aaron, as he reached up and slipped the collar first onto the horse's muzzle and then put the strap over its head and buckled it under its neck. He looped the leading rein through the bottom of the collar and started to lead the horse to the five-bar gate. Holding the rein in one hand he slowly eased the gate ajar with the other. With great difficulty, he managed to squeeze the big animal though the half-open gate without allowing the other horses to follow.

The boy led the mare to the stable and tied her up in a stall. He then made up some barley mash and put a bowlful on the ground under its head. While she was occupied with the mash the boy took a stiff hand brush and worked hard brushing and combing out the mud and dust on the horse's coat. Then, one by one, he lifted the horse's hooves and used a hoof pick to clean out stones and compounded chalk inside the shoes. Finally, he got a bucket of water and gave the horse a drink.

When he was ready, he sat on a bench and waited for the arrival of Mr Newman. His anxiety was mounting. He had committed himself to this venture, but now he was very, very nervous.

It was eerily quiet. Normally the farm workers would be busy at their tasks, for Saturday was a normal workday. But this was the one day in the year when the manager would have some forbearance for workers arriving late. Soon he heard footsteps, and since he did not expect any of the farm workers to make an appearance yet, he knew that the sound heralded the arrival of the man he was waiting for.

"Morning, Master Aaron, you have a fine day for a good walk. I'm glad to see you here on time – I suppose the other lazy beggars are sleeping off the ale. They'd best be here soon, the cows need to be in for milking."

"Morning, sir, the hoss is ready."

The manager clapped the mare on its rump and appraised Aaron's work.

"She looks good, lad. How about the hooves?"

Before Aaron could reply the manager had lifted one of the horse's back legs to inspect the shoe.

"Looks alright."

He dropped the leg and turned to Aaron.

"Here's the paper which you must sign when you have counted the money. You then give it to Mr Briggs."

"Yes, sir, that I will."

"Remember, not until you have counted the money."

"Twelve pounds, sir."

"That's right. Do you remember where you are to meet him?"

"At the Red Lion and Cross Keys Inn, sir."

"And where is that?"

"Er, um…At the end of the cathedral wall, sir?"

"No, no. At the end of the wall you keep going in the same direction until you, you…Look, when you get to the end of the wall ask someone the way. There is always a crowd outside the White Hart Inn at the end of the wall."

"Right, sir. Don't worry, I'll find it alright."

"Best you get going then."

Aaron unhitched his bag from the hook and put it on his shoulder. He then untied the leading rein from a ring on the wall and gently pushed the horse in the chest to make her go backwards until she could turn and exit the stall and then the stable.

"Bye, lad. When you get back, come over to my cottage with the money."

"Yes, sir, I will."

Boy and horse made their way slowly up the hill, passing the field where the accident had happened the evening before. The rabbits once more darted into the hedgerow as he approached. His shadow was shorter now that the sun was higher and there was the promise of a fine day. He began to feel more at ease. As he led the mare along the lane towards the road which would take him to Salisbury, he met two of the farmhands on their way to work.

"A big job for a little lad," remarked one of them.

"I bet he ain't even shaving yet," joked the other.

Aaron replied indignantly, "I do, on Sundays, like me dad. At least I get to work on time, not like some I could mention."

One of the men pretended to cuff the boy as he passed them. He called after Aaron, "Look out for them Salisbury girls. They'd have ye for breakfast."

Twenty minutes later the horse and her temporary master reached the farm lane junction and turned left onto the highway to Salisbury.

As they started to make their way north on the dusty road, Aaron soon realised that he was not alone in journeying to Salisbury. Today, Saturday, was market day in the city and not a few farmers, traders and tinkers were making their way to sell and buy. The farmers and small holders in particular had much to sell, for this was the time of plenty in the year – the time of harvest both in the fields and in the orchards.

As he led the horse, Aaron was amazed at how busy the road was. Often he was overtaken by others. Some of those travelling faster were on horseback, but most were travelling in horse-drawn vehicles. He stared in awe at an elegant post-chaise – a four-wheeled carriage – with finely attired occupants and a liveried driver, as it passed. Although by the time he had remembered to touch his forelock in respect to the obviously fine folk in the carriage, it was too late for them to notice. But most of the horse-drawn traffic consisted of farm carts which were creaking under heavy loads and were driven by simple farm folk. The carts carried cargoes of animals and chickens. Frightened pigs squealed, calves bellowed and lambs bleated as they peered out from wooden barred cages on their way to an uncertain future.

And the horseback riders were just as varied as the wheeled vehicles. Many aroused wonderment in the boy. There were traders with their wares strapped astride their mounts; fine gentlemen with white breeches, long black riding boots, splendid jackets and top hats; and even one naval officer in full uniform. The boy pondered about who they were and where they had travelled from and if they were all going to Salisbury. He wondered if, perhaps, when he was a blacksmith he might have a fine jacket and his own horse.

Although his progress seemed slower than most others, Aaron gradually began to get closer and closer to a flock of sheep which was being shepherded along the road in front of him. Eventually, he caught up with the end of the flock. The girl who was responsible for seeing that the tail-enders kept up with the others had noticed him coming up from behind some time ago. She knew that the boy and the horse had caught up with her from the increasing volume of the steady plod of the cart horse, but she did not turn her head. Aaron's senses quickened; he had only spoken to girls from his own village before. There was a thrill in meeting one who was a stranger. His excitement overcame his shyness.

"It be hard for you, miss, to be at the back, all that dust they be raising," he said.

The girl spoke very softly, so quietly that Aaron could hardly hear what she was saying as her voice competed with the baaing of the sheep. Aaron stooped forward to listen to her reply. She turned her head towards him and he felt a tingle of excitement when he saw how pretty she was.

"We take turns, my sister and me, turn and turnabout." She pointed up the road and following her indication Aaron saw that another girl was walking at the head of the flock beside a man in a shepherd's smock.

"Nevertheless, it's dusty work. You going to Salisbury?"

"We be that. There ain't work enough for two and mother at home. Too many mouths to feed. So my job today is to help father, but not for much longer. I'm to stay in Salisbury when we have sold the flock."

"What you be doing there then?"

"I'm to go into service for my aunt. She keeps the Saracen's

Head Inn in Blue Boar Row." The girl was casting cautious glances forward to the man leading the flock.

"Where's that then?"

"Ain't you never been in Salisbury then?"

"Na, never had cause to afore now."

Just then the shepherd turned round to check the progress of the flock behind him and noticed Aaron for the first time.

"Here you, boy, you got no business talking to me daughter. Come on past and get on yer way."

Aaron quickly glanced at the girl and said, "What's your name?"

Turning towards Aaron she said, just loudly enough for him to hear, "Peggy."

"Might see you in Salisbury then, Peggy. I be Aaron."

The girl smiled at him and then turned her head back to watch the progress of the sheep ahead of her.

The boy started to walk more quickly as he had understood that the shepherd was not pleased to have a stranger talk to his daughter. While he was not worried on his own account, Aaron feared that the father might take his anger out on his daughter. When he reached the front of the flock he found that her father was leading a ram to make the ewes follow him. The boy tried to ingratiate himself with the shepherd.

"Them be fine ewes you are leading, sir."

"Happen they are, let's hope the market traders think so. How come a young lad like you is leading such a handsome hoss?"

Aaron explained his mission with some pride. As he did so he noticed that the girl by the shepherd's side was very interested, and indeed impressed, by what he had to say. Aware of this, the shepherd decided that the conversation had gone on long enough.

"Thee'd better be going on then. Better not miss your appointment."

"Ah, yes. Yes, I should be getting on, that's quite so."

He took a last lingering look at the girl, but she did not respond to his smile. He turned to the shepherd and said, "May see you in the market then. I bid you adieu."

"Bye, lad," said the shepherd.

Aaron moved on down the road ahead of the sheep, slowly increasing the distance between them. Almost all of the traffic was going in the direction of Salisbury and, apart from the flock, most was going faster than him. As he strolled on, the horse plodding beside him, he began to get increasingly concerned about the fact that it was getting unseasonably warm and the horse really needed a drink, as indeed did he. When he saw a milestone he paused to see if he could read how much further he had to go to the village of Downton, where Mr Newman had said there was a horse trough. On the milestone he recognised the number 6 and the letter 'S' with which the word began and asked himself, "If Mr Newman said Downton was halfway to Salisbury and there are six miles left in a ten-mile walk, how far is left to Downton?" He quickly came to the conclusion that the answer was one mile, but checked by using his fingers to count on. The fact that they should be at the village in twenty minutes or so eased his anxiety about the thirsty horse. However, as he got further and further from home he felt more and more insecure and his confidence about the whole enterprise was beginning to wane. Could he really find the Red Lion and Cross Keys and would he be able to find his way home again? His belief that he would find a water trough soon was also shaken as he walked on and on with no sign of a village. And then, as he came around a bend, he saw a group of several cottages and as he got closer, what looked like an inn.

When he reached the first house he saw that there was a woman picking apples in the garden. Aaron stopped and called out, "Good day, mistress, be this Downton?"

"That it be, lad. Leastways round the corner it is."

She walked towards him and pointed down the road to where there was a smaller road going to the right.

"Is that where the trough is?" asked Aaron.

"Aye, by the White Horse."

"I'm beholden to you, mistress, bye."

Aaron made a click sound with his tongue against the roof of his mouth to get the horse walking again. When they reached the junction, turning right they came to a row of houses along the edge of a wide grassy area, at the end of which was another inn. On the grass there were several booths where traders were selling vegetables, meat and items of haberdashery. Interspersed between them there were gardeners and farmers selling their produce. They walked past the little market and stopped at the inn which had a painting on a board of a white horse, hanging from the wall.

There were a number of riding horses tied up outside the inn as well as several in the traces of carts by the side of the walkway. Aaron walked the mare up to the trough, but saw immediately that it was almost dry. Clearly, the trough had been much used by the horses already there. He looked up and realised that several of the carters were watching him and exchanging comments about his dilemma. He felt very uncertain of himself as some of the men seemed to be sharing a joke at his expense. He summoned up his courage, stood square in front of them, and in the most confident voice he could muster he said to the nearest carter, "Could you direct me to where I can water the horse in the river?"

"That I can, lad. Follow the road down there and you will see a turning going north next to the river. Follow it for five minutes and there's a shallow opening between the reeds in the river bank. That be the place."

Another carter chimed in, "Look out, lad, the river is empty on Saturdays."

The other men roared with laughter and Aaron was perplexed as he stood watching them.

"Empty?"

The man who had spoken first said, "Don't pay no attention, lad, they be just joking."

Aaron was beginning to feel anger rising. He bit his bottom lip, thought for a moment, and realising that at least one of the men had been kind to him, said, "I'm obliged to you."

Aaron turned the disappointed horse's head and led it off as directed.

He set off down the road and soon came to the river, where he turned left and followed a wide track which ran parallel with the riverbank. Just as the carter had described, there was a long gap in the embankment and the water lapped the grass on the side of the track. The place was clearly a popular watering hole as there were numerous hoof prints in the mud. He let the animal drink its fill and then gave it one of his apples before letting it off its halter to graze on the grass between the river and the trail.

On the other side of the road there was a hurdle fence enclosing a meadow. Aaron sat on the ground leaning his back against the gate in the fence and ate some of his bread and cheese. The scene was very quiet for the while and Aaron started to doze until he was disturbed by the flap-flap of strong wings. He opened his eyes and saw a heron lifting from the reeds on one side of the opening to the river, where he had watered the horse. The bird traversed a length of the river in front of him, announcing its presence with a loud screeching sound to ward off competitors. It then effortlessly circled above the river looking for any movement in the water. All at once it dropped onto a rock by the reed bed and stood perfectly still. Suddenly, its head jerked forward into the water. When it was withdrawn, a writhing silvery object was in the bird's beak. There was a short struggle and then a loud flapping of wings as the bird rose laboriously into the sky with its finny prey.

Then, Aaron became aware of another sound – the bleating of sheep. Looking down the road in the direction of Downton he could see dust rising and sheep running towards him. They were being pursued by two girls and it was soon obvious that these were the girls whom he had seen earlier. Clearly, something had panicked the sheep.

As they came closer, Aaron considered what he could do to hinder their headlong charge. Wrenching the gate open he swung it across the track and stood with his arms stretched wide in the gap between the end of the gate and the river. He let out a loud yell and the leading sheep immediately diverted into the field, whence the remainder followed. The two girls came up puffing behind them; further down the road the shepherd was trotting along, being dragged by the ram.

The girls said nothing, but both smiled and looked at Aaron with relief on their faces and some admiration for his effort. Seeing both together, Aaron could see the strong family likeness, but he was in no doubt that it was Peggy's smile which was warmest. When the shepherd caught up with the girls he tied the ram to the gate, which by now had been closed, walked up to Aaron and slapped him on the back.

"We're truly grateful to you, lad."

"What happened?" asked Aaron.

"It was them soldiers. We heard them coming and tried to

move out of their way, but the sheep were proper scared of their tramp-tramp as they come down the road and the rattling of that drum – 'twas more than the beasts could bear, they just run for it."

"Where are the soldiers?"

"They ain't far behind us."

"Why are they coming this way instead of following the main road past Downton?"

"Same as us, lad, and you too I shouldn't wonder. To water their animals."

Aaron had become aware of a noise further down the road, and looking down it he saw some uniformed riders coming into view round a bend. A cloud of dust rose behind them. As he watched he saw a column of soldiers coming following the riders, their red jackets bright in the sunlight. The sound he could hear was the steady rat-a-tat of a drummer beating the marching pace on his drum.

The shepherd uttered a growling sound and said, "This is a confounded nuisance. We'll have to wait to water the sheep until they've gone. It's going to cause me to be late to market."

He turned from watching the approaching column and slapped Aaron on the back again. He continued, "Anyway, I'm beholden to you, lad, for your help. I shall see that you get a good draught of ale for this service. Wait for me at the Saracen's Head when you get to Salisbury."

"I can't do that, sir, I have business at the Red Lion and Cross Keys."

"Then come to the Saracen's when your dealings are done."

"Will you still be there this afternoon?"

"Well, I plan to walk back tonight, but I'll leave word with my sister, the innkeeper, to look out for you."

"I'm not sure. I, too, plan to return this afternoon."

"You go in and ask for Mrs Tomkins, she'll see you right with some victuals for the journey home."

Aaron's hesitation was overcome by the knowledge that Peggy would be working for her aunt in that inn. He smiled and nodded to the shepherd just as the riders were approaching them. As they got nearer the drummer started playing his drum more loudly. Aaron was suddenly seized with panic – his horse was grazing untethered

33

by the riverside, on the other side of the road. Surely it would bolt at the sight and the noise of the column of marching men. He dashed across the road directly in front of the four officers on horseback at the head of the column. One horse took fright and reared up, throwing an officer with a fringed epaulette on his right shoulder off its back onto the dusty road.

A soldier in the first row of some rank which was denoted by a crimson sash with a buff stripe knotted on his left hip, quickly turned and bellowed, "Company halt! Be easy!" The order came as a surprise to the majority of the marching men who could not see what had happened in front of them, and there was some disorder as many reacted too slowly.

One of the other soldiers on horseback drew his sword and rode over to where Aaron was now standing, holding the mare.

"You stupid oaf, see how this feels."

The officer tried to swing the flat side of the sword across Aaron's back, but the lad was too quick for him and dodged the weapon. He was not quick enough to elude the two soldiers who, having passed their firelocks to comrades, chased after him and dragged him back to face the officer.

The mounted officer seemed to have regained his composure when he said with a calm voice, "What is your name, lad?"

"Aaron, Aaron Mew, sir."

"You are indeed fortunate that you are not in the army, Master Mew, for if you were I would have had you flogged."

He turned and nodded to the soldier who had ordered the column to halt.

"Deal with it, Serjeant," said the officer.

The Serjeant removed his black tricorn hat which matched the colour of his hair, though it was beginning to go grey, and handed the hat and his halberd to the soldier next to him. He stepped forward to where Aaron was being held. At close quarters the prisoner could see the man's bloodshot brown eyes and the grey stubble on his face. It was doubtful if this man could ever look friendly. He was brutish and added to his threatening mien by contorting his face with a look of disdain as he regarded the youth in front of him. Without comment he swung a hard punch which landed just above the boy's belt. Aaron was winded, but saw the next punch coming – it was aimed at his face. He bent his head forward in an attempt to duck it, causing it to land with a heavy thump to the side of his head. The blow hit his left ear and the boy reeled backwards against his captors in an attempt to dodge further blows. There were screams from the other side of the road where the horror-struck girls were watching. Perhaps because of this, the assailant became concerned that there were witnesses to the assault. He looked round at the officer who, indicating by shaking his head that the punishment had been sufficient, beckoned to the two men holding the boy to let go. They and the hatless man moved back into the ranks, while the dismounted officer, having dusted himself off, climbed back on to his horse, which was being held by a soldier.

Aaron had been momentarily stunned, but lurched back and with one hand nursing his ear, used the other to grab the mare's halter. One of the officers turned and spoke to the Serjeant who had hit him and who had shouted the previous command. He stepped out of rank, turned and shouted, "Company, common time, march!"

The long procession started moving on down the road in the direction of Salisbury. The four officers left the column and walked their mounts to the riverside to let them drink before resuming their journey towards Salisbury.

Aaron spoke comforting words in the ear of the mare and watched the soldiers as they tramped past. The marching men wore red jackets, though some of them had very well worn ones, with long turned-up white cuffs, some decorated with buttons. Their breeches must have at one time been white too, but now most were stained and darkened with road dust, the same dust which had removed the shine from their black boots and coated their tricorn hats. Each soldier carried a firelock over his left shoulder, and on the other shoulder a haversack; they each also had a knapsack on their backs with a rolled coat on top. On their left hips they had a bayonet frog with the handle of the weapon protruding. On the other hip each of them had a leather pouch and a circular wooden water container.

The drummer was no more than a boy; certainly a lot younger than Aaron. He strode at the head of the marchers, beating the pace of the march. He had a distinctive uniform and a different type of hat from the others.

It took a while for the column to pass; Aaron thought he counted sixty marching men. When they had gone by, there followed a procession of three horse-drawn vehicles. The loads on the carts were covered by oilskin sheets, but though he could not see the cargo, Aaron assumed that the goods being transported must be supplies for the company of soldiers. Each cart stopped for a while to let the horses drink. Then, when each carter decided that their animals had had enough, they backed the carts onto the track and turned to follow the marching men. All the while, Aaron had been holding the mare well out of the way of the military convoy.

As soon as the last cart had left, Peggy and the shepherd rushed across the road to him.

"Are you alright, boy?" he asked.

"Yes, I'm fine. My ear is burning from that punch – it's given me a noise in my head, sounds like an angry beehive, but I'm sure it will pass soon enough."

"Those brutes had no call to treat you so, but there ain't no arguing with them. Good thing you be a well-built lad."

Aaron agreed and said, "Right, I'd best be off then, or do you need help to gather up the ewes?"

"No, they be settled now and it shouldn't be difficult to get them back to following the ram."

"I'll bid you good day, then."

"Don't forget, come over to the Saracen's Head when you've done your business."

Aaron smiled and waved his hand indicating agreement. As he got further away, more than once he turned to see if he could get another glimpse of Peggy so that he could wave to her, but she was now too busy in the field helping to get the sheep to the riverside.

Aaron's head was in turmoil with a violent mix of emotions. He had met the prettiest of girls, he was furious about the cruel assault, and while he was increasingly excited about the prospect of seeing the big city, he was also getting more and more nervous.

Chapter 3

While the side of his head was tender and his ear felt as if it were on fire, it was the sound of a thousand bees in his head which caused Aaron most distress. But his discomfort did not distract him from his mission and he continued the long walk. He knew he had spent too long by the riverside and was beginning to feel anxious about keeping good time. So he walked onwards, with purpose and such speed as the horse allowed, slowing only once, when he reached the hamlet of Harnham on the outskirts of Salisbury and saw the miraculous pinnacle which was the spire of the mighty cathedral. His astonishment grew as the huge proportions of the stonework became apparent as he made his way towards the city.

The sun was almost at its zenith when Aaron saw a large inn across a field. His way to the bridge was straight ahead, but he was intrigued by the crowd of people and animals surrounding the building and he made a short detour on a path from the road to the inn to have a look. He saw from the picture on the inn sign that he had reached the Rose and Crown. The thatched inn was a busy place. Here there was all manner of conveyances parked in the field by the inn. It was a place where travellers rested before passing over the toll bridge and entering the city, or for those about to embark on the long journey to Dorchester or even Exeter in the opposite direction, it was the last opportunity to obtain refreshment and water horses for a considerable distance. There were many travellers milling around tending to their own needs and those of their animals.

Aaron did not stop, but he slowed his pace to look at the other travellers and their vehicles, and there were many looking at him as he led the fine animal. Just as he was passing the inn, two men leaning on a fence called out to him. Aaron looked at them carefully, but as he did not recognise them he carried on walking.

They left the fence and walked quickly in the same direction. Soon they caught up with Aaron and his horse.

"Fine hoss, son. You going to market?" said one of the men.

Aaron whispered "Whooa" to the horse and stopped to see what the men wanted.

One of them was hatless. He was tall and thin with what seemed a very long neck. There was considerably more hair on his face than on his head; in fact he was almost completely bald. He wore a threadbare brown jacket with tails and worn black breeches. The other man looked more prosperous. He had a black cocked hat, a long black jacket, grey breeches and white hose.

"You selling her at the market, lad?" asked the tall one.

"No, sir, I am selling her to Mr Briggs of Wilton."

"But we could save you a journey and give you a good price for her," said the man in the black jacket.

Aaron was feeling somewhat pressured by the two men and decided that it was best to move on. He went forward to the toll gate in front of a bridge.

One of the men called after him, "You would save money on the tolls too, if you sold her to us."

The boy paid them no heed and stopped beside a woman who was obviously waiting to cross the bridge. She looked at Aaron and said, "You done the right thing. Them forestallers are a menace. They would have cheated you, mark my words."

"Forestallers? What do that mean?" asked Aaron.

"Why, ain't you heard? They hang around on the road to market and offer to buy goods and animals from those who is going to Salisbury to sell them."

"Why do they do that?"

"Well, they make a handsome profit. They buy from the unsuspecting farmers, paying little, and then sell the selfsame items in the market at a higher price. But it is quite illegal – the charter of the market forbids forestallers."

"How can they do it then?"

"They take the risk, don't they? But I know the constable. I'll tell him when I get to town."

The gate keeper was busy directing the traffic while Aaron and the woman were standing talking behind him. When he turned round, the woman, who clearly passed this way often, greeted him. Then Aaron said, "I got to pay for the hoss and me, sir."

"Big horse for a young lad, ain't she?"

"I can handle her, sir."

"Sixpence, but wait here until those two carts have come over the bridge, for there ain't room for all of ye."

Aaron held the six pennies tightly in his clenched left hand and waited. When the carts had passed, the gate keeper directed Aaron and several other travellers to proceed over the bridge. As he walked across he realised what the man had meant by two bridges: there was one after the other, with two houses on the island between them. The construction of the first bridge greatly impressed him; it was the biggest bridge he had ever seen. Made of stone, it spanned the wide river flowing underneath. At the end of the first bridge the tollmaster was standing waiting for the travellers from the south. Aaron gave the man his six pennies and nervously asked him the way to the city centre.

"You can't go wrong, lad, just follow the crowd past St Nicholas Hospital," he said, pointing at several large buildings on the right side of the road beyond the bridge.

Aaron then proceeded over the second, smaller bridge. There was a stone wall on each side with two small, wider sections, almost like alcoves, where pedestrians could find refuge when a wide cart came across the bridge. Ahead of him the cathedral rose like a gigantic spearhead pointing heavenwards. He was becoming overawed by the scale of his new experiences. The boy's heart was beating so loudly with the excitement of entering the city that he could almost hear it. The horse too seemed to be affected by the busy atmosphere and Aaron had to keep patting and gently speaking to her to calm the beast.

It was now obvious from the stream of people and transport in both directions where the main thoroughfare to the centre of the city was. He passed several fine buildings before the road reached the high stone wall which surrounded the Cathedral Close, the wall described by the farm manager. Nevertheless he felt uncertain and when a woman carrying a basket hurrying in the same direction drew beside him he said, "Good day, mistress. Can you tell me which street this is?"

The woman slowed and turned to face Aaron. He saw that her face, topped by a high bonnet, was red from the exertion of walking. Catching her breath, she said, "This, my lad, is Draghall Street. Where you be going?"

"I'm taking the horse to the Red Lion and Cross Keys."

"Well, go over this bridge, and turn left."

In front of Aaron was another bridge, which though much smaller than the previous two bridges crossed a stream.

"You'll see Brickett's Hospital on the other side of the road. Just keep walking. It ain't far."

"Thank you, ma'am," said Aaron as he negotiated the bridge.

Looking down at the stream running under the bridge he could see that it carried all manner of rubbish and filth with it.

Walking down Draghall Street following the line of the Cathedral Close wall, he soon saw the fine building which must've been Brickett's Hospital, after which there were some cottages. The further he went, the bigger the houses became. He passed an opening in the Close wall with two massive gates pushed back to allow pedestrians to pass through. Opposite the gate was an inn with the sign of a bell, and then another with a king's head and next to that another, larger inn. People were crowding around the entrances to these hostelries and there was much shouting, laughter and some arguments. At the end of the wall, on the opposite corner, there was another ale house where several men were lifting barrels off of a dray and rolling them down a ramp into the ale house cellar. Aaron waited until one of the men walked past him to get on the dray and then asked the way to the Red Lion and Cross Keys.

As he walked down the street he was amazed at the size of the houses and all his senses were variously assaulted by the sights, sounds and smells of the city. He was almost overcome by the busyness of the streets and the noise. The excitement he felt dulled the irritation of the endless buzzing sound in his ear. He was jostled by other travellers and implored by hawkers trying to sell items from trays they held on their bellies, supported by a band round their necks.

The boy was well used to the smell of a farmyard, but the stench of the filthy street, which was covered in stale and fresh animal dung and the contents of domestic latrines, was overwhelming. The drainage system seemed ineffectual. The waste was only slowly being carried away by water in the ditch which ran along the side of the road. Soon, he came to the road junction where he had been told to turn right. Here the smell was just as bad – the ditch he had been walking alongside emptied into a canal which ran along the middle of the road. It was polluted and almost blocked by detritus of every kind. The waterway carried the refuse of the city to the river, which he had been following on his way to Salisbury. However, because of the period of dry weather which had been so favourable for the harvest, there was insufficient water in the canal to dispose quickly of the foul contents.

Ahead of him he saw a large sign mounted on an archway on the front of a big building. The sign showed a red lion and two keys crossed diagonally. This was his destination. He waited while a coach was manoeuvered out of the inn courtyard under the arch and into the road, watched it set off on its journey and then he led the mare under the sign and into a cobbled inner yard.

There were many horses tethered in the yard for this was a coaching inn where transports could swap their tired horses for fresh ones. The mare he was leading reacted to the other animals and became nervous and difficult to control. Seeing that he was having difficulties, a man wearing a leather apron who was using a shovel to clear the horse dung stopped what he was doing, propped his tool against the wall and hurried over to help Aaron. The boy was glad of the assistance of the hostler.

"We've been expecting you, well, that is to say, we've been expecting the horse, but Mr Mew usually deals with the horse trading. Where is he?"

"He had an accident last evening. Got stuck on a pitchfork. I'm his son."

"Nasty, sounds very nasty. Give him the good wishes of John the hostler – that's me," he added.

"Where can I find Mr Briggs?"

"He'll be in the bar. Ask the serving girl, she'll direct you. Give me the halter, I'll put this lady in a stall and give her a feed and some water," he said, grabbing the rope from Aaron.

The boy gave the horse a farewell pat and walked across the courtyard in the direction indicated by the hostler. In front of him was a large black door with some writing on; he lifted the latch and pushed it open. The scene that greeted him was one he had not expected. He had assumed that he would find Mr Briggs waiting for him in salubrious circumstances. Instead, there was an atmosphere of raucous revelry and it was anything but obvious which of these gentlemen before him could be Mr Briggs. The bar was packed with small groups of people sitting at tables speaking to each other in raised voices. Some sang, some cursed, some shouted, many laughed. Here and there some figures appeared to be sleeping with their heads resting on their arms folded on the tables. The beer-stained tables supported wooden tankards and the occasional pewter one. Yet there were no wretches here; everyone seemed to be well clothed and of respectable appearance.

It was quite difficult to see the far side of the room. There was only one window which gave little natural light. Visibility was further hampered by the foul smoky atmosphere. The air was choking, partly with the smell of beer, but mainly from the heavy aroma of tobacco smoke. Many of the drinkers had clay pipes in their hands, on the table in front of them or in their mouths. Flitting between the tables were serving wenches carrying tankards overflowing with froth.

Aaron was aghast, yet mesmerised by the scene. However, he quickly came to his senses when a man sitting at the table next to where he was standing grabbed him by the arm.

The man addressed the others at his table: "Well, here's a fine young lad. Shouldn't wonder if he's bin sent by his mother to fetch his dad home!"

His companions roared with laughter. One of them shouted, "Come, lad, have a taste of the hops." The speaker held up his tankard to the boy.

"Thank you, sir, but I'm 'ere on business."

"Oh, lads, did you hear that? He's here on business!"

There was further laughter round the table.

"And what business might a whippersnapper like you have in this fine hostelry?"

"I am to sell a horse."

The ribaldry at the table got even more intense.

Aaron had heard enough – he wrenched his arm from the man's grip and moved quickly across to one of the serving girls. She was busy, but paused when he called out to her, "Can you direct me to Mr Briggs of Wilton?"

The girl turned towards him and he was surprised to see that although she wore the clothes of a girl, she was quite old, perhaps in her thirties. She wore long brightly coloured skirts and a blouse with a very low cut over her bosom.

"Well, my love, what dealings would a young gentleman like you have with a man of such status?"

"I am here to receive payment for a draught mare I have brought from my master."

The woman eyed the boy up and down, enjoying seeing him blush at the sight of her.

"Over there, in the corner – the gentleman with the black wig." She pointed to the darkest corner of the room.

Aaron made his way to the table. He could see that Mr Briggs was sitting with two other men and a woman. He was puffing at a long clay pipe and in front of him was a pewter tankard. The man looked up as Aaron arrived at his table.

"Please, sir, I am the son of Mr Mew. He has been injured and I have brought the mare to Salisbury instead of him." Aaron had to raise his voice to make himself heard.

"Not injured badly, I hope?"

"Badly enough, sir. He had a pitchfork through his shoulder."

"How unfortunate. You say that you have brought the mare?"

"Yes, sir, she be outside."

"Then let's take a look at her."

Mr Briggs drained his tankard and excused himself to his company. When he stood up Aaron noticed that he was very tall and well proportioned. He had the air of a man of authority; he spoke very loudly and people seemed to show deference to him. He put his pipe on the table, straightened his jacket, put on his tricorn hat and then the two of them wended their way around the tables in the bar room to the door. As they proceeded, drinkers at several tables greeted or made comments to the estate manager as he passed. Clearly he was very well known.

Aaron was glad to be outside again. The air, corrupted as it was by the fumes of the city, seemed pure in comparison with the stench of the bar.

They made their way to the stall. Aaron opened the gate and held it open for the older man, who went in and untied the animal. The boy was suddenly seized with terror; he thought, what if I have walked her too fast and she is lame – did I give her enough water? He felt a sweat break out as the mare was ushered past him.

Mr Briggs led the mare out into the daylight. Without saying a word he expertly pinched, prodded and squeezed different parts of the horse while Aaron held the halter.

"Lead her across the yard, lad."

Aaron understood that the buyer wanted to be sure that the horse was not lame. He did as instructed and hoped against hope that all was well.

There was a long tormenting pause and then Mr Briggs said, "Yes, apart from the road dust she is in as fine fettle as when I saw her on your master's farm. Next time you sell a horse, lad, give her a grooming before the purchaser checks her over."

Aaron led the mare back into the stall and closed the gate. His heart was again thumping loudly. He had to ask for the money now.

"Begging pardon, sir, but um…I should take the sales price back to my master."

"Yes, of course. Let's go back inside. You must be thirsty after your long walk. I'll buy you an ale."

Aaron was embarrassed. He knew that his mother would not approve of him drinking beer, but Mr Briggs was a man of substance and status; he could not offend him by refusing his offer. And indeed, he was really very thirsty.

"Well, that is kind of you, sir," he replied.

Mr Briggs led the way back to the bar room door. He opened it and they made their way through the almost impenetrable fug towards his table. As they passed a serving woman, Mr Briggs put his hand on her backside and said, "Two of your best ales, my tankard is on the table."

The woman giggled and said, "Of course, Mr Briggs, I always reserve the best for you."

When they arrived at the table one of the men had gone and Aaron took his chair. The estate manager took off his hat and addressed the couple at the table.

"My young friend has indeed done well to bring a very powerful animal nigh on ten miles for it to begin work on our estate. Master Mew, my companions are Mr and Mistress Dawson, tenant farmers on his Lordship's estate. They have sold their porkers at the pig market this morning."

"Pleased to meet you I am sure," said Aaron respectfully.

The couple nodded at him, but clearly they were somewhat in awe of the ebullient Mr Briggs and made no conversation.

"So, young Master Mew, your employer trusts you to carry money to him. A lot of money."

"Yes, sir, I be honest and trustworthy."

"Very good indeed, I am sure you are."

"I must return to the village this evening and on my arrival I will take the money directly to the estate manager's house."

"Good. Well here is the sum agreed."

He reached into a pouch at his side and pulled out a leather purse. He pushed it across the table to the boy.

"It is all there," he added.

Aaron was perplexed. His master had told him to count the money before accepting it and signing the bill of sale. However, he sensed that Mr Briggs would be offended if he made such a show of doubting the manager's honesty. He picked up the purse and held it in his hand. It was impossible for him to judge whether the amount was right by its weight. He had to count it. Salvation was at hand: Mr Briggs stood up and said, "I must go for a piss."

Aaron quickly, but carefully, tipped the contents of the purse onto the table. Ignoring the man and woman at the table he started to methodically count the coins. When he was halfway through, the serving woman came with the two ales. She paused for a while, looking at the coins on the table, and then moved off to deal with other orders.

"Twelve, that's right," he said to himself.

He pulled out the cord around his neck, opened the pouch and put the purse inside. He then put the pouch back inside his shirt.

Mr Briggs came back and sat down.

"Your good health, Master Mew, and a speedy recovery for your father!"

The man pushed the full wooden tankard towards the boy and raised his ale. Aaron picked up the tankard and took a long swallow of the beer. He found it somewhat bitter, but not objectionably so and took a second draught.

"Now, Master Mew, a second bit of advice for you. Don't trust anyone, especially your elders and betters!"

Despite their respect for the estate manager, the man and woman laughed and agreed volubly.

"Always count the money you are paid. There could be a pig in the poke."

Mr Briggs' companions laughed even louder. Querulously, the man said, "The joke's on you, Mr Briggs."

"How so?"

"Master Mew counted the money while you were away!"

The manager leant forward, slapped Aaron on the back and said, "You are clearly wiser than I had thought. We'll have another."

"But, sir, I am not finished with the drink I have."

"Make the most of it. I have to leave shortly and I would not like you to return to your father and say that Mr Briggs was any less generous with his son than he is with his father."

Mr Briggs shouted above the noise of the crowd to attract the attention of a serving woman. When she arrived he said, "Two more ales and I can settle my account."

When the fresh tankards had been placed on the table, he turned to Aaron and said, "Now, you have a bill of sale for me."

Aaron had almost forgotten the final part of the sales act.

"Oh yes, sir, that I have."

He fumbled in his shoulder bag and pulled out a creased paper. He passed it to the manager who shouted to the serving woman for a pen and ink.

"Seems in order. When she brings the pen you should sign it here."

He held his finger in the space provided in anticipation that the boy would not be able to read the paper. When the pen arrived he dipped it into the ink, shook off the drip on the sharpened quill and passed it to the boy who slowly scribed his name.

"What is your job on the farm that the manager trusts you so well?"

"I am not working on the farm, sir. I am apprenticed to the blacksmith in the village. I have been for three years."

"How old are you now?"

"Almost eighteen, sir."

"Contact me when you have finished your apprenticeship. We can always find work for a good blacksmith."

So saying, he knocked out his pipe by inverting it and gently tapping it on the table. He stood up, once again put on his hat and said to his companions, "Come then if you wish to join me in my carriage to Wilton."

The man and the woman got up from the table to leave with Mr Briggs.

"Farewell, Master Mew, pass my respects to your father."

"Goodbye, sir, and thank you."

The three of them departed and Aaron was left alone with his second tankard of ale. As Mr Briggs made his way across the floor Aaron noticed that the manager singled out one of the serving wenches, gave her some coins, and glancing round at Aaron, leant forward and had a word in her ear.

The boy sat contemplating what Mr Briggs had said about the possibility of employment. It seemed unreal, but then everything was beginning to seem unreal. He was feeling light-headed; perhaps he should leave the rest of the ale where it was. But then his parents had always taught him not to be wasteful. Mr Briggs had been kind enough to buy it for him. He should be grateful he thought, as he took another long swallow.

As he sat gazing at the tankard, increasingly unaware of what was going on around him, he felt a movement in the air and heard a noise close at hand – the rustle of cloth. He looked up and saw that one of the serving women, the one Mr Briggs had spoken to, had sat down on the chair next to his.

"I heard tell that you have walked all but ten miles today with a girt hoss."

The woman leant forward across the table revealing more bosom than Aaron had ever seen in his life, apart from when his mother fed the baby. He tried to fidget to the far side of his chair.

"You must be real tired, I'm thinking."

Aaron had indeed begun to feel somewhat dozy, but that was before the woman had sat beside him.

"Now my pretty, you likes what you sees, don't ye? You want to see more?"

"Miss, I've got to be going shortly to be home afore sundown."

He suddenly became aware, under the table, of her hand on his thigh. He tried to move further away, but in response she gripped him. The hand moved further up towards his groin and a battle commenced between his instinct to reject this advance and his enjoyment of the pleasure he was feeling. He struggled, but as the hand explored further he began to concede.

"Why don't we go to the hay loft where we can be more comfortable, my lovely?" said the woman. She began to stand up, saying, "Follow me."

Aaron picked up his bag and tamely, but with some enthusiasm, followed her out of a door adjacent to where they were sitting. She held the door open for him and then closed and locked it. It was quite dark in the passageway through which she led him, but he could see daylight under the door at the end of it. Immediately before she reached this door, they passed a dark turning which went off to the right. By the light coming under the door Aaron saw the woman turn towards him and reach to pull him towards her. She threw her arms around his shoulders; as she did so, he was conscious of a noise behind him.

The first blow to his head only stunned him, but he felt his legs giving way. He was too weak to resist. The woman held him up so that the assailant could hit him again.

Chapter 4

The buzz in his ear woke Aaron. He opened his eyes. The iridescence of something moving in front of his head was the first thing that came into focus, but the drowsiness he felt caused him to stay still. The object moved into his field of vision again. Now he was becoming more aware of his surroundings. He was lying on grass. The source of the iridescence was a pigeon's neck as the late afternoon sun caught it.

Aaron jerked his head up to survey his surroundings while still lying on the ground. He was in some sort of field with tall trees, but he was not alone. There were several men prostrate on the ground and some sitting with earthenware flasks, which they occasionally held to their mouths, and not far away there was a group of men having an altercation.

He sat up slowly. He could see rows of cottages in front of him and turning round he saw a long grass rampart behind. A shadow fell across him.

"You look to be a bloody mess, boy. Bit young to be here, ain't ye?"

Aaron looked up and saw a wretchedly dressed hatless man clinging to a bottle, leaning over him.

"Where is this?" he asked.

"This is purgatory, my son, this be where those as no one will have in the city have to quench their thirst. Be thankful that it is a fine day."

Aaron could tell from the way the man slurred his words that he was very drunk. But he was only one of many in the same state who were occupying the grassy area.

The man continued, "What happened to your head, young fella?"

Aaron put his hand to the back of his head and very gingerly felt the tender lump. When he withdrew his hand and looked at it he saw that it was covered in blood. He then became conscious that the back of his collar was wet and sticky from the same fluid.

"Ain't so bad as it looks, knocks to the head always bleed like a stuck pig. Ask me, an old soldier who has had a few bangs."

"What time is it?"

"That's difficult to say," he said as he took a swig from his bottle. "I heard the bells from the church for evensong some while back, but I've had a nap since then."

The man sat down beside him and Aaron became aware of the foul stench of his companion. As he turned to Aaron the boy could see in detail the swollen red nose with streaks of burst blood vessels, the blotchy cheeks and his grey uneven whiskers penetrating the filth on a face unwashed for many days. The man moved even closer.

Aaron began to wonder if the man was going to attack him. His instinct was to move away to protect himself and the pouch inside his shirt. He grasped at the pouch. At first he thought that it had slipped or fallen off of the cord inside his shirt for it was not in the right place. Frantically he felt around the shirt, where it was tucked into his breeches. There was no pouch!

A sensation of terror shot through the young man's spine. He frantically searched again, and again. He looked for his shoulder bag – it was gone, as was his jacket. He was distraught. He was penniless in a city he did not know. His anger grew as he thought back to what had happened to him, but nevertheless his brain was still too slow to connect his encounter with the woman with the disappearance of the money. He turned to his drunken sot of a companion and seized the old man by the ragged lapels of his jacket.

"You have stolen my money, give it back."

The man blinked; his inebriated state prevented him from reacting quickly. He fell backwards and Aaron rolled across to sit astride the man. He held his fist up threateningly above him.

"Give me my money back!"

The drunk was sobering fast and shouted, "Lay off me you mad bastard, I haven't got your money. Do you think that I would hang around this cesspit of a place if I had money?"

The shouting had attracted others from the serried groups of drinkers. Several men waddled over to watch the action, but one of their number, a brutish looking figure, came more quickly than the others. He grabbed Aaron by the shoulder and dragged him off the man on the ground.

"Leave the old feller alone, there's no harm in him. What's wrong anyway?"

"He stole my money pouch. I had twelve pounds from Mr Briggs."

"You hear that lads? He had twelve pounds, he says!"

There was raucous laughter from the gathering crowd.

"Son, do you think old Harry would hang around here if he had twelve pounds in his pockets?"

There was more laughter from the crowd.

"Now we be peaceable folk enjoying the evening air on market day and spending our wages the way we like. You can join us or push off."

Aaron stood up and surveyed the wrecks of humanity gathered around him. He felt slightly dizzy.

"But where has it gone then? I had a cord round my neck with a money pouch."

"By the looks of your head you've been waylaid, lad. You should never keep all your money in one place."

In a flash Aaron realised what had happened – he had been robbed in the inn. He remembered being held while someone hit him. Greater anger now welled up inside of him.

"Which way is it to the Red Lion and Cross Keys?" he demanded of everyone in general.

One of the crowd answered, "You won't be welcome there, that's an inn for fine folk."

The man who had dragged him off the drunk called Harry said, "Is that where you were waylaid, lad?"

"It has to be."

"What happened then?"

"I was talking to a woman and…" His voice tailed off. He was too ashamed to explain any further.

"That explains a lot, don't it!" shouted one of the crowd.

"I have to go there and find the woman," said Aaron.

The man who had previously asked him to relate what had happened said, "I should go down to the pump in the lane over there and wash the blood out of your hair before you go. You look a sight fit to frighten God-fearing folk."

Pointing in the direction of the pump again, he said, "That lane leads through to Milford Street. You go down the hill and you will see the sign of the Red Lion and Cross Keys."

Aaron, grateful for having found kindness in an unexpected place amongst these drunks, down and outs and ne'er-do-wells, nodded and raised his hand in thanks. He trudged off in the direction shown him towards the pump. There he joined a queue of adults and children with different types of receptacles, all waiting to get water from the post with a handle on one side and a spout on the other. Some helped each other, one pumping and the other holding a bucket or whatever they had brought to collect the water. When it came to his turn, Aaron pumped quickly and hard knowing that there would be a flow of water sufficient for him to leave the handle and run to the spout with his head under it. He did this twice, enjoying the refreshing sensation of the cold water. He flicked his long hair several times and then left the pump and followed the lane towards the inn.

By the time he reached the door of the bar room, his anger had reasserted itself. He pushed the door open violently and marched in. The scene was the same with the drinkers sitting around the tables and many of them contributing to the foul air as they puffed on their pipes. Aaron looked around to see if he could identify the woman, the authoress of his predicament. The light outside was failing and inside was worse. After spending some time looking at the serving women he could not see the one he sought. His sense of justice tinged with a large measure of desperation drove him to go to the bar.

"I have been robbed by one of the serving women!" he shouted to one of the men standing by the large ale barrels.

"Not here you haven't, this is a respectable establishment," replied a man passing two tankards to a woman.

Aaron's anger spilled over. He raised his fist to the man.

"One of your serving women took the twelve pounds Mr Briggs gave me. I want it back – I must get it back."

"Steady, lad," said the barman as he looked round and called out to get the attention of a very large man with rolled-up sleeves who was hammering a tap into a barrel lying horizontally beside several others.

The bigger man stepped over and tried to grab Aaron, but the boy pulled away and shouted, "You must help me, I have to find my master's money."

The man tried again to grab Aaron, but the boy kicked out at him. "The little bugger!"

He lunged at Aaron and pushed him backwards so that he fell over a wooden crate on the floor. He bent down and grabbed him by his shirt, held his clenched fist over the boy and said, "On your feet, before I give you reason to lie on the ground."

Aaron struggled to get up and did so partly propelled by the man, who had hold of his shirt. When he was on his feet, the barman punched him on the side of his ribcage. By this time the disruption had been noted by those sitting closest to the barrels and they began to crowd around to view the spectacle. Others were craning over heads trying to see what was happening. The barman hit Aaron again and then he was aware of the other man dragging him towards the door which was opened by one of the onlookers.

"Back to the street with you where filthy beggars belong," said the man as he pushed Aaron under the high archway of the coaching inn and into the roadway. He gave the boy a kick which caused him to fall into the filth of the gutter. The man turned and went back inside. Aaron felt tears welling up, but he had not cried since he had clung to his mother's skirts and he fought not to do so now.

He dragged himself back to the wall of the inn and sat there a while. He was aching from the punches; his head throbbed from the injury and his ear was still buzzing. He tried to gather his thoughts. He realised that though he was bruised, he was not badly injured, and after a while the pain from the punches began to subside. It was getting dark; he wondered what was to become of him. He could try walking home in the dark; it should not be too difficult. However, he had no money for the toll road – he would have to cross the fields and find a way over the river. And then he suddenly realised that part of the reason that he was feeling weak and sorry for himself was that he was hungry. He had not eaten since he had enjoyed his lunch by the side of the river. It seemed like a lifetime ago. He had to find food if he was going to walk home. Home, home…What would happen when he had to tell the estate manager that he had lost the money, all twelve pounds?

There would be disgrace for him and probably for his father too. Perhaps his father would have to pay the money back. It would take him years to do so, and at what cost to the family?

Aaron sat and watched what he could see of the market evening revelers passing; some had lanterns, others held flaming torches. Two flaming torches had been placed on pillars outside of the inn. There was a babble of noise and conversation. People seemed to be enjoying themselves; some were turning to go into the inn, and others were going to their homes or other inns. Then he heard a different sound. It was a sound he had heard earlier in the day – the tramp of men marching to the beat of a drum. The sound got louder and then around the corner, by the light of lanterns and the lighted torches, he saw the four mounted officers appear, soon followed by a column of marching men paired two abreast. As they appeared, people stopped and started cheering. The marching men were in step and clearly trying to look their best as they marched past the inn towards the market place. As they passed, many men and women and some children fell in behind them and followed. Aaron got to his feet and joined the throng.

The column passed a huge building which was surrounded by a wooden scaffold. Aaron recognised from the estate manager's description that this must be the Bishop's Hall which was being repaired. In front of it was another large building. The column marched between them both and on to the market square. Had Aaron seen the place earlier, he would have been impressed by the number of market stalls and the animals in pens, but now the square had been cleared and cleaned and many burning torches lit up the area. He stopped by the stocks in front of the Bishops Hall. By the light of the flares he saw a man sitting with his legs trapped in the wooden construction. Despite the filth with which he must have been bombarded, he recognised the bald man with the long neck sitting in the stocks – it was one of the forestallers. It seemed that the constable had done his work.

The soldiers filed into the square led by the drummer boy and then some of them formed into two short lines. The men in each line carried their weapons across their bodies and gradually in measured paces approached each other as if attacking. Although the light of the torches did not permit him to see all the people, Aaron was aware that there was a large crowd watching the military drill.

An order was shouted: "Halt", then a second, "Cock firelock", then a third, "Make ready". The men took a short step back with their right legs. The order "Present" was followed by "Fire". All the soldiers had pointed their firelocks at an angle into the air. The volley echoed loudly around the square.

There was a cheer from the crowd, and the officers on horseback struggling with their nervous animals, made a perfunctory bow. Then all the men formed up again in ranks and marched past a point in the square where a table and chairs had been arranged. Just beyond it they placed their firelocks in groups of three, standing leaning against each other. Once they had disarmed, the soldiers in the line broke off and gathered in informal groups, some headed off in different directions.

Aaron was much taken by the demonstration and joined in the cheering. Then one of the officers standing behind the table stood upon a chair and addressed those of the crowd remaining.

"Good people of Salisbury. You have seen a fine demonstration by this recruiting company of magnificent men of the 62nd Regiment of Foot. Fear not, they were firing blanks. Men, you too can wear the red jacket of this brave band. We need more men to face down the enemies of our Sovereign George the Third in our thirteen colonies of America. There, brave Loyalists endure the attacks of the perfidious rebels who reject the rule of His Most Gracious Majesty. Join us as we march to glorious victories against these villains. Leave your worries about poverty, hunger and lack of purpose behind you. In the army you will be fed, clothed and taken care of. Take the King's shilling and join the courageous redcoats."

There was a ripple of applause. Aaron noticed several couples nearby where women tugged at husbands' or sweethearts' arms and drew them away from any temptation to accede to the persuasive speaker. When an officer started walking around addressing people individually in the dwindling crowd, Aaron took fright and found his way out of the light, to the edge of the square. But then his attention was caught again by activity near to the table. He heard orders being shouted and turned to see three manacled men being led by two others, one of whom was carrying a lantern. The crowd started gathering again to watch the spectacle. The three prisoners were pushed towards the table and an officer asked them something, the answer to which he appeared to be writing down.

Aaron moved forward with the small crowd, which surged towards the table to watch. He turned to a youth about his own age who was also watching the spectacle and asked, "What is happening to the men?"

The boy said, "They have been brought from the County Gaol at Fisherton Bridge. They are criminals. The two watchmen are taking them to sign up for the army."

"But why?"

"The gaol is overfull and they have been given a choice – a crowded rat-ridden riverside prison or the army." He laughed and continued, "Most of the King's army is made up of convicts, debtors, lunatics and Irishmen."

Aaron reflected on what he had seen and heard; it seemed a harsh fate for the three men. But then he remembered his own situation – he had become a debtor himself. How could he repay his master the twelve pounds? What was he to do? He was hungry, had no jacket and was sore, although not in serious pain now, and he had no money. Neither did he know anyone in the city. He stood considering his plight and then turned round to watch some of the soldiers going into the three inns across the roadway. There were flaming torches outside each of them. The one directly opposite where he was standing had a painted sign which he could see by the light of the flames. It showed a man with a cloth around his head. He walked over the road.

"What inn is this?" he asked a fellow who was walking towards him.

"Why, can you not see? It is the Saracen's Head."

Aaron immediately remembered and said to himself, Saracen, the Saracen's Head! That was the inn where the shepherdess Peggy was to work for her aunt!

Apart from Mr Briggs, who was now in Wilton, the only people he was acquainted with at all in the area were the girls and their father, though the shepherd had probably left Salisbury by now. Perhaps Peggy would help him! He walked across the road and found a way through the throng of drinkers standing outside the inn. The door to the tavern was wide open and looking in, it seemed to him at first to be much the same as the previous inn he had visited, though more crowded. Once again there was a thick layer of tobacco smoke above the heads of the drinkers who were sitting and standing around with tankards. But the noise level was much higher than in the Red Lion and Cross Keys, with shouts, laughter, cursing and some song. And then he noticed that the people were different; here the customers seemed to be less salubrious. Many were simply dressed and some wore tattered clothing. As he stood looking through the doorway, two burly men pushed past him dragging a customer who was worse for drink. They unceremoniously threw him onto the walkway before returning inside.

Aaron got closer and peered in to see if he could identify Peggy among the serving women. The only light was that from candles on the tables and he could not easily see the features of the women. From where he stood he saw no one resembling Peggy. He plucked up courage and sidled up to one of the women as she walked past.

"Pardon me, miss, but is there a girl called Peggy working here?"

The woman turned and smiled at him. Even in the poor light Aaron could see that the woman was much older than Peggy.

"Who is asking, my love?"

The crepuscular light hid the fact that Aaron was blushing.

"Er…I am a friend of her father's."

"Then you had better ask him where she is. He is over there," she said pointing.

Aaron's eyes followed the direction of her arm and he saw, not far away, sitting at a table by the wall, the shepherd. The boy was surprised as he thought that the man was going to return to his farm that evening. Aaron walked over to the table. The shepherd sat with two women; both of them were smoking pipes. He was leaning forward in discussion with the women and did not notice Aaron until the boy said in a loud voice to combat the noise in the bar, "Excuse me, sir. I am Aaron, the one who helped you to recover your flock."

The shepherd turned slowly and looked up at the boy. He gazed for a while and then in a slurred tone shouted, "The lad with the big hoss?"

"Yes sir, the same."

"Well, there's happenstance!"

"How so, sir?"

"I was just describing the event which caused me to nearly lose my flock. My companions are so taken with the presence of our brave soldiers that they will hear no ill spoken of them. But they almost ruined me!"

The shepherd was clearly much the worse for the drink and his words were, though loud, quite difficult to interpret.

"But you did get them safely to market, sir?"

"Only by the grace of God – and your help."

"I was happy to help, sir."

"Pull up a chair, boy, and sit with us. This is my sister, Widow Tomkins the innkeeper, and her friend, Miss Attril."

Aaron nodded to the two ladies and then took an unoccupied chair from an adjacent table and sat down.

"Shouldn't you have walked home this afternoon?" asked the shepherd.

"Indeed I should have, sir, but I have been robbed."

Miss Attril shouted across the table in a shrill voice, "Robbed – robbed? How were you robbed?"

Aaron paused for a moment, considering his reply. The whole truth would do nothing to enhance his prospect of gaining sympathy from the listeners.

"'Twas when I returned from the privy that I was fallen upon and beaten."

"What privy, where?" asked the sister.

"In the Red Lion and Cross Keys. I had to transact the sale of the horse with Mr Briggs there."

"So much for the so-called fine folk who give custom to that establishment," said Miss Attril of the rival inn.

"But what of the money from the sale?" asked the shepherd.

"Gone, all gone. All twelve pounds, even the pennies my mother gave me to spend. And gone with it is my jacket and my shoulder bag. I have nothing."

The innkeeper addressed the shepherd: "Ezra, order an ale for the boy, you owes him." She turned to Aaron. "And I dare say you haven't eaten, have you?"

"No mistress, not since noon."

The woman called one of the serving women over to the table and spoke to her. She turned back to Aaron.

"You'll get some bread and mutton presently. You can sleep in the hay loft tonight afore ye return tomorrow. It'll be too cold to walk abroad without a jacket. But come to think of it, I have a jacket of my late dear husband's, God rest his soul. He were a hefty blighter like you. It will fit a treat."

"You are very kind, Mistress Tomkins."

As they were talking, more and more soldiers were coming into the inn. They were now off duty and carried their hats under their arms. Indeed had they not, they would have been knocked off by the low beams. Most stood around in groups holding tankards; by royal decree public houses had to give serving soldiers two pints of ale free.

"There will be little profit made here this evening," said Widow Tomkins.

"Perchance they may buy ale when they have had their free share," said Ezra.

"No, they will move on to the Chough and claim their beer there too," she replied.

The atmosphere was very jolly and most were well behaved, but one small group of three were loudly abusive to the people nearby to where Aaron was sitting and demanded that they should move to another table so that this group of three could sit together.

The innkeeper looked across to the table considering whether any action should be taken and decided against it. She turned to the shepherd. "You might expect that the officers would give the men a good example of gentlemanly behaviour."

"Those three young ones be officers?"

"Yes, you see the sashes they are wearing and their lace. The two boys are ensigns."

"Some rich father paid their commissions to make men of them."

There was a loud shout as one of the three tried to get the attention of one of the serving women.

Aaron paid the men no attention; he was more concerned with the possibility of food and a comfortable lodging for the night. He was feeling huge relief at having found some sympathetic support; his mind had also moved to wondering where Peggy might be.

"I hope that your daughters were not too fatigued by the long walk today, sir."

"They been long since sent to bed. A man can't have a decent wet while being nagged by family."

"Ezra, you know they have your best at heart."

"That's as maybe, but I don't want them down here in this rough company."

Just then there was a scream. They looked up just in time to see the woman serving the officers give one of them a slap. The slap had been observed by many others including a large group of soldiers. From them came a loud cheer.

The officer who had been slapped stood up and grabbed the fleeing woman by the arm. He flung her to the ground and kicked her. Immediately, pandemonium broke loose in the room. Everyone it seemed wanted to exceed the volume and severity of the curses of his or her neighbour as they verbally attacked the officer.

Mistress Tomkins stood up and marched over to the table amid a great cheer from the customers. It was clear from her gesticulation that she was demanding that the men should leave. One of them, with a fringed epaulette on his left shoulder, stood and roughly pushed her backwards. As he did so the two burly men whom Aaron had previously seen eject a drinker, arrived at the table. The three officers started trading blows with these two.

Aaron stood up and, weaving his way round the tables and chairs, ran up to the fracas and grabbed the officer with the epaulette by the shoulder. The man, who was short but stout, turned to face Aaron and raised his fist, but Aaron was faster and landed a blow squarely on the officer's nose. The red-jacketed officer fell backwards over his chair and crashed to the sawdust covered floor. The cheering of the crowd reached a crescendo.

The officer stood up and glared at Aaron. Then he jerked his head as if in disbelief, strained forward and said, "I know you, you whelp. We have met before. Mark my words, we will meet again."

He spat at Aaron, who was about to hit him again when Mistress Tomkins grabbed the boy's shoulder and said, "No, Aaron, it is not necessary, these gentlemen are leaving."

As the three were manhandled out, the bloodied one turned and shouted, "Until next time, Master Aaron."

The inn quietened down and Aaron resumed his place. Mistress Tomkins sat down, taking deep breaths while she struggled to relight her pipe and said, "Thank you for your help, Master Aaron, but I fear that you have made an enemy this evening."

"That's as maybe, but I have nothing on my conscience."

"Apart from losing your master's twelve pounds," Miss Attril reminded him.

The remark brought Aaron back to the reality of his situation. He supped his ale and then to his delight a platter of bread and meat was put before him. Then another tankard of ale appeared. The serving woman leaned forward and said, "The foot soldiers over there sent you a beer as a reward for your effort. They enjoyed watching the officers getting some of their own medicine."

Aaron looked across to the largest group of soldiers; many were still laughing and joking about the recent event and several raised their tankards to him. Then, suddenly, these men went quiet. Another soldier had come into the inn and Aaron immediately recognised him as the officer who had hit him earlier in the day. The Serjeant leant forward to the nearest soldier and asked him something. The man shook his head at the officer who then grabbed him by the lapels of his jacket and pulled him so that their faces were almost touching. The trembling man lifted an arm and pointed across the room to where Aaron was sitting.

Serjeant Granville ordered a beer and then stood apart from the others with his tankard, sipping the ale and ignoring those around him. He looked resplendent with his red sash of office tied in a knot on his left hip. Running through the sash was a buff coloured stripe, the colour of the uniform facings for the regiment; other parts of his jacket had markings of the same hue. His buttons were polished and it was clear that the cloth of his red jacket was of a better quality than that of the men, and unlike the men, he carried a sword. From time to time he glanced across to where the innkeeper and her company were sitting. When he had finished his beer he called a serving woman, spoke to her and waited until she came back with two tankards. He took the two tankards in one hand and did something with one of them. He then pushed his way through the throng of people, and moved across the room towards the table where Aaron was sitting.

Serjeant Granville beamed a genial smile and addressed Aaron, "Hail to the hero of the evening. No hard feelings I hope, lad. Here with the complements of the army, to wash down your supper."

He placed one of the tankards on the table alongside the one which was already there.

Aaron looked up at the soldier, impressed by his civility compared with the behaviour of the officers. Ezra too was taken by the sentiments of the man, despite his irritation about what had happened to his sheep in the morning.

Ezra tried to engage the soldier in conversation and asked, "Have you been in the army long?"

"That I have, sir, these last twenty years."

"And have you seen much action?"

"Enough, sir, for I was one of the two hundred gallant men of the Carrickfergus garrison who held out against the French army in 1760."

"What happened?"

"We were besieged for weeks and eventually ran out of food and ammunition. But we fought as long as we could. We even melted our coat buttons to make bullets. When we surrendered, it was with honour. The French commander allowed us to march out of the castle with our weapons and he promised not to sack the town."

The company was listening with rapt attention.

"Sit down, sir, and tell us more of your regiment's endeavors."

"That's kind of you, sir, but I must rejoin my companions."

"Before you go, can you tell me who those officers were who caused the trouble?" asked
the innkeeper.

Somewhat reluctantly, he replied, "Oh, it was the Lieutenant and two ensigns."

"Is the Lieutenant your senior officer?" asked the shepherd.

"Oh no, the company commander is Captain Trowbridge – you wouldn't see the likes of him in here, sir, meaning no disrespect, ma'am. He will be dining with his wealthy friends somewhere in the city."

With that the soldier moved back across the room and once more stood alone. From time to time, Aaron found himself glancing across at the Serjeant and each time he felt some discomfort about the fact that the man appeared to be watching their table.

Conversation flowed as Aaron's companions filled and refilled their glasses. He himself, being unused to the drink and now mindful of how it had contributed to his downfall earlier in the day, drank slowly and with small draughts. He was in any case feeling tired and somewhat unwell. His head throbbed from the effects of the robber's blows, and he was still troubled by the buzzing in his ear.

"Mistress Tomkins, if it pleases you I would like to take my leave and use your hayloft."

"Of course my lad, you finish up the beer the gentleman has bought you and I will show you the way."

Aaron's hand stretched out for the full tankard and he pulled it towards him. He looked at the brown liquid, thought for a while, took a deep breath and then resigned himself to the fact that good manners dictated that he should do as Mistress Tomkins had said. He hesitated for a moment, then picked up the tankard and put it to his lips. He was tired of the drink; the more he drank the less he enjoyed it. He took a sip and decided to take one long swallow and pretend that he had finished, for his companions could not easily see how much was in the container. When he put the tankard down, he found that Serjeant Granville was at his shoulder.

"Welcome my lad, welcome to our company, otherwise called the 62nd Regiment of Foot."

"What do you mean?" asked Aaron. His companions all looked quizzically at the soldier.

Without saying a word, the soldier took the tankard from Aaron's hand and very slowly decanted it into the empty one next to it. When the liquid had been emptied he held out his hand and into it dropped a coin.

"Here my lad, you took the King's shilling. King's regulations say that having the coin in your drink is the same as having it presented to the palm of your hand."

"But, but, how do you mean? I can't join the army, I have to go home."

"The army is your new home, lad."

"No, no, I don't want to."

"So you mean that he has taken the King's shilling to join the army?" the innkeeper demanded.

"Yes, mistress."

"But that is outrageous."

"No, madam, it is regulations. He will make a fine soldier I am sure, to serve his King and Country."

The other soldiers in the tavern had fallen silent as they observed the scene at the shepherd's table. The Serjeant looked up and waved to two of them to come to the table.

"You two, escort Master Aaron out to the square to await the rest of the men. We return to the camp within the hour."

The Serjeant yanked Aaron out of his chair.

"But I can't leave. I must go back to my work and my family."

"You have new work and a new family. Now move!"

The Serjeant pushed Aaron towards the door between the escorts.

Chapter 5

Aaron turned back to look imploringly at the shepherd and his company, but he caught just a glimpse of them remonstrating with the Serjeant, before he was out into the street. The two soldiers each held one of his arms and took him over to where the table still stood in the centre of the market with two lanterns placed on it. The manacled prisoners whom he had previously seen were standing uneasily together with two other men who were so drunk that they could hardly stand. After a few minutes the officers appeared – one of them Aaron immediately recognised as the man he had punched. Even if he had not recognised the man's face in the poor light, he would have realised who it was once the man had sat down and the lanterns picked up the blood stains on his lace cravat.

The seated man was handed a book by one of the others, together with a pen and ink. The Serjeant had arrived and was standing behind him.

"Name?" growled the seated officer.

"Aaron Mew, sir."

"When were you born?"

There was a silence while Aaron tried to remember his birthday.

"Michaelmas, seventeen hundred and fifty-seven."

The Lieutenant wrote down the details.

"You have taken the King's shilling, Private Mew. Welcome to His Majesty's 62nd Regiment of Foot."

"But sir, I did not wish to…"

Aaron felt a hand grab the back of his shirt collar and pull him violently backwards towards the mouth of the assailant.

"Mew, you speak only when the Lieutenant asks you to. Understood?"

Aaron recognised the loud voice of the Serjeant who by now had his mouth against his ear.

"But I…"

The Serjeant howled in Aaron's ear, "Understood, Mew?"

"Yes," said Aaron timidly.

With an even louder voice, came the instruction, "Yes, Serjeant!"

"Yes, Serjeant."

The Lieutenant pulled a purse out of his pocket and counted out some money on the table.

"Mew, his Gracious Majesty has seen fit to pay recruits to this regiment ten guineas in bounty. Take this."

He pushed a paper note and two coins across the table. Aaron hesitated.

"Are you deaf, Mew!" screamed the Serjeant.

"But what is this for? What is the paper?"

"Tell him, Serjeant," said the Lieutenant.

"That there is a ten pound note and two crowns, making in total ten pounds and ten shillings, the same as ten guineas. Now pick it up, you bumpkin."

The two soldiers holding Aaron's arms let go and he took a pace forward and scooped up the two coins after folding the ten pound note. He put the money into his pocket.

"On Monday morning you will be taken before the magistrate to swear the enlistment oath along with the other new recruits. Tomorrow you will buy your 'necessaries' with your bounty money."

Aaron was about to ask what necessaries were, but with the fearsome Serjeant breathing down his neck, thought better of it.

The Lieutenant spoke: "Serjeant, keep him handcuffed tonight, just in case." Then, referring to the two drunken men, he said, "You deal with those two sorry creatures – they'll get their bounty tomorrow."

He got up from the chair, leaving it vacant for the Serjeant to act as his clerk in getting names and dates of birth from the inebriated recruits.

"Yes, sir," snapped the Serjeant as he moved round to the other side of the table. As he did so he said, "Corporal, take Mew and the three released prisoners to the camp. How many are in your tent?"

"Me and two others, Serjeant."

"Take Mew and two of these in with you, then. Find another

tent for the other one. No blankets for them tonight. That'll make them appreciate such comforts all the more when they buy their necessaries tomorrow. Keep Mew handcuffed to a tent pole."

The two men who had been holding Aaron before, one of whom was the Corporal, seized his arms again.

"Let's go then," said the Corporal, giving Aaron a push. The three prisoners who were still manacled followed, for there was no risk of them absconding.

Their walk took them back the way Aaron had previously come from the Red Lion and Cross Keys. They walked past the inn and then turned right. They followed the road by the light of a pale moon until they came to a field by the river. By the light of lanterns and a camp fire, Aaron could see several tents and two bell tents. The camp site was quiet as most of the soldiers were still in town, but they were challenged by a sentry as they approached.

"Halt. Who goes there?" shouted the sentry.

"Corporal Reid and new recruits."

"Advance, Corporal, and give the parole."

"Wessex."

"Pass on, Corporal, all is well."

Aaron's two captors led him to one of the tents; the Corporal lifted the flap and pushed him in. Reid said to his companion, "Keep him in there while I get the handcuffs, then we can go and have a drop of rum."

Later, by the light of a lantern, Aaron sat awkwardly, his right arm retained by the iron cuffs behind his back. The cuffs had been locked, with one part on his wrist and the other round the tent pole. The two prisoners were already asleep on the cold ground sheet which was the only thing between the sleeper and the hard earth. He looked enviously at the blanket rolls which were awaiting use from the other occupants of the tent, who had yet to arrive. His head was spinning. It had been a day like no other in his life and he was having difficulty in comprehending all the events which had taken place since he had bidden farewell to his mother that morning. He suddenly realised that there was no way that his mother and father would know what had happened to him. The only people who knew were the shepherd and his company, but they did not know where he lived; they would not be able to recount to his parents how he had been inveigled into joining the army. Then the thought occurred to him that if he did not come home, it would look as if he had absconded with his master's twelve pounds. He would be branded a thief.

The more he reflected on it, the more desperate he became. His mother, who had always taught him that he must be honest, even with farthings, would think that he had stolen the twelve pounds and run away. A thief, yes; she would think him to be a thief and so would all the village folk. The shame he had brought on his family! And little Matthew, who always looked up to him, he would grow up thinking that his big brother was a disgrace to the family. And what of his father? He might have to pay the money back to the Squire, but how? But then despite his anguish, a solution suddenly occurred to him. He had ten guineas in his pocket. If he could get home he would at least be able to repay most of the money. If he could get home! He tried pulling at the tent pole. It was possible to move it a little, but if he pulled the base out, the tent would collapse and surely the Corporal or his companion would hear. He tried lifting the pole instead. Although the pole was restrained by the guy ropes outside, it was possible to push it up slightly.

Aaron changed his position. He slid his right hand to the bottom of the pole so that the handcuffs were on the ground. With his left hand he gripped the pole and pulled it vertically with all his might and then dragged the cuffs out through the gap so formed. He was free!

Quietly opening the tent flap he looked around and saw two figures standing by the camp fire, some twenty paces away. He sneaked out of the tent and headed for the darkness of the river bank. He had to get across the river to find the road back to his home. He knew that there were only two ways: to swim across the river or to cross the toll bridge. The tollhouse would be closed until daybreak and the gates shut. He decided to try the river.

Aaron had never learned to swim, but he had noticed earlier, when crossing the bridge, that he could see the bottom of the river. Hoping to be able to wade across, he first sat on the river bank and then let himself slide into the water. With the river up to his chest he could feel the stony bottom under his feet. But the fast flowing water was already trying to drag him downstream. He attempted to take a step forward across the river, but immediately lost his foothold and was swept along with the water sometimes going over his head. Gasping for breath he waved his arms in an attempt to direct his progress towards the bank. The weight of the handcuffs on his right wrist was pulling him down into the water on one side. He began to realise that the cold water was sapping his strength. Suddenly, the current carried him into a bush which was overhanging the water. He desperately grabbed at the bush, but realised immediately that it was a bramble. The thorns pierced his hands, which had been softened by immersion in water. Aware that he was getting badly scratched, but not caring, he pulled himself along the bush to the shore. He heaved himself up on the river bank and collapsed into the long grass trying to recover his breath. After a few minutes, during which time he tried to extract thorns from his hands, he considered his options. He could clearly see the camp fire upstream. He guessed that soon the rest of the soldiers would be returning from town and that this was when his escape would be discovered. His only remaining option was to try to get across the bridges.

Keeping as close to the river bank as possible, Aaron crept back towards the camp. It was very dark; the moon had disappeared. Suddenly, there was the sound of a horse loudly neighing nearby. It was followed by a general chorus of horses all unsettled by the stranger who had inadvertently walked into the horse lines. Aaron started to run, frequently stumbling. By the firelight he saw the two men heading to investigate the reason for the horses' discomfort. He also heard the distant noise of the drummer leading the off-duty soldiers back to their camp. Skirting round the camp he followed the river to where his way was blocked by a large building; it was St Nicholas Hospital. He walked round it and found the road which he had taken into the city in the morning. Hurrying up to the bridge, he could just make out the shape of a gate which was closed across the road. It was not particularly high, and looked easily climbable.

He was within a few paces of the gate when he heard first a snarling sound and then a loud, deep toned bark. The dog was obviously very big, but it did not seem to be about to chase him. It just stood its ground in front of the gate. Aaron immediately assumed that the animal was tethered there, so he tried to approach the end of the gate where he could not be reached. The sound of a chain rattling brought home to him that the dog was indeed tethered, but it was on a line in front of the gate, permitting it to run from side to side.

As Aaron stood wondering how to get past the mastiff, he became aware of a noise behind him. People were running up the road. He turned and saw a man with a lantern which illuminated his and his companion's white breeches. Aaron's escape had been discovered and the Serjeant must have realised that he would try to return on the same road which he had taken to Salisbury. His situation was hopeless. He dropped his arms to his side and waited for the inevitable retribution.

To his relief, the soldiers who grabbed him and frogmarched him back to the camp did not include the Serjeant or the Corporal. Neither were they angry with him; indeed they were in a jovial frame of mind. This arose partly from the alcohol which they had consumed during the evening, but also because Aaron seemed to have assumed some celebrity status.

"You're a clever lad. First, you unseat the Captain from his horse, then you give the Lieutenant a bloody nose," said one.

"And then you have the nerve to make a run for it with His Majesty's bounty in your pocket!" said another, to the accompaniment of laughter from the others.

"But what really riled the Serjeant was that you didn't go down when he punched you by the river. There ain't many as is left standing when Granville swings one," added another.

"Anyway me boy, you'll be having a right bundle of trouble when we get back," said one who had not spoken before. This man had a strange accent which Aaron recognised was the same as the tinkers who were regularly chased from his village. He was Irish.

"Shouldn't wonder if he won't get the 'D'."

A soldier with a voice which sounded like the parson in Aaron's village refuted this. "My dear Jamie, it would hardly be politic to give the D to one who has not yet entered formally into our illustrious company. He has not yet taken the oath of enlistment."

"I wouldn't put anything past Lieutenant Stephens, Rev."

"It would be a travesty of military regulations, but then I suppose that heaven and hell hath no fury like a Lieutenant wronged."

"What's D?" asked Aaron.

"I don't think that young Mewie needs to have that elaborated at this stage," said the soldier who had been addressed as Rev.

Aaron was taken to wait outside one of the bell tents. By this time the Serjeant had met up with the returning group. Without saying a word to Aaron he called into the bell tent, "Private Mew is here, sir."

The tent flap opened and the Lieutenant, wearing only breeches with braces over his stained shirt, poked his head out. Aaron immediately recognised him as the officer he had punched. He stepped out of the tent, a glass in hand.

"You, young Mew, are badly in need of the Serjeant's discipline. As you will learn from the oath of enlistment, the punishment for desertion is death by shot, as it is for striking an officer. But we would prefer to keep you alive — I have no doubt that a colt as high-spirited as you will take some breaking, but break you we will. Serjeant, give Private Mew something heavy to carry. Other punishment can wait until after the oath."

"Yes, sir," exclaimed the Serjeant with undisguised glee. "Corporal Reid, you two come with me, bring that lantern."

They led Aaron over to where one of the carts was standing.

"Reid, get the looped ball."

The Private lifted a heavy canvas cover and while the Corporal held up the lantern he searched among some wooden boxes. He lifted out a cannon ball which had a metal loop attached to it. The Serjeant took a key out of his pocket and unlocked the side of Aaron's handcuffs which had previously been on the tent pole. He locked the cuff to the loop on the iron ball which was being held by the Corporal. The Serjeant took the ball out of the Corporal's hand and gave it to Aaron.

"Right, Mew, let's see you make a run for it with a four pound shot in your arms!" he guffawed sadistically. "Run you bastard, run." He gave Aaron a kick in the backside and the other two jogged with Aaron between them, back to the tent which he had escaped from.

He entered the tent followed by the Corporal. The lantern was still burning and he recognised the faces of the two soldiers already there beside the sleeping prisoners. Sitting with his back to the tent pole, reading, was the one who had been addressed as Rev and the other, Jamie, was lying wrapped in a blanket with his head on his greatcoat.

The Corporal took off his jacket and folded it beside the piece of ground sheet which he intended to occupy. He unrolled his blanket and put his greatcoat in place as a pillow.

"I'm going for a piss. You want to come, Mewie?" he said.

"Yes please, sir."

"You don't need to call me sir, just Corporal. Come on."

They both left the tent and went over to the river's edge. Aaron had some difficulty undoing his breeches and the procedure took him some time. The Corporal waited impatiently for him.

"I daren't let you out of my sight. I got a tirade from the Serjeant last time you made a run for it."

They returned to the tent. The Corporal took off his breeches and, forming his blanket into an envelope, crawled inside the flap. Aaron was still very wet and the cold of the evening added to his discomfort. He could not easily take off his clothes and so decided to sleep with them on.

"Jamie, give Mewie your greatcoat to cover him."

"But, Corporal, I need it, and anyway, it'll get wet."

"Do as I say. You've got a nice soft knapsack you can use as a pillow."

"Oh, how gratifying to see the milk of human kindness flowing in this bleak desert of misery and selfishness which is the army," observed Rev.

"Shut up, Rev, and put that lantern out," ordered the Corporal.

The reader snapped the book closed and then knelt by the tent pole for a while with his hands together in prayer, before lifting the lid of the lantern and blowing out the light.

Although he was desperately tired, Aaron lay awake for a long time, partly because of discomfort from the effect of the hard ground on his bruises, and his wet clothes, but mainly because of his concern about the turn of events which had befallen him. He had been beaten, robbed and nearly drowned. Now he had lost his liberty. He could see no way of escaping from his new situation. His previous thoughts about the shame he felt ran through his head again. His mother, a woman who had tried to protect him from the vices of the world, would now think of him as a thief who had abandoned his family for twelve pounds. After waking that morning in his secure and comfortable home he now found himself sharing a tent with at least two convicted felons. He wondered too what the morrow had in store for him. What were the necessities and the D? Clearly, he had much to learn of and much to fear about the new world in which he found himself.

Chapter 6

Aaron was woken by the sound of men getting dressed around him. The air was foul with the smell of farts and sweat. He sat up and with bleary eyes looked around the tent.

"Isaiah sixty, Mewie: 'Arise, shine, for your light has come'."

"Shut up, Rev," said the Corporal, who was already in his breeches and shirt.

"Come on, Mewie, ablution time."

Aaron stood up, though he had to bend his head to avoid the tent roof. With cannon ball cradled in his right arm he followed the Corporal out into the field. They joined other men standing around a makeshift table, on which were several metal bowls. Two men were shaving; others were washing themselves. The Corporal took one of the bowls and, walking upstream of where men were peeing into the river, filled it with water. He put it on the table in front of Aaron.

A voice boomed out from behind Aaron, "Don't treat him like a nurse maid, Corporal – let him get the bloody water himself."

"Yes, Serjeant."

The Serjeant pushed past the Corporal, reached out and grabbed the bowl. He poured the water onto the ground. Aaron watched, shocked and angry. He considered whether he could swing the ball and hit the Serjeant with it. Fortunately for him, the Serjeant moved on, berating other soldiers for various other perceived misdeeds.

Aaron struggled with the bowl in his left hand and the heavy burden in his right, to scoop up some river water. The only way for him to do it was to kneel on the bank and to reach down. Jamie had come out of the tent and was standing beside him. He kept looking round to see if he was being observed by the Serjeant, as he leant down to help Aaron.

"Cutler! What the hell do you think you are doing! Did you not hear my order to Corporal Reid!"

"No, Serjeant."

"Report to the Lieutenant's tent for disciplining after parade."

"Yes, Serjeant."

Jamie leant forward to Aaron and whispered, "You're on your own, Mewie."

By the time Aaron found his way back to the table with the bowl, the three prisoners and two other men, whom he presumed were the couple rendered incapable by drink the evening before, were being shown where to wash and clean themselves up. The prisoner's manacles had been removed as had their shirts.

"Corporal Reid, see that these men's clothes are burned before we get an infestation of prison fleas in the camp. Then take them to the store wagons to arrange fatigues. Take Mew with you too. You can get second clothes for him, but as he is the one most likely to make a soldier, get his necessaries as well," bellowed the Serjeant.

Aaron looked at the five men; the prisoners were emaciated and looked wretched. The other two, although the worse for their evening activities, were well fed to the point of being overweight. He dried himself on his shirt, which he had not been able to take off completely because of the weight he was carrying, and followed the Corporal and the five men.

One of the carts had a roof of canvas strung over bent hazel branches. Corporal Reid stopped by the wagon and called in, "You there, Barton?"

A man poked his head out of a flap at the back of the canvas cover.

"Yes, Corporal." He let the platform gate at the end of the cart down, revealing to the men standing outside an array of boxes and packing cases inside the wagon.

"Six outfits of second clothes."

Barton slowly looked the men up and down deciding on sizes. He then went back inside the cover while the Corporal and the other six waited outside. When he emerged he was carrying a pile of off-white linen breeches.

"Here, you try these," he said as he handed out the first three pairs to the felons. "And these are for the fat fellows, and this pair for the big lad."

The transition of the six men from their various previous lives was completed as the last vestiges of civilian life – their clothes – were taken from them and replaced by military garb.

Aaron awaited further attention from the Corporal. Reid called out to the Serjeant, "Serjeant, can you unlock these cuffs so that we can get him kitted out?"

The Serjeant ambled over to the cart and roughly dealt with the lock. He dropped the weight to the ground and Aaron had to move smartly to avoid it falling on his foot.

"Lock them again when you have finished," he ordered the Corporal, giving him the key as he left.

"Right, Barton, necessaries for the farmer," shouted the Corporal.

"I'm not a farmer, I'm a blacksmith," said Aaron.

"Now that's good to know, you could be useful."

While the Corporal had been speaking, Barton was in the wagon opening and closing various wooden boxes. He reappeared with his arms full and called out, "One knapsack, one greatcoat, two pairs of shoes, two pairs of stockings, two shirts and three waistcoats. Get him to try the shoes, Corporal."

Aaron sat on the ground and pulled his shoes off. He tried the army shoes while the Corporal looked on.

"They be a bit tight, Corporal," said Aaron.

"That's on account of the wet socks you have on, the army stockings are thinner. They be fine, Barton."

Aaron took his new shoes off and put his damp ones back on.

"Mew, watch me carefully because I only demonstrate this once."

The Corporal opened the knapsack as wide as it would go.

"You puts the heavy things in first, yer shoes and tent pegs. Barton, let's have the other stuff for the knapsack," he called out and paused while the man rummaged round inside.

"Four brushes and button stick, two tent pegs, pipe clay and chalk, pencil and paper. That's it, Corporal."

"What's the pipe clay and chalk for?" asked the new recruit.

"They are for whitening your straps and keeping your uniform spruce. Watch now."

The Corporal carefully placed the non-clothes items in the bottom of the bag and then folded the clothes, placing them uppermost.

"Right, Mew, you see how I done it? Remember because the Serjeant checks knapsacks and he ain't as patient as me."

"Yes, Corporal."

"Barton — a mess tin, ammunition pouch, water bottle and breadbag. Then you had better measure up the blacksmith for his jacket. Oh, and his hat, too."

The soldier busied around getting the remaining items and then dumped them on the platform at the back of the wagon. The mess tin rattled from the utensils inside it as he dropped it onto the flat surface. The Corporal attached the ammunition pouch to the knapsack and said, "You ain't getting no ammunition till you learnt firelock drill. When we get to Galway, you'll get a warrant for a Stand of Arms." Looking up at Barton he said, "Make sharp and get him measured. It'll be parade shortly."

Barton jumped down and used a tape to carefully measure the new recruit. He pulled a piece of paper out of his pocket and jotted down figures.

"You see, Mew, your shoes can 'urt, your back can be breaking and your belly burblin' with hunger, just as long as your uniform looks good, the officers will be happy. So we pays great attention to getting that right."

"I'll have it ready tomorrow, Corporal. Here's the docket." He handed the Corporal a piece of paper and climbed back onto the wagon tail gate.

"Put on one of the white shirts and your fatigues, Mewie, you only gets to wear the dress uniform on Wednesdays and Sundays and when we wants to impress men that they would like to join the army. Leave your farmer's clothes by the cart." The Corporal knew that Barton would check Aaron's clothes and those of the others to see if there was anything worth selling.

When Aaron had put on the grey fatigues and carefully transferred the still wet ten pound note and the two coins to the pocket in his new breeches, the Corporal once more locked the cannon ball on a chain to his arm. As he was doing so there was the rattle of a drum being beaten. The noise galvanized those around the camp and soldiers rushed to form up in two lines, one behind the other.

Aaron dragged his knapsack and greatcoat using his left arm and cradled the ball on his right. The two of them found Jamie and the two prisoners and lined up beside them. The Serjeant was prowling around behind their line.

"The company is at ease, Corporal, show them what that means."
Corporal Reid walked in front of the new men and told them
to put their hands clasped together behind their backs. Aaron placed
his bag and coat in front of him and imitated the action of the others
to the extent he could.

"Company, be alert!" commanded the Serjeant.

The recruits quickly, though clumsily, copied the action of the
rank in front of them.

"Let's try again for the new boys. Company, be at ease!"

Once more the action of the back line was slower than that of
the others. The Serjeant practised the 'at ease to be alert' several
times before marching past the rows and calling at the door of the
adjacent bell tent, "Company ready for inspection, sir!"

The tent flap opened and the Lieutenant, followed by the two
ensigns, stepped out. The officers walked around the square of the
paraded soldiers. When they got to the back row, the Lieutenant
turned to the Serjeant and said, "Who are the new men?"

"Sir, Private Mew, whom you have met. Private Pierce and
Private Goddard, two volunteers, and Privates Graham, Bell and
Huhne, late of the city gaol."

"Thank you, Serjeant. What does that bring our number up to?"

"Seventy, sir. That is, sixty-one men, seven Corporals, Serjeant
Ryan and me."

"Very good. I want you and the Corporals to report to my tent
for orders for the day after the punishment detail."

"Yes, sir."

"Carry on, Serjeant."

When the officers had retreated back to their tent, the Serjeant
shouted, "Be at ease." Then after a pause he called out, "Company
dismiss."

The ranks broke up and Aaron began to saunter towards his
tent to stow away his kit.

"Mew, report back here soon as you have put your stuff away."

"Yes, Serjeant."

Inside the tent, Rev was already in his favourite position with
his back to the pole, reading.

"Ah, young Mewie. Are you ready for retribution? For vengeance will be mine sayeth the Lieutenant."

"I have to report to the officers' tent."

"Ah, I wish you fortitude. I believe that Jamie will be joining you."

"I don't know," said Aaron as he left the tent.

When he arrived at the bell tent there were two soldiers standing either side of a third, their hands firmly holding his wrists. The man in the middle was dishevelled and had no jacket. Behind them stood Jamie.

The tent flap opened and the officers came out. The short and stout Lieutenant looked the detained man up and down disdainfully.

"Oh no, not you again, Mallone. Don't you ever learn?"

"Oh, your honour, it is me weakness I know, but when I sees the ladies, me knees come all of a tremble and me desires can't be denied."

"I hope that she was worth it."

"Ah, sir, she had skin like finest linen and bubs that felt like a silk purse of goose down. I never dipped my machine in a fairer canal."

The tent flap opened again and the Captain came forward to stand at the Lieutenant's shoulder. He asked, "And what did that cost you, Mallone?"

"'Twas all of eight pence your honour, and never was a day's pay spent so well."

With difficulty the officers tried to restrain a smile. They were aware that Mallone, like many of the Irish soldiers, had a way with words which made it difficult to be angry with him. The Captain's putative smile turned to a scowl.

"Private Mallone, I could call your night's absence desertion, in which case, because of your record you would be shot. However, since His Majesty's need for soldiers is great at the moment, I find you guilty of taking absence without leave. Serjeant, he is to be brought to the halberd – thirty lashes. Prisoner dismissed."

The two soldiers holding Mallone turned him round and marched him off towards where the carts were parked.

The Serjeant looked round at Jamie and shouted, "Private Cutler come forward."

Jamie stepped forward three paces and stood to alert in front of the officer.

"What is the charge, Serjeant?"

"Insubordination, sir."

"What's his previous record?"

"Good, sir."

"Private Cutler, you are to lose one day's pay and work on latrine duty for a week."

"Yes, sir, thank you, sir."

Jamie saluted and marched away from the tent.

"Private Mew, forward."

Aaron attempted to emulate the way that Jamie had marched up to the officer but was hindered by the weight he was carrying. He was very nervous and the buzzing sound in his ear had started again.

"Private Mew, you are in the fortunate position of not yet having taken the oath of enlistment. King's regulations do not permit me to punish you until you have done so, but I can direct the Serjeant with regard to your duties today. Serjeant, Private Mew will assist Private Cutler with the latrines. You can remove the weight."

"Yes, sir," said the Serjeant. He remembered that the Corporal had the key. "Beggin' your pardon, sir, I have to collect the key from Corporal Reid."

"Now, before you go, there is the matter of your kit to be paid for. Has he been issued with his full equipment, Lieutenant?"

"Serjeant?"

"Yes, sir."

The Lieutenant turned to one of the ensigns and asked him a question. He turned back to face Aaron and said, "You will give the Serjeant ten pounds to cover your uniform and equipment."

Aaron was aghast. "But, sir, that's almost all the bounty money."

"Quite so, dismiss," answered the officer.

Aaron's anger began to build and the buzz in his ear seemed to get louder, but he realised that he was in an impossible situation and begrudgingly, he handed over the damp ten pound note and then stood facing the Lieutenant.

"Move, Private Mew!" barked the Serjeant.

And so, after the weight had been removed, Aaron began his duties serving King George by filling in latrine pits and digging new ones, together with Jamie. This gave the new recruit the chance to get answers to some of the many questions which he had been longing to ask.

"Jamie, what is to become of me now? I mean, after we have finished this work?"

"That depends on the orders that the Serjeants get from the Lieutenant. Maybe we will move on to another town."

"What for?"

"This is a recruitment party – that is a beating party. We travel from place to place enlisting what you might call volunteers. The 62nd is short of men – we have lost quite a few and the Captain is trying to build up the numbers in case we are shipped to the American colonies."

"Were the men killed?"

"No, we haven't seen any action for years. The regiment is stationed in Ireland, in Galway, and life is very quiet there at the moment. No, we have lost men from sickness and desertion. A lot of the recruits are Irish. Some save a bit of money and then make a run for it. They have to run fast for if they are caught, it's the firing squad or the noose for them."

Their conversation was interrupted by the rattle of the snare drum.

"Look lively. Leave the spade there, we have to go and watch the poor bastard."

"Look at what?" said Aaron, brushing the soil off his fatigues.

"Mallone's comeuppance for dipping his wick."

"How do you mean?"

"You'll see. Hurry up or the Serjeant will be bawling at us."

By the time they had arrived, the other soldiers had fallen into line, as they were all required to watch the punishment. They were formed into a hollow square on the open area where they had previously had the parade. Serjeant Granville stood in the middle of the assembled men together with the Captain, the Lieutenant and another officer. This officer, who like Granville wore a red sash with a buff line through it around his waist, was Serjeant Ryan. There was a tripod made up of three halberds – Mallone was tied up between them. A fourth one was placed across his front and he was faced inwards with his back bared. The young drummer boy took a green cloth bag from Serjeant Ryan. From it he pulled out the cat-o'-nine-tails. He shook the whip to loosen the tails which were tangled up.

Serjeant Granville turned to the Captain, saluted and said, "Ready, sir."

Captain Trowbridge wasted no words; he called out, "Private Mallone, as sentenced, for absence without leave, thirty lashes."

The Irishman did not respond. Serjeant Ryan walked round to face his countryman and tried to put the stick into the man's mouth.

"What's he doing?" Aaron whispered to Jamie.

"He's giving him a stick to bite on to stop him screaming with the pain. But Mallone's no nightingale."

"What's a nightingale?"

"Someone who shouts when he is being beaten."

Mallone spat the stick out and let it fall to the ground. The drummer took up position behind him, then raised his arm and swung the cat onto Mallone's back. The man's body flinched as the nine tails of the cat smacked across his shoulder blades, but he did not struggle and there was no sound from his mouth. Every man in the watching ranks followed intently the count called out by Serjeant Granville, willing the Captain to stop the punishment early, as often happened, for they knew that the next one between the halberds might be them.

Weals started to appear on the white back and soon they crisscrossed each other as the lashes struck the man with a slightly different trajectory. After ten lashes, Granville handed Ryan his jacket, stepped forward and took the lash from the drummer boy. The older man then continued the punishment and it was clear that his flogging was heavier than that of the drummer. Then, as the count of twenty was reached, there was a shout from the Captain. "That will do, Serjeant Granville." There was an audible exhaling of air from the lungs of the assembled soldiers.

Serjeant Granville, now breathing heavily from the effort of his endeavor, walked back to the other Serjeant, handed him the cat and retrieved his jacket. He put it on and then turned to the paraded soldiers.

"Be alert."

He waited a few seconds and then shouted, "Dismiss!"

Two men rushed up to the halberds and began to untie Mallone.

They carefully lifted him, put one of his arms round each of them and led him off to his tent.

"Come on, Mewie, let's get back to work before we find ourselves in the same position."

Aaron did not answer and when Jamie turned to look at him he saw a young man, his face drained of colour resulting from his state of shock.

"Come on, lad, come on."

"That Serjeant is a brute. We wouldn't beat a rabid dog like that at home."

"Well, he has a job to do, and anyway, Mallone was lucky to get away with just twenty. The Captain has to enforce discipline. Really he should not sentence a man to lashing without a full Court Martial, but we are a long way from where he could hold one and in any case he wanted to make an example to the men before others take the same liberties as Mallone."

"Have you been beaten, Jamie?"

"Oh no, I am careful, for once the Serjeant takes a dislike to you, you are sure to get to the halberds sooner or later. You would do well to remember that."

"One day I will get revenge for the way he cheated me."

"Forget about it, you can't win against officers. Here, take the spade."

So saying, he handed Aaron his spade and the boy thrust it into the turf with such vigour that it was clear that he was venting his anger against the man who had tricked him into taking the King's shilling.

Chapter 7

"Jamie, how long do we have to go on doing this?"

Both of them had stopped digging after ensuring that the Serjeants were nowhere near and were watching men being drilled on the open ground in front of the tents.

"Why? Are you getting tired?"

"No, just wondering if this is what life is like in the army."

"You can be sure there are worse jobs than this."

They both started digging again and as they continued, Aaron became more and more aware that the smell of the smoke from the stoves behind the carts was gradually being replaced by the aroma of food.

"When do we get some food, Jamie?" asked Aaron.

"We eat when the senior Serjeant says so, but that should be soon. Usually the drummer lets us know, so when he starts a rattle then we can down tools."

"Which Serjeant is that then?"

"Grabber Granville, he is the senior Serjeant here."

"Why do you call him grabber?"

"He is the main recruiting officer – he grabs anyone he can find, like he did you. Gets paid well for it too. As a senior Serjeant he gets one shilling and sixpence a day. But he gets payment for every poor sod he enlists."

"What, for me too?"

"Without doubt. But he won't get his money for you and the others until you all take your oath of enlistment tomorrow. The oath can't be taken until at least a day after you have taken the King's shilling."

"Can I refuse to take the oath?"

Jamie slapped Aaron on the back and laughed saying, "Once they have got you, you are like a fly in a spider's web, there are only two ways to get out – in a shroud or as an invalid. Tomorrow, you will have to swear the oath in front of a Justice of the Peace and you can wager that he has been paid too."

"But I don't want to be in the army."

"You should have been careful about what you drank." Then after a pause, he said, "Many if not most you see here are where they are because of a weak moment when befuddled by the drink."

Aaron had realised some time ago that Jamie expressed himself very well, just like a gentleman of some standing; a man with an education. He had a fine unpockmarked face, a square chin and appeared to have all his teeth. His thick black hair had been gathered at the back of his head, bent back on itself and tied with a black bow, and despite his current occupation, he seemed to take a pride in his appearance.

"Why are you here, Jamie?"

The Private laughed and said, "Most of us prefer to keep our reasons for joining the army to ourselves, but I can tell you that I joined willingly. Despite the dangers and discomforts it is preferable to being transported to Australia."

"Was your crime so serious?"

Jamie's mood changed and with sarcasm he said, "I shouldn't wonder that you are in trouble with the Justices too. How did you come to get into such a sorry state? When you came in yesterday you had a bloody shirt, a cut head and your hair was a rare tangle."

As Aaron dug, he related his experiences of the day before, carefully omitting the detail about his encounter with the serving wench in the Red Lion.

"My lad, you should be thankful to Serjeant Granville for recruiting you. For if you had gone home without the twelve pounds, your master could have handed you to the Justices to be tried for theft, and then you would have at best have been transported and at worst hung. Be thankful that wearing the red jacket will protect you from accusations and pay you eight pence a day."

Aaron laboured on in resentful silence until he heard the rattle of the drum.

Planks had been unloaded from one of the carts and set up as makeshift tables and benches. Seated with the others from his tent, Aaron had his first army meal: beef broth and potatoes washed down with small beer.

"You say what you like about the army, young Mew, but we eat well," said Corporal Reid.

"I can't argue with that, Corporal, 'twas good," said Aaron as he reached for more bread.

"You'll get two good meals a day and five pints of small beer as well as a regular tot of rum. We get pies and stews as well as broths."

A solemn voice from down the table chimed in, "Corporal, you should enlighten this young man about the fact that this beneficence is not the gift of a grateful country – he will have to pay almost half of his daily wage for the feast you describe."

There was laughter around the table and the Corporal said tersely, "Shut up, Rev. I tell the boy what he needs to know, not you."

There was a silence which was eventually broken when the Corporal said, "Mew, go back to the tent after we've finished. I got to deal with your hair."

"My hair, Corporal?"

"Yes, your hair's got to be clubbed, like mine and the others. It's got to be folded up to make like a sausage, and then tied with a black ribbon. Your hair will have to grow a bit afore it will be quite right."

"Why?"

"Well, lad, look around you. We have to have a ten-inch pigtail what is tied just below the upper part of your uniform collar. If it ain't, you got trouble coming. And while we are on recruiting duty we got to look as smart as we can, to make fellows like you want to join."

Aaron's hair was duly arranged to fulfil the requirement of the regiment and later he rejoined Jamie to complete the digging of the new latrines. After the tea meal, the Corporal called the occupants of his tent together. They sat on a bench in front of the tent, Reid standing in front of them. Rev was delayed, so he paced back and forth for a few minutes waiting for the latecomer. Aaron noted that Corporal Reid had a slight limp. The man was thin and wiry and fairly short; he did not have the air of one who could command other men, but as Aaron was to learn, Reid brooked no challenge to his authority and frequently resorted to sarcasm to avenge any perceived affront to his rank. His situation was an inversion of the normal order, as clearly Jamie and Rev were of a higher social and educational status than him.

When Rev appeared and sat down he started, "Right lads, the Captain has decided that we've done a good job here. All together, including you six new boys, we got twenty-nine recruits on this beating order in Wessex. We'll be going back to rejoin the regiment in Galway to await orders."

"But, Corporal, while many wait but few are chosen. Are we to take this chosen few to be quartered in that detestable Popish bog again, doomed to military obscurity?"

"Rev, be careful what you wish for. His Gracious Majesty may see fit to send the 62nd to help quell the rebellion in the thirteen colonies of America. Our quarters in Galway will seem your vision of heaven compared with a two month on a bloody leaking troop transport ship."

There was silence while the group considered with disquiet the Corporal's repost to Rev.

"When are we leaving, Corporal?" asked Jamie.

"Tomorrow, directly after the oath swearing for the new men."

"And how do we travel?"

"The same way we come, Jamie. We march to Holyhead and take the packet to Kingstown. Then over the hills to Galway."

"I shall fervently pray that the Lord stills the tempest for us," said Rev.

The Corporal grinned and said, "You never prayed hard enough on the way over did you!"

Rev was about to reply, but before he could, the Corporal added, "The Serjeant wants all kit cleaned and packed ready to break camp after breakfast. Mew, you ain't got a firelock have you?"

"No, Corporal."

"We can't have you marching to Holyhead without a brown bess. The new recruits have borrowed old firelocks to march with. You'll get your Stand of Arms in Ireland. I'll see if we got an old one left for you."

The Corporal left the soldiers and headed for the supply wagon. As he left, he looked over his shoulder and shouted, "Get on with it then, rag fair before bed."

Aaron looked at Jamie and asked, "What's a rag fair?"

"A kit inspection. If you think the Serjeant was cruel before, just wait to see his humour if he doesn't like the look of your kit."

With that, Jamie and Rev disappeared into the tent and soon reappeared carrying their firelocks and the ones issued to Privates Huhne and Graham, and a handful of rags.

"Right, lads, we start with the firelocks. Give them a good clean and a polish. We try to see who can remove His Majesty first," said Jamie, referring to the fact that the etching of G III R on the barrel of the gun could eventually, after many years of use, disappear with frequent and hard rubbing. Soon after the others started polishing their weapons, Corporal Reid returned with a firelock for Aaron.

"T'aint ever going to work, but it will serve its purpose on the march."

Jamie looked at the weapon and whispered to Rev, "By God, he'll have some work to do on that, look at the rust."

The Corporal thrust the gun at Aaron and said, "Well, get on with it then. It won't hurt you."

The group set about rubbing and dusting the firelocks. Aaron tried with little success to remove the patches of rust on his gun barrel. The rag he was using was not abrasive enough and so he left the others and looked for a small piece of flint to scrape the rust. This treatment was more effective but left scratch marks on the gun. The men stacked their firelocks with the stocks on the ground, barrels pointing upwards, in the shape of a cone.

Then, item by item the two experienced soldiers and the Corporal showed the three novices how to clean and present their uniform and kit for inspection.

As they stood and waited for the two Serjeants to come to their tent – outside of which all their equipment was displayed, a stack for each man – they could hear the bellowing of Serjeant Granville as he cursed and swore at soldiers outside of other tents.

"Here they come," cautioned the Corporal.

The five men, dressed in their fatigues, lined up, each behind their pile of kit.

The two Serjeants came round the side of the tent and stood in front of the men, looking them up and down.

Addressing the two ex-prisoners, Granville growled, "By Zeus, we've got to put some flesh on your bones if you are ever to face the Frenchies."

"Were they the best you could find in the gaol?" asked Serjeant Ryan.

"You should have seen the others. Well, at least they top five foot four and half inches, so they can be soldiers," scoffed Granville.

The Serjeants started to walk along the line of soldiers, looking at the stacks in front of them.

"Mew, where's your uniform?"

Aaron attempted to answer – the buzz had started in his ear again – and he stuttered. The Corporal intervened.

"It will be ready in the morning, Serjeant, he's a big lad."

The Serjeant said nothing and then the two of them walked over to where the firelocks were stacked. Granville picked up one, inspected it carefully, replaced it and then picked up another.

"What the hell has happened to this weapon, Corporal?"

"It's an old one."

"I can see that.Who has damaged it?"

"Mew, sir."

Granville carried the firelock up to where Aaron was standing and held it under his nose.

"It was rusty, Serjeant."

"And now it is scratched. Damaged, you have damaged His Majesty's property. You can thank God that you ain't taken the oath yet, for if you had, it would be the halberds for you. I'm watching you, lad, and waiting for you to put a foot wrong after the Justice has done his work."

The Serjeant thrust the levelled weapon hard against Aaron's chest.

"Here, take it. Next time, use brick dust to take off rust."

With that, the two Serjeants marched off in the direction of the next tent.

When they were out of earshot, Aaron leaned over to Jamie and said, "What does he mean about the Justice?"

Jamie looked across to the Corporal and said, "When is the lad's oath taking?"

"Probably tomorrow morning, along with the others, before we leave. Mewie, we've got to get your uniform first thing and then either the Justice of the Peace will come here or we will go past the Council House to see him on our way out of the city."

Aaron stood in silence considering the awful fact that tomorrow he would have to take a binding oath from which only death, incapacity or old age could release him.

The men picked up their belongings and their firelocks and took everything inside the tent. They each arranged their blankets in their appointed sleeping positions. In ones and twos they went out to relieve themselves and then everyone started to settle for the night. The lantern attached to the tent pole was lit and Rev assumed his usual position sitting with his back to the pole, his book in his hands.

"Don't we get a nightshirt, for sleeping in?" queried Aaron.

Jamie and the Corporal exploded with laughter and the Rev put his book down, a smile on his face.

"Mewie, you get two white shirts. They've got to last you a month before washing time, or shorter if they get soiled. They are both your day shirt and your night shirt," said Jamie, trying to control his laughter.

"And they got a good long shirt tail to keep yer arse and yer wedding tackle warm, because we don't have nothing else under our breeches do we?" added the Corporal.

"You are bloody lucky, Mewie – in the gaol we wore the same threadbare clothes for months, night and day. And by God, that Fisherton gaol was cold," said Graham. This was the first time that either of the ex-prisoners had joined the others in conversation.

"What were you there for?" asked the Corporal.

"I was falsely accused of coining."

"Ah, a coin clipper! And what about you, Huhne?"

"Um, well let's just say that I spent more than I earned and my creditors did not take kindly to this."

"What about the other felon?"

"Tingaling Bell? He's a thief. He'd steal from his own poor widowed mother, given the chance."

It was quiet in the tent while the men considered what had been said.

The Corporal broke the silence. "Come on Rev, out with the light, we got an early start."

After a few seconds there was the sound of a book being snapped shut. Several watched as Rev turned and knelt with his head towards the tent pole, hands clasped. After a minute, he sat down on his blanket and pulled off his breeches. He then leaned over and lifted the lid off the lantern and blew out the flame, before covering himself with his blanket.

Aaron gazed at the roof of the tent, though it was far too dark to see it. The chorus of snores increased in volume as the choir grew in size. The buzzing in his ear had diminished considerably, but he was now aware that his hearing seemed somewhat muffled on that side. It would be some days before he recognised the fact that the torment in his head, caused by the blow from the Serjeant, was made worse by mental strain or fear. He touched his ear – there was no pain. He felt the back of his head; it was still very sore from when he had been struck in the Red Lion, and he was conscious too of some bruises on his body which troubled him when he lay in particular positions. Sleep did not come easily to him. He had so much to think about.

He considered what Jamie had said about what would happen to him if he returned home; that he would be brought before the Justices and charged with the theft of the twelve pounds. He was even more appalled by the disgrace that this would heap on his family. But then he had disgraced them anyway. Transported to Australia! Could that happen? Jamie seemed to be an educated man; he certainly knew about these things. Was there any way of avoiding taking the oath tomorrow? And if he did avoid it, what would he do? He could not countenance going home in shame.

And what of his companions? Jamie was already like a friend to him, the Corporal wasn't too bad, and Rev treated him well, almost like a father really. He seemed to understand his difficulties. The only really bad thing so far was Serjeant Granville – he was detestable. The more Aaron thought the more he became convinced that he had to reconcile himself, though sadly, to his new situation. He might never be able to see his mother and father and his brother and sisters again. He really had no alternative. The army was his new family.

Aaron was not the only one in the tent to whom sleep did not come easily. Rev noticed that the young man was fidgeting, trying to get comfortable. After a while he whispered, "You can't sleep, Mewie?"

"I'm not easy with my situation, Rev."

"Well, my boy, joining up is like a kind of redemption. The redcoat protects you from your past. We all start equal here – the judgment made about you is how good a soldier you are. It is not based on what you did before you took the oath."

"Is that the way it was for you?"

"That is of no matter. But you have taken your mess of pottage – tomorrow you must forfeit your birthright. Now stop worrying and get some sleep, we have a long march ahead of us."

Neither man spoke again but both reflected on what they had heard and said, until sleep overtook them.

Chapter 8

"I swear to be true to our Sovereign Lord King George, and serve Him honestly and faithfully in Defence of his Person, Crown, and Dignity, against all His Enemies or Opposers whatsoever: And to observe and obey His Majesty's Orders, and the Orders of the Generals and Officers set over me by His Majesty."

The words rang out as the Justice did his best to make an impression on the small crowd which had gathered in front of the Council House early on Monday morning to watch the ceremony. The six new recruits stood awkwardly in a line facing the official. Their packs with rolled-up greatcoats on top of each were placed on the ground behind them. Their temporary weapons, the ancient firelocks, were stacked in the conventional way in a cone shape. The line of men was incongruous. The two plump merchants amply filled the white waistcoats under their fatigue jackets, while the uniforms of the three gaunt ex-prisoners hung on them like clothes on a scarecrow. Aaron, standing at the end of the line on the Justice's right, wearing his new uniform, looked every bit a soldier. Behind the row, Serjeant Granville prowled around, ensuring that all was done by the book and that the oath taking went smoothly. For if it did, he stood to earn a good bounty on his new recruits. Behind him were the four officers; they sat as still as they could on their fidgeting horses, impatiently awaiting the opportunity to start the journey northwards towards Holyhead. The company was paraded in two lines behind the horses. The men had their full packs on their backs. When the order was given they would turn and set off in twos on the long march to the port, with the new recruits joining at the rear.

At the beginning of the ceremony, Aaron was trying to concentrate on and understand the words being intoned by the Justice, but he soon found his mind wandering. He looked across the market square and saw a small knot of people outside the tavern where his fate had been sealed. And there, among them, standing next to her aunt, was Peggy. He felt a thrill run through him and lifted his right hand as much as he dared, in a wave. To his delight the two women acknowledged him by waving. Peggy's face, which he had found so pretty, was framed by the same bonnet that she was wearing when he had first seen her. Aaron got even more excited when the two women crossed the road to witness the event more closely.

"...*mutiny or desertion is punishable by death.*"

The Justice had noticed that he had lost the attention of several of those before him. He raised his voice in the last sentence and betrayed his irritation when he said, "Do you all understand what I have read to you?"

The men mumbled and nodded.

He took a pace towards Aaron.

"Your name?"

"Aaron Mew, sir."

An assistant standing behind the Justice referred to a large ledger book, the one which the officer had written in the night Aaron had been taken from the tavern.

"Your age?"

"Seventeen, sir, well that's, er, um, coming up to eighteen soon, sir."

"Your occupation and place of birth?"

"I be a blacksmith, sir. What was the other question?"

"Your place of birth, boy. Where were you born?"

"In Fordingbridge, sir, in the county of Hampshire, down past Downton."

"I know where it is, thank you very much."

From the sarcasm in his voice, it was clear that the Justice was getting exasperated.

"Master Mew, listen carefully. Say 'no' after each of these questions unless you have any of these afflictions."

The buzzing had started in Aaron's ear. He turned his head slightly so that his good ear, the right one, was more towards the Justice and nodded.

"Do you suffer from the fits?"

"No, sir."

"Rupture?"

"No, sir."

"Lameness?"

"No, sir."

The Justice lowered his voice, "Deafness?"

Aaron hesitated. He was too nervous to realise that this was a trick question. He did indeed find it difficult to hear when the buzzing was haunting him.

"Yes, sir."

"You say that you are deaf, boy, yet you can hear the question!"

There was some laughter from the crowd. Those soldiers within earshot smiled, but knew better than to arouse the ire of Serjeant Granville by laughing.

"Last question, are you an apprentice?"

"Yes, sir."

This unexpected response evoked an irritated reaction from the Justice. He looked across to the Serjeant and said loudly, "Are you trying to enlist an apprentice? You know that this is not permitted. His first duty is to his master."

The Serjeant stepped forward and glared at the back of Aaron's head.

"Boy, who is your master?" demanded the Justice.

"Thomas Sykes in Fordingbridge."

One of the ensigns kicked his horse and walked it forward to stand by the side of the Serjeant. He leant down from the saddle and quietly said something to the Serjeant who nodded and then walked forward to the Justice.

"A word please, sir," he said, beckoning to a spot a few yards away from where the Justice had previously been standing.

The two men conferred for a short while and then the Justice resumed his position.

"Master Mew, the King's regulations do not permit an apprentice to be enlisted into the army, unless they volunteer. Did you volunteer?"

The buzz in his head was louder than it had ever been as he sought an answer.

"No, sir, I did not."

"Then on repayment of your bounty money of ten guineas

and another twenty shillings to defray expenses, you may return to your master."

Aaron was in huge discomfort from the nagging noise in his head, but also from the embarrassment of being the attention of the impatient Justice, the waiting officers, the assembled ranks behind him, the crowd, and in particular he now felt foolish in front of the two women he recognised. He tried to analyse what had been said to him and then blurted, "Sir, I spent the bounty, all but ten shillings and—"

The Justice interrupted him scoffingly, "Drank it all I'll be bound!"

There was laughter from the crowd which increased the torment the boy felt.

"No, sir, I—"

He was interrupted again: "Do you have ten guineas and twenty shillings or not?"

"Well…well, no, sir, I ain't."

"Then your only course of action is to volunteer to join up!"

"No, sir, I don't want to."

"You are trying my patience, Master Mew, and that of your officers. I will ask you one more time before I decide that you are in contempt. Do you wish to volunteer or do you wish to put yourself in the position of a debtor – a debtor, boy, to his most Gracious King George, your Sovereign."

Aaron stared at the ground. He had never felt so alone, so crushed and totally outmanoeuvered. His head was almost bursting; he was angry, confused and helpless. He raised his head and looked at the glowering official in front of him. "Yes, sir," he whispered.

"Then I declare you enlisted."

He immediately turned his attention to Graham, who was on Aaron's left.

"You man, your name?"

And so it went on, though in the cases of the next five men the Justice had no such difficulties as he had had with the blacksmith's apprentice. When the last man, Private Pierce, had been enlisted, the Serjeant turned and waved to the drummer boy who was standing on the far right of the parade; the position which, when the company turned left, would be the head of the marching column.

The boy hoisted his drum to his hip and began a rhythmic beat at the pace the men were to march. His uniform was quite different from that of the other men. He had red and white stockings. His jacket, which was white, was more elaborate than that of the other men, with buff coloured stripes and lace. On his head he wore a bearskin mitre cap, on the front of which was the King's crest and the Latin motto, *Nec aspera terrent*.

The Serjeant turned to the line of six newly enlisted men who were standing awkwardly betraying the fact that they were uncertain what to do, and bellowed, "You men, pick up your packs, get your firelocks and fall in on the left of the parade."

The six men turned and hastily lifted their packs onto their backs before scurrying off as directed.

The mounted officers rode forward to the Justice; the ensign who had previously spoken to the Serjeant dismounted. He passed a small package to the Justice and retrieved the ledger with the men's details. He then remounted and the four of them walked their horses to the far right of the parade.

"Company! Turn left! Form up in pairs," shouted the Serjeant.

The soldiers turned. Some spread out, others closed up, to form marching order with eighteen inches distance between each man. The new recruits copied the others, but since there was an uneven number, Aaron was left with no partner to march alongside.

"62nd!" bellowed Serjeant Granville.

The men responded by bracing up, firelocks tight between body and right arm.

"Company will shoulder…Arms!"

As the last word was spoken, the men tossed their firelocks across their bodies with their right hands and placed the brass plates on the butts of their firelocks into their left hands and took the weight of the forty-two-inch barrels on their left shoulders. Their right hands slapped down smartly to their right thighs. Some of the men were slow in this operation, but the Serjeant did not comment while they were in this public place. There was no doubt, however, that he had noted which men he would be dealing with later.

"By the front, double time, march!"

The drummer boy beat out a rhythm which equated as near as possible to seventy-five paces to the minute and the soldiers marched with the regulation thirty-inch steps.

Aaron was about to turn to wave to Peggy and her aunt, when he was alarmed to find that Serjeant Granville had fallen in next to him at the end of the column. It soon became apparent that from this position the officer could observe the performance and demeanor of his charges, and as he considered necessary, act to improve both. The Serjeant did not carry a firelock; instead he had a short halberd which betokened his rank.

Aaron had confusion of emotions: fear of the Serjeant marching next to him, trepidation about being forced to go far away from his home, dreadful apprehension and anger about the consequences of the oath he had just been forced to take; but dominant at this moment was sadness and regret that he had no chance to say goodbye to Peggy. But there was little chance to dwell on the latter as he tried to match the marching feet of the men in front of him.

The column headed north through the city and as they did so people came out of the small houses which backed onto the river to watch the procession. Some cheered, others just watched. Small children ran alongside the column; some marched in imitation of the soldiers.

The further they got from the market square the smaller the properties were, until finally there were only hovels by the riverside. The tollgate was opened for the company and only then, when there were no further habitations by the Avon, the Serjeant bellowed, "Company, halt."

The column stopped rather more raggedly than the Serjeant would have wished.

"Be easy."

When Aaron joined the other men from his tent, the Corporal said, "We stopped here because the water in the river is cleanest before it reaches the city. Rev and Jamie will show you how to fill your water bottles. The bottles hold exactly three pints, and you are going to need them filled right up for we have a hard march to Marlborough today – twenty-five miles across an open plain with only one other chance on the way to get water.

"When you have filled your bottles go to the sutler's wagon and get your ration of bread and salt beef. We will stop on the march when the Serjeant tells us, to eat our victuals."

Aaron followed the others to fill his wooden water bottle and then got his food ration. The Serjeant busied round trying to hurry everyone, telling them in threatening tones that the march was long and that they were starting late.

Eventually, the company reformed into marching order and Aaron once more found himself in position next to the Serjeant.

"Company, will shoulder...Arms!"

This time the Serjeant, now unobserved by onlookers, could express his feelings about the performance of some of the men in shouldering arms. He left his place and strode forward. He prodded one man with the blunt end of his halberd and shouted, "Watch the others, you bastard, and keep in time."

He then walked back to his place and shouted, "62nd, follow the drumbeat, by the front, march at ease!"

The drummer boy struck up, but this time the rhythm was slower and marked the pace the men would be expected to proceed with for the next twenty-five miles.

As they left the riverside and followed the road north, they found themselves walking uphill. Occasionally, through the trees they could see the extent of the climb which was marked by a ruined castle, far off at the top of the hill. As they walked, the incline got steeper.

Directly in front of Aaron were Graham and Huhne, late of Fisherton gaol. It soon became apparent that these two undernourished men who had been incarcerated without any exercise for several months, were having difficulty keeping up, even at the slower pace that the column was now marching.

Several times the Serjeant cajoled them, "Keep up, move on, damn you."

Eventually, he started using the blunt end of his halberd to prod them by pushing it into their packs.

It was indeed fortunate for Pierce and Goddard that they had the three ex-prisoners behind them, for they too were finding the climb exacting, though not to the same extent. Their plight was masked by the worse performance of the other two. But it was not long before the Serjeant noticed the gap opening up between them and the more seasoned soldiers in front. He stepped out of line and hastened to come level with the two men who just two nights before had been junketing in Salisbury taverns.

"Get a move on you lousy merchants, or it will be the worse for you. Look lively, keep up!"

The two men, who were sweating profusely, hastened their step. The Serjeant resumed his position and his tormenting of Graham and Huhne. However, it was becoming increasingly clear that both of them were no longer responding to the taunts and the prods. Further forward Bell was having the same problem.

Aaron, who was younger and very much fitter than the other new recruits, was experiencing no difficulty with the ascent. The Serjeant addressed him without turning towards him, saying, "Private Mew, take the firelocks from the men in front and carry them for them."

Both men turned without stopping and handed Aaron their weapons. It was impossible for him to shoulder the guns and so he carried all three, cradled in his arms as he marched. The young soldier was now carrying an extra weight of twenty-one pounds awkwardly in his arms. While at first this was no difficulty for him, as time went on the burden began to tell.

The Serjeant seemed to take delight in addressing two of his immediate concerns in one go, easing the load for two of the weaker men and inflicting discomfort on the young recruit. Again, without turning, he spoke to Aaron, "Heavy is it, Mew? Think what a kindness you are doing to your comrades."

But even with a lighter load the two men dropped back further and further from the main column, as did Bell, and to a lesser extent, the two merchants. The Serjeant had no other choice but to accept that the main column would reach the top of the hill far in advance of the group of stragglers. The recognition of this situation did not ease his temper or moderate the expletives used to shout at the new recruits as they laboured up the hill. The only thing which eased his anguish was to see Aaron's increasing distress caused by the extra weight he was carrying.

On reaching the top of the hill the officers had ordered the main column to stop to await the arrival of the stragglers. Not surprisingly, the three wagons were also far behind the column, though not far behind the slower walkers.

As they approached the waiting column, an ensign rode to meet them.

"Serjeant, put the five men's weapons and packs in the wagons to lighten their load."

The day was a long one, especially for the five unfit men. They had had a welcome rest when the company stopped on the bleak plain to eat their rations, but it was not until, in the dusk, they raised their tents by a stream in a clearing in the Savernake forest, just south of Marlborough, that they had more refreshment. The same six messmates shared a tent, as they had in Salisbury. Immediately after supper Graham and Huhne collapsed on their blankets and fell asleep. The other four sat on their packs in the tent chatting quietly, though Rev had a book open and now and again, when the conversation did not interest him, he read from it. The reason for speaking in lowered tones was not out of respect for the two sleeping soldiers, but because they knew that the Serjeants snooped around the tents listening to conversations.

"How do you feel after your first day of soldiering, Mewie?" asked the Corporal.

"I'd feel happier if I weren't marching with that brute next to me."

"Shhh…You never know when he is lurking around outside."

Aaron spoke again, now almost whispering, "He's going to kill someone with that halberd ere long."

Rev looked up from his book and quietly contributed, "Corporal, tell our young comrade how much our good shepherd Grabber needs to deliver the new lambs in his flock to the Galway fold."

"Rev's right, Mewie, we've been trudging round the south of England trying to find new recruits. The Serjeant ain't going to risk losing any of the ones we got. Especially you."

"Why me?"

"Well, look at the other sods, they ain't exactly thoroughbred racehorses are they? Oh yes, he'll make soldiers of them, but you are a much better prospect. That's why you got to get a new uniform."

"I don't understand."

"Look, Mewie, I've been in the army for, well, nigh on twenty years. I'll be forty in five years' time and there ain't many men who see that age while still on active duty. But the army will have got twenty-five years' service out of me. It'll nearly be the same with you, but the others are at least in their mid-twenties, they ain't going to give anything like the service to His Majesty that you will."

Jamie interjected, "And the state they are in it is doubtful whether they have many years of soldiering in them."

Rev looked up again. "So, Mewie, Serjeant Grabber may make your life a misery, but he won't do anything to impair your ability to make a good soldier. You must remember too that he has received his thirty pieces of silver to betray you to the army, as indeed he has for the others. His embarrassment would be total if, perchance, harm should befall any of you before he delivers you into the safekeeping of the regiment."

"So, where are we going?"

"Tell him, good Corporal. Tell him of the halcyon paradise which is our headquarters on the Isle of Hibernian. And do not neglect to mention the balmy Atlantic winter breezes which soothe our cheeks and the gentle, life-giving rain that never, never stops and renders every garment sodden."

"Shut up. Get on with your book, Rev. We are going to our headquarters in Galway. The regiment has been stationed in Ireland since we came back from Dominica in the West Indies six years ago."

"Those of them that came back!" said Jamie.

"What do you mean?"

"Well, Dominica you might say wasn't a very healthy place and a lot of the men were taken sick. There were just seventy-five fit men when we arrived back in Ireland. The regiment should have nigh on five hundred," said the Corporal.

There was a silence while Aaron anxiously considered this worrying information.

"How far is it to this Galway?"

"A long march. It is over two hundred and fifty miles to Holyhead where we embark on a ship for Dublin. From there we have another march of over a hundred miles across Ireland."

"Don't worry, Mewie, you're a strong lad, you'll make out well."

Aaron was awake for some time, his thoughts just as confused as they were the previous night. He would be forty in about twenty-two years – no, he did not want to stay in the army that long. Embark…on a ship on the sea! He was nervous, but excited about that. And then to be in another country, what would his parents say? Yes…what were his parents saying now? They thought he was a thief. Would his parents have to pay the money back? Every now and again the image of the shepherd girl Peggy came into his mind and momentarily lifted his spirits.

Gradually, his weariness overtook him and he slept.

Aaron was woken by the patter of rain on the canvas roof. Rev was already awake and was untying his greatcoat from the roll on his pack.

"Good morning, young Mewie, the elements have turned against us. Fortunately, the army provides for all eventualities. Today, I fancy, will be positively diluvian and requiring the use of this most useful accoutrement."

Aaron had decided some time ago that he could not expect to understand the larger portion of Rev's comments; indeed, it seemed that no one else except Jamie did either, but he grasped that it would be a day for the use of the greatcoats. As he was pulling on his, he heard the now familiar bark of Serjeant Granville. He was going from tent to tent bellowing a morning greeting.

"Look lively, time for a good walk. Let's have you now."

As soon as he had passed by, Graham asked, "How far are we going today, Corporal?"

"Why, you tired, Clipper?"

"It seems that you are to be saddled with a nickname relating to your alleged nefarious activities, Private Graham," observed Rev.

"No, I just wondered. Where are we going anyway?"

The Corporal opened his knapsack and took out a sheet of paper.

"Right, you listenin'?"

The men stopped eating their porridge and each turned to look at the Corporal.

"The Serjeant give me this yesterday. The Lieutenant has split up the march into twenty-five-mile parts. He reckons that it will take eleven days to get to Holyhead. In normal times we march twelve miles a day, but the Lieutenant got an order to get us over to the regiment double quick on account of the need for training should we be going to America."

There were gasps from the two weakest messmates.

"Where are we going today?" asked Aaron.

"Today we march through Marlborough and on to Ciren… Can't read 'is writing."

"Would you permit me to help, Corporal?" asked Rev unctuously.

With some annoyance, he replied, "Yeah, you got younger eyes than me."

Rev took the paper and spent a moment looking at it before saying, "Gentlemen, our excursion this day will be to Cirencester. The following day, having tired of the delights of that fair town we proceed to Tewksbury, a place renowned for its abbey. Our tour continues the next day to the city of Hereford, site of a splendid cathedral, though I doubt if the Serjeant has planned for us to inspect it. Thence we walk to Ludlow, a place of which I know nothing. Indeed I am not even sure if it is in England or Wales."

"Get on with it, Rev, we have to strike the tent soon."

"Right, Ludlow to Shrewsbury, and then good folk, we really are going to be in Wales, for we will spend the night at Llangollen. Ah, I remember that place, we camped by a river on the way here. The river was the only memorable thing about the village. And by then, and I speak from experience, I do hope that Private Huhnie and Private Clipper Graham will have developed thighs like an oxen, for we have mountains to traverse, two days to Capel Curig and thence to Menai and the raging torrent which is to be crossed before we march on to the port of Holyhead."

The flap of the tent was thrown open. The glowering face of the Serjeant was framed by the opening.

"Get this tent down and be in line with your packs before I get back here again. Look sharp, you lazy asswipes."

Rev folded up the paper and gave it back to the Corporal, who barked, "You heard the Serjeant. Mewie, collect the bowls and take them to the wagon. The rest of you help with the tent – like Rev says, we got a long way to go."

And thus continued the journey for the seasoned soldiers and the new recruits. The day started well with the long descent down to Marlborough, but the weaknesses of the previous day showed themselves again when the company started the ascent out of the town. However, each day the fitness of the Salisbury recruits improved and before they reached Ludlow, no more exceptions were made regarding the carrying of weapons and equipment. Ten days later as dusk fell, the men followed the four officers on horseback, down the slope which led to an inn by the Menai Straits near to Porthaethwy.

Chapter 9

The officers dismounted, handed their horses to a hostler and went into the inn. The company was lined up in two rows in their marching order. A light drizzle had started and some of the men began to take off their knapsacks to untie their rolled greatcoats.

"Leave your bloody coats where they are and look lively with the tents," bellowed Serjeant Granville. The ranks broke up and the men began grouping with their Corporals and the men with whom they shared a tent.

"Aren't we going to cross tonight, Corporal?" whispered Jamie.

"Not while the officers have the chance of a nice warm bed in the inn!" answered Corporal Reid.

He turned to Aaron and said, "Get off to the wagon with Clipper and Huhnie and unload our tent."

The young soldier was slow to react; he was mesmerised by the view in front of him. The wide stretch of turbulent water was both exciting and frightening to him.

"Didn't you hear what the Corporal said, Mew, you stupid bastard! Get your ass up the track to the wagon afore all your messmates get soaked."

"Yes, yes, Serjeant," he replied, trying to hide his loathing for the man who took every opportunity to taunt and belittle him.

The supply wagons were still a short way from the main company as the drivers gingerly brought them down the steep slope. As soon as the horses were stopped the soldiers ripped back the canvas cover on the cart which carried the tents. There was some disorder as men tried to be first to grab a tent and a set of poles. Aaron, who was one of the biggest of them, tried to push his way up to the edge of the cart, followed by his two messmates. As he reached out to grab one of the rolled tents he felt a sharp blow to his ribs. He turned and saw that the perpetrator was aiming another punch, this time at his head. Aaron ducked and parried by swinging his left fist at the face of the man he recognised as one of the new recruits, a man called Kemp. He was a bull of a man. His massive rounded shoulders, just like a bull's, seemed to run directly to his head, with no intervening neck. The only sign of a joint between the back of his cranium and body was a deep furrow lining the skin, which would have been hidden had he not been bald. His round face was dominated by an overhanging brow, at the base of which bushy eyebrows failed to hide bulging eyes. These contemptuous eyes seemed to be constantly roving to find objects and people on which he could possibly give vent to his violent nature.

The crowd milling around the cart parted as soon as it was seen that there was the potential entertainment of a brawl. The young soldier's punch had landed on Kemp's cheek and temporarily dazed the man. But the respite was short.

"Time you had a lesson you dirty farmer," said Kemp as he squared up in front of Aaron with his fists raised. He threw several punches, all of which the younger man easily avoided. The crowd around the pair began to chant, some shouting "Kempy" but most "Mewie". As Kemp swung a right hand, Aaron ducked and, taking advantage of the fact that the older man's right side was thus unprotected, shot his left fist into the man's nose. There was a loud grunt from the man and a roar from the crowd. By this time the buzzing in Aaron's ear had reached an almost unbearable level. He shook his head to try to be rid of it, but this hesitation cost him dearly. The now bloody Kemp was beside himself with anger. He launched himself directly at Aaron, grabbing his throat as the two men fell to the ground. Falling backwards with the heavy man on top of him, Aaron was completely winded and defenceless. The older man sat astride him and twice punched his head mercilessly. He would have continued had he not received a tremendous kick in his kidneys from a tall lean figure. Kemp screamed and turned his attention to the new assailant, Rev.

As the bleeding man tried to stand, Aaron's unlikely saviour swung a tent pole at Kemp's head and there was a thud as it connected. Kemp fell forward and lay stunned beside his victim.

Friends helped the two men to their feet. With bloodied faces they glowered at each other until the Serjeant, who had been observing but had not intervened, shouted, "That's enough, now get them bloody tents up."

Later, by the light of the lantern, the messmates discussed the evening's event.

"You done well, Mewie. Kemp is a bully, but be careful of him."

Jamie agreed, "Yes my friend, keep well clear of him. You have made an enemy this evening and he won't forgive you."

"Where is Rev, Jamie?" asked Aaron.

"He went up to the chapel we passed. He'll get wet through, but he is a tough one. Don't be fooled by his praying and reading and the like, he is afeared of naught."

"Well, I am certainly beholden to him. I hope that Kemp does not take revenge on him."

"No, the Serjeant has no reason to let that happen. He needs Rev. He is the only one who can preside at the burials."

"Burials?"

"Yes, well, we have been lucky so far – no injuries, no fevers. But mark what I say, you will lose many more of your comrades to sickness and accidents than will ever be killed by an enemy."

"Shut up, Jamie, don't scare the lad," said the Corporal.

"He is going to find out soon enough."

"Shut up, I said."

The tent flap opened and Rev's head appeared in the opening. He took off his greatcoat and shook it outside.

"The rain has stopped, gentlemen. Let us hope for a fine day for our excursion on the brine."

"Rev, I would just like to…" stuttered Aaron.

"Not a word, young Mewie, vengeance was mine, as the good book states. How are you recovering from the ministrations of our pugilistic comrade?"

"I'm alright."

"What happens tomorrow then?" asked Clipper.

"We've got to get over to Anglesey. It ain't far, but they'll have to make several trips to take us all and the carts. And the water has to be running right, or rather it ain't got to be running too much."

"Why?"

"The tide runs something savage and if the ferry gets caught by it we could get wet or worse."

There was silence in the tent while they contemplated the prospect of a watery grave. Rev unpacked his book and assumed his usual place. Others made themselves comfortable for the night and waited until the usual irritated request was forthcoming from the Corporal for Rev to cease his reading and douse the lantern.

Next morning, standing outside of their tent they noticed the Serjeants giving the order to the drummer before they heard the familiar and often despised rattle of the drum. Despised because for the last ten days, each morning, it had summoned the weary soldiers to form up for the next leg of the march.

Aaron and his comrades lifted their knapsacks from the damp grass and heaved them onto their backs, then picked up their firelocks, before moving off to join the column of twos forming a serpentlike procession down the slope. They had been standing higher up the hill than most of the others and thus found themselves joining the tail end of the queue.

Soon, they heard an order barked and the column moved off towards the jetty. When those at the head reached the waterside, they stopped in front of the first of two bargelike vessels which were moored alongside and the column halted. When about twenty men had been loaded on the first boat it was immediately pushed away from the landing stage and rowed out into the strait. There were four oarsmen who propelled the vessel from the shore. Meanwhile, another group of men had embarked on the second boat, and Aaron and his messmates shuffled further down, almost to the water's edge.

Eventually, they saw the boats coming back for them. The Serjeant shouted, "Corporals Bryant and Reid, you and your men are to load the baggage on the second of the two boats when they come back. Then stay here to get the carts on. The rest of you embark on the first boat with Captain Trowbridge and the other officers."

There was a groan from the soldiers at the back of the column. They would be doing the heavy work while their comrades on the other side could relax with a waterway between them and the Serjeants.

As soon as the boats had arrived, Serjeant Granville bellowed, "Look lively now, if we miss the tide we will be here for another twelve hours."

The men milled around the three carts, unloading them and

carrying their contents to the second of the two boats, while the first craft departed for the far shore. But the cooperation between the two teams of men was uneasy, for among Corporal Bryant's men was Private Kemp. The operation became somewhat fraught with much pushing and shoving. Nor did the inevitable comments made, supposedly out of the Serjeant's earshot, by the men of the two tents, assuage the ill feeling. Several references to the colour of Aaron's right eye were met with comments about the crooked appearance of Kemp's nose.

Serjeant Granville was well aware of the antagonism between the men and while he normally enjoyed fomenting confrontation and watching the results – which he always regarded as part of the men's toughening up process – he could not afford to be blamed by his superiors for missing the tidal opportunity. With regret, he decided to put a stop to the growing tension between the occupants of the two tents.

"Right you bastards, put your backs into it. If I hear another comment or see any lack of love between you I'll guarantee your appearance at the halberds."

The threat of the cat-o'-nine-tails was sufficient to calm the situation and the work continued in an uneasy peace at a quicker pace. The barge was full to capacity when it left the jetty, and there was only just enough space for Serjeant Ryan to squeeze aboard. He was to supervise the unloading when they reached Anglesey. Serjeant Granville, the ten men and the carters remained to await the return of the boats.

There was an air of great excitement among all the men, especially the new recruits, most of whom had never seen the sea before and none of whom had been on a ferry. There was no one more charged with excitement, and to some extent fear, than Aaron, when he uneasily felt the rocking of the boat as it was pulled from the shore.

Within a few minutes the boat grounded on a wide slipway at Porth y Wrach. The boat's lines were taken ashore to secure them from being dragged off by the accelerating tide. Here, the job of disembarking the carts was made cumbersome by the fact that they had to be lifted over the side of the boats and dragged through the knee-deep water onto the land.

By mid-afternoon, the carts had been reloaded and the fresh horses put in their traces. The order was passed on that the company would march as far as they could towards Holyhead before nightfall.

That night there was much discussion about the day's happenings. As usual, Rev was sitting with his book, half listening to the conversation. He noted that despite his earlier excitement, Aaron was not contributing much to the comments about the day and their transport across the water.

"Did you see the waves on the strait when we crossed it?" asked Clipper.

"You call those waves? You just wait until we leave Holyhead for Kingstown," retorted Jamie.

"Why, will it be rough?"

"I don't doubt you'll see yer breakfast twice," intervened the Corporal.

"How do you mean?" asked Huhne.

"Well, you see it first when you eat it and then again when you heave it up!"

Jamie laughed, but the comment made the others pensive.

"Come now, Corporal, if the weather is clement the voyage will be a most pleasable day excursion," said Rev.

"Yea, but if it ain't we are depending on you stilling the storm, like our Lord did."

The Rev turned back to his book.

"Mind you, the Irish Sea ain't nothing compared with the Atlantic. Now that is a sea. I never thought we would see the end of it when we come home from Dominica."

"And that's the truth," observed Jamie.

"At least the three of us survived that pestilential place and, by the grace of God, returned safely to our own shores, unlike most of our comrades."

There was silence. This last remark reminded all the occupants of the tent that the likelihood that they would ever see their homes again was remote.

Later, after the lantern had been blown out and the chorus of snores had begun, Rev said softly, "You awake, Mewie?"

"Yea, I can't sleep."

"Is your concern about Private Kemp?"

"No, not really."

"What is it then?"

"Well…well, I fear that I may never see my parents again. And then again, I know that I can't go home anyway unless I can take twelve pounds."

"Why are you thinking about that now?"

"Well…well it was like as if crossing the water today made me feel further away from them than ever."

"I understand. Can you write?"

"Well, I never paid too much heed to reading and writing at school. I never thought to have much use for it."

"Would you like to learn?"

"How?"

Rev chuckled and said, "I would be happy to teach you. Then you could write to your parents and tell them what happened to you."

"I'm beholden to you for the offer, but I ain't a clever learner."

"I wouldn't have deigned to make the offer if I had not detected a glimmer of intellect in you."

"When could you teach me then?"

"We get stand easy time each evening. You can spend a short period of study each day."

There was a long period of silence and then Aaron said, "Can we send letters from Ireland?"

"It can be arranged. We can get a letter taken to Dublin with dispatches. From there it would go by ship's letter to Holyhead. A post boy would take it to London and then transfer it to a delivery to your village."

"Would they have to pay?"

"No, with the new system you can pay for it when it is sent, though it will cost you a day's pay. By the way, can your parents read?"

"Mother be the clever one, she can read, but father never had use for it."

Aaron was suddenly charged with an enthusiasm which he had not had during his school days. The thought that he might be able to explain to his parents his plight and current situation motivated him to say, "Well then, if you please, I should like to do that."

"On the morrow we shall sharpen our sticks of plumbago and start by practising letters."

"Plumbago?"

"Yes, my dear fellow. Mined in Borrowdale in Cumbria. Better known as pencillus, or pencil. The army has seen fit to provide us all with one."

And thus it was that the next evening Rev began to instruct his pupil. The learning materials consisted of an army notebook, a well-thumbed Bible, a copy of *Pilgrim's Progress*, and a pencil.

Chapter 10

The soldiers, who had just had breakfast, were sitting on whatever was convenient in the morning sunshine on the dockside at Holyhead, watching the workers using a derrick to load the carts into the hold of the ship. Aaron was sitting on a packing case. He was torn between watching the men on the quay, staring with admiration at the two-masted ship which was to carry them to Ireland, and looking at the various signs on the walls of the storehouses. He tried to read the wordings letter by letter to understand what service or commodity was being offered by the advertiser. He had had two sessions with Rev to rectify the shortcomings of his school education. Several of his comrades taunted him, especially the Corporal. Though it was unsaid, Rev and Jamie recognised that their Corporal was envious and already felt threatened by the fact that of all his charges, apart from Aaron, he was the most poorly educated and least literate. This educational handicap would forever prevent him being promoted to Serjeant.

The wooden panels which would cover the hold during the voyage were replaced and covered by a large canvas sheet. This was fastened in place with wooden chocks which were hammered into loops surrounding the hold.

"Stand to you lazy asswipes, time to go. Form up in twos."

The Serjeant strutted along the line of soldiers and looked them up and down.

"Now hear this. We share these seas with others, and though as we are told, there is presently peace between us and them, if we meet any Frenchies we've got to be ready to give an account of ourselves. Bear in mind too that American privateers frequent the waters around our country. Those as are trained with the firelock shall have ammunition at the ready during the journey and pass the voyage on deck. It's going to be crowded on board. New recruits will be travelling in the hold. Serjeant Ryan will direct you as you get on board."

Granville beckoned to the head of the column to begin embarkation. Gradually, the men shuffled forward to the gangplank and, as commanded, most followed the leaders to an open hatch where a ladder protruded.

As their eyes got used to the darkness down below, the recruits nervously looked around for a comfortable place to pass the voyage. Several climbed up into the carts which had been lashed down in the hold for the journey. On the floor against a bulkhead, adjacent to the ladder, there was a row of buckets. Each was lashed to a hook in the woodwork.

After what seemed a long wait in the increasingly stuffy hold, the bulky shape of Serjeant Ryan blocked the natural light coming through the hatch and then descended the ladder.

"Listen up! We shall shortly be leaving on the tide. The wind is fair for Kingstown – we hope to be there by midnight. As long as it is safe to do so, the hatch will be left open. The weather will also decide if you can have your midday porridge on deck or in the hold. You have no other call to go on deck. And to be sure, you see there are buckets here for you to do your business."

The Serjeant turned and climbed up the ladder. His departure occasioned a loud buzz of conversation among the new soldiers. Some joked, but many made anxious remarks to those within earshot, for none of them had ever embarked on a sea voyage before. As the noise subsided they heard orders being shouted on deck and a rattling sound which, although they did not know it, was the noise of the rings attached to the triangular sail being hoisted up the main mast. The offshore breeze meeting the resistance of the increasingly big sail caused the boat to lean slightly. Amid a crescendo of curses and foul language, the men below tried to grab at anything which could steady them and prevent them sliding or falling towards the lower side of the hull. More orders were shouted and unseen by the recruits, the ship's lines were loosed and pulled aboard. Released from the quayside, the ship became more upright, to the relief of the soldiers.

The soldiers on deck were able to watch the activities of the ship's hands as they bent the two square foresails on the mast nearest the bow. The ship accelerated with the wind fine on the port quarter, but now instead of leaning over in one direction, the ship rolled in the following wind.

On the scale of good to bad weather, the conditions were favourable for a quick passage. The weather was dry and the wind was from a useful direction and not strong enough to cause the Captain any concern about shortening sail. For the men below, such information was of little consequence as they were first pushed and then pulled by whatever steadying handhold they had. Like anyone on their first sea voyage, unaware of the abilities of the ship and having no knowledge of what is normal on a sailing vessel and what is exceptional and therefore cause for concern, the recruits, from the bravest to the most cowardly, had feelings ranging from anxiousness to terror.

Aaron was beginning to learn to live with the annoying noise in his head which appeared every time he was anxious or distressed. He had developed a mannerism of placing his left hand over his ear and pressing his palm against his head when it started. This gave slight relief, so in his present position on the ship he sat with one arm round the ladder and his other hand on his ear.

The vexed men became silent as they tried to come to terms with the discomfort and uncertainty of the sea journey. Some had found comfortable corners where they could wedge themselves in, others sat holding the wheels of the carts or some other convenient object of a steadfast nature. There was little talking, but a medley of other sounds: the rush and swish of the sea, the creaking of timbers and the occasional flap of a sail. As the vessel drew away from the shore it became subject to the waves created by the stiff breeze and began to pitch as well as roll. Aaron sat on one side of the ladder and folded his right arm though the upright. Clipper was on the other side of the ladder clinging on likewise. The advantage of their position, as long as there was no rain, was that they had a plentiful supply of fresh air from the open hatch. Such was not the case for those further in. The combination of stagnant air and the movement of the ship soon claimed its first victims. Their discomfort was first signaled by a sound of retching and then cursing by the men who were being trampled on in the rush of one of their companions to reach the buckets. The careering of the ship maximized their plight and amplified the wretchedness of their situation. Nor was the environment improved when men started to attempt to use the buckets for other, more normal purposes.

After what seemed to be an interminable time, Serjeant Ryan's head was once more framed by the opening. "Those of you with a stomach for porridge can come up now. To be sure the air would do you good for there is a smell most foul emanating from below. Oh, you'll not be forgetting your spoons."

Most of the men did not move, but gradually some started weaving their precarious way towards the ladder. Aaron and Clipper climbed up and though the sun was not shining, it took a time for their eyes to adjust to the light of day. The sight which greeted the two men astounded them. Whichever way they looked there was sea – no sign whatever of the land they had left or the one which they were to go to. Ropes had been tied between the two masts and the redcoats were sitting on the hold cover with their arms linked round the ropes for safety. Before the foremast there was a tripod from which swung a large pot. A soldier was standing with a ladle in one hand and gripping a line with the other. A second soldier stood by two barrels which were lashed down on a bench. Beside each of the latter was a wooden cup on a chain.

Serjeant Ryan called to those who had emerged from the hold, "Come lads, come. For 'tis the finest of food that awaits you and the Captain has ordered a double tot of rum."

A short queue formed, the men trying to keep their balance as the ship sought to make this an impossibility. When each man reached the tripod, which was fixed to the deck, they picked up a bowl from a rack and held it out with one hand while grasping at any available support with the other. The purveyor of porridge plunged his ladle into the swaying pot, pulled out a portion and slapped it down in the bowl. Each soldier then moved across to the barrel where the cup was filled with a double tot of rum for immediate consumption. Next, as best they could, they turned a tap on the next barrel for a cup full of small beer.

Aaron and Clipper waddled over to where Jamie and Rev were sitting.

"So, you have survived and still have an appetite, Mewie," said Jamie.

"You need an appetite to eat this stuff," intervened Clipper.

"Enjoy it while you can. I rather fancy that we will not be seeing food again until we breakfast on Hibernian," suggested Rev. "Anyway, how are things in the bowels of the boat?" he added.

"It's a stinking hell hole. You are very fortunate."

"We are, unless it rains," said Jamie.

"Where's Grabber?" asked Clipper.

"A malicious rumour has circulated that our senior non-commissioned officer has retired, a victim of *mal de mer*."

"What's that, Rev?" asked Aaron.

"Seasickness, dear boy. Naturally, few regret the Serjeant being thus incommoded. How uncharitable of them."

"Come now, lads, look lively. When you have finished, take your bowls back and then get yourselves back below," called Serjeant Ryan.

Aaron and Clipper, in common with several others, ate as slowly as they could to prolong their stay on deck. The Serjeant was clearly getting annoyed. He moved around the eaters with as much dignity as the rolling deck allowed, telling each of them to hurry up. He did not want the officers to appear on deck and find it crowded with the recruits who should be below. Then he called out again, "Now me patience is stretched as thin as a fiddle string. Get ye all below, now. Now, I said! Mew, Graham – be off with ye."

The two of them returned their bowls and reluctantly made their way to the hatch. As they climbed down they were met by an awful stench – a combination of vomit, urine and sweat. The situation was made worse by the fact that in their absence their prime positions by the ladder had been occupied by Pierce and Goddard, the Salisbury merchants. Aaron and Clipper had to find their way into the dark recesses of the hold for a clean place to sit.

After some time when the men were dozing, some soundly and loudly, others fitfully, they were woken by the sound of men running on deck and raised voices. Shortly after they heard the rattle of a heavy chain and a splash. Pierce climbed up the dark ladder and looked around. He came straight down again.

"We're there, lads, I can see lamps on the shore. I think we have anchored," he called out to the others.

There were cheers, not reflecting enthusiasm, but relief. Their current ordeal was over. Within an hour the ship had been towed to a jetty and even though it was late in the evening, unloading began so that the soldiers could recover their tents and make a camp for their accommodation. Aaron and his comrade new recruits spent the first of many nights in Ireland.

Chapter 11

Long before they reached Galway the officers on horseback had left them and gone on ahead to enjoy the comfort of the officers' mess. The column marched up the hill to the old castle; their trek across Ireland was over, but the sight of the dilapidated stonework of the building filled the new recruits with foreboding.

"Jamie, is this where we are going to live?" asked Aaron with some trepidation.

"Well, it will be until the Serjeant has decided that you can 'pass the guard'."

"What does that mean?"

"That he considers that you act like a soldier and look like one too. Until then, you won't be able to leave the barracks in the castle. Later, you will probably be billeted in the town – there isn't enough space in the castle for the whole regiment."

While Aaron was considering the prospect of incarceration within the grey walls, they approached the castle gate. Serjeant Granville shouted, "Company, halt!"

Outside the gate was an armed sentry. He saluted the Serjeant.

Granville turned and addressed the column. "Take heed now, you new men. This here is the sentry. He is part of the unit on guard duty. There are twelve men in the guard, a Serjeant and a drummer. They are all armed and stay on duty for twenty-four hours before handing over to the next unit. The others are in the guard room. Their job is to check on everyone coming in and that no one goes out without permission and in a proper state of dress. You new men won't be getting the aforementioned permission until I say so."

The company was ordered to continue their march and they entered through the gate. The Serjeant saluted an officer and the column moved on. Inside there was a large square around which were long wooden huts. They were ordered to halt in the square.

Most members of the original beating party, including Rev and Jamie, were dismissed and given permission to return to their billets in the town. The circumstances were such that no comments or farewells could be made, but as they passed, both Jamie and Rev winked at Aaron. He watched with his hand on his ear, as the two men on whom he had so much reliance made their way towards the guard room and the gate. The Corporals remained with the company, but without the two older men who had given him so much guidance and understanding, he felt very alone.

The recruits were kept waiting in the square while the two Serjeants conferred first with each other and then with the Lieutenant, who had appeared from one of the buildings carrying a paper. All the time soldiers were coming and going, doing various chores and carrying boxes and equipment. In one corner of the square a company was doing physical exercises. In pairs they were throwing a cannon ball to each other. A Serjeant barked derisive remarks at individuals who were doing this too slowly and occasionally uttered a scornful expletive to anyone dropping a ball.

Paying little heed to these distractions, the new recruits all had their eyes on the two Serjeants and the Lieutenant, anxiously awaiting to hear what was to happen to them next. Serjeant Granville looked up from the paper which the three of them had been studying and said, "Now listen up, men. This is your home for the next few months. There are twelve men, including a Corporal, to a hut. I will read your names in groups of eleven and then allocate a Corporal who will show you to your billets and instruct you about living in them. He will show you your beds and help with other things. The Lieutenant has kindly allowed you to rest this evening. Your training starts tomorrow. Any questions?"

There was a silence, then the Serjeant continued and started to read out names. The first group went off with a Corporal and then the names of the second group were called: "For 'ut seven, Huhne, Pierce, Mew, Goddard, Graham, Turner, Harris, Bell and Brooks, O'Driscoll and…" he paused to get maximum effect, "And Kemp, go with Corporal Reid."

Aaron was relieved to hear that he would at least be billeted with some of the recruits he knew, even if they were not close friends, but was horrified to hear Kemp's name.

The eleven recruits followed the Corporal to a row of huts behind the one they had first seen. He opened the door and ushered the men in. The room was illuminated by the light from the one window, but this did not suffice for them to see the detail of the room until their eyes had become accustomed to the gloom. However, what struck the men first was not through the use of their eyes, but through their noses. There was an almost chokingly strong stale smell of smoke, lamp oil and urine.

In a long row, parallel to each other on the floor, were twelve straw-filled palliasses, with about a foot between each. At the far end of the room was a long wooden table with the same number of chairs. Behind that was a cooking range and two cupboards.

The Corporal broke the silence: "Brooks, open the window, let's try to freshen the place up. My bed is the one nearest the table. The rest of you can choose whichever one pleases you most. You keep your packs to the left of the head of your bed. Take your pick now – put your haversacks as instructed and be easy at the foot of your bed."

There was some commotion as men took possession as ordered. Aaron tried to place himself as far from Kemp as possible, taking the bed nearest the door and next to Huhne. He noticed that there was a hook on the wall over his bed and hung his coat on it. Then he positioned himself at the foot of the bed as ordered.

"Come on, come on, O'Driscoll, we haven't got all night."

"But to be sure, Corporal, 'twas the time it took to find the drawing of me loving mother."

There was laughter around the room which to an extent lightened the anxiety of the recruits, but it was quickly cut short by the Corporal. "This here is the accommodation his Gracious Majesty has seen fit to provide you men. Here you will sleep, eat, cook, clean your kit and when the Serjeant affords you the opportunity, relax."

He paused, considering the order to give further information. "As I said, here you will sleep and for them as needs a pee in the night there is the 'sip pot'. He pointed to a large open wooden tub which was at the back of the door. All too late, Aaron realised that he had chosen the bed next to the night urinal.

"Any questions, men?"

"What about food, Corporal?"

"An important question, Pierce. This here, that is you lot, is a mess. Each mess takes charge of its own food, that is, getting it from the sutlers and cooking it. So we take it in turns to cook."

Pierce intervened again. "What if we can't cook, Corporal?"

"Then you had better learn double quick 'cause there's no one so unpopular with his messmates as a man who don't provide a good dinner. And if you make a real bad job of it you risks a company Court Martial. I will explain that should the need arise. Right, food. Food is provided as prescribed by army regulations. The cook of the day will be allocated, for each man, a pound of bread, a pound of beef or pork, a pound of pease or turnips, an ounce of butter or cheese and an ounce of rice. He also gets a sack of potatoes to share out. This is the food you pay for by deduction from your pay. Any questions?"

"What about drink?" growled Kemp.

"The cook will get a barrel of small beer a day to be shared as required. In the cupboard are tin mugs for the beer. You each of you already have your wooden trenchers, your bowls and your spoon. You bring them to the table."

"When do we eat, Corporal?"

"Don't you think about anything else than food, Pierce? Well, first is breakfast – bread and small beer, then at midday you gets your boiled beef and potatoes and the pease or turnips. At about five o'clock we have tea meal, usually small beer and bread with the cheese or butter. Now, if this ain't enough for you, you are at liberty to buy extra food from the hawkers who the guard let into the castle in the evenings."

"What about rum, Corporal?"

"Keen on your drink, ain't you, Kemp? As he sees fit, the Captain will order an issue of rum ration for each mess. If and when we are on active duty, we get rum every day. Any other questions?"

The Corporal waited for a few seconds and then continued, "Tomorrow you start your training and you will get your proper firelocks and equipment. Barrack duties tomorrow – Mew to empty and clean the sip pot, Huhne to cook. The ablutions and the cess pits are round the back of this hut. Check and clean all your kit and your uniform ready for tomorrow, the Serjeant will be particular about having his new recruits looking like hopefuls."

It was dark; all of the occupants of the hut were soundly asleep. This was the first time that any of them had slept in anything like a bed since they had left civilian life. The crash of the hut door being thrown open and banging back onto the pot brought most of the sleepers to consciousness. The booming voice of Serjeant Granville resounded round the hut as he held up a lantern. "It is five o'clock. By Bob's rattle the sun's burning holes in your blankets. Turn out you gutter rats, you unchristened sons of mendicants. Bless your eyes! Bless your souls." He paused and then continued, "You filthy asswipes, out of bed and up to wash. I want you all lined on the square washed, hair clubbed, breakfasted and in fatigues at six o'clock."

He thumped the lantern down on the table, turned, walked out and left the door open allowing the chill air to challenge the fetid air of the hut.

Amid a chorus of cursing and yawning, men scrabbled for their clothes. Corporal Reid's voice penetrated the discord: "Huhne, get over to the sutler's wagon and ask for the bread and beer for hut seven. Pierce, go and help him."

As soon as he had put on his breeches and boots, Aaron grabbed the wet rope handles of the sip pot and carefully lifted it. He put his foot in the door which was still ajar from having been opened by Huhne and carried the pot out. Without the benefit of light he stumbled around to the back of the hut and there by the light of a hanging lantern, was guided by men from other huts on the same mission as his. After having emptied and scrubbed the pot he returned to the hut, but as he tried to enter, a bulky frame barred his way.

"You and me got some unfinished business, farmer," growled Kemp, who was silhouetted against the light of the lantern inside. He pushed Aaron roughly as he exited the doorway. The younger man bit his bottom lip and carried on with his task.

As soon as Huhne and Pierce appeared, one carrying a bread sack and the other a churn, the men sat down to breakfast. The meal was hurried by the fretful Corporal who was concerned that his mess should not be last to make an appearance on the square.

"Pair up with the man on the next bed to yours to do each other's hair, and do it quick," he instructed.

The men had had several weeks of practice now of clubbing each other's hair, but nevertheless Huhne fumbled awkwardly trying to grapple with Aaron's hair.

"Having trouble with the farmer's haystack, Huhnie?" shouted Kemp. There was laughter around the hut as others sycophantically appreciated Kemp's joke.

"Shut up, Kemp, and get on with your own," interjected the Corporal. The men continued in silence which was only occasionally broken by grunts and complaints about hair being pulled too tightly.

Shortly before the drummer announced that it was six o'clock, the men from hut seven were formed up in line on the square with the other recruits. To the east were the first signs of a breaking dawn and from the west the autumn wind brought a chill to the paraded men. A feeling which was not to last, for after a roll call and cursory inspection by Lieutenant Stephens, the Serjeants got to work. The men were marched and drilled continuously for three hours. During the session two men, including Pierce, collapsed and were dragged off to their beds after their names had been taken by Serjeant Ryan. After a break the men began their first session of physical exercises, a session which produced another casualty when one man ran into another. However, one recruit who did not suffer the extremities of the session was Huhne, as he was excused to go to prepare the midday meal for the hut.

The exertions of the morning, and the hunger so induced, broadened the tolerance of the diners to the quality of the food. There were no complaints about Huhne's cooking, but a tirade of grumbling about the morning's activities. There were further complaints about the fact that Pierce was allowed to rest on his bed to recuperate.

In the afternoon the drilling continued and it was a very weary group of men who quietly rejoiced as they were dismissed shortly before five to have their tea meal. The refreshment helped the men to recover their spirits and soon there was lively ribaldry around the room; this continued until Kemp once more started taunting Aaron. Few of the men dared not to laugh at the young man's discomfort.

There came a point when the Corporal had heard enough.

"Out with you all, take your beds and shake them outside, get the fleas out of them. Come in when I call you. Not you, Kemp, you stay here."

No one heard what fiery Corporal Reid had to say to Kemp, but afterwards there was a temporary marked decline in his bullying of Aaron. Three days later, Reid's warning forgotten, Kemp was sitting at the table in the hut with two of his most ardent henchmen, Bell and Brooks, all cleaning their boots. The Corporal and the other men were outside the hut. It was Tuesday evening; all kit had to be in good order for the Wednesday parade. Aaron had no choice but to join the other three at the table to clean his footwear.

"Who says you can sit with us, farmer?"

"I don't have to ask you, Kemp. I've got the same right as you."

"What do you think, Brooksy?"

"He could at least say please."

"That's right, Brooksy. Say please, farmer."

"No I ain't, and I bain't a farmer, I'm a blacksmith."

Kemp reached forward to snatch at Aaron's shoulder, but the boy was too fast for him and leant back quickly. In doing so his chair fell backwards and Aaron landed heavily on the floor. His boots were still on the table. Brooks grabbed them and threw them over to Kemp. He passed them to Bell and then moved quickly round the table. He put a foot on Aaron's chest to hold him on the ground.

"Fill them up, Ting," shouted Kemp.

Bell grabbed the jug of small beer and started to fill one of Aaron's boots with the liquid. Before he could fill the boot, there was a rattle as the hut door opened. Two of the men walked in followed by Corporal Reid.

"What the hell is going on in here?" demanded Reid.

On hearing the sound at the door, Kemp had removed his foot from Aaron's chest and pretended to be helping him to his feet. Bell tried to hide the sodden boot.

"He fell off his chair, Corporal, nasty accident. I was helping him," muttered Kemp.

By this time Aaron was on his feet. His fury was clear to be seen, but he was biting his bottom lip hard and rubbing his left ear.

"You alright, son?" asked Reid.

"Yes, Corporal," he said as he grabbed his boot from the table.

"Where's your other boot, Mew?"

It was obvious to all that Bell was trying to hide the object in his hand; he had no option but to put it on the table.

"I was helping him to clean it, Corporal."

Reid snatched the wet boot from the Private and poured the beer which was left in it onto the floor.

"Helping were you? Give me your boots."

Bell passed his newly cleaned boots to the Corporal.

"Here, Mew, are some nice clean boots for you to wear tomorrow. They'd be a bit tight I shouldn't wonder, but they will do until yours dry out. Bell, you put on Mew's tomorrow."

No words were said to Kemp. The Corporal knew from bitter experience that no further words from him would have any effect.

The next day, the Corporal took Aaron aside.

"Kemp been giving you a rough time, lad, ain't he?"

"He doesn't seem to like me much," said Aaron.

"Every hut has a boss man, and it ain't the Corporal. It's the one that others are afraid of. And in hut seven that'd be Kemp."

"I bain't afraid of him."

"Yes, that's the problem. You got to decide to be afraid of him, otherwise you got to smash him up a bit and take his place."

"How do you mean?"

"Well, you ain't heard this from me, but the only way to deal with a man like him is to take his place. You'd have to take him off guard somehow."

The conversation continued and when it had finished, Aaron knew what had to be done.

Every Saturday evening a double rum ration was issued to the recruits. The effect on them was different, ranging from morose ramblings about loved ones missed, to petulance about the army, and sometimes the more aggressive ones looked for fights. The Corporal knew who to watch through the evening to avoid the latter. And even though he was relatively small in stature he had easy recourse to reinforcements from the guard room.

On the Saturday following his conversation with Aaron, Reid issued the rum ration to the men seated around the table. Huhne and Aaron refused their ration.

"Here, Kemp, you want Mew's ration?" asked the Corporal.

"You are damned right I do," he said as he grabbed the metal cup measure and tipped it into his mug.

"Then you might as well have Huhne's as well."

Only Huhne, Aaron and the Corporal knew that each measure had been increased twofold and by the time he had greedily emptied his mug, the bully had consumed the equivalent of five double rums in a short time. The effect of the drink was noticeable as the volume of Kemp's voice and the profanity of his curses increased.

Corporal Reid stood up and walked past Aaron, who was standing at the end of the table. As he passed him he winked and whispered, "The club is under your bed." He turned to the men at the table and said, "I'll leave you gentlemen for a while to visit Corporal Bryant."

As soon as the Corporal had left the noise level increased further, and almost as soon as Aaron sat down Kemp turned his invective on him.

"Who said you could sit with me and my friends, you stinking farmer?" said Kemp.

There were calls from his friends of, "Yeah, who said?"

"I don't need to ask no lousy weaver where I can sit," replied Aaron, alluding to Kemp's previous trade.

The noise level around the table instantly dropped. All sensed that a boundary had been crossed. An irreversible assertion had been made and there could only be one outcome. Despite his inebriation, Kemp had recognised this too and rejoiced in it. He put his hands on the arms of his chair and laboriously pushed his huge body to its feet. He stood swaying pendulum-like, his bloodshot eyes staring venomously at the youth at the end of the table.

"Now you'll get your comeuppance, you blasted whelp."

As he spoke, he ponderously found his way along the table to the far end where Aaron had started to raise himself. Meanwhile, Huhne had quickly made his way to the far end of the hut where Reid had secreted a heavy ash club for Aaron to defend himself with.

When faced to each other, it was clear that they were about the same height, but despite Aaron's sturdy frame the other man was unmistakably heavier in build. Aaron raised his fists to defend himself as the older man grabbed his shoulders. He brought his head down surprisingly quickly trying to smash his forehead on the younger opponent's nose. But he was not quick enough and as the heavy head descended, Aaron dodged sideways and the man's head landed on his right shoulder. This put Kemp off balance and he staggered forward. As he did so, he received a stinging left-hand punch to his right cheek as Aaron broke away.

The younger man backed away and moved further down towards the darker end of the hut, where Huhne was standing with the club in hand. The crowd around the table started to boo Aaron as they perceived that he was running away.

"The club, for God's sake take the club, before he kills you, Mewie," pleaded Huhne.

But Aaron ignored his friend and stood his ground halfway down the hut where he had more space to use the advantage of his agility. The approaching shape of the seething Kemp was silhouetted by the lanterns on the table. He was breathing heavily as he tried again to grab the subject of his anger, but Aaron had realised that he must use the advantage bestowed on him by virtue of his youth and clarity of mind to keep the pugnacious soldier at a distance. As the man tried to grab him he shot out his right arm and connected with Kemp's face, square between the eyes. The big man staggered at the shock, and his trauma was compounded when a left was landed on his right ear. He was now beside himself with rage and as Aaron tried another right-hand punch Kemp managed to grab his arm with his left hand. He held it vice-like and swung the younger man round so that his back was against the wall. Aaron writhed, but could not free himself as, despite the poor light, he saw the huge clenched right fist swing towards him. At the last second, before the battering ram of a punch crashed into his face, he bent his knees, lowering his body. The assailant, his mind slowed by the drink, was too slow to alter the trajectory of his arm.

Despite the roar of the spectators, one sound was clearly identifiable: the howl of pain as Kemp's wrist broke. The wild punch had impacted on the Irish oak frame of the hut with every iota of strength the heavy man could muster. But then another, different sound caught the attention of the crowd. The hut door rattled, and in the dim light, first the figure of Serjeant Granville and then that of Corporal Reid, who was carrying a lantern, appeared.

"What in the name of Jesse is going on in here? By your beds, all of you, now," bellowed Granville.

In the confusion which followed, Huhne replaced the club into its hiding place. The men scrambled to stand at the ends of their straw mattresses waiting for the inevitable interrogation, each of them determined not to be singled out as the one who betrayed the others. However, it was already quite obvious to Granville what had happened although he did not know of the Corporal's connivance.

As the Corporal held the lantern up to the man standing at the end of the first bed it was clear to the Serjeant, from his dishevelled appearance and his heavy breathing, that Aaron had recently been involved in some exertion.

Granville walked briskly past the other men up towards the far end. He stopped by Kemp.

"Bring the lantern, Corporal, let's have a close look."

Reid held the lamp up to the soldier's face. There was a swelling in the middle of his forehead and the man was shaking from the effect of shock. He was supporting his right forearm with his left hand. Blood was dripping from the lacerated knuckles, but what most caught the Serjeant's attention was the odd angle at which Kemp's right hand hung from his arm.

"Struth, Kemp, what happened to you?"

"I was violently attacked, Serjeant, and that's the truth."

"Who attacked you?"

"The farmer, Serjeant."

Pointing at Kemp, the senior officer said, "Corporal, arrange for this man to see the surgeon."

Then striding down to Aaron he said brusquely, "Mew, you are on a charge, come with me."

The Serjeant led Aaron to the guard house.

Three days later the boy from Wessex was led out to the waiting halberds. All the recruits were paraded in a hollow square waiting for the punishment to be administered. But there were others watching too. A number of regular soldiers, who although not paraded, had stopped their work to watch. Jamie and Rev, who were unloading supplies from a sutler's wagon, put their boxes down and gazed down from the wagon at the scene in the square.

The Captain had sentenced Aaron to fifty lashes for brawling in the billet. Many reflected that at last the Lieutenant had achieved retribution for the treatment he had received at the Private's hand in the Saracen's Head in Salisbury, others that the punishment seemed unduly harsh, but all agreed that the aggrieved Lieutenant had influenced the Captain's decision.

One drummer boy was beating a steady rhythm as the prisoner walked up to the halberds. When he reached them, Serjeant Granville shouted the traditional instruction, the only time an officer called a Private 'sir'.

"Strip, sir."

The recruit did as instructed and the surgeon who always attended such punishments quickly appraised that the prisoner was in good physical condition. Two Corporals tied Aaron to the frame and then stood back as the Serjeant pulled the cat-o'-nine-tails out of the green baize bag he was carrying. He flicked it to free the tangled tails and handed the cat to a second drummer boy who was standing by the halberds.

The Captain read out the charge and the punishment awarded. Then Granville went round to the back of the halberds and tried to put a bullet into Aaron's mouth for him to bite on. The prisoner refused and spat it out.

Then the drummer boy started his work. The sickening whoosh of the cat was followed by the slap of the leathers thrashing the bare back. At the first lash Aaron's body jolted, at the second it jerked less and eventually the young recruit's body no longer reacted to the lashes. As the strokes continued the Serjeant counted each one out loud.

After ten strokes, the drummers changed places. The younger of the two, who had been beating the drum all through the punishment, stopped, took off the strap and gave the drum to the boy who had been administering the lashing. The punishment continued for five more strokes when Aaron's body suddenly sagged as if he were unconscious. The surgeon stepped forward, waved at the boy to stop the flogging and peered round to look at Aaron's face. Satisfied with his examination, he waved the drummer boy to continue, even though some of the weals on the victim's back were now oozing blood.

Ten more lashes were administered before the surgeon put

up his hand and stopped the beating. He turned and whispered something to the Serjeant.

"The punishment is judged to have been administered," shouted Granville. "Parade, dismiss!"

The two Corporals came forward to untie the prisoner. As they did so Aaron slumped down onto his knees. But he fell no further, as Huhne, Jamie and Rev grabbed him. The two regular soldiers took one of Aaron's arms each and put them over their shoulders. They gently bore him to hut seven, followed by Huhne, who had picked up Aaron's shirt.

This was the first time Aaron had been in the hut since the fateful evening when he had been dragged off to solitary confinement in the guard house. Though he was only vaguely aware of it, the atmosphere had changed and he was welcomed back by messmates who but a few days ago were his tormentors. Kemp's bed was gone; it had been taken to the sick bay where the surgeon was trying to treat him for a compound fracture of the wrist, with little success.

Later, the surgeon appeared to inspect the lacerations on Aaron's back and declared to Reid, "Corporal, see that the wounds are washed with salted water. He will be fit for duties again in two days."

The drill training continued unabated for three more weeks, the only relief being the Wednesday full dress parade and the Sunday church parade.

In December, the recruits were told that they were to be inoculated, one mess each week. The Corporals were given the task of explaining the procedure to the men in their hut. When the rota indicated that the treatment was imminent for the occupants of hut seven, Corporal Reid gathered the men and addressed them.

"You have all heard that you are to be given a treatment to protect you against smallpox. Have any of you had it before? Because if you have, you already have immunity. You can't catch it twice."

"I've had it, Corporal," volunteered Bell.

"Right, you can stay to listen anyway."

"What's the treatment, Corporal?" asked O'Driscoll. "For I'm not sure as I want it."

"Wait for me to explain, and you will be having it whether you want it or not."

There were nervous mumblings amongst the listeners.

"Quiet, quiet, let me explain." The Corporal waited for silence and then continued.

"You get infected with a mild dose of the smallpox, very mild mind you. This infection will give you some discomfort for a couple of days, and then you will be as healthy as ever and never catch this awful disease."

"Jesse, Corporal, how do we know that we won't catch the real illness?" pleaded Huhne.

"You won't catch it. Look, I have had the treatment, as have all the other soldiers here."

"And could you be telling me, Corporal, just how this, this treatment works?" asked the doubtful Irishman.

The Corporal now had a silent audience in front of him. "The surgeon takes a small amount of fluid from a smallpox sore on someone with the disease, and then he puts it into your blood."

The silence continued for a few seconds – the men were aghast at the concept just described to them. Then the Corporal was assaulted by a barrage of questions and curses. He shouted loudly, "Shut up, shut up. Look, would you prefer that I ask Serjeant Granville to come to explain this to you?"

The crowd went quiet again, and then the silence was broken by O'Driscoll. "And could you be telling us, Corporal, just how does this, this, this fluid, get into our blood, for it would seem to me that this idea smacks of the black arts. Would the surgeon be coming on a broomstick?"

The laughter around the room eased the atmosphere enough for Reid to continue. "The surgeon will cut a small hole in your arm with a scalpel and insert the fluid. It is almost painless."

"Painless! You'll be making a hole in my arm and you say painless. This was not in the oath we took when we joined up. I think I'd be preferring to have smallpox."

"The oath did say that you would obey orders, O'Driscoll, and if the army says you are to have the treatment, you will damned well have it."

The men could tell by the Corporal's voice that he was now much incensed; no one dared to add to the Irishman's objection. There was a pause, and then the Corporal addressed them further.

"Now the good news. After the treatment you get a holiday. No work, no drills."

"Oh, the magnanimity of the army knows no bounds," grumbled O'Driscoll.

"Yes, for one week after the treatment you are to be confined to quarters to rest."

There were many exchanged glances and a few comments between the listeners.

"You mean that we have to stay in here for a whole week without going outside?" asked Huhne.

"Yes, that exactly. Your food will be brought to you and the sip pot will be emptied by one of the soldiers."

"But why, why in the name of the Maker would we be locked up for a week?" asked a dazed O'Driscoll.

"I've told you all you need to know. After breakfast tomorrow you should all report to the regimental hospital."

With that the Corporal quickly made his way out of the hut for a quiet pipe in the cold air. He realised that sooner or later the men would find out why they would be isolated for a week after the treatment. Because of the opposition he had encountered, he had decided not to tell them that besides getting some mild symptoms of the illness itself, they would be infectious to others for a time and had to be kept away from those who had not yet had the treatment.

Just before dusk at the end of December, after a physical training session, Serjeant Granville addressed all the recruits.

"Now you gentlemen have had a taste of army life, it's time for you to learn how to defend King and Country. Tomorrow, we begin flintlock training."

There was a buzz of enthusiasm among the men.

"What's that I hear? I did not ask for anyone to speak. Tonight, you will all clean your firelocks and check your flints. And check them carefully, because one day your lives will depend on the spark. Tomorrow morning your Corporals will give instruction in the huts and introduce you to the Drill Manual of 1764. Dismiss."

Next morning, Corporal Reid and the eleven recruits sat around the table. In front of him was a firelock.

"This here is the weapon. It will be your best friend and as the

Serjeant said, your life will depend on it. This is how it works. First, the parts."

The Corporal went on to show how a small gunpowder charge in the flash pan was ignited by a flint gripped by the hammer, scraping against a steel cover, the frizzen. The flash in the pan in turn ignited the main charge of gunpowder in the breech of the gun barrel, which shot the ball out.

"Your firelock has to be well maintained and cleaned or it can kill you. When you put the charge in the pan you first pull back the hammer halfway, one click, that's half-cock. If you ain't looked after your weapon proper, the gun can go off at half-cock."

"Where do you get the powder for the pan, Corporal?" asked Huhne.

"This is the procedure, though as you are going to see later, there are very strict rules about loading. You take a cartridge from your cartridge box, which you has on your right hip, with your thumb and forefinger. You put the end of the cartridge in your mouth and tear off the top. You then lift the frizzen with your other fingers and put a small amount of the powder into the pan, and then close it."

"What about the ball?" persisted Huhne.

"The ball is in the cartridge with the rest of the powder. You empty it into the barrel and push it in with your ramrod. Not hard, just gentle like."

While describing this, the Corporal used the weapon to demonstrate the actions.

"Then if you were given the order, you cock the firelock, that is, the hammer is lifted out of the half-cock position, and you are ready to fire at the Frenchies. Now get your own firelocks and go through the procedure. When you have finished your training you should be able to load and fire at least three shots in a minute."

The men collected their weapons and practised the loading routine they had been shown. What none of them yet knew was the vast extent of their waking hours for the next few months would be spent doing exactly the same thing – learning the commands and actions for loading and firing the flintlocks and later, in using their bayonets. After the midday meal in light drizzle, they were called to order on the parade ground.

"Form up in line, two ranks deep," shouted Granville.

The Corporals busied round arranging the recruits, each of the men with a flintlock in hand. When the two ranks had been formed, the Serjeant stepped out in front of them. He roughly grabbed the flintlock from a soldier in the front row and shouted, "Be at ease. I want you motley crew to put your firelock butts on the ground on your right side, holding the barrel with your left hand. Goddard, do you know which is your right side?"

"Yes, Serjeant."

"Then what are you waiting for!"

There was some shuffling around as the recruits all made sure not to be the focus of the Serjeant's ire.

"Corporal Bryant, would you be good enough to do the honours and be fugleman?"

"Yes, Serjeant."

Bryant was hardly taller than the five foot four and a half inch, army-minimum height. But what he lacked in height he made up for in breadth. He looked like a mastiff with square shoulders and a bulging chest. He marched from the left flank of the line of recruits, where he had been keeping a watchful eye on the men furthest from the Serjeant's attention, just as Reid had been doing on the right side, and took the firelock offered him by Granville.

The Serjeant ran his eyes along the line of men in front of him and when he was satisfied that he had their riveted attention he shouted slowly and deliberately, "This morning in your cosy huts, you learnt the parts of your firelock and how to achieve its intended purpose. And what would that be, Mew?"

Aaron put his hand to his ear as he stumbled to find an answer.

"To explode the powder in the barrel, Serjeant."

"Corporal Reid, you have my full sympathy. I hope you have the patience of Job to make a soldier of this man."

The Serjeant paused and then marched up to where Aaron was standing in the second row. He leant forward and shouted, "The purpose of your firelock is to propel a bleeding bullet at the enemy and to do so without hurting the man firing it. Got that, Mew? Got that the rest of you?"

The Serjeant glowered round at the men and then walked back to where Corporal Bryant was standing.

"What you are going to see now is what you men are going to be able to do before you leave here, even with your eyes closed. Listen to the orders I give and watch what the Corporal does. In battle, the Lieutenant will say the orders to a Serjeant, and the Serjeant will call out each order in turn to the men. Ready, Corporal?"

"Yes, Serjeant."

"Shoulder firelock."

The Corporal took the butt in his left hand with the arm extended and the firelock stock leaning on his left shoulder.

"Recover."

He lifted the weapon from his shoulder so that the firing mechanism was in front of his face.

"To the position of prime."

The gun was now horizontally across his body at waist height.

"Half-cock firelock."

Bryant pulled back the cocking arm one click.

"Handle cartridge."

The Corporal put his right hand round to his cartridge box and slapped it loudly.

The Serjeant turned to the recruits and said, "Why do you think he gave the cartridge box a slap?"

There was silence. The Serjeant scanned the ranks, waited for a few moments and then turned to Bryant.

"Tell them, Corporal."

Bryant had a very deep voice which did not lack volume.

"Well, it is a fact that sometimes the cartridges can stick in the box – the slap loosens them up."

"You got that, men? If you see the French dragoons bearing down on you, you don't want to have your cartridges all jammed up in the box." He paused for effect and then said, "Carry on, Corporal."

He pulled out a cartridge and bit off the end, which he spat out and held level with his chin.

"Prime."

He poured some powder into the pan and waited.

"Shut pan, cast."

The frizzen was closed and the firelock rested vertically on his left side.

"Load."

He poured the remainder of the powder into the barrel, dropped in the cartridge as wadding and slapped the ramrod which was attached to the firelock.

"Withdraw ramrod, enter."

Bryant detached the ramrod and held it just inside the barrel.

"Ram home cartridge."

When he had done this he held the ramrod ready to return it.

"Return and recover."

After he had replaced the rod the Corporal lifted the firelock up in front of his face. At the order "Cock firelock" he pulled the hammer back from the safety position.

"Make ready."

The stout figure shifted his right foot back about the length of his foot and lifted the barrel to his right shoulder. When the Serjeant bellowed, "Present!" the Corporal lifted the butt to his shoulder, aiming at the leaden sky over the recruits' heads.

"Fire."

There was an immediate response from the weapon. It belched smoke and flame, a bullet passed harmlessly over the ranks of soldiers and some black flakes of the cartridge case fluttered down on those in the front row. The effect of the blast was electrifying; some men ducked, others fell to their haunches, a few were transfixed.

The Serjeant called them to order.

"Stand firm in your places. That was just one bang. In battle the whole of the front rank would fire at once, and your enemy will do the same and you will not flinch. You men will not get to fire a bullet until your first action in battle, but as part of your training you are permitted to fire two blanks each year. Thank you, Corporal."

The firelock was handed back to the recruit.

"As I said, you will not be firing your firelocks live until you are in battle. In the meantime, you saw the procedure what has to be second nature to you. What the Corporal has just shown you, you will have to do at least three times to the minute before I decide that you can walk out of 'ere. You will know it so well that you can do it in the dark. You will dream about it, you will have nightmares about it. It will be as natural to you as having a piss."

He paused; his glowering eyes ran right along the rows of recruits. When he was satisfied that he had made an impression, he boomed, "So, we begin with the shoulder position. Shoulder firelocks!"

And so began weapons drill training for the recruits. It continued day after day, week after week as the days got shorter and colder, interspersed only by fitness and tactical formation training, meals and sleep, until the officers were satisfied with their performance. It was to be February before Aaron and Huhne were deemed to be capable soldiers and allowed to 'pass the guard'. Even so, they were among the first of the recruits to be given this privilege.

Chapter 12

The old oak door to Mrs Delany's lodging house, which had not received the attention of a paintbrush for many summers, creaked open. A well-dressed man stepped out into the biting wind of a Galway February Sunday afternoon. As ever the wind was in the west and so he turned east, after first forcing his black round hat with a semicircular crown onto his head. After turning he then fastened his cape, which was of the same colour as his hat.

Josiah Smee belied the expression by which his kind was known in the army: 'a boiled lobster'. Such sea creatures when alive were black, but when cooked in boiling water became red. And thus it was that when a churchman, who always in his calling wore black, was disgraced by defrocking and took the not unusual route to obscurity by accepting the King's shilling, his uniform changed from black to red. While Josiah Smee did in theory fit this epithet, in practice he seldom wore a redcoat. In the army's desperate quest to find recruits, he had been welcomed to the service and the fact that he had weak lungs was carefully concealed by him until the hard physical nature of the training made it impossible to do so any longer.

When the commander of the 62nd Regiment, Lieutenant-Colonel John Anstruther, was informed that Private Smee was to be discharged because of poor health, he halted the process and appointed Smee to be his personal servant. The arrangement was one of great convenience to all, for the army frowned strongly on wasting an able-bodied soldier as an officer's servant, and Private Smee was not only literate, but could also be expected to provide some level of decorum and good manners in the circles in which the commander moved. The fact that the position also gave the incumbent an extra shilling a week in army pay eased Private Smee's misgivings about serving in a menial role. An officer's servant was only required to wear uniform on certain special occasions and more unusually, when required to by his master. Thus it was that Smee's attire seldom matched the colour of a cooked lobster.

As he turned back to face the wind and walk down the muddy garden path to the street, he glanced anxiously about him, for while he was perfectly free to come and go in the town in the few hours he was given off from his duties he did not wish his movements to be traced to this address. Not that there was anything particularly insalubrious about the premises apart from the usual dilapidation and squalor of army billets, but Private Smee enjoyed a good chat with others of his intellectual level and from time to time and when he could he often sought the company of Rev and Jamie. Gobbets of table chat from the commander's dining room were inevitably dropped into conversation with his off-duty companions and his tongue was not always as guarded as his master might have wished. Today he had a slightly guilty conscience that he might have said more than he should. Thus, when he reached the junction of the path and the street he was concerned when he was called by a young Private who was standing in the street with a companion. The soldiers were resplendent in their scarlet coats with the yellowish buff facings of the 62nd Regiment: waistcoats, white breeches and gaiters, which had clearly been very recently cleaned for a visit to the town.

"Excuse me, sir," called the soldier. "Be this the lodgings of Private Jamie Cutler?"

Pulling his hat down ostensibly to avoid it being removed by the wind, but in reality to hide his face, the ex-parson said, "It is. If you pull the bell rope by the door, Mrs Delany will let you in and direct you."

"Thank you, sir," said Aaron as he and Huhne passed the man and headed for the door.

They found Jamie and Rev together with a third soldier sitting around a table in the small room, which obviously served as bedroom and living room for the three of them. Rev had a book open on the table, though a much larger one than he had had with him on their long journey. The other two men were playing cards. The air was thick with the smoke of Jamie's and the other privates' pipes and would have been insufferable but for the fact that the window was slightly ajar, allowing the west wind to provide some ventilation.

"Mewie! Huhnie! What an unexpected pleasure. And my word, you both do look unspeakably fine in your uniforms. Come, come join us, we have news. News which should thrill such ardent looking soldiers as you two. 'Be dressed ready for service and keep your lamps burning, like men waiting for their master to return from the wedding banquet', as the good gospel of Luke tells us."

Jamie interrupted, "What Rev is trying to say is that the regiment is commanded to go to Canada. Sit down, and hear."

"Huzzah! But where is Canada, Rev? How do you know?"

There was only one spare chair – Huhne, who had asked the question, grabbed it. Aaron sat balanced on the window sill.

Excitedly, Aaron asked, "When, what's happened there?"

"Wait, wait, the two of you. First of all, this is very confidential." Jamie looked across at Rev, and then continued, "Can we rely on you two not to tell a soul?"

"Yes, yes, of course. But how do you know?" asked Aaron.

"Let's just say we have a friend who knows about these things."

Rev turned the book on the table around so that the two visitors could see it.

"This, gentlemen, is a map of the Atlantic Ocean. No, but how remiss of me, I have not introduced you to our companion. Privates Huhne and Mew, this is Private Seamus Beardon, recently Corporal Seamus Beardon but, regrettably, owing to bacchanalian excesses, now in reduced circumstances. To all, now known as Beardie."

The three men shook hands and Rev, pointing at the map on the open page, continued, "This is where we are today, on the west coast of Hibernian, as you see, the extremity of Europe. And that, gentlemen, is Canada."

"And that is all sea?" asked Aaron.

"Yes, indeed. And we, lock, stock and barrel will have to be transported across it."

"How far is it, Rev?"

"Well, as we discovered on our way to our late sojourn in the West Indies, the distance is of little consequence. What is of more importance is how long it will take, despite inclement weather, to get there. The estimation is at least a month."

"A month on a ship?"

"At least, Mewie, probably a lot longer."

"But why are we going?"

"Jamie, perhaps you could enlighten our two guests about the predicament General Sir Guy Carleton finds himself in."

"Who's he?"

"He, Mewie, is the Governor of His Majesty's colony of Canada and commander of the army there, such as is left of it."

"Yes, as Rev says, Carleton is in trouble. We heard, um, that is our friend heard, that dispatches have been received from the city of Quebec that a rebel American army under a General Montgomery, who by the way was once a British officer, and General Benedict Arnold, have taken possession of the whole of the colony and is currently besieging Quebec, where Carleton is. Three quarters of the twelve thousand redcoats in Ireland are to be transported across the Atlantic – some to New York, but most, including us, to relieve the city of Quebec in Canada, and give chase to the rebels."

"But when?"

"As soon as we can be equipped and ships found to transport us. Our friend told us that the British government is seeking to charter hundreds of vessels."

"But when will that be?"

"Who knows, at least two months I should think. Apparently, the regiment has got a warrant from Dublin castle to receive a complete new Stand of Arms. It will take a while to get all that transported here in winter, and then we will have to get down to Cork where we are to embark."

"So we get new firelocks?"

"Everything. Bayonets, scabbards, cartridge boxes, belts, the lot."

There was silence in the room as the five of them considered the enormity of the news. Aaron was first to interrupt the contemplation of the others.

"But why are the Americans rebelling?"

Rev looked up, glanced at his room-mates and then said, "As soldiers we don't ask questions like that, Mewie, we do as ordered. But if truth were told, the whole sorry situation has as its genesis the fact that our government tried to tax the Americans more than they would tolerate to pay for the cost of the war in America against the French and their allies, the savages. A few misguided American individuals then protested that they should not be taxed by a country where they have no parliamentary representation, and acts of civil disobedience ensued."

Seamus slapped his hand on the table and spoke with a raised voice, "Oh come on, Rev, that's not the whole truth. The rebels are greedy for land. They want to take the territory west of the Proclamation Line, the lands the British have allocated for the savages. And anyway, it's well known that very few Americans pay their taxes, which by the by are lower than the British pay."

"As you see, dear friends, the situation is very complicated..."

Jamie interrupted Rev and said, "His Majesty was much infuriated by his errant subjects across the water and persuaded Parliament to issue decrees to punish them by limiting trade and generally making life more tedious for them. Now we are to enforce these decrees."

"Alright, Jamie, that's enough. As I said, soldiers shouldn't ask such questions. We serve our Sovereign as required."

"And that's the truth of it. As required," added Seamus with a broad Irish accent. "Will the two of ye stay to have tea meal with us?"

"Thanks, but we would like to look around the town before it gets dark. This is the first time we have been given permission to pass the guard."

Rev closed the book and said, "Well, we will see more of you now because you will be allotted to a company and be on general duties like the rest of us. Shouldn't wonder if they billet you out in the town. But perhaps not if we are leaving soon."

As the pair stood up, Jamie exclaimed, "I almost forgot to tell you. Captain Hawker is forming a Light Company – you might like to volunteer for it."

The two men had already heard about the duties of 'light bobs', as they were called.

"It's true enough, a good chance it is for young fellas the likes of ye. They get the best weapons, and I daresay the best victuals," added Seamus.

"An announcement will probably be made soon. But say nothing about it to your friends."

"Yes, Jamie is right. What you have heard here must stay between us. Remember what the St James Gospel says, 'The tongue is an unruly member'. By the way, Mewie, how are things in your mess now that Kemp has been declared unfit for the army?"

"Well, we all get on alright, even the ones who were closest to Kemp."

"Ah there, you see, as Matthew's gospel tells us, 'I will strike the shepherd and the flock of sheep will be scattered'. Kemp's acolytes were lost without him. By the by, Mewie, you can now start your reading studies again. Come on Sunday afternoons at this time."

"I should like that, Rev. I dearly want to be able to write a letter to my mother and father."

"Good, that is decided then. Farewell to you both."

As they were about to go through the door, Jamie called, "Be careful in the town, there are many girls about who will offer you everything for a day's pay, but the 'everything' will likely include the pox."

"Is that experience speaking, Jamie?" asked Huhne.

"Get on, be off with the two of you."

Two days later the announcement was made that the regiment was to be posted to Quebec. Shortly after, all the new men were paraded and Serjeant Ryan addressed them. It was immediately clear that there was no question of volunteering to join the Light Company; the men had been selected.

"For those of ye who can read the written word, there is a list of the men volunteered to join Captain Hawker's Light Company, on the wall by the guard room. For them as can't read, ask the Serjeant of the guard to read it for ye. The company is to assemble tomorrow morn here at seven-thirty with full kit and a day's ration in their haversacks. Dismiss."

There was a rush of feet towards the guard room and soon a crowd had surrounded the notice. The gathering quickly gained the disapproval of the Serjeant of the guard who commanded them to move back while he read the notice aloud for them.

"Captain Hawker's Company. Commissioned officers – Lieutenant Spicer and one other Lieutenant to be appointed. Ensign Munbury. Non-commissioned officers – Serjeant Granville and two others to be appointed. Corporals – White, Cole and Cutler."

Aaron's alarm when he heard Granville's name was tempered when he thought he recognised Jamie's surname. He shouted, "Please, Serjeant, be that Jamie Cutler?"

"Yes, Corporal James Cutler. To continue, Bugler Boy Taylor."

The Serjeant then read out a list of forty-four names, most of whom were not new recruits, but included Mew, Graham, Bell and Huhne.

When he had finished reading out the names, most of the men dispersed; those who remained talked excitedly to each other, for they were some of those on the list.

The following morning at seven-thirty, by the pale light of the February morning, the soldiers were lined up, standing at ease, in four ranks of eleven men. The Corporals fussed round the gathering making sure that all looked as it should, before the Serjeants made an inspection prior to roll call. Aaron and Huhne exchanged grins with Jamie as he passed by them in his new role as a non-commissioned officer, wearing the white cord on his right shoulder which denoted his rank. The Corporals exchanged salutes with Granville who then checked the names of those present. This completed, he addressed the men.

"As you all know, we will be going to Canada. The commander of the force, Lieutenant-General Burgoyne, has issued an order that every regiment must have at least one Light Company. You men have all been trained to fight in tight formation. In line formation the Light Company forms up on the left flank, the grenadiers on the right and generally eight other companies in the middle."

He paused, scouring the faces of the men to judge whether his words were being listened to and noted. He knew that all ears would be sharpened for fear of verbal retribution if he asked a question.

"Which side will you be on, Huhne?"

"Um…the left, Serjeant."

"Good, I am honoured that someone is listening. In a few minutes Captain Hawker will be here to tell you about the role of the Light Company. Meanwhile, a few points to remember. First off, you may think that you are lucky bastards to be training while the others are doing the 'eavy work, sorting, packing and carrying, ready for departure to Cork. Let me assure you, you 'aven't got the easy option. Second, you got a lot to learn in a short time including accuracy with the flintlock. Only you, as Light Company men, will be firing real bullets in practice – remember all the safety procedures. Thirdly, in a Light Company, all the orders are relayed by bugle, not by drum, a bugle being much easier to hear in the noise of battle and at a distance. There are many bugle commands which you will have to learn by heart. Fourthly…"

Granville noticed the Captain walking towards him with Lieutenant Spicer. He straightened his back and dropped his arms to his side, saluted and then turned to the men.

"Light Company, be alert!"

The men did as ordered.

"Tell the men to be easy, Serjeant. Do carry on with what you were saying."

"Thank you, sir. Light Company, be easy! Fourthly, the role of a Light Company soldier requires maximum ease of movement and to aid this, your uniform redcoats should be shortened to this length."

The Serjeant pointed to his hip.

"The regimental tailor will not be called upon to perform this alteration. You will do it yourselves."

Turning to the Captain he said, "Sir, forty-four men, three Corporals and myself present."

"Thank you, Serjeant." Clearing his throat, he raised his voice and addressed the ranks. "Men, you have been honoured to perform a vital role for the regiment. The nature of the terrain in America is such that much of the fighting we can anticipate will not be in set battles of the type we see in Europe, but it will involve loose formation action where fighters need to use initiative, self-discipline and such advantages as the rough wilderness provides in terms of cover. An important part of your job will be skirmishing, harassing the enemy's rearguard when we have them on the run, and should it ever happen that they turn to face us, you will be probing their defences.

"In your training here you have learnt to fire at an enemy, in formation. The task of light infantry is different. It is, when commanded to do so, to fire at will at targets of opportunity. You men have been selected to join this company because of your proven abilities, or the promise you have shown in training.

"We do not yet know when we will be leaving for Canada, but you will be using the time between then and now for intensive training for the duties I have outlined."

He turned to the Serjeant and said, "Carry on, Serjeant."

Granville saluted, as did the Captain, who then strode off with the Lieutenant. The Serjeant waited until the Captain was out of earshot and then turned to the ranks.

"Today we are going for a trip in the country, but before we start the march, while still assembled here I want to group you in fours. Look to it – get a bloody move on, Mew. In each group choose a partner. Your partner is the man on whom your bleeding lives will depend. In action one of you will always have a loaded firelock. You listening, Huhne? That is, that when in action, one of you does not fire before you are certain that your partner has reloaded."

He paused as he fiercely scanned the men in front of him.

"Mew, Huhne, come over here. Corporal Cutler, please join me."

The men took position as ordered.

"These two bold Englishmen, Huhne and Mew, are chasing two Frenchies – the Corporal and me."

The two officers pretended to be fleeing in front of the soldiers. Granville turned and said, "They both fire their firelocks and miss us. What's going to happen then, Mew?"

"Fix bayonets, Serjeant?"

Granville marched up to Aaron and with his face only a few inches in front of the soldier's he bellowed, "Fix bloody bayonets! No, you fool, we will have turned round and shot you both because we know you can't defend yourselves."

He paused to look at the effect of his words on the men.

"Now if only one of you fires, and then the other soldier waits for you to reload before he fires, them Frenchies ain't going to be strolling, they are going to be running because they know that you are dangerous! Though it is beyond imagination that you two could ever look dangerous. Get back into line."

After giving a few more instructions the men were told to collect their flintlocks in readiness to leave. When instructed, they shouldered their knapsacks and marched past the guard room, through the town and out into the bleak winter countryside for their initial training.

Despite the intensive training, Aaron was able to keep his appointments with Rev on Sunday afternoons. But they were in a hurry – the young light infantryman wanted to write to his parents before facing the dangers of the ocean and the uncertain future of soldiering in a hostile country. After several attempts with pencil and paper, Rev guided him in the use of the quill and ink to copy his pencilled draft. It was a draft which owed more to Rev's prose than Aaron's clumsy attempts to express himself, but the tutor hoped that the young man's style would improve with age and experience. After several attempts, the copied version of the letter with the fewest number of alterations and crossings out was accepted by the patient benefactor, in the knowledge that further improvement would take more hours of work than the pair had at their disposal.

Dear Father and Mother,
My fervent hope is that this, my first letter, finds you both in good health. I am indeed fortunate that the Good Lord has blessed me in this respect.

My heart is heavy with the shame of not accomplishing the task allotted me by Mr Newman. I did indeed deliver the mare as instructed, but later I was robbed by perfidious ne'er-do-wells in Salisbury. They stole the Squire's money and left me penniless. In my thus inflicted pitiful situation there was but one solution, to take the King's shilling. To this end I now find myself in Ireland serving his Gracious Majesty as a soldier in the 62nd Regiment of Foot.

In the last months I have seen many wondrous things, castles, ships and seas. I have also been fortunate to find friends who are honourable people. Soon we are to depart for Canada where I hope to acquit myself well as a soldier, so that you may be proud of me.

Father and Mother I crave your forgiveness and I pray that one day I may return in a sufficient state of affluence to repay Mr Newman.

Your humble son,
Galway, Ireland, 31st March, 1776

Chapter 13

On Wednesday 3rd April, 1776, Lieutenant-Colonel John Anstruther was sitting on his chestnut mare on a hillock, surveying the scene on the busy quayside below him at Monkstown, near Cork. Around him were several other officers on horseback and some on foot. All shared the same anxiety that the three ships on the quay should be loaded quickly while the weather remained clement, so that the 62nd Regiment of Foot could start its journey to Canada in fair conditions. The forest of masts offshore belonged to the fifty-one troop transport ships already loaded. Thousands of soldiers from various regiments had already embarked on the vessels which were waiting at anchor in the bay. In the distance, the two naval vessels, *Caresford and Pearl*, which would escort the convoy to Canada, were impatiently prowling back and forth beyond them outside of Haulbowline Island. But there was another important matter of concern to the officers on the hill, and that was that the men should be loaded on the ships as fast as possible so that none of them had an opportunity to desert; this in view of the fact that the regiment was still not up to full strength.

The night before, all men had been confined to camp to minimise the risk of desertions. One of the likely reasons for men to desert was that they had to leave their wives behind. Officers were permitted to take their wives and families when posted abroad, but not so the men. Normally, the procedure was that six wives per company were allowed to travel with their soldier husbands. However, General Burgoyne had decreed that for this expeditionary force, the wives of only three men in each company would be permitted to travel on the ships. The draw of lots to decide which three soldiers in each company of just over forty men could take their wives was not made until six hours before boarding to limit the possibility of men having a chance to desert.

And not only were some of the men unenthusiastic for various reasons about a long-distance posting over the dangerous Atlantic, two officers had today requested to remain in Ireland on half- pay. A Captain and an ensign had bent the commander's ear in the morning about how delicate their wives were, and how they would not survive the rigours of crossing the ocean or manage to live alone at home. But their superior officer was well aware of the real reason for their requests. He knew all too well of the opposition in Britain against the war in America. Several high-ranking officers had refused to serve there and many politicians railed against taking up arms against people in America, whom they regarded as fellow citizens.

The senior officer turned to his adjutant. "What can you tell me about our ships, Percival?"

"Well, sir, the *Monmouth*, the largest of the three ships, the three-masted one nearest us, is 560 tons. She was built in 1720 and sailed for the East India Company until 1733. Since then she has been used on charter as a troop transport to the West Indies."

"Struth, Percival, you mean she is almost fifty years old?"

"I am assured, sir, that she is most seaworthy. Based on the Navy Board regulation of allocating a maximum of 100 men per 200 tons of ship, we should be able to load 280 officers and men on her, just more than half the regiment. The women are not counted in the Navy Board regulation, neither the children. As normal, they will live on the lower decks."

"And the second ship?"

"The *British Queen*. This is the ship you will be on, sir. 350 tons, so we will have 175 men on her. The master is Captain James Hodge."

"How old is she?"

"Built, um, let me see, 1715, sir."

"I suppose with the Navy Board having to find ships for us and the Germans, and chartering at just thirteen shillings a ton per month, choice is limited."

The sixteen thousand German soldiers who had been employed by the British government to strengthen the army in America and Canada were to be transported from English ports, after arriving from Germany. Three thousand of these, mainly from Brunswick, under the command of General Riedesel were expected to leave

Portsmouth on 4th April, for Quebec. The remainder would be travelling to New York to reinforce the army there.

"Yes, sir. The third ship is *Princess Anne*, 250 tons. Our supplies and cannon have all been loaded on her and she is ready to sail. Twenty men and a Serjeant are sailing on her as a guard detail."

"Very necessary, we can't afford to lose our supplies to Conyngham and his ilk."

The Lieutenant-Colonel was referring to the American Privateer Captain Gustavus Conyngham, who in his ship, *Charming Peggy*, was the scourge of European waters, having captured sixty British merchant vessels in the last two years. As the fleet from Ireland approached the American coast the risk of the lightly armed merchant transport ships being attacked by American privateers was severe. The only defence each transport had was one or two cannons, and the firepower available from the men's firelocks.

"I had hoped that we could have seen the General's flotilla pass. He was due to leave at the end of March. It would have been fortunate indeed if we could have joined our convoys. According to dispatches, he is travelling on the thirty-two gun naval frigate *Blonde*, with the famous Captain Philemon Pownoll in command."

Pownoll was well known as the dashing commander who, with a very much smaller vessel, took one of the richest prizes in history, the Spanish treasure ship *Hermione* in 1762. However, unbeknown to the commander of the 62nd, Lieutenant-General Burgoyne was delayed and did not leave Spithead with his convoy of thirty ships until 5th April.

"Come, gentlemen, we must board our ship and bid farewell to our wives and horses."

Lieutenant-Colonel John Anstruther turned his mare's head and kicked her into a trot down the gentle slope.

The scene on the quayside was a strange contrast between the orderliness of the queue of soldiers patiently waiting their turn to board the ships, and the chaos of the women, many with children, busying about carrying all manner of chattels, trying to board the same ships as their menfolk. Serjeant Granville was supervising a working party engaged in trying to keep order, checking which family members had the right to travel and helping the women to board. The latter included his own wife and fifteen-year-old daughter. Unlike the commissioned officers' wives who shared cabins with their husbands, all the non-commissioned officers' and soldiers' womenfolk and children were ushered down to the lower decks, separated from their menfolk. For on board ship, unlike on land when they often shared a tent with the soldiers, the camp followers were berthed separately. One reason given for this was that they would be safer on the lower decks, but the fact was that keeping discipline amongst the men was difficult enough in the cramped quarters on a ship without the diversion of the women and children sharing the cabins.

Those women being left behind on the quay, through choice or because of the lottery result, were waving handkerchiefs and scarves and calling out last messages to their departing husbands and sweethearts.

Aaron was oblivious to the noise around him as he stood in the line of men, gazing up in wonderment at the tall masts of the *Monmouth*. He was anxious about the long voyage ahead of him, but also thrilled at the prospect. As he stood with his palm pressed against his ear, he watched the seamen working in the rigging, making preparations for departure. Then his attention was directed towards the hull of the ship alongside which they were standing.

"They ain't real," said a man two places ahead of him in the queue. He was pointing at the white squares which had been painted on the hull of the vessel.

"No, you are right, Ting. Many of the transports have painted gun ports to fool privateers into thinking that they are men-o'-war. Let's hope that they have that effect," commented Corporal Jamie Cutler, who was standing nearby to Bell.

Real or not, it was the sheer size of the ship which gave Aaron and his comrades a degree of confidence about the safety of the journey ahead of them. Surely such a vessel must guarantee a secure passage. Eventually, the Light Company men reached the gangplank and set foot on the vessel which would be their home for at least four weeks. The first thing Aaron noticed as he stepped aboard was the strong smell of oak and tar, but his attention was quickly caught by the sailors who were standing round looking disdainfully at the new arrivals and waiting impatiently for their human cargo to be loaded. They wore loose canvas breeches, which as he was to learn, they called 'trowsers', white checked linen shirts, many with a brightly coloured knotted kerchief around their necks, and blue jackets. The latter led to them being referred to by the soldiers as 'blue bottles'. But the insults were not delivered only in one direction; the sailors referred to their passengers as 'live lumber' and 'lobsters'.

The soldiers were led below by one of the Serjeants marshalling the passengers. Even the shortest of the soldiers had to bend down to avoid hitting their heads on the woodwork as they made their way along a lower deck in single file, past rough wooden cabins, which judging from the raucous noise and laughter emanating from them, were already occupied.

"You boys are the lucky ones, you get to have a cabin. Number forty-two." The Serjeant had stopped by an open door.

He continued, "The last ones in the queue will be sleeping in hammocks on the between decks."

He pointed at the door opening. "Regulation, six foot by six foot. Four beds, each with a bolster, a blanket and a coverlet. The hatch in the ceiling has a grating to keep the air sweet, but will be covered in the event of bad weather."

The men crowded round the door opening to look in.

"There are two seats of easement over there and two piss dales. When the ship is leaning over use the ones on the lee side, we don't want shit all over the hull. There's a tow rag on a line by each seat of easement. Firelocks go in the rack over there." He pointed to the side of the ship.

"In the eventuality that you feel well enough to eat, you get called to collect your food. You return to your cabin to eat it. Therefore, when ordered to do so by myself or another Serjeant, one of your number should go up to the cook house on deck and collect the food cans for your cabin. See up when moving around the ship in heavy weather. If you drop the food you don't get more. Every day you have bread, butter, cheese and small beer. Rum as apportioned by the Lieutenant. Three days out of seven you have salt beef or salt pork as long as it lasts. Now move on in you four."

Aaron, Huhne, Bell and Graham stacked their firelocks on the rack and then lowered their heads even further to get through the doorway and squeeze into the cabin with their kit.

Two hours after boarding the ship, as they lay on their straw palliasses, the four men were aware of feeling some motion, but from their cabin and even in the narrow corridor between it and the hull, there was no chance of them observing what was happening. Had they been on deck they would have seen the ship's hawsers being pulled on board, this after a line had been passed to the large rowing boat in which eight oarsmen strained to turn the *Monmouth's* head so that such sails as had been set could catch the wind and carry the ship out into the deep harbour.

The Captains of the transport ships had been called to a meeting with the commander of the naval vessels two days ago and each of them had been given strict instructions about their position in the convoy. The importance of maintaining station in relation to the other vessels was stressed to the extent that they were told that if any ship edged in front of the convoy, one of the naval ships would fire a live round close across its bows. Each Captain was given a sealed envelope which was only to be opened if, as a result of the weather, they got separated from the convoy for more than twenty-four hours. The contents of the envelope gave the name and position of the secret island rendezvous where lost ships should await orders.

As soon as the *Princess Anne* had likewise departed the quay, all of the ships in the convoy started to weigh anchor in the prescribed order to form up in their respective positions. By late afternoon when this had been done, the wind being fair, the fleet departed and negotiated its way past Haulbowline and Spike Islands before passing Crosshaven and turning west into the Atlantic.

There were anxious whoops and shouts from the cabins as the ship settled on a starboard tack in the fresh northerly breeze. While the *Monmouth* was not leaning heavily, it was enough for Aaron and his companions berthed on the port side of the ship to feel themselves slightly pushed feet first towards the door, as several loose items of their equipment tumbled in the same direction. This, and the reverse on the port tack, was something that they had several weeks to get used to. But what some unfortunates never got used to was the effect of the ship's motion on their stomachs. Most vomited during the early stages of the journey and then adapted to the rolling and pitching, but a few never did. While seasickness was never terminal, a man who became dehydrated or near starved because of it was often too weak to survive other dangers.

The messmates soon got used to the signal from the *Caresford*, the firing of two cannons, which gave the fleet the instruction to tack or gybe. This gave them fair warning, in particular in strong winds, that they should brace themselves differently. At night, the four men were wedged into each other so tightly that there was little danger of them being thrown about.

By dint of the skylight in cabin forty-two, the occupants were able to tell day from night. That was apart from the times when it rained. Then an unseen hand on deck placed covers on the skylights. They were fortunate, for not all of the cabins had skylights and some soldiers would hardly see daylight apart from when called on deck, collecting food or using the seats of easement. The chance of regular daylight and the many passive hours encouraged Aaron in his ambition to improve his reading and writing. To this end he had started to keep a journal of his experiences to send to his parents, but his enthusiasm for it varied as often there was nothing of note to add to his description of the departure from Ireland.

Life in the ship settled into a tedious pattern of sleeping, eating, drilling and inspections. The only break in the routine was when each company in turn, according to a timetable, was on watch duty. At these times the men waited in their cabins ready to be called should the need arise to defend the ship. This happened after two weeks at sea. At noon on 19th April, the bugler called the watchmen to stations on deck. There was a rush to put on boots and grab firelocks. When Aaron emerged from the hatch, blinking in the daylight, Serjeant Granville was already on deck. The *Monmouth* was sailing on a port tack to the south and windward of the *Princess Anne*. The Serjeant had his hand to his brow, shading his eyes and peering in a southerly direction. The soldiers arriving on deck automatically did the same. There was much excitement as they made out a large number of ships to windward. The soldiers had been at sea long enough to realise that the ponderous *Monmouth* would have little chance of escape from a man-o'-war to windward.

"Jesse, there's a whole fleet bearing down on us!" shouted the Serjeant. "Men, form up in two ranks and shoulder firelocks."

He paused while the men did their best to form up on the rolling deck. Then he very calmly shouted, "Recover." A pause, then, "To the position of prime," and so on through the whole sequence until the men were all shouldering loaded firelocks and waiting for them to be required as the sails on the port beam got larger. They noted that the *Caresford* had left her station at the head of the convoy and had gone about on to the starboard tack to place herself between the approaching fleet and her charges.

There was what seemed to be an interminable wait, during which time Captain Hawker and Lieutenant Spicer appeared on deck, quickly followed by the highest ranking army officer on the ship, Major Harnage. Then the men heard a call from the main top mast head, but they could not make out what was said. A seaman hurried down from the poop deck and said something to the senior officer; he leant forward and spoke to the Captain who then strode over to pass the information to Serjeant Granville. The latter, looking almost disappointed, shouted, "Be at ease."

Soon, the soldiers, still lined up smartly on deck, could make out the British flag on the leading ship, which they were to learn was the frigate *Blonde*. Captain Hawker came across and spoke once more to Serjeant Granville, at the behest of their senior officer.

"Now you have a chance to impress and show the style of the 62nd," shouted the Serjeant, "for on the *Blonde* is Lieutenant-General Burgoyne."

The fleet of thirty ships, led by the *Blonde* and several other naval vessels, was the convoy transporting mainly German officers and men from Portsmouth via Plymouth to Canada. The two fleets sailed together for two days, while the General issued a number of orders to the army officers in the convoy, the last of which was 'double rum ration today', an order which initiated what was to be a lasting and increasing popularity of the Lieutenant-General with his men. The two fleets then diverged and each headed their separate ways to the same destination, according to the sailing abilities of their ships and the inclinations of the naval commanders leading them.

From the first day on board ship it became apparent that the animosity between the crew of the ship and the soldiers would be a constant irritant. For the crew were merchant sailors, not subject to the extreme discipline of their naval counterparts. Sometimes their scorn manifested itself as name calling and insults, but from time to time there was pushing, tripping and shoving, and occasionally scuffles fuelled by rum broke out. The situation reached a crisis point when several of the sailors found excuses to go to the lower decks so that they could try their chances with the soldiers' women. On one occasion, several of the husbands attacked the seamen and a brawl ensued which had to be broken up by a party of grenadiers under the direction of a Lieutenant. But then this particular problem suddenly ceased to exist. A rumour started to circulate regarding the seamen's superstition about women on board a ship bringing bad luck, and how disaster would befall. And disaster had befallen, for the crew had recognised an illness among the women. The reason they now shunned the lower decks was 'ship fever'.

The women and children inhabited the stuffy, cramped part of the ship below sea level, which they shared with vermin. Sanitary conditions were primitive as there could be no seats of easement below the line of the surface of the sea. The inhabitants of these decks used wooden buckets which had to be taken on deck to be emptied over the side.

With these conditions and little chance of exercise or fresh air, it was no wonder that less than halfway into the voyage several women and children succumbed to illness for which the sailors used the general term 'the fever', though there were also cases of smallpox. And neither did the fever limit itself to the women, for in particular those men who had denied themselves sustenance because of seasickness became prey to the infection. Victims had similar symptoms; the first sign was a headache and loss of appetite followed by an increasing temperature with chills, exhaustion and nausea as a rash appeared all over the body. Some recovered after two weeks, but others got gangrene on their fingers, nose and ears, which was eventually followed by heart failure. The regimental surgeon tried various remedies to cure the victims, but almost invariably unsuccessfully. His wish to bring the sick camp followers up to recuperate on the same deck as was inhabited by the men was resisted by the officers who feared that some contagion might decimate the number of soldiers resident there. Only in the case of smallpox did they allow it, as all the men had received inoculation. But this was untrue of the sailors. As soon as patients started being placed in the between decks, their faces covered by the characteristic fluid-filled, pimple-like beads, the area was quickly eschewed by the crew, for they knew that at least a third of the smallpox victims would die, and those who did not would have deep scars.

There was, however, one positive outcome in response to the epidemics. The surgeon recommended to the Major that in the interest of communal health the men be allowed to take the air once a day, a company at a time spending half an hour leisure time on deck. Acceptance of this proposal permitted the men to have a relaxation period with a view of the sea and the sky. The women and children were afforded the same benefit when the men had gone below. Sometimes as the Light Company men were going back to their cabins after a session on deck they passed the women and children being shepherded up the steps to breathe the fresh air. It was on one such occasion that Jamie surreptitiously pointed out Serjeant Granville's wife and daughter to Aaron and his companions.

"How could a woman live with that ogre," commented Bell when they got back to their cabin.

"Ting, there is no accounting for love," said Graham.

"Skinny wasn't she?" added Bell.

"Well, none of the women are going to get fat on the half rations that they are allocated."

"You are right, Clipper. Jesse, if they are getting only half of the scraps we have to eat, God help them."

Bell was alluding to the fact that as the voyage had progressed, the quality and quantity of the food provided for them at each meal had declined, despite the fact that he had found ways to 'acquire' extra rations for him and his messmates. It was many days ago since they last had fresh bread; now hard biscuit had taken its place, and the smoked meat slices were getting thinner and thinner at the same time that the meat was becoming more and more discoloured by aging. Cheese and butter was now rancid and no one could remember when they last had fruit or vegetables. Porridge was fast becoming the staple food, with little to provide variation.

"But as you well know, Ting, because of your thieving, we are eating better than most."

"Yes, well a man has to look out for opportunities."

Graham was still thinking about Granville's wife and daughter and said, "You are right, Ting, that girl was thin, even thinner than her mother, poor girl. God, imagine having Granville as a father."

"But she was a fair maid, despite having him as her father," commented Aaron.

"You lustful bastard, Mewy. I tell you that any female looks fair to a man who has been at sea for three weeks," replied Graham.

Aaron closed his eyes, but try as he might he could no longer see an image of Peggy. After a while, he asked, "Does anyone know what her name is?"

There were some jibes at Aaron before Graham terminated the conversation by saying, "I don't know her first name, but her second is Granville, and that's warning enough to show no further interest."

Only twice before landfall were there any items of interest for those on deck to view, apart from the routine goings-on of the crew. On 4th May, to the north but close by, huge islands of ice were sighted. The amazing towering ice castles several times higher than the ships filled the men with awe and fear. Not without reason did the *Caresford* signal to the convoy to turn to a more southerly course to avoid collisions with them. At last Aaron had something to write about and indeed, two days later there was more when the fleet fell in with a French fishing boat. One of the crew explained to the men that French and Basque fishermen were regularly to be found fishing for cod on the Newfoundland banks, something they had been doing for hundreds of years. However, since England and France were currently at peace with each other, the craft was allowed to continue on its way unhindered. The occurrence did initiate another spectacle for the men to observe. Several of the officers tried running fishing lines behind the ship, and on one occasion the four messmates saw a large cod which was landed, thrashing on the deck.

The burials of the fever victims were at first formal affairs attended by all the officers, but as their frequency increased only the ship's Captain, friends and occasionally, when there were any, relatives attended. In the absence of a regimental padre on board, the tall lean figure of Rev was present to officiate at each committal. Whether the deceased was male or female, he used the same words on each occasion from St Peter's Gospel; he knew them by heart. This was just as well for the burials took place just after sunset and it would have been impossible to read in the failing light.

"All men are like grass and all their glory is like the flowers of the field. The grass withers and the flowers fall, but the word of the Lord stands for ever…"

The bodies, some of them very small, lay on a horizontal plank, one end resting on the gunnels, the other end held by two soldiers. Each corpse was covered by the union flag, which was retained by one of the soldiers holding the end of it as the plank was lifted by them and the body slid over the side and into the dark sea below. The soldiers then folded the flag and stowed the plank in readiness for the next requirement and the Captain of the ship retired to his cabin to note in the ship's log the date and the name of the deceased.

The soldiers were not allowed lanterns or candles in their cabins in the evenings and so the only chance to have light enough to play cards, dice or to read was to sit on the deck under one of the lanterns in the narrow passageway outside the cabins. It was here that Aaron often had his reading and writing lessons with Rev, who was billeted not far from number forty-two. This particular evening, the four messmates were playing dice when Rev appeared down the stairs from the upper deck.

"Want to join us, Rev?" asked Graham.

"Not really a pastime I embrace or endorse, Clipper. In any case, I find myself somewhat wearied both mentally and spiritually from my late occupation this evening."

"Anyone we know?" asked Huhne.

"Indirectly, yes. I fear to tell you that this evening I have had to commit Mrs Granville to the deep."

The players stopped their game and gazed up at the man looking down at them.

"What, the Serjeant's wife?" asked Aaron.

"The very same. And may I suggest that while none of us has a great affection for the officer, we should show Christian charity and sympathise with him in this, his dark hour."

After a few moments of silence while the men considered separately whether Granville as a widower would be more or less ruthless and detestable, Aaron asked, "What about his daughter?"

"Yes, indeed, Alice, the poor waif, she was quite inconsolable. How will she fare without a mother to guide her to womanhood?"

Alice, thought Aaron. So that is her name. But he said nothing to his companions.

"One of us ought to offer condolences on behalf of the company," suggested Clipper Graham.

"Quite so, but I fear that the one who does that publicly will be accused of being the Sergeant's lickspittle. It might be better coming from the good Corporal Cutler, who is but one rank removed from the grieving officer. I leave you to consider the possibility. Goodnight."

The four of them sat in silence pondering what had been said.

"By Jesse, it's cold, it gets colder every day. Struth, this is springtime but doesn't feel like it."

"It was even worse when it was foggy this morning. Chills a man right through. Yeah, I think I'll go to bed too," said Bell, agreeing with Graham.

With that the four men retired to their darkened room. The cover had been placed on the skylight auguring the fact that the crew expected the night to be cold. At midnight the sleeping men were jolted by the ship suddenly being put about.

"I was awake, I heard no cannon. What's about?" said Graham anxiously.

The four men struggled to sit up in their beds. They waited anxiously to see if there was any other indication that something untoward was happening. Unseen by them and indeed almost all those on the ship, the Captain, on his own initiative, had ordered the helmsman and the bosun to change course. He had been waiting for a signal from *Caresford* for he feared that the convoy, according to his reckoning, must be very near their anticipated landfall, Cape Race on Newfoundland. While his new course would hold them from rocks on the coast, the danger now was that the ship might collide with one of the other vessels in the dark. Most fortunately, the night was clear and moonlit, indeed light enough for the masthead watch to see surf breaking on the starboard beam. As soon as this information was relayed to the Captain, he ordered their two cannons to be fired twice to warn the other ships of the imminent danger.

If the men below decks were concerned before they heard the two cannons roar, they were terrified afterwards. Cursing men started to open the doors of their cabins and pour out into the passageway. The women below decks were in an even worse state of panic confined as they were below the waterline. Some of them started to appear in the passageway with their children. Aaron looked around in the weak lantern light, but did not see Alice. The Captain had anticipated that there would be confusion below decks and hastily sent the bosun below to try to allay the fears of the landsmen. He held up a lantern on the steps from the hatch and shouted, "Land ahoy! And all is well."

The Serjeants quickly restored order and commanded the men back to their cabins and hammocks. The soldiers did as ordered, not only relieved that all was well, but overjoyed that their sea journey would continue in safer waters and should soon be over.

As dawn broke, the Captain found his ship behind most of the convoy. To the north the crew could see the breakers on the Cape and very close to the rocks, three of the transports struggling to make to windward and avoid disaster. Later they learnt that these were the *Henry* and the *Sister,* each carrying men of the 53rd Regiment and the *Lithy* with a company from the 31st. Miraculously, the three ships clawed their way off the coast and rejoined the convoy which had slowed off the island of St Pierre, for these three and *Monmouth* to catch up. The fleet then continued past the island of St Paul and into the great Gulf of St Lawrence.

Chapter 14

From 8th May, the men who had previously had so little to observe when they had their daily period on deck now looked forward to seeing a new vista each day. Soon after they lost sight of St Paul's Island the Birds' Islands came into view. Even from the distance they were offshore, they could see the seemingly millions of sea birds darkening the skies around the islands as they hunted for fish to feed their new broods. A day later, with the wind in their favour they cruised along the coast of the near-barren Anticosti Island and entered the St Lawrence River. Paradoxically, the voyage was now entering a period of greater danger, for even though the river was very wide for some distance, the convoy was more restricted in terms of space to manoeuvre. In addition, the weather turned against them with gales and heavy swell. Two of the ships, the *Providence* and the *Woodcock,* collided and a grenadier from the 53rd Regiment was crushed to death before the ships could be disentangled. And then fog descended on the ships, which further increased the danger of collisions. The clanging of ships' bells penetrating the murk warned of their proximity to others.

By 24th May, with the fog behind them, the fleet at last got news of the situation in Quebec City. A small vessel sailing down river bore the tidings that although the city had been under siege all winter and was in a parlous state, it was still in British hands. Furthermore, that an assault on 31st December, led by the American General, the Irishman Richard Montgomery, had been repulsed and he had been killed. It was indeed due to the perverse fortunes of war that the defender of Quebec City, General Carlton, had been a friend and fellow soldier of Montgomery in the recent war against the French.

Two days later, the fleet anchored off the volcanic island of Coudres awaiting pilots to take them up the river to Quebec to lift the siege. But even before they got there, news was received that General Carlton had broken out of the city and chased the Americans up river to their stronghold at Sorel. The enemy were in a pitiful state. Their long winter siege outside the walls of Quebec and the unsuccessful storming of the city had taken an awful toll on them. They were starving and many had succumbed to a smallpox epidemic.

On 30th May, they passed the verdant island of Orleans, with its rows of grapevines just in leaf, and to the north, those on deck at the time were lucky enough to see the huge Montmorency waterfall, which was at its most impressive after the winter snow melt. Shortly after, the *Monmouth* dropped anchor two cable lengths off Quebec harbour and awaited the order for troops to disembark. The Light Company and the grenadiers were to be given priority to land, as it was anticipated that they would be needed first. The men stood on deck with their equipment, amid much excitement about going into action for the first time. Before them they could see a huge walled settlement on top of a high hill. At the bottom of the hill was a forest of masts belonging to ships from which cannon and supplies were being unloaded onto the dockside. The uninformed comments of the men waiting on the *Monmouth's* deck attracted the attention of an old sailor who was working with several other crew. They were preparing nets to put over the side of the ship for the soldiers to clamber down on to reach the smaller craft which would ferry them to the shore.

"Behind all the ships alongside the harbour is Place Royal, the oldest part of Quebec. There used to be about five hundred or so people living there. There were houses and businesses concerned with shipping and of course, the soldiers' and sailors' taverns, but now as you can see, all the buildings have been burnt down by the damned Americans. Most people, more than ten times as many, and mark my words most are Frenchies, more than ten times as many as I said, live up on the hill." The sailor was keen to assume an air of superiority using the knowledge gained on his previous Atlantic voyages.

"What's that over there?" asked Corporal Jamie Cutler.

"If I am not mistaken, those are the tents of the savages. Beware of them. They have learned the white man's vices, but they have retained their own ferocity."

There was a silence while the soldiers surveyed the walls, earthworks and the seemingly impregnable massive redoubt at the top of the cliffs. Cannon were peeping over the parapet pointing at the river and the approach that any seaborne invasion would have to take. Several of the older soldiers wondered how the British could have wrested such a well-defended place from the French.

"Where was General Wolfe's battle?" enquired Jamie.

"You see the western cliffs," he said pointing. "Twenty-four British volunteers climbed up that gulley and surprised the French outpost. They never expected anyone to be able to get up that way, you understand. Well, with the outpost overrun, all the other troops attacked by the same route."

The soldiers gazed at the rock formation, silently considering the audacity of the attack.

"Look lively now, Light Company. Form in two ranks and hear up," bellowed Serjeant Granville.

The men did as they were told and waited for orders.

"You men ain't goin' to be treadin' the streets of this fair city tonight, for General Carlton has ordered us all up river, towards the enemy stronghold. We stay here to await supplies and a new pilot and then continue our voyage to a village called Trois Rivieres, some thirty leagues up river. The 62nd are to join a brigade of infantry commanded by Brigadier-General Fraser. So, take all your equipment back to your cabins, for the voyage will probably take a week."

As soon as the Serjeant departed in the direction of the quarter deck, there were groans and some moaning from many of the men. Most started dispersing and going back to the cabins they thought they would never see again. But a few dallied on deck.

"Jesse, boys. It took us nigh on sixty days to get here from Ireland and now another seven just to go up for a cruise on the river." O'Driscoll aimed his complaint at the crew members still standing by the nets.

"Yeah, why should it take a ship a week to go thirty leagues?" added another discontent.

The same old sailor who had spoken to them earlier was clearly irritated at the slur on the performance of his ship. He growled at the soldiers, "Ye land lubbers understand nothin' of the sea. The

St Lawrence is a tidal river, a tidal river I say, ye understand what that means? Do you?" He shook a fist at the Irishman. "I'll tell you bloody lobsters what it means. The water rises and falls up to eighteen feet, twice a day. There are terrible currents here. And because of the snow melt, the strongest of them is going the opposite way to us. It is going to be damned hard work for we sailors to work the ship upstream."

The tense atmosphere was suddenly calmed when the bosun shouted to the sailors, "Standby lads, there's a transport alongside with fresh provisions for the galley."

The soldiers nearest the gunnels looked over the side and saw a barge alongside, its deck covered with boxes, on top of which were whole carcasses of meat. One turned round and shouted to the others, "Struth, it looks like we got beef again."

There was a cheer and the men turned to find their way back to the maritime lodgings.

It was, as the sailors had predicted, a difficult voyage, for with the restricted width of the river, there was no chance of tacking the fleet up the waterway and so they had to await a fair wind to combat the tidal currents. The going was so difficult that on 1st June the Captain of the leading ship, the *Woodcock,* decided to anchor and disembark the 53rd Regiment so that they could save time by marching to Trois Rivieres.

The *Monmouth* eventually anchored off the village on 7th June, the first of the transports to arrive, though several naval vessels were already there. One of them, *HBMS Martin,* had anchored further upstream, past the town. From the *Monmouth* the soldiers could see the neat village on the hill. There were about two hundred houses and the settlement was dominated by the high cross on top of the Ursuline Convent as well as the lower one on a nearby church. As many soldiers in pain and distress were later to find out, the nuns who were noted for their piety and care of the community had medical skills which they practised in the Convent hospital.

As soon as the ship had dropped anchor, barges were rowed out from the shore to quickly disembark the troops. Company by company the men on the *Monmouth* were brought on deck to await their turn to scramble down the rope nets to the ferries. They had been given orders to only take with them their essential marching equipment. Thus, as well as his firelock, each man had a knapsack on his back containing his necessaries, with his blanket rolled up on top. Attached to the knapsack was his ammunition pouch with at least thirty cartridges. When in action the pouch, with its heavy leather flap to keep the ammunition dry, would be transferred to his right hip. Now he usually carried his water bottle and a haversack with two days' supply of bread, beef, rum and biscuit on this hip. On his left hip was his bayonet in a frog, and in the case of the Serjeants, a short sword.

Thus encumbered, the men stood on deck waiting impatiently. As they did so, their attention was diverted to the noise of three Indians with two militia soldier passengers in their canoe. The Indians were making a whooping sound as they guided the canoe downstream with the current. They steered for the naval frigate moored near the shore and scrambled on board.

"A scouting party, I'll wager," said Jamie to those nearby. "Judging by their excitement, they have important news."

The men had observed Indians, who the Europeans referred to as 'savages', in canoes while on their way upstream and had admired the way the light canoes were deftly managed by the strange- looking native people, but so far the soldiers had had no close contact with them.

"Are they fighting on our side?" asked Aaron.

"I heard that many of them fought with the French in the last war, but Rev says that there are different families or tribes of savages with varying loyalties."

"Well, those three must be with us, they have gone with the militiamen onto the naval ship."

"Come on you men, look lively, over the side now," called Granville.

As they were ferried ashore Aaron and his companions noticed a flurry of activity around the ship which the Indians had gone aboard. Longboats were pulling away; one headed for the *Monmouth*, one for the shore and one in the direction of the *Martin*.

The barges landed the men on the steps to the short quay and they quickly climbed up them and ashore, though many had problems balancing since they had not walked on solid ground for eight weeks. From the quay the troops were directed to a piece of scrub land adjoining the forest, west of the town and a hundred paces from the river. Eventually, when all the 62nd were gathered on this strip of land, the men were split into working parties and as their tents, tools and equipment were ferried to the shore they started to clear bushes and trees to make space for their encampment. The 53rd Regiment had already made their camp a little further up the hill, inland.

The level of excitement was high, for the news borne by the two Quebec militiamen they had seen in the canoe had spread during the afternoon. These scouts had seen over forty vessels plying back and forth across the St Lawrence from the American stronghold at Sorel to Point du Lac on the northern shore, just nine miles west of Trois Rivieres. It was obvious that the retreating enemy had been reinforced by several thousand new troops and they were now only a day's march away. Sentries were posted and scouting parties were being sent forward to search out the enemy.

It was while the soldiers were working that they saw some of the Indians at close quarters. A Native American scouting party of about twenty men passed the labouring soldiers. The Indians were trotting, firelocks in hand, towards the forest and had to cross the area where the encampment was being set up.

"Stand back, Ting, our allies are coming," said Jamie.

"Jesse, look at them. Would you believe that any of God's children could paint their faces like that?" exclaimed O'Driscoll, as he leant on a spade.

Other soldiers put their tools aside to watch the strange procession as the Indians leapt over the trees felled by the soldiers, which were obstructing their path.

"And nimble they are. And to be sure, what is it they are wearing?"

"Seems to be leather, but some have cloth shirts," observed Huhne.

"And running in slippers they are too."

"Do you see what they do with their hair?"

"Well, strike me down, it's fine feathers they have as a hat."

"How very interesting. I feel that we should learn more about these noble savages and their unconventional garb," added Rev.

As soon as the runners had passed there was a shout from a familiar voice, "Get on with the work, the enemy is not going to wait for you to get comfortable."

The men continued slashing saplings, felling trees and levelling ground for several hours. They frequently cast anxious glances at the thick canopy of forest. The only movements were the scampering chipmunks, the occasional black squirrel leaping across branches, and the swaying of the tall trees. Aaron had long since noticed that many of the trees in the Canadian forest were of a type he had never seen before. He had no names for the red oak with its spiky leaves, the tall cottonwood with its yellow-grey bark, the white elm and the white pine with its bundles of evergreen needles, but he frequently stopped to gaze in wonderment at the sheer size of them.

Work continued, with only one interruption, until late afternoon, by which time the tents had been set up for the men and officers. When they had finished the work, the soldiers were shocked to see some men wearing green jackets coming down the hill from the direction of the town. Several of the labouring soldiers recovered their flintlocks from where they were stacked and awaited orders to load. However, their fears were allayed when they saw a red-coated officer with the four men. Captain Hawker went out to meet the group as they arrived.

"Be they enemy prisoners, Corporal?" Aaron asked Corporal Cole, who happened to be nearby.

"Don't look like prisoners, but they aren't uniforms we have seen before."

"Who are they then?"

Apart from the green jackets, the men had buff breeches, white stockings and black tricorn hats with a white trim. Each had side arms – a curved sword. They clearly had the respect of the Captain.

"Come on, come on, get back to yer work, we have a war to fight," called Serjeant Ryan.

As ever, rumours soon spread amongst the men about the identity of the visitors and later it was confirmed that they were American Loyalist officers; men who supported the British against the uprising in their native land. The newcomers had much to learn of the men and the uniforms of diverse people who fought for the King, and they had yet to see the range of German uniforms. But, it was how to identify the enemy which was now of greatest concern to the tired soldiers, for they had been warned that many of the Americans fought in either normal clothing or in any uniforms they were able to obtain, such was the haste with which many of the Americans had been recruited to their cause.

As dusk fell the men really were very weary, for they had had eight weeks of relative inactivity, losing the high degree of fitness gained from their intensive training in Ireland, and during this day they had been involved in heavy manual work. In the gathering darkness as they relaxed by their fires, they were cheered to see the arrival of several other troop transport ships. Since it was now late, these would sit at anchor and be unloaded the next day.

There were nearly a thousand men in the two tented encampments. But sleep did not come easy to them. Apart from the many new impressions gained from the sights and sounds of the day which partly occupied their minds, their primary concern was that the enemy was nearby and ere long they would be in action. Most experienced and new soldiers alike felt degrees of anxiety ranging from mild apprehension to terror. Many had thoughts of home, of loved ones; some wondered about their wives still on the ships, for the women and children had been kept on board until the situation in the area became stable. The soldiers tried to put out of their minds the dread idea that they may never again see the faces and places they knew so well. Few talked, many thought. Aaron was no exception; he lay awake thinking of home. What would they be doing? Had his father recovered from his injury? It was early June, he should be busy with the hoeing at this time of the year; too early yet for the haymaking. And what of his brother and sisters? They would have grown. Would Mother have told Matthew about his elder brother's disgrace? Aaron shuddered when he reminded himself of how he had let his parents down and tried to block out the memory of this by thinking of Peggy. Would she still be at the Saracen's Head when he got home?

"God's teeth, what the hell was that!" shouted Huhne as he quickly sat up, throwing his blanket off. The others followed suit and in the early dawn light which was just penetrating their tent canvas, they grabbed for their breeches, stockings and boots.

Then they heard the sound of several heavy cannon again.

"Jesse, we are under fire!" called Bell excitedly.

The rat-a-tat of a drummer calling men to action coincided with the next volley, by which time the men were outside of the tent doing up waistcoats and coats and strapping on equipment. Hundreds of others all over the encampment were doing the same thing.

Aaron could feel the buzz starting in his ear as he asked, "Where is the shot falling?" for there was no sign of any damage around the camp.

"We'll find out soon enough. Be at ease outside the tent and wait for orders," said Jamie.

A messenger came running from one of the tents nearest the river. From the position of these tents the occupants could see some way upstream.

He was shouting to groups of soldiers as he passed, "It's the *Martin,* she has opened fire onto the forest shore."

Messengers were running hither and thither, back and forth to the officers' tents. Very soon it was clear that General Fraser had ordered the troops on the ships to start disembarking with all haste, for the fear was that the force ashore was vastly outnumbered by the approaching Americans.

Just after five in the morning with the sun just appearing over the river, Serjeant Granville stood on the east side of the encampment and addressed the Light Company with the orders they had been waiting for.

"With loaded firelocks at the trail, follow me to join the 53rd Light Company and advance into the forest to seek out the enemy. The grenadiers will support the advance. The other eight companies of the regiment are to build breastworks on the camp perimeter around all the openings from the village to the forest and prepare a defence. Meanwhile, reinforcements will be transferred to the shore with all haste and be led along the road by General Fraser, to counter any American advance by that route. Carry on."

As directed the men loaded their firelocks and, carrying them horizontally in their right hands as ordered, they followed the Serjeant and the other officers and linked up with the other Light Company. Then in their groups of four, they plunged into the forest. The trees were so close together and the undergrowth so thick that their progress was immediately slowed. It was almost impossible to believe that an army could traverse through it. Unseen by the soldiers, but clear to the sailors on the *Martin,* the Americans would have no choice but to penetrate the forest. For every time they attempted to progress along the narrow strip of land between the forest and the river, they were at the mercy of the hundreds of small lead balls of grape shot fired from the ship. And on the road to the village, General Fraser's troops stood their ground and prevented passage.

As they fought their way through the tangle of bushes, undergrowth and saplings which blocked their way between the trunks of the huge trees, they slowly made their way towards the enemy. After a while, the soldiers came to hollows in the forest floor which were filled with shallow black water. A little further on these developed into swamps which were covered by aquatic weeds. Here the trees were much more sparse and they could see a greater distance. With the muddy water already over their knees they prepared to make their way through the swamp, but no sooner had they started moving forward than they heard splashing, shouts and gunfire as three columns of soldiers wading towards them on the other side of the swamp came into view from behind the low bushes. Aaron had been confused about where sounds were coming from since he always heard better with his right ear. He had long since learned to watch for the reactions of others, so that he was seldom caught out by this problem. Now they could see that the men were wearing dark blue jackets and tricorn hats, both with white facings. They had obviously seen the vivid red uniforms before Aaron and his comrades had seen them. Although they had no cover, the centre column spread out and opened fire. It was immediately evident that the eighty men of the two light companies were outnumbered and with the two outside columns approaching them from the left and right, they were in severe danger of being outflanked. The bugler sounded the retreat and Granville shouted, "Back, back. Mew and your group stay with me to form a rearguard while the others retreat."

Terrified and with his left ear almost making him demented, Aaron found cover behind a tree with Huhne and they fell into their well-practised routine of load and fire. The Americans' centre column, now four or five men across, was approaching the middle of the swamp and with no cover they were vulnerable. The leading men began to fall as the five redcoats fired into them. Realising the desperation of their situation the column broke and men began to scramble back to safety, but not so the two outside columns, which began to skirt the swamp on either side. Fortunately, they were slowed by the morass of tangled bushes round the edge of the water. They were hindered enough for Granville to order a withdraw. The five men turned and rushed as best they could through the knotted and twisted undergrowth, weaving between the huge tree trunks and using such glimpses of the sun as they had to assure themselves that they were heading east, all the time fearing that the men behind them would soon be upon them.

When they broke through the cover of the forest and out into the open they found themselves close to the river and easily identified the defensive positions thrown up by the regiment. They raced for the piles of logs and cut brushwood set up as breastworks behind which the soldiers were taking cover and threw themselves on the grass beyond, hearts racing and lungs almost bursting.

Granville was first to get up. He found the energy to run to report the situation to the Captain and to receive orders from him. He returned and briefed the Corporals. Each of them moved along giving orders to the men.

"Glad you got back safely, lads, but it is not over yet – that was just the beginning. From the description Granville gave, the American Loyalist officer thinks that the men we met in the forest were from the 4th Pennsylvania Regiment under Anthony Wayne, a fine commander."

There was a crack of gunfire behind him and he shouted, "Wait for it! Await the command."

The soldiers of the 53rd Regiment on top of the hill had the first sight of figures emerging from the forest. Three six-pounder cannon had been wheeled into position in vantage points, but the terrain was unsuitable for their use, for men began to appear from different parts of the woods and there was no group at which to aim effectively. The waiting soldiers were fondling their flintlocks awaiting the order; they too had no solid line of enemy to aim at. Then more shots began to ring out from in front of the Light Company. Serjeant Granville was standing behind the breastworks and part protected by them, his sword held up in his hand indicating to anyone who saw him that they should await his order.

More and more Americans emerged through the undergrowth

and into the open. Each man in the defensive position was longing for the order to fire. As the attackers came closer and closer, they heard shot impacting on the logs in the breastworks. When the first Americans were not more than fifty paces away, Granville bellowed through the cracking of the enemy guns, "Light Company, choose your man and fire at will."

The defenders fired and mechanically went through the reloading drill they knew so well. Already there was a large cloud of gun smoke hanging over the battle scene. A scream from beside him made Aaron glance sideways. Huhne had his hand over a gushing wound under his shoulder. For the first time the young soldier's fear left him – now he felt anger, anger that his friend should have been wounded. He knew that he could not stop firing to help the injured man and so heartlessly ignored his cries and reloaded.

More Americans were valiantly fighting their way through the overhanging branches of the forest to join the assault, but gradually the newcomers became tangled up with the retreating wounded and found their way hindered by the bodies on the ground.

Then the order came for the company to leave the relative shelter of their breastworks. The order echoed up the line as the Serjeants called, "62nd, fix bayonets."

Aaron and the others took their bayonets from the frog on their belts and slotted them on the end of their flintlocks. The bugle call sounded and its call was echoed by the sound of the drummers also sounding the advance.

"Forward!" ordered the Serjeants. The men left their defensive positions and the whole line of the regiment climbed over the various obstructions and moved towards the forest. In many places the Americans bravely stood their ground, their Colonel courageously encouraging them until he saw that it would be suicidal to resist further as many were falling victim to the bayonets before given a chance to reload their flintlocks.

"Light Company forward in groups of four," shouted Granville. His sword was back in its sheath and he waved the men forward with his left hand, his flintlock with a bayonet in the other. The well-rehearsed teams of four formed and plunged into the undergrowth in pursuit of the fleeing Americans. They had not gone far when a dozen or so Indians overtook them in the pursuit. The warriors were far faster than the soldiers, with natural agility, no equipment encumbering them and lacking the caution of the advancing redcoats.

Aaron found himself being distracted and sickened by the sight of the dead and dying and the plight of the wounded enemy, but thoughts of the injury and death he was causing to fellow humans was deeply subsumed by the frenzy of the hunt as the Serjeant urged the company on to chase the retreating soldiers. Some of the Americans were hiding behind trees and firing at the advancing redcoats, whose bright uniforms stood out well against the greenery. Gun smoke betrayed the position of the snipers and they soon found themselves isolated and either killed or captured. Here and there the men found enemy bodies with the top of their heads cut off – nothing in their training could have prepared them for the gruesome sights they saw as they traversed the forest.

Gradually, the firing stopped, though there was much shouting and cursing as men were captured or dispatched with the bayonet. Some of the redcoats started taking the prisoners back through the forest to the encampment, after in many cases stealing effects from them. The Light Company continued its westward sweep through the trees. The going was very slow because of the wide swamps, the need to avoid the occasional sniping of the American rearguard and a fear of losing their way. The latter problem was solved when they were joined by a party of Indians. They moved slightly ahead of the soldiers, showing them the way towards where it was assumed that the Americans would try to retreat back across the St Lawrence, Point du Lac, where they had left their boats. The American commander, General Thompson, had left two hundred and fifty men to defend the landing stage to ensure a line of communication. However, unknown to both the British in the forest and the Americans desperately trying to reach their boats, naval ships had made their way up to the river and had bombarded the boats and sent the guard fleeing westwards.

By nightfall the Light Company had reached a clearing in the forest in the middle of which was a small farm building. The officers made this their headquarters and the men prepared for a night in the open. Sentries were posted at several strategic points around the clearing and both officers and men rested fully clothed, their weapons beside them. The soldiers made the most of such timbers and branches as they could find to make simple shelters for the night. Not wishing to attract attention to themselves they did not light fires and relied on the contents of their haversacks for nourishment. The night was in any case mild and clear, and well before it was completely dark the half-moon was rising and faintly illuminating the ground.

The Indians did likewise, though they held themselves separate from the redcoats. Since they had no blankets with them they covered themselves with branches, using such protection as the leaves afforded against the elements. There were always two of them sitting silently smoking their pipes, listening to the sounds of the forest and any sign of approaching danger.

It was a nervous night. From time to time there was a distant firelock shot, but more frequently there were shouts, screams and the sound of people calling to each other; clearly there were some men still lost in the forest.

"Did you see what happened to Huhnie, Ting?" whispered Aaron.

"I saw him fall, he got one in the shoulder I think."

"I hope someone got him to the regimental hospital, it was just behind the lines."

"No such luck for the poor sods in the forest. The wolves will be well fed tonight. That's probably what the screams are about."

Aaron quietly reflected on the awful possibility of wolves gnawing human flesh and shuddered. It could have been him lying wounded in the dense forest. But then he thought about what he had done; there was no doubt that he had done his duty well, but at what cost? He had maimed and probably killed Americans; he had seen them up close, and they just looked like any other men he had ever met. The ones without uniforms looked like the villagers at home. They had mothers, brothers and perhaps wives who they would never see again. He salved his conscience and hid his revulsion by turning his thoughts to the fact that his friend had been shot, perhaps even killed, and then he became haunted by the fact that the ball which had struck Huhne could have easily embedded itself in him instead.

Eventually, he dozed restlessly until he was roused shortly before dawn by the sentries coming off duty to take his turn on one of the outposts on the forest edge together with Jamie.

The sun rose far behind the leafy barrier of the forest trees and it would be some time before it rose high enough to reach them and to take the chill off the morning air. Before that happened, the two sentries saw the Indians coming down to the forest edge. Aaron noticed the mops of hair each attached to a bloody lump of flesh, which were hanging from their belts. He immediately realised that these were the missing parts of some of the dead they had seen in the forest – their scalps. The soldiers exchanged glances acknowledging that they had both seen the same thing, but said nothing as clearly the Indians were listening intently to something which was not apparent to the Europeans. The silence was broken when the Indian leader said something to the others in their own language. Then he turned and said something in French to the Corporal.

"What did he say, Jamie?" asked Aaron anxiously.

"He said that people are coming towards us."

No sooner were the words out of Jamie's mouth before there was a call from among the trees, "We are surrendering."

The Indians rushed into the forest and within a few seconds they returned, pushing in front of them three men. They looked haggard and dishevelled, showing that they had spent the night in the forest.

"Stand or I fire!" shouted Jamie at the men, as he pushed through the Indians before any of them had a chance to take a scalp.

Two of the captives with pistols threw them to the ground, relieved that they were to be prisoners of the redcoats and not the Indians. An officer standing behind the other two stepped forward. He was wearing an unbuttoned tattered civilian frock coat, but under this and on top of his waistcoat he had a pink sash which he wore diagonally across his chest. This was the sash of an American Brigadier-General. He pulled out his sword and handed it to Jamie.

"Corporal, would you be good enough to take me to your commanding officer. I am General William Thompson of the 1st Pennsylvania Regiment. This is my adjutant, Captain Grainger, and this is Lieutenant Parker."

The pursuit of the American soldiers continued for several days until it became clear that those who had escaped had managed to cross the river to the relative safety of their own stronghold. The campaign had been a great tragedy for the attackers. The rebels had lost heavily with about three hundred taken prisoner, many killed or wounded and some perished, undiscovered, in the forest. The British Army had lost five killed and fourteen wounded.

However, the 62nd Light Company did not spend more time looking for escaping rebels. On 9th June the company was placed into a force of twelve hundred men comprising the light companies and grenadiers of all the regiments. They were called the 'Advance Corps' and General Fraser took command. Two days later they had crossed to the south shore of the river pursuing the retreating enemy. The American commanders, Generals John Sullivan and Benedict Arnold, had decided that the pitiful physical state of their four thousand strong army with a large proportion of the men sick or wounded and numbers further threatened by a smallpox epidemic as well as desertions, prevented them from resisting the British.

The Advance Corps led a fast advance of the army south along the bank of the Richelieu River, often just hours behind the enemy until they reached Chambly, only to find the fort there had burned to the ground. The pursuit was slowed when it was discovered that the twelve-mile track south to St Johns over the many rivulets through the wilderness was almost impassable as the Americans had destroyed the many bridges. Eventually, as the Advance Corps neared St Johns, scouts reported that they had seen the Americans requisitioning all the vessels they could find to evacuate the exhausted army south along the waterway to Lake Champlain.

Chapter 15

Three miles north from St Johns, news reached the Advance Corps that the American rearguard had been sighted. Three companies of light infantry under the command of Captain Craig were ordered to pursue them at the trot. The men ran as fast as their heavy packs would allow them, trying to catch up with the Americans. When they arrived at the village, the fort was in flames. The soldiers split up to hunt for any enemy who had not yet been evacuated.

Corporal Cutler's three men hurried out of the cover of the tall pines, and made their way towards the river. A pistol shot echoed through the clearing leading to the waterway and then they heard the splash of oars. All four men ran, to the best of their abilities, towards the sound, though the older soldier soon fell behind.

As they rounded the bushes and joined the track recently churned by hundreds of feet they saw a dead horse by the beach, and beyond the horse, four men furiously rowing out into the river. A fifth man sat in the stern of the vessel. They were already beyond accurate range of a firelock, but nevertheless the four redcoats discharged their guns at the craft, two at a time. The rowers visibly ducked as they heard the reports, but needlessly as none of the shot came near them.

The breathless soldiers on the beach were shocked when they heard a croaky voice call, "That, my friends, was General Benedict Arnold. And there is his horse."

The tones were those of a man who was suffering. "He was last to leave and did not want to give his horse to the British. There was no room for me in the boat, or rather no one wanted to be near me, for surely I am doomed."

The four of them looked at the man lying on the shore. He had no uniform and looked to be what he probably was – a farmer. His face was a mass of pustules, his lips split and bloody. The hands loosely cradling his knapsack were studded with the same small and round red and white lumps.

Aaron gazed at the wretched young man for a few seconds wondering what strength of feeling had made him venture his future by joining the rebel army and then said, "They have left him to try to infect our troops with the smallpox. We'll have to kill him."

"But Mewie, we have to take him prisoner," argued Bell.

"We can't. A lot of our men haven't been inoculated. We have to shoot him. I'll do it if you won't."

Aaron looked at the man again; he was obviously suffering terribly. Like many other rebel soldiers they had seen, he was wearing a thick linen shirt and a waistcoat, breeches buckled below the knee, and knitted stockings. His large floppy hat was on the ground beside him. The man had heard what the soldiers had said and held his arms open wide, not imploring mercy but inviting them to end his suffering.

Aaron lifted his firelock slowly to do what had to be done, but before he got to the firing position he heard a click behind him, the sound of a gun being cocked. Jamie had caught up with them and there was a boom as he fired at the defenceless cripple. At point blank range the ball smashed the man's face open, revealing his brain.

"He was going to die anyway, best he did so without taking others with him," mumbled Jamie as he reloaded. "Now cover him with some branches, we can bury him later. Let's see if anyone else has been left by the Yankees."

Just then they heard people running through the bushes – Captain Craig and some other soldiers had arrived.

"Where are they? We heard a shot."

"Gone, sir," said Jamie, pointing out into the river where a figure was standing in the back of a rowing boat waving his hat. "All we have is a dead man and a dead horse, and no boats to give chase."

"Then they have escaped and we have no means to catch them unless we can bring our ships up to St Johns."

After the Captain had moved away to discuss the situation with the other officers, Jamie said to the other three, "You saw for yourselves the rapids between Chambly and St Johns – not even a rowing boat could pass them."

"Then we have to march round the lake to catch up with them," said Aaron.

"We will have to wait and see what Gentleman Johnny decides."

General Burgoyne had become a popular figure with his soldiers. He moved freely among them encouraging them and giving praise for achievements. Despite his reliance on the material comforts provided by an extensive baggage train with his personal effects, the men admired his well-publicised love of drink and his predilection for female company. Although overall command of the army was General Carlton's, Gentleman Johnny was the men's favourite.

The light companies and other troops were all stationed near to St Johns to await orders, although several sorties were made against the American rearguard, which was waiting for boat transport south while inhabiting an island called Isle aux Noix. Several of these expeditions were led by Canadian and Indian forces who had acquired a reputation for cruelty. When the British later took over Isle aux Noix, they found this inscription on a gravestone:

Beneath this humble sod lie Capt. Adams, Lieut. Cuthbertson and two Privates of the 6th Pennsylvania Regt. Not hirelings but patriots. They fell not in battle, but unarmed, were basely murdered and inhumanly scalped by the barbarous emissary, of the once just but now abandoned Kingdom of Britain.

At the end of June the General issued orders intended to progress the campaign.

"Construction of a fleet? What, here, Mewie?" asked Bell.

"Yes, that's what the rumour is."

"That's what I heard too – we are going to drag the ships over land to bypass the rapids and they are going to build some new ships here too," added Graham.

"That's impossible, Clipper, you saw how big even the smallest naval vessels are."

"There's the Corporal, ask him, Ting."

"Corporal, is it true about the boats?"

"I don't know, but we are being paraded later today, perhaps the Serjeant will have news."

As the men of the company stood at the alert in two ranks, Captain Hawker stepped forward to address them.

"Serjeant, tell the men to be easy."

"Light Company, be easy!"

"As you know, we have rid Canada of the American menace. Now we must continue with our campaign to rout the Congress Army of America. Benedict, the so called General of the Army we are chasing, has mobilised a fleet of ships at the south end of Lake Champlain, a very large body of water to the south of us. To pursue our purpose we must destroy this fleet which is blocking our progress. To this end, the army will build a shipyard here in St Johns. Several hundred sailors and any soldiers with skills in the necessary trades will prepare a fleet to engage Benedict's."

"Carry on, Serjeant."

The next day when the men were paraded Aaron was informed that since the boat builders needed blacksmiths, he was to be transferred to the shipyard. The remainder of the men were to be occupied with tree felling to supply timber for the boats.

Aaron took leave of his old friends, Graham, Bell and Corporal Cutler, saying, "Sorry you are to be mosquito bait! If you hear anything of Huhnie, get a message to me."

Aaron had tried fruitlessly to get news of Huhnie, who had been shot at Trois Rivieres. Communications were very difficult if not impossible, but he hoped that one day his friend might reappear. The reference to mosquitoes was occasioned by the fact that ever since they had arrived in the village they had been plagued by the insects. In particular in swampy ground and forest, many men had suffered from the constant itching produced by the attention of these creatures. It was said that the Indians prevented being plagued by covering their skin with red ochre, but the soldiers had found no way of protecting themselves. These flying tormentors were just one type of wildlife now experienced by the men. While the racoons and chipmunks were entertaining and harmless, the snakes raised terror in many. The call of the wolves at night when they were hunting deer caused many a nightmare and not infrequently men on sentry duty nervously fingered the triggers on their firelocks when packs of wolves howled nearby.

At Chambly, Aaron reported for duty to help with the preparation of the ships waiting to be transported the twelve miles between the two villages. He was told to join a crowd of men standing by a ship to hear what had to be done. There he noticed that he was only one of three soldiers amongst all the sailors who were gathered in front of the officer, Naval Lieutenant William Brown of *HBMS Apollo*, as he briefed the work force. When he had finished he said, "So men, this is the task ahead of us. I will ask the officer supervising the work, Lieutenant John Schanck, to give you the details."

Schanck pointed at the vessel. "This is the *Inflexible* – 180 tons, armed with eighteen twelve-pounder cannon. She is to be dismantled, the parts ported to St Johns and then reassembled there."

There were some exclamations among those listening as they gazed up at the ship and
the towering masts.

He continued, "The schooners, *Maria*, fourteen six-pounder cannon and the *Carlton*, eighteen twelve-pounder cannon, are also to be transported in the same way."

Pointing up at the rigging he said, "We start by building a tripod shear to lower the masts. While that is being done all the cannon should be unloaded and prepared to be transported. Your officers will assign your duties."

Aaron returned to the forge to start his work, enthused by the opportunity to practise his trade. There he learnt that his commanding officer was the blacksmith, Master Smith Robert Jones.

The forge was far from complete. A gang of sailors was sitting in various places on the timbers of a building frame, passing up sapling trunks to form a roof. Under them, several men were busy using stones to build four hearths, one of which was nearing completion. Another group were disassembling the bellows from a farrier's cart. These carts followed the army to provide a shoeing service for the horses and carried a complete forge.

Work slowed as the naval personnel looked with curiosity at the soldier who was talking to the smith.

"What's your name, Private?"

"Aaron Mew, sir."

"And what experience do you have?"

"I've done three years of my apprenticeship with Mr Thomas Sykes in Fordingbridge."

"Where's that?"

"In Wessex, sir, down Hampshire way."

"Can you read and write?"

"Yes, sir, that I can."

"Well, Private Mew, I think we can use you. All of the iron fittings on the ships are to be removed and to be refitted when the ships are reassembled. Many will break. Our job is to carefully remove these fittings and where necessary to make new ones. We have to keep written records with drawings and measurements of all the details to be made. As soon as they have the masts down on the ships we can get started. Until then you can join the men over there making nails – we'll need many hundreds of them.

"You can mess with some of the sailors."

And so began Aaron's reintroduction to the work he had once been training for. He was thrilled to be part of the huge team of men busying about in the yard. The smell of the forge transported him back to another life; a time seemingly long gone and a village far away. Memories of the place he called home were evoked, with the bitter sweetness of good times remembered, and the recollection of his shame.

Gradually the carcasses of the three ships began to diminish in size as the disassembly proceeded. There was a constant stream of horses and carts carrying everything from the timbers to the ships' bells along to St Johns. All the time, more naval crew and a few more soldiers arrived to help with the prodigious task. Meanwhile, the army remained stationed around St Johns. Hundreds of men there were building an even bigger shipyard for reassembly of the three ships and the construction of rafts and small gunships. Teams of soldiers scoured the forest for suitable timbers for the new craft while others worked as sawyers and carpenters. All the while there was some skirmishing with small parties of Congress troops who were probing defences and scouting for intelligence.

There came a time in early August when the blacksmiths and carpenters at Chambly transferred to the shipyard at St Johns and Aaron found himself once more able to meet with his old friends. The first evening he was permitted time to do so he sought out his erstwhile companions and found them sitting in the sutler's tent sharing a bowl of punch and between sips, puffing on their pipes.

"Hello, gentlemen."

"My dear boy, we are so pleased to see you return to us. We have sallied forth and expelled the enemy from the Isle aux Noix, a veritable snake pit, felled trees amidst multitudes of mosquitoes and chased deserters, of whom there have been a number. What have you been doing?"

"Did you see action at Isle aux Noix?"

"The enemy showed the presence of mind to vacate the island at our approach. We now have another three hundred of the savages with us who threaten the foe with their barbarism. But we did have action with the snakes. Much of the island is swamp, which seemed to suit the slithering kind. St Matthew was right when he said, 'Ye serpents, ye generation of vipers, how can ye escape the damnation of hell?'"

"You killed them then?"

"By the score. This wilderness seems a hostile, devilish place. The antithesis of Christian civilization."

"What have you been doing, Mewie?" asked Graham.

"I was lucky. The Master Smith took me on and I been working in the forge at Chambly. It's hard work but I have learned very much.

"Are you coming back to join us now?"

"No, Clipper, now starts the biggest job as we must reassemble the ships in all haste, for the whole campaign is delayed for want of ships. We have three large craft to be made and we await the arrival of twelve gun boats from England. They are all in pieces and we are to build them too. Each will be armed with one cannon. There is much to be done and in a mighty hurry."

"Tis true, Clipper. We can go no further while Arnold controls the lake. We have heard dire tales of the American winter and we must move on before the snow impedes our progress and closes the trail south."

"How are they going to supply us through the winter if the roads are not passable, Rev?"

The good Mr Smee was still a regular visitor to his friend although the circumstances of their meetings were in stark contrast to those in the town billet in Galway.

"Ah, I have it on good authority that we will overwinter at a place the Indians call Cheonderoga, meaning 'brawling waters'.

The fortification there constructed by the French and taken by the British in the last war is Fort Ticonderoga. There we will find shelter and good sources of supply, when we have won it from the Americans."

"Where is it, Rev?"

"I have no map, but I am led to believe that it is at the southern end of the Lake Champlain, the very lake on which we are planning to engage the enemy with the inchoate fleet on whose construction Mewie is engaged."

"And does Grabber treat you well, Ting?"

"As ever, Mewie. We have been on several missions past Isle aux Noix with the savages, to try to find prisoners. The General wants us to capture rebels when they come ashore to get wood, so that he can gain intelligence from them."

"But Granville is much distracted by concerns for his daughter. It does nothing for his temper."

"Where is she?" asked Aaron.

"With the older women and like them she makes some money doing the cleaning and washing for the men. The Serjeant fears that it is no good company for the girl, for many of the women are as pot valiant from the rum as the men."

There was a pause for thought while several of the men refilled their pipes.

"What news of Huhnie?" asked Aaron.

There was another silence. Rev and Graham glanced at each other and then Rev said, "The Lord giveth and the Lord taketh away. Huhnie has gone to a better place."

"What do you mean? Is he dead?"

"I am sorry, dear boy, I know that you two were very close. We got news eventually from one of the men of the 53rd who had been wounded at Trois and had now returned to duty. He told us that Huhnie died in the hospital at the nunnery. He had taken a shot in his right lung. The nuns have buried him in their cemetery."

Aaron was speechless, reflecting on how Huhne had met his end and how the shot came so near to killing him. He took a deep breath and said, "Would you give me a sip of your punch bowl please, my mouth is very dry."

Aaron retired early to bed. The news of Huhne's death had

shocked him and he had no appetite for company while he tried to come to terms with the news. He had seen death at close quarters several times since Trois Rivieres, but the victims were strangers to him. Huhnie had been his companion through all the tribulations as well as joys, since the day he was enlisted. They had experienced so much together; he was the partner on whom Aaron's life depended in battle, and now he was no more. For the first time in his life the young smith grieved for the loss of someone close to him.

By mid-August over seven hundred sailors as well as soldier artisans were working feverishly in the shipyard. The biggest new vessel was a fortified raft destined to be called the *Thunderer.* The craft measured one hundred feet long and was thirty feet wide. She carried six 24-pounder and four 12-pounder cannon as well as four howitzers. Despite severe storms during late August, on 15th September, with several of the smaller craft already in the river, the *Inflexible* was launched twenty- eight days after laying her keel. But near disaster followed when the first of the three masts was raised.

Aaron was on board the ship working on the iron fixings for the main shrouds as the tripod shear was put in place. The work was being directed by a tall naval officer.

"Who is the big fellow, Jack? I've seen him about before," Aaron asked of his naval companion.

"That's Edward Pellew, Master's Mate. He was a midshipman on the *Blonde*, but he got demoted for some reason."

"He seems very sure of himself."

"Some would say, 'with all right'."

"Why?"

"He is as strong as an ox and seems to be able to succeed at everything he tries. But like an ox he bellows loud, too loud for my liking. Look out, here comes Schanck, he will want to supervise this task."

They paused to watch as two groups of sailors, one at the bottom of each leg of the shear, gradually edged the poles further forward, as gently as possible raising the mast. When the mast was part of the way up Lieutenant Schanck took Pellew aside and gave him an instruction. The Master's Mate put a large coil of rope around his shoulders and balancing carefully on the mast, walked to the top, and sat astride it after tying one end of the rope to a loop. The

Lieutenant then spoke to the bosun who proceeded to call orders to the groups of men.

"What's he doing?" asked Aaron.

"He is going to make fast the mast to the shear poles when it is upright. They support it until the shrouds are in place. So we had better hurry with our work."

"I have written the measures, I will go back to the forge to get one more fixing made."

Just as Aaron turned to go there was a roar from the men pushing the poles and a boom as one of them crashed to the deck. Pellew was left desperately holding the top of the mast as it careered off to one side. All hands gazed skyward as they waited for the Master's Mate to fall to his death.

"Jesse, he's finished," shouted Aaron.

"Poor sod is doomed!"

But Pellew was not about to commit himself to a fatal fall onto the deck. He leapt sideways with a force which allowed him to clear the gunnels and land in the river.

"Pellew! He's gone!" shouted Schanck, his assumption being that like almost all sailors, Pellew would not be able to swim. But then there was a cheer as the Master's Mate's head emerged from the water and he began to swim to the side of the ship.

At the beginning of October, a flotilla of vessels sailed from St Johns to moor nearer to the lake. They included the *Carleton, Maria, Thunderer* and twelve gunboats. The fleet was under the command of Captain Thomas Pringle on the *Maria*. The *Carleton* was manned by twenty men from the *Blonde* with Lieutenant Dacres in command.

The waterway was too shallow for *Inflexible* to sail fully laden, so she was sailed to the south of Isle aux Noix where her guns were taken on board. With Lieutenant Schanck in command the ship joined the other vessels, and on 10th October, the fleet set sail with a strong following wind to find the enemy.

With the work at the shipyard finished, Aaron rejoined his unit when they set up camp on a piece of land called Point au-Faire, where the river broadened out into the great lake. There they waited for news of the outcome of the sea battle.

The first indication of the outcome of the confrontation came on 12th October with the arrival of a small boat carrying wounded sailors. They reported that the Americans had drawn up their fleet in a crescent between Valcour Island and the mainland, but they had not been seen by the British fleet which sailed down the centre of the lake. When they were eventually noticed, on account of some of their ships opening fire, the fleet was too far downwind to engage them. The British turned and started to tack slowly back towards the enemy.

The first ship to come within cannon shot of the American fleet of fourteen vessels was the *Carleton*. She anchored in front of the crescent and opened fire. The ship took a terrible punishment from the attention of the whole fleet in front of her. First, Lieutenant Dacres was badly wounded and then the second in command. The next in line to command the ship was Master's Mate, Pellew. The ship then came under additional fire from soldiers on the shore. In a desperate situation, the *Carleton* was ordered to withdraw before the *Maria* and the *Inflexible* arrived and took over the attack. Eight of the *Carleton*'s crew of twenty were dead and six wounded, but the ship was unable to steer clear of the action because the foresails would not set. Pellew had climbed on to the bowsprit and dragged the sail until the wind caught it and they could retire. Several broadsides from the schooners silenced the American guns and several ships were sunk. During the night, under cover of fog, the remainder of Benedict Arnold's fleet escaped, only to be later caught by the British. At the end of the action only four American ships remained.

The news of the victory was carried to Point au-Faire by an officer travelling in a canoe waving a captured American flag. The flag had thirteen red stripes on a white background with a rattlesnake motif diagonally across it. The design represented the thirteen American colonies and the snake signified that they should not be trodden on.

With enthusiasm the whole army moved south to the site of a ruined British fort at Crown Point, just twelve miles north of Ticonderoga. Crown Point had been one of the biggest forts built by the British in America, but some years before it had been destroyed by an accidental fire. After weeks of living in forests, the men were now camped on open land around the site of the fort. The weather was wet, but spirits were high for they were now just twelve miles from their objective.

"Mewie, come into the tent. We have double rum ration to celebrate and Ting has bought spruce beer from the sutler."

"Damnable weather, Clipper, pass it to me, I need something to keep out the cold."

"Time to light the lantern, Rev. We won't be doing any more work today."

"You're right, Clipper, no more digging today. The rain washes away the earthworks as fast as we can build them. Unless we get some dry weather soon I can't see how we can build up defences."

"Ting, God will provide, all in good time. And remember, the rain which falls on us also falls on our enemies."

"Ah, but they are in the warm and dry fort, but four leagues away. Sure they won't be suffering like us," complained O'Driscoll.

"Surely the officers are comfortable, but just as surely the men will be under canvas experiencing the same vicissitudes of the weather as we are," said Rev.

"But we have to be able to fortify this place if we are to launch an assault."

"Man proposes, but God disposes, Clipper."

"Mewie, have you heard about the rebel prisoners captured during the sea battle?" asked Graham.

"No, what's happened then?"

"You tell him, Clipper. Tell him of the foolishness of the men who lead us," said O'Driscoll.

"Lord Carleton has had them all released and Captain Craig has escorted them all the way to Ticonderoga to hand them personally to General Gates, the rebel commander."

"Why did he do that?"

"To show what he called magnanimity, dear Mewie."

"How do you mean?"

"As the book of Romans tells us: 'If your enemy is hungry, feed him, if he is thirsty, give him something to drink. In doing that, you will heap burning coals on his head'," replied Rev.

"Doesn't seem fair when more than sixty of our sailors were killed or wounded," said Aaron.

"And one of the prisoners was a General, too," added Graham.

"Mmm, apparently the prisoners have given their parole promising to take no further part in the revolt against us. I fear that the honesty and dependability of the rebels may be overestimated," said Rev.

The tent flap was thrown open and a woman with wet and bedraggled brown hair poked her head in.

"Can we join you gentlemen? Our tent is sodden wet."

"Mistress Saunders, you have smelled the rum I take it?" said Graham sarcastically.

"I have that, but fear not gentlemen, for I have my own."

She turned and called to someone behind her, "Come on in, Alice, bring the flask."

She pushed the girl in through the tent door and pulled the flap down. The woman was wearing a long tattered dress and her shoulders were covered by a wet shawl which she took off, folded and threw to the ground to sit on. Her appearance was by no means unique, for the hundreds of women camp followers were unable to obtain new cloth because of the long supply chain back to the nearest shops and the fact that military supplies took absolute precedence. Even needles and thread were in very short supply as they were rationed for the soldiers to repair their uniforms.

"You all know young Alice Granville, don't you? She's sharing with me and Mr Saunders on account of her not having female family. Here, give me the flask, Alice."

Rev stood up and taking his pipe out of his mouth said, "Gentlemen of the Light Company, I am beholden to you for your hospitality. I shall find my way back to my tent before dark."

So saying he left the tent.

"He doesn't like me does he?" said the woman.

Graham answered, "I am sure you misunderstand him, he is a good man. And where is your good man, Private Saunders, this evening?"

"He's on sentry duty. He'll be wet as a tow rag when he gets back to the tent."

"I fancy he will be looking for his rum."

"Well, he ain't going to find it because here it is."

The woman sat down on her wet shawl and beckoned to the girl. "Go sit over there with the boy, he'll keep you warm a while."

Aaron looked at Alice. The lantern light was too weak for him to discern her features very clearly, but he detected by her hesitant movement that she was frightened. He moved over to give her space to sit down, but was careful to keep distance between them.

The woman cackled at the girl and taunted her, "He won't keep you warm like that!" Addressing the others she said, "She ain't got over her ma being tipped into the briny on account of the fever, poor soul. Here, give me a drop of the spruce to wash the rum down."

She took a swig from the flask she had brought with her and then grabbed the tankard in Bell's hand.

"This damned weather is going to be the death of me. Chilled I am, chilled to the bone."

She took another draught from the flask, dipped her hand inside her bodice and pulled out a pipe.

"Give me some baccy, Clipper, I forgot mine."

She took the tobacco pouch offered her and Graham passed her a wooden spill which he had lighted from the lantern.

"Like I say, the girl mopes around and some days don't stop crying. She's got to earn her keep so I makes her help with the laundry I take in, tears or no tears. Say something then, Alice." She waited a few moments and then added, "Ain't the greatest of company is she?"

The tent flap opened again and Corporal Cutler poked his head in. "Orders have just been posted. We are to withdraw!"

He pushed his way through the tent door and stood bending his head in the low tent.

"What's going on in here then? A celebration? The tent smells like a rum bottle."

"How do you mean withdraw?" asked Aaron.

"Just that. The Serjeant is coming to explain."

The flap opened again and the sitting soldiers sprang to their feet when the figure of Granville appeared in the opening.

"Be at ease men." He paused, and then looking shocked, shouted, "Private Mew, outside."

As Aaron made to go the Serjeant hissed, "Mistress Saunders, it does not become you to keep company here when your husband is on duty. I will thank you to take my daughter back to your quarters."

The woman got up, gathered her shawl and sullenly shuffled past the officer. Alice tamely followed her. When they had gone he turned to the men and muttered, "I'll be back shortly," as he too exited the tent. Aaron was standing in the rain and the rapidly disappearing daylight.

Granville took three steps and then launched himself at the soldier and grabbed his lapels; he brought his forehead down on Aaron's nose. Fortunately, the Private moved back swiftly and the blow was not as hard as it might otherwise have been. A crescendo of noise erupted in Aaron's ear and he bit his bottom lip hard to contain his anger. He knew that to strike an officer could lead to the death penalty.

Holding on to the lapels, and with his face just a few inches from Aaron's, the Serjeant growled, "If I see you with my daughter again without my permission, you will wish you had never been born."

"But, Serjeant…"

"Shut up and get back into the tent."

Inside there was a deathly silence, for Granville's words had easily penetrated the canvas. He followed Aaron inside and stood leaning forward because of the restricted height.

"Sit down, Mew."

Aaron was searching his knapsack to find some item of old clothing he could use to wipe the blood from his nostrils.

"Owing to the inclement weather and the current impossibility to hold a parade to publish orders, the Captain has asked the Serjeants to go round the tents to pass them on. It will have been noticed that the winter is approaching, making it difficult for us to fortify this place. Thus, in his wisdom, His Excellency, General Lord Carleton, has decided that we can't defend Crown Point. Further, spies and scouts have estimated that a force of some twenty thousand rebels awaits us at the stronghold of Ticonderoga. More than twice the size of our army.

"Any questions?"

The men were silent.

"Tomorrow we begin a general withdraw back up the lake using the small craft, and then march back to winter quarters by the St Lawrence. The Light Companies and the grenadiers will form a rearguard and be last to leave, after the women and children. Other tents will be struck as and when boat transport is available for the occupants.

"Any questions?"

"With respect, Serjeant, are we to give up all the territory we have gained?" The Corporal was the only one who dared to voice the concerns they all felt.

"The enemy is not expected to campaign during the winter and therefore we hope to march back here to Crown Point next summer with no opposition, and continue our march south."

"Thank you, Serjeant."

"That's all. I bid you goodnight."

Bell was first to break the silence. "Jesse, after five months campaigning, we are to give up and march back whence we started."

O'Driscoll could not contain his anger and shouted, "I can't believe it! We have walked over half a continent through forest and swamps, mountain and strand. Threatened by serpents, bitten by mosquitoes and fired at by the enemy. This is a bloody disgrace. The spirits of the rebel dead must be laughing, for what they could not make us do when they lived our generals have done, and that to be sure is to make us engage in a dishonourable retreat."

"Shh, Patrick, the canvas is thin and others may hear you."

"The devil take them, I care not."

There was a silence after O'Driscoll's tirade, then Aaron added, "And all that work to build a fleet seems wasted."

The men sat in silence balancing their feelings of relief about avoiding a battle for Ticonderoga in wet and cold weather with an enemy superior in numbers and well entrenched, against thoughts of the blood spilled, the discomforts, the death of their friend and the risks they had taken to arrive within twelve miles of their objective.

On 24th October, General Burgoyne sailed for St Johns in the *Washington*, a ship captured in the sea battle, and then rode to Quebec, where a navy frigate was waiting to take him back to England for the winter. On the 30th, the *Thunderer* was sent north and on board were letters from soldiers; it was hoped that the mail would reach a naval vessel bound for England before the ice formed in Quebec harbour. Amongst the mail was Aaron's second letter to his parents; this time he wrote without the help of his mentor.

Dear Father and Mother,
My ardent hope is that this letter finds you in the finest of health. I have been blessed so despite the intensities of the climate in America. The summer was very hot and we are warned that the winter will be long and cold.
    I hope this letter reaches you safely, it was consigned with the

help of my friend Rev to the Thunderer and he gives me some level of hope that it will reach you.

Me and my friends have been campaigning all summer long and into the autumn over as very great a distance as you could ever imagine. Life in the army is hard and unrelenting for it is our officers' ambition that we should be the finest of soldiers. I have to confess that while it was never my intention to be in this army and the very thought that I must exercise violent retribution to the King's foes at times appals me, there is great satisfaction to be doing my duty for my country and I hope that you are proud of that. I am happy to relate that for a time I had work in the smithy at the shipyard. Now all but one of my companions from Salisbury is still with life for my good friend perished at Three Rivers. We have been triumphant over the rebellious scoundrels until the rains stopped our progress.

I have seen so many things what I had never imagined. Here the deer are plentiful and hunted by great packs of wolfs the call of which chills the blood of a man. And bears and other beasts roam the big forests at will not knowing to fear man for they have never seen them. That is except the savages which thanks be to God fight beside us. For they know the forests and where an Englishman would be lost in the wilderness they find their way directly with no let or hindrance.

The country is wonderously beautiful. We live at this time on open land which is Crown Point but to the east and west there are great mountains. Those on the east are green and to the west were until the leaf fall red like fire. The savages call them the Adirondacks.

I pray that you have forgiven me my disgrace for the thought of it still bothers me greatly.

Your humble and loving son,
Aaron Mew
Crown Point 29th inst.

Chapter 16

"God's teeth it's bloody cold. Corporal, where are we going?" asked Graham.

"A place called St Nicholas. Some of our line regiment are already there."

Corporal Cutler had just been briefed by Serjeant Granville about where the men in the Light Infantry Company were to spend the winter. They had formed a rearguard while the rest of the army had been transported across the lake from Crown Point. On 8th November they had been the last to leave and now ten days later they had stopped for a rest in their march east along the south bank of the St Lawrence towards Quebec. Although most of the light companies were to overwinter together at La Prairie and several other villages near to Montreal, the men of the 62nd were to rejoin their regiment.

"Are they all there?"

"No, there is not enough room for us all. Men have been placed in six different villages," said the Corporal.

"Why can't we stay in Quebec town?" asked Aaron.

"Now, that would be comfortable, wouldn't it! But the fact is that the barracks there will only house sixteen hundred men and it is full. So the whole army is spread around lots of different towns and villages."

"How will we be housed?"

"I don't know, neither did the Serjeant, but it can't be under canvas. We would freeze to death."

"Is it going to get worse than last night?" asked Bell.

"Ting, last night there was just a little snow, during the winter there will be snow up to your arse. Come on, let's get moving before it gets dark."

The company shouldered their packs, picked up their firelocks and continued on the muddy trail.

The next day, just as the Serjeant was considering ordering the men to pitch their tents for the night, they saw the village they were looking for. As they approached the settlement a sentry called out the challenge and then let them pass. News of their approach had quickly spread and a number of soldiers appeared from several of the small houses built around a square next to a tiny wooden church.

The new arrivals were lined up in the square to await instructions about where they would be billeted. Lieutenant Stephen, an ensign, and Serjeant Granville, stood out of earshot of the men deep in discussion. Clearly, there was some sort of problem. Eventually, Granville came over to the men.

"Almost all the billets in the village are occupied. The men here have been repairing a barn which was burned last year. This is to house our company when it is ready, but the roof is not yet on. So half of you will double up with the billets in the village, the other half are going to take over a longhouse abandoned by the savages. The longhouse is on the other side of the village."

The Serjeant stepped forward and counted twenty-one men including two Corporals, Cutler and Bryant.

"You men follow Serjeant Ryan, he will show you where the longhouse is. The sutler will be there later with victuals."

Aaron and his companions once more lifted their knapsacks and in the fading light, followed the two officers. They passed a small farm and what they assumed was the barn which was being repaired, and then saw what looked like a forest of spiked poles. As they got closer they realised that the poles, each of which was three times the height of a man, were formed into a very large circular wall. They were placed in such a way that it was very difficult, from any distance, to see how to gain entrance through the wall. They all stopped and gazed at the construction.

Serjeant Ryan turned to the men and said, "This men, is a Wendat longhouse. The Wendat are the tribe the French call Huron. It is, as you cannot fail to see, mightily well protected by this palisade. Follow me."

The Serjeant led the men, who were forced to go in single file, through a skilfully disguised entrance into the enclosure. They stood staring with amazement at the building in front of them.

"The likeness is to a giant woodlouse," he said as he slapped the shell of the large building.

It was indeed the shape of a woodlouse, though in height it was almost up to the level of the spikes on the fortifications and in length almost forty paces. The shell appeared to be covered with the bark of a tree, giving it a smooth appearance.

"Inside, you will find that a fire has been started for you to warm the place. We enter over there at the end of the building, though there is an entrance at each end. Come on."

He led them through a hanging curtain of birch bark strips which functioned as a door, into the cavernous longhouse. Inside, the atmosphere was very smoky, although there was a hole in the roof above the blazing fire. Beside the fire an Indian was standing facing the arrivals.

"This is George, or that's what we call him. He is one of our Haudenosaunee scouts, or Iroquois as they are better known. The Iroquois are the enemies of the Huron and they have turned out the families of the latter who previously resided here so that we can use it. He has picked up some of our tongue. He will look after you here."

The Indian was standing behind the fire cradling a firelock. He was wearing a decorated long leather waistcoat over a grey shirt. The waistcoat was gathered in above his hips by a red sash, from which on the left side hung a large knife, and across his chest was the strap of a cloth bag which was worn on the opposite side. On his legs he wore leather leggings, the bottoms of which covered the top of his soft shoes. From the angle he was standing it appeared that he was bald. He nodded unsmilingly at the newcomers as they all looked at him before surveying what they could see of the house by the firelight.

"As you see, on each side of the centre there is a structure at two levels. The benches on the lower level are where savages sit to eat and work and also sleep. And it is so that on the next level they store things. So choose a part of the bench to sleep on and put your things on the shelf above."

The men spread out to choose a sleeping space and claimed one by placing their knapsacks on the timber shelf above it. Though many tried to get near the fire in the centre of the house, most had to be satisfied with a place some distance away. Aaron found himself positioned with Jamie on one side and a bench, which to judge from the point blanket spread on it, the Iroquois warrior had claimed on the other. The soldiers had already learnt that point blankets were one of the Indians' most treasured possessions. They were produced by the Hudson Bay Company and the Indians obtained them by trading. The number of woven coloured threads in a corner of the white blanket indicated its size and quality.

That the warrior was indeed Aaron's neighbour was confirmed when the former put his firelock on the blanket, before returning to the fireplace.

"Aaron, it looks as if he is cooking something for us," said Graham. "What is it? I hope that it is for us, there is no sign of the sutler yet."

The two men approached the fire and looked into the large pot which was hanging over it on a metal tripod. George, who had started stirring the pot with a wooden stick, looked up and said, "We eat sagamite, it very good to welcome guests."

"What is in it, George?" asked Graham.

"What?"

"What do you make it with?"

The warrior walked over to his part of the bench and from the shelf above, pulled a sack down. He carried it to the fire, and dipped his hand inside. He withdrew some of the contents and opened his hand in front of the two men, though by this time several other inquisitive soldiers had joined them.

"It's maize, ain't it?" said one of them.

"Yea, they call it Indian corn don't they?" said Aaron.

The Indian put some of the corn on a flat stone and used a round one to demonstrate how he had ground the maize.

"Also pumpkin and fish, and many beans," stated the warrior.

Their discussion was interrupted by the arrival of the sutler.

"Gentlemen, I have bread for you, small beer and rum, but I am certain that the Serjeant will decide on the distribution of the rum."

"What, no beef?" demanded Corporal Cutler.

"No, we will arrange your usual victuals tomorrow."

There was a chorus of disapproval from the men which was quietened by the Serjeant's voice. "Alright men, we have a tea meal ready for us on the fire. After a tumbler of the rum you'll forget about the beef."

The tired soldiers began to crowd around the Serjeant with their metal cups.

"Alright, alright, let's have some order here. Stand by your beds and wait for the Corporals to serve you a drop."

The atmosphere changed as the men waited for the wooden cask to do its round and the air of conviviality was only interrupted when Corporal Bryant walked past the Indian warrior without stopping to give him a portion. George grabbed the Corporal by the arm and shouted something in his own language. The room went silent as the warrior reached across his stomach with his right hand, towards the sheathed knife.

"Let me be, you savage," shouted the Corporal.

"Me have rum too!" demanded the Indian, now with his knife in his hand.

"Yes, yes, you shall have rum too," said the shaken officer.

The Indian put his knife back and grabbed a dried gourd which was hanging from his belt. He yanked it off and held it to the cask. The Corporal gave him a more than normal portion and resumed his round of the room.

Jamie leant forward to Aaron and whispered, "You can see why the Americans are terrified of our Iroquois warriors."

"Don't they have savages fighting for them too?"

"Yes, Rev is most preoccupied in studying the savages' ways and loyalties and he says there is one tribe, I think called the Oneida, which supports the rebels, but we have not seen them in any action."

"Do you think that we will see Rev this winter?" said Aaron.

"He might be here in St Nicholas, but Granville told me our regiment is spread out in six different villages."

"By the by, how could George have had the food prepared? How could he have known that we had arrived?"

"The Lord has given these savages a gift of hearing which is far better than ours. I assume that he heard us coming long before we arrived in the village. That is one of the reasons, apart from their unnatural powers of navigation, that they are such good scouts," said the Corporal.

"But why do they cut the scalps from their dead enemies?"

"You will have to ask George."

"Come, eat," said the warrior as he beckoned to the soldiers.

With no hesitation the hungry men pulled their wooden plates from their knapsacks and made their way to the cooking pot. Later, when they had all finished, they sat on the benches nearest to the fire, many smoking their pipes, deep in conversation in small groups. The Indian sat alone on a large log in the centre of the house, behind to fire. He neither moved nor spoke and just gazed impassively at the far end of the house.

"Corporal Cutler and Corporal Bryant, a word if you please," ordered Serjeant Granville. He stood up and walked towards the doorway whence they had entered, followed by the two Corporals. When they reappeared the Serjeant stood on the opposite side of the fire from the Indian and shouted, "Right men, listen up. We will have two sentries outside the fence. It is possible that the tribe which has been displaced from this house might return to reclaim it. Sentries to have loaded firelocks at all times."

He read a list of names and times when they would be on duty and then proceeded to issue other duties including cook duty, the fetching of water from a nearby stream and the cleaning of the sip pots.

"And on the morrow, all the men except those on sentry duty will help with the work of rebuilding the barn."

The soldiers passed their first night in the longhouse and there was general consensus that the accommodation was superior to that afforded by the tents they were used to. When they reported for duty at the barn, Jamie and Aaron were delighted to see the gaunt figure of Rev at one end of the double-ended plank saw, as he and his companion alternately pushed and pulled the tool along a log. Rev let go of the saw and rushed over to the two newcomers and embraced both of them.

"My dear friends, I am delighted to see you. How was your perambulation from Crown Point? We feared that the snow might cause you encumbrance or that the enemy might wreak revenge for their humiliation."

"It was a long walk and we constantly feared that the Americans might pursue our rearguard, but apart from the rain, the cold, occasional snow showers and mud, the march was pursued in the utmost tranquillity," said Jamie.

"Were there any casualties?"

"No, not on the route but before we left Crown Point, O'Driscoll disappeared."

"How do you mean disappeared?"

"Well, he was seething angry about what he regarded as our retreat. In fact, we were afraid that he might be charged with insubordination. Then one evening when he was on sentry duty by the river, he just, well, disappeared."

"And you, Aaron, how goes it with you?"

"They do say that it will get even colder."

"Without doubt that is the case, dear friends. You must furnish yourselves with a blanket coat. You see those men over there wearing them."

He pointed to three men who had just arrived. Over their greatcoats they wore a point blanket which had been made into a long coat with a hood. Down the front was a series of loops on one side and wooden pegs sewn to the other. The pegs passed through the loops to fasten both sides of the coat.

"One of those would have been good on sentry duty last night," said Aaron, "but I can't sew."

"One of the women will doubtless provide such a service for a modest remuneration. Oh yes, how is your commodious Wendat accommodation?"

"Get on with your work, Rev, and leave those lazy devils be." There was no mistaking the voice; Serjeant Granville had arrived at the site. As instructed, their friend returned to the saw.

"Mew, your skills are needed in the smithy. We are short of nails and iron brackets. You will find the forge at the back of the farmhouse over there."

"Yes, Sergeant." Aaron was thrilled that he was once again going to have a chance to put into practice the skills taught him by Thomas Sykes in a village many hundreds of miles away.

Granville pointed to the farmhouse, a simple building which showed signs of having recently been repaired with new planks nailed to the existing walls. Aaron could see smoke rising from a building behind it and enthusiastically made his way towards the smithy. It was in a simple building with a flat roof and open on three sides. The forge was one of the type which had been used at St Johns, taken from a farrier's cart. The Master Smith, Jacob Francis, had the rank of Serjeant, but Aaron could tell by the warmth of his greeting and his general informality that the smith would rely more on his experience and skills than on his rank to exert his authority.

So the soldier's new routine was defined and the days began to pass in relatively settled circumstances compared with the transient life of the company during the previous six months. Aaron had the benefit of a job under cover, often with the benefit of the warmth of the blacksmith's hearth. Jacob Francis was benign and generous with his time, recognising that his new helper was a hard worker and keen to progress in the trade. Over the period of five weeks while Aaron worked on details for the building, he helped the younger man to develop his competence. During the same period they were often visited by a young boy of perhaps five or six. From the footsteps in the snow, it was clear that he lived in the little farmhouse. Occasionally his mother came looking for him and dragged the unwilling lad away and back towards the building.

On one such occasion Aaron was alone in the forge, the Master and the other workers being at the building site to deliver some ironwork.

"He ain't any trouble, missus, he can watch and warm himself by the fire if he wants."

"I don't want him hurt, or burned, he's all I got left. But we got precious little warmth in the house, not having a man to cut logs for us. I do what I can."

Aaron was puzzled by the woman's dialect; it was one he had not heard before. He smiled at her and said, "I'll keep an eye on him, missus, that I vouch to you."

"Well, just for a little while, while I go to the miller's to see if he got any flour left."

"I'll bring him to the farmhouse afore it gets dark."

When Francis returned, Aaron explained that he had allowed the boy to stay while his mother was away.

"The poor little devil is hungry more than likely, I shouldn't wonder." The smith opened his bread bag and took out a crust. He held it to the boy who immediately snatched it and crammed it into his mouth.

"What's your name, boy?" asked Francis.

"Isaac, sir."

"Isaac, son of Abraham. Aaron, did they teach you that in church school?"

"I don't recall, sir. What happened to the boy's father, sir?"

"I don't know, perhaps he is in the rebel army."

They both continued with their work. Suddenly, Aaron remembered that he had promised to take the boy back to his house.

"Sir, I promised to take Isaac back to his house afore dark. May I do so?"

"Yes, go on. Find out what happened to his father."

"Thank you, sir. Come on, Isaac, time to go home to your mother."

The house, which was hardly more than a shack, was little more than fifty paces from the forge, but since it was getting dark, Aaron took a firebrand with him. In the gathering dusk, Aaron beat his fist on the front door. There was no answer. The boy pushed the latch down and the door swung open. Not wanting to take the firebrand into the house, he stood awkwardly peering inside whence the boy had gone.

I can't leave the boy alone here in the dark, he thought, and then called to Isaac, "Have you got a candle?"

The boy reappeared carrying a metal candle holder, his finger through the loop on the side of it.

"Here, let me light it for you."

He lit the candle, stuck the firebrand in the snow outside and went into the house with the boy. Despite the freezing temperature, there was no fire in the hearth. From the light of the candle, he could see that the furnishings were very simple: a table with three chairs, a cot against one wall and a cupboard in front of which, on the bare wooden floor, was a worn mat. On the table there were signs that the occupant had recently been sewing or repairing Isaac's clothes, for lying on it, as well as needle and thread, there was a small pair of breeches. There were two pictures on the wall depicting bible stories: over the cot was a line drawing of Adam and Eve in the Garden of Eden and on the other wall a picture of Jesus surrounded by children. Aaron was able to read the title, 'Suffer the little children to come unto me'. There were various household utensils hanging from hooks over a bench where it looked as if food was prepared. From the patched-up woodwork on one wall it was clear that the house had been damaged, probably by a small cannon ball.

"Isaac, come with me. We will get some wood from the smithy

to light a fire before your mother returns."

They went back to the forge. It had started to snow as they retraced their steps. Aaron explained the situation to the smith and asked if he could take some of the timber offcuts which they used to light the charcoal in the hearth. The older man agreed and said, "Come back and get some of the logs, too."

"Come on, Isaac, you carry some wood too," said Aaron.

They walked back to the house and after making some wood shavings with his knife to start the fire, Aaron soon had a blaze going which was starting to warm the room. They were just about to leave to get the logs when the door opened and the woman stood in the doorway carrying a heavy sack on her back.

"Well, I do declare! What's this then?"

"Sorry, missus, I thought that it might warm the place up a bit for you and the boy."

The woman swung the sack off her back and let it down heavily on the floor. The boy ran to her and she put her arm round him.

"I am mighty obliged, Private, for tonight will be very cold. I never expected any generosity from the King's men for my kind."

"How do you mean, missus?"

"Well, you can see what Carleton's men did last year on their march from Montreal to Quebec. Near destroyed my house, took my animals, burnt my barn and, and..." She paused, half sobbing, running her fingers through her tangled black hair, "...robbed me of my man, Abraham. All I got left of him is the boy and a grave mound in the meadow. My parents brought me here from Holland when I was a girl. We were wealthy, but look at me now."

Aaron was embarrassed by the emotional state of the woman and decided to make avoidance by saying, "I got to go to get logs for you, missus."

He rushed out and hurried over to the forge. When he returned, the woman was ladling flour out of the sack and into a bin. The boy was holding the sack open for her.

"I'm beholden to you, Private."

"I'm Aaron missus, you can call me Aaron. I'll bring you some more logs tomorrow."

"I thank you for your kindness, Aaron. I be Widow Rasmussen, Sarah Rasmussen."

Aaron paused for a while and then said, "Do you have food?"

"This is the last of my flour. Got to get it in the bin afore the rats come looking for it. I couldn't pay the miller so he kept half my corn. But we get by – I take in washing and clothes repairs from the soldiers, at least those as are civil to me who they see as a rebel's wife."

There was an awkward silence and then Aaron asked, "Was your husband in the rebel army?"

"No, he never had the chance, but he spoke out for freedom from the crown and defended our farm from the Tories, and that was our undoing."

Aaron thought for a moment and then said, "Why did he not want to be British?"

"Well, we are Dutch like many other settlers around here. There are lots of Germans and Swedes too. We have no allegiance to the British King."

There was another protracted silence. Aaron realised that this was something he had not considered before, but he was nervous about offending the widow by asking more questions. He stepped towards the door, patted Isaac on the head and said, "I must get back to work. I bid you goodnight, Widow Rasmussen."

Aaron walked back through the increasingly heavy snow storm and continued with his work until the smith permitted him to leave for the longhouse. However, he did not go back directly to the billet, instead he went to the sutler's hut. There he bought a point blanket as well as some chocolate.

The next day, after seeking permission from the smith, he plodded through the deep snow carrying a load of logs to the house. In his greatcoat pocket he had the chocolate. While encumbered with the logs he struggled to knock at the door, but before he did so it was opened by the widow.

"Good day to you, missus, I got some logs for you and um… I got some chocolate for the boy."

Isaac bounded across the room, glad to see Aaron.

"Stand back, lad, this is heavy. I don't want to drop it on you."

He unloaded the wood and then reached inside his pocket for the chocolate which he tried to give to the boy, but his mother snatched it.

"I don't hold with begging. It ain't right that he scrounges off you."

"But he ain't scrounging, missus. I tell you what, tomorrow, Sunday, after church parade I've got time before the tea meal to come here to saw some of those tree trunks you've got round the side of the house. He can help me and earn his chocolate."

"But why should you be wanting to help the likes of us?"

"Well, Widow Rasmussen, I was thinkin'..." He paused awkwardly, and then continued, "Could you sew me a blanket coat? I mean, like, I could pay you by making a stack of logs from that timber. Is it well seasoned?"

"Yes, it's been lying there untended since last year. Do you have a blanket yet?"

"Yes, missus, I got it at the sutlers."

"Well, bring it over on Sunday then and I will measure you for the coat."

Just then there was a bang at the door. When the widow opened it, the distinctive figure of Serjeant Granville stood in the doorway; he had a sack over his shoulder from which protruded several shirts.

"Widow Rasmussen, some laundry if you please." He caught sight of Aaron. "What the hell are you doing here, Mew, ain't you working?"

"The smith sent me over with some logs for the widow, Serjeant," he lied.

The Serjeant looked around the room suspiciously, saw the logs and then said, "Then there is nothing to detain you. Off you go."

He stepped back to let Aaron pass and then went into the room with his sack of clothes.

Soon after returning to the forge, Aaron saw the Serjeant making his way towards the barn which was now nearing completion. Addressing the smith, he said, "I was wondering, sir, now with the building next to being finished, will I continue to work here?"

"Do you want to?"

"Indeed I do, sir."

"We have a lot of work coming up with the shoeing of all the draught horses before the spring campaign gets started. I will speak to Serjeant Granville."

When Aaron was on his way back to the longhouse he happened upon Rev outside of the barn which was to be the new barracks.

"Hello, Mewie, I've been looking for you. I understand you are to shortly move in with the rest of us in the new barracks."

"Yes, Rev. The day after tomorrow, on Monday."

"Tell me, the savage who resides in your current quarters, does he speak English?"

"What, George, you mean? Yes, he does, but he ain't got much to say for himself. He sleeps next to me, but in all the time I have been in the longhouse I have never seen him asleep. He always seems to be listening and alert."

"Have you not asked him about the ways of the native people?"

"Not really. We asked him about the carving on the outside of the house, over the door. But not much else."

"What carving is that?"

"It's a sea creature called a turtle."

"Ah, this is most interesting. I have seen references to such creatures in my study of these people. I have my rations with me. May I join you for tea meal this evening? Since you know George, perhaps you could introduce me."

And so it was that Rev brought his food ration to the longhouse, and after the meal, together with Aaron, sought to talk with George. At first the Indian was not forthcoming, but when he realised that the questioner was showing a genuine interest in his culture, rather than adopting the generally scoffing attitude of the soldiers who often taunted him about his customs, he beckoned to his sleeping bench and the two soldiers joined him there, sitting next to him. Aaron listened intently while Rev asked a number of questions.

Eventually, Rev seemed to have found out what he wanted to know. He and Aaron walked over to the other men who were sitting near the fire, chatting and puffing on their pipes.

"Gentlemen, thank you for your hospitality. The evening has been most enlightening though the heathen beliefs of the savages do increasingly concern me."

"What did you find out from George?" asked Graham.

"Well, George is Iroquois as you probably already knew, but the tribe is really called the Haudenosaunee."

"Did he tell you what it means?" asked Graham.

Aaron looked across at Rev, who said, "You tell them, Mewie."

"It means 'the people of the longhouse', and the name Iroquois was given to them by their enemies – it means rattlesnake."

Aaron held the floor and said, "We now know why they have the turtle carving."

"Yes, indeed we do, and therein lay the nub of the heathen contradiction of our Christian beliefs."

"How do you mean, Rev?" asked Jamie.

"The Iroquois believe that the world was created by the 'Sky Woman'. She fell to earth from the sky, but there was no land, only water. A bird tried to stop her falling, but could not, so it called to all the creatures of the deep to find some firm ground for the Sky Woman to fall on. The fish and the ducks collected soil from under the sea and heaped it onto the turtle's back. Eventually, all the animals joined in and made a huge land, and it was all carried on the back of the turtle. This creature became the most venerated of all animals to these pagans."

There was a long silence as the listeners tried to comprehend what had been said and then Bell asked, "So they don't believe in Adam and Eve?"

"No, indeed they do not. And in their wayward way they use the turtle to symbolise their deity. George tells me that the turtle has thirteen plates on its shell and these represent the thirteen moons in one year. Aaron, I suggest that you count the plates on the carving in daylight tomorrow, to see if he is correct."

Rev put on his greatcoat and bade his listeners goodnight.

Chapter 17

The next day, Sunday, the men spent the early part of the morning clearing snow from the area used as a parade square before the service. Afterwards, Aaron returned to the longhouse to collect the blanket. He then made his way to the farmhouse after picking up a saw and an axe from the forge.

"Good day, Widow Rasmussen, I have come to cut the wood for you. Here is my blanket."

"Good day, Aaron. Isaac, say hello to the Private."

The boy shyly greeted the visitor.

"Come in and close the door. Let's have a look at the blanket. Um…it's a good one, quite heavy."

"It cost me nigh on a week's pay."

"I'm sure it did. Now let's get you measured. Stand over here."

As she measured his shoulder width and the length of his arms, Aaron became acutely aware that he had not been this close to a woman since that fateful day in Salisbury which had led to his current situation; apart from when he sat next to the girl, Alice. His blood began to race and he felt excitement as she ran her tape along his arm and around his chest. Had he recognised it, she too was affected. This was the first close encounter she had had with a man for over a year and she was consciously taking more time over the measurements than she needed to.

She walked round in front of him, looked up into his blue eyes and said softly, "That'll do for now."

He looked down at her, conscious that the boy was with them, and in a way grateful for it. Somewhat breathlessly, he said, "I can whittle the pegs to button up the coat."

"If you get them ready in time, bring them to me this evening."

"That I will. Now come, Isaac, put your coat on, we have work to do."

Before dusk, the soldier and the boy stood before a neat stack of fire logs which were lined up along the side of the farmhouse. Having said his farewells, he returned to the longhouse.

"Where you been, Mewie? The Serjeant has been looking for you. Ting is sick and the sentry duty roster has been changed. You got from eight to midnight."

Aaron was crestfallen. He had already begun to feel a tingling excitement about the prospect of his evening assignation.

"Damn, I had other plans. You sure about it, Clipper?"

"That I am – I'm on duty with you. The Serjeant has given us permission to light a brazier to keep warm."

"And this is our last night here. Why did it have to happen now?"

"What's these 'other plans', Mewie? You really are shook up, ain't you."

"'Tis of no importance," said Aaron, trying to disguise his real feelings.

"And you had best get your kit cleaned and in order – there will be an inspection tomorrow morning before we move out to the barracks."

Later, the two men went on duty and spent four hours by the side of their fire. Aaron was angry and disappointed, completely oblivious to the sheer beauty of the landscape with a three-quarter moon shining over the pristine snow of the meadow leading down to the frozen St Lawrence. His firelock propped up by his side, he carefully chipped and cut away at the birch branch he had taken from the longhouse wood store and by midnight he had made five pegs.

The whole of the next day the company was involved with the move into the new billet, installing and moving furniture and arranging the sleeping quarters. It was first on Tuesday that he started again at the forge. As he worked, he frequently glanced towards the house and after the noon meal, he was delighted to see Isaac making his way towards the smithy.

"Ma told me to say thank you for the chocolate and that she needs you to try on the coat this evening."

The boy's high-pitched voice and childish lack of discretion caught the attention of the smith and the other men working in the forge.

"What's this, Mewie? You makin' merry with the rebel widow?" said one of them.

"Shut up, I just helped her get some firewood and she is making a blanket coat for me."

Aaron hoped that his blushes would be mistaken for the redness occasioned by his proximity to the hearth. However, later when the widow came to collect her son there was no disguising the discomfort the young blacksmith felt as all eyes were upon him to gauge his reaction to her presence. She gave nothing away and said nothing to Aaron; the message had been delivered and so her only words were to thank Jacob Francis for allowing her son to be at the forge.

Aaron was detailed to do a number of chores after the tea meal and it had been dark for some time before he slipped away from the barracks, the pegs deposited in one of his greatcoat pockets. The temperature was well below freezing and there was a crust on the top of the snow which made a loud crunching sound as his boots walked over it. It was this noise which alerted the widow to the approach of the visitor and as Aaron climbed the steps to the door, it opened before him and was quickly pushed closed after he had walked through it.

In the candlelight the widow's night shift looked very white, almost ghostlike.

"Sorry, missus, I didn't know that you was a bed," Aaron mumbled as he turned to make for the door, but she caught his arm.

"Shh, Isaac is asleep in the other room. You got the pegs?"

Aaron swallowed hard and reached for his pocket, "Well, yes, um…here they be."

He held out his right hand. She took it, removed the pegs with her other hand and placed his right hand on her breast. The noise in Aaron's ear which had been silent for weeks began to roar. She unbuttoned his greatcoat and jacket and pulled him towards the cot.

"Uh, but the coat."

"We can look at the coat later. Come, come keep me warm."

It was much later when Aaron eventually tried on the blanket coat and he was pleased when she told him that he would need to try it on again the next night, after she had sewn the panels together. Within a day or so, the blanket coat was no longer needed as an excuse for the Private's nocturnal visits to the farm.

Aaron became more and more besotted with the widow woman and his secret became common knowledge with the other men. But the fact of the matter was that his affair was no sensation, as many of the company had female companionships; some with wives, some with the widows of dead soldiers and others with American camp followers who had chosen to follow the army back into Canada to avoid reprisals for supporting the royal cause in their homeland. Many of the women had moved into the barracks.

Despite the days being taken with his labours in the forge and his evenings being spent in the company of Sarah, Aaron had found time to record some of his impressions of the winter. The previous week, the New Year had been ushered in – seventeen-seventy-seven. Ominously, it had already been named the year of the gibbet, for the sevens looked like a row of gibbets: 1777. The weather, though exceptionally harsh, provided the men with many new and often exciting experiences. Over several weeks Aaron had composed the letter he hoped to send to his parents when the ice broke and ships once more provided communication with England.

Dear Mother and Father,

I hope that this letter finds you well. I am billeted for the winter in a village called Saint Nicholas in Canada. The weather here is most exceptionally cold. But do not fear for my health, we have gloves, coats and caps to protect us. Nevertheless, it is necessary to be prudent. One of my friends got frostbite and his fingers and toes went black. When he died we could not bury him as the ground was frozen hard to many feet deep. His frozen corpse waits in a shed near the church for the spring.

Here we see the most remarkable things what you could never imagine. We store our meat in the ice and when we come to cook it we pour water over to recover it from the ice. And there is much of the previous for the whole river is frozen to such a depth that horses and carts can traverse over the water. Also some officers have carrioling races. For some time I lived in a savages' longhouse which was more comfortable than might be imagined. Now I live in the barracks. And the hares turn white in the winter. Not long ago I met a fine Dutch lady and we are stepping out together. She is very kind and cooks

exceedingly well. I am sure you would like her. In the spring we will
continue our campaign against the rebellious Americans.
I pray nightly that you have forgiven my great transgression.

Your humble and loving son,
Aaron Mew
St Nicholas
January 1777

The winter seemed interminable and only the increasing daylight
gave indication that at some time in the future the cold season
would give way to a warmer one.

It was seven-thirty in the morning; light was just discernible in
the east for it was now late March and dawn was getting earlier each
day. Aaron had been on duty as sentry on the south perimeter of the
camp since two in the morning. Frost had formed on his blanket
coat, making the white woollen garment inflexible and shell-like.
A short while ago it had started to snow.

A few days ago, it had suddenly got warmer and a thaw had
set in. Everyone had thought that winter was over, but the relief
was short lived and winter had returned with a vengeance. Aaron's
hands were so cold, despite his fur mittens, that he was unable to
hold the barrel of his firelock and instead had it propped up beside
him. He had loaded it when he came on duty and had put pig's
grease round the frizzen to keep the damp out of the pan. His relief
was due before first light so he was not anxious when he heard
footsteps coming towards him. The advancing feet were crunching
on the ice-covered slush and then squelching as they pierced the
crusty covering and became immersed in the wet snow underneath.
He grabbed his firelock and shouted, "Halt, who goes there?"

"It's me, Mewie, Rev."

"Advance, Private, and give the parole."

"Petersfield!"

"Pass on, Private, all is well."

Then he whispered, "I didn't expect them to send you as my
relief, Rev."

"Mewie, they haven't. I have a mission from the Lord. The poor
misguided savages must be taught the ways of God and the true

story of the creation. And have you seen the Wendat savages' finger rings? They wear the rings given to them by Jesuits – French Jesuits who would win their souls. Each Catholic ring has the insignia IHS, with a cross over the H. These noble savages, these spiritual innocents are being enslaved into popery. They must be saved and shown the true path to Godliness."

"Shh, Rev. Struth, what do you mean?"

"It does not become you, Mewie, to ask God's truth in this situation. I mean that I am sent here to show the savages the right way. The way of the Protestant Church. I implore you to let me pass and to go to do the work I must to save souls. Give me but five minutes to reach the horse lines, where my footsteps in the snow will be unidentifiable with those of the hundreds of others who have walked there. Count to sixty, five times, and then fire your firelock. Thus you will be held to no blame when you report that an unidentified figure passed you in the dark."

"But, Rev, you will be shot for desertion. Get back to the camp."

"Fear not for me, I am about God's work."

Thus saying, the older man continued to crunch the snow crust away from the camp. Aaron was shocked by the occurrence and only after a while remembered to start counting. Before he had reached the fifth sequence of sixties, he heard other footsteps coming towards him. As they grew very close he realised that he must act quickly, or the plot would be discovered. He shouted, "Halt, who goes there," raised his firelock and discharged it into the air.

"Struth, Mewie, what's about?" shouted the approaching Private Graham.

"I don't know, a deserter I think, he ran past me in the dark going south."

It was not many minutes before the guard had been called out together with some Indian scouts. As the day got lighter, the Native Americans started to follow the tracks. But the search was hindered by the snowfall – a precipitation which quickly became heavier and heavier, laying a white blanket on the footsteps of the fugitive soldier. At muster it was quickly established who the deserter was, and those searching were told that there would be a payment for capture of the veteran soldier. Hopes of catching him, however, were dampened when Indians returned reporting that one of the horses had been stolen and because of the snowfall they were unable to trace the direction the rider had taken.

"Private Mew, you were on duty as sentry when the deserter made his escape. What do you have to say?"

The Captain was seated in his hut flanked by a Lieutenant. Serjeant Granville stood to one side glowering at the Private standing to attention. He longed to put his hand to his ear to try to get some relief, but knew that it would not go well for him if he moved. He tried to concentrate on responding to the question.

"Sir, I heard footsteps. My task was to be attentive to dangers from outside of the camp and thus, I assumed that the footsteps behind me were of my relief."

There was a silence as the two senior officers considered the logic in the Private's reply.

"Private Mew, a sentry's duty is to challenge any person approaching from whatever direction."

"Yes, sir, and I did call the challenge."

"And what was the parole?"

"Petersfield, sir."

"Did you recognise the voice?"

Aaron hesitated. He knew that he would have to answer yes, but knew equally well that such a reply could damn him. He lifted his left hand to his ear.

"Stand to attention, Private Mew!" growled the Serjeant.

"Well, did you?" asked the Captain.

"I thought that I did, sir. But I was not sure."

"You know the sentence for abetting a deserter?"

"Yes, sir, but I didn't. I fired at him, or at least towards where I heard the voice."

"Did you indeed," said the Captain in a disbelieving fashion. "Serjeant, I believe that this man has a good service record."

"Yes, sir, apart from an occurrence of brawling for which he went to the halberds."

"Private, you are to lose a week's pay and to do double sentry duty. Perhaps you will learn to be more vigilant in future."

"Yes, sir, thank you, sir."

Aaron saluted, turned, and followed by Serjeant Granville, marched out of the hut.

"Get back to the snow clearing detail, Mew."

Aaron carefully made his way over to the parade square, trying not to slip on the icy surface. He picked up a spade and joined his friends at their work.

Graham looked up and said quietly, "How did it go, Mewie?"

"Alright, I suppose. Cost me a week's pay."

Jamie overheard what he said and came over to stand very close by him.

"Did Rev tell you anything?"

"Yes, he talked about saving the souls of the Wendats."

"I thought as much. He did the same thing when we were on Dominica – that time it was African slaves."

"What do you think he will do, Jamie?"

"Oh, he will do as he says, or he will try to. But the Wendat are no friends of the British. They still have strong sympathies with the French."

"Will he be in danger?"

"Of course. If he is lucky, the chief will have him brought back here alive, to get a reward. Otherwise, they may just bring his scalp – they get paid anyway."

"Oh God, I should have stopped him."

As he worked, he thought about Rev. Their relationship was strange – he the son of a farmhand, Rev a very clever and well educated man who clearly had had a high social standing. Yet the older man had mentored him, taught him to read and write, and seemed to have great regard for his welfare and his company. He was like a father figure or an elder brother, but though he was obviously very religious, he had never tried to press his spiritual views on him. Although the young soldier was confused about their relationship he realised that as well as the respect and liking he had for him he had much to be grateful to the deserter for. He blamed himself for not being more determined in stopping Rev deserting; he was concerned for the older man's welfare and it worried him greatly.

A week later, the men working at the forge became aware of a commotion near the parade square. They put their tools down and went to see what was happening. A large group of Indian warriors had arrived in the village. Most of the visitors had painted faces. Unlike the Iroquois scouts, they wore coloured ribbons and turkey feathers in the patch of long hair at the back of their otherwise bald heads. The man leading the procession had a crown headdress with bundles of turkey feathers and several eagle feathers at the front. They were armed with short flintlocks and axes. Behind the leader came two warriors roughly steering Rev with bound hands, between them. He was wearing a tattered army greatcoat and his head had been shaved so that just a bunch of hair on the back of his head remained.

The arrival of the warriors had quickly got the attention of the officers, and the Lieutenant, quickly followed by the Captain who was hastily buckling on his sword, came out to greet them. He shook hands with the chief who loudly greeted the Captain in French. Clearly, the officer was unable to respond in the same language even if he had understood the greeting. He looked round at the Lieutenant who shook his head. Serjeant Granville marched across the square past the warriors, attracted the officer's attention, saluted and leant forward to speak to the Lieutenant. The two men scanned the crowd of soldiers, who had stopped their various tasks, and then the Serjeant marched across to where Corporal Cutler was standing and said, "Corporal Cutler, the Lieutenant would like a word."

The two men marched back to the Lieutenant. After a consultation, Jamie quietly addressed the Indian chief in French and then turned and translated for the Captain, who then instructed the Corporal about what he wanted to reply. And thus the conversation continued until they reached a point where the chief turned to the two warriors holding Rev and gave an instruction which was obviously that they should release the Private into the custody of the army.

"Alright you men, back to work," instructed Serjeant Granville. The command was echoed by the other non-commissioned officers. The various groups of soldiers broke up and they returned to their tasks. Meanwhile the conversation with the Indians continued, although clearly some agreement with regard to their reward had been reached.

Later, in the barracks, Corporal Cutler was the centre of attention as he was questioned about what had transpired between the Captain and the Indian leader.

"I can't tell you the details, the Captain would not approve of me breaking his trust. But I can tell you that the savages told him that if this man comes to their camp again with his ranting and raving, they will bring his scalp next time."

"But what about the price? What did they want?" asked Graham.

"I can't tell you the details, but it included a cask of rum."

"There is bound to be a full court martial," said Aaron.

Those who knew and respected the recalcitrant Private quietly contemplated the fact that he might be shot for desertion.

The following day, Aaron was summoned to the officers' headquarters. Granville had come to get him at the forge.

"Put your coat on, lad, and look smart. The Lieutenant wants to speak to you. Remember to stand alert and to salute."

The Serjeant marched the soldier to the building and knocked on the door. It was opened and the two of them entered. The Lieutenant was seated at a desk.

"Be easy. Now, Private Mew, you are to be a prosecution witness at the court martial of Private Fabian Villiers."

Aaron had only heard Rev called by his real name on one or two occasions and was at first confused. His ear started bothering him and he was reminded once again that the man who had caused this discomfort was standing next to him.

"The court martial will be held in Quebec City as soon as possible. I will be attending the trial and will travel with you and the prisoner, together with a Corporal and a guard. The river is still well frozen. We will walk with snowshoes along the river and then approach the city through the Plains of Abraham where it is not too steep. It will be impossible to get up the hills from the harbour as the tracks are covered in ice. Do you understand? Any questions?"

Aaron was shocked by the prospect of the trial and hesitatingly asked, "But what shall I say, sir?"

"You just have to answer the Judge Advocate General's questions truthfully."

"What is the distance to Quebec, sir?"

"It's just five leagues – only a day's journey. We leave at first light tomorrow. Oh, and Serjeant, can you see that Private Mew's appearance does credit to our regiment."

"Yes, sir."

The two men saluted the Lieutenant and marched out of the building.

The next few days were filled with trauma for Aaron. Uppermost in his mind was the conflict he felt at having to testify against his mentor, but there was also the terrible drama of being called to face a panel of high ranking officers. Added to this was the discomfort of the day's march in the company of the Lieutenant, but then too there was the excitement of visiting the city of Quebec. As regards the latter, although the stay in Quebec lasted ten days while the arrangements were made, he saw very little of the city as he was quartered in the barracks at the castle and spent most of his time there. When the trial was over, he had wanted to speak to Rev and be present while the sentence was administered, but he and the Corporal were sent straight back to Saint Nicholas. The Lieutenant had been invited to stay in the officers' quarters at the castle while waiting to watch the sentence being carried out and to await delivery of the transcript of the court martial, which he would take back to the Captain.

Chapter 18

On his return from Quebec, as they walked up the track from the river to the village, Aaron knew that his friends would be waiting to quiz him and Corporal Reid about the court martial and whether they knew the verdict of the court. However, in the fading daylight he decided to go straight to the farmhouse to surprise Sarah. He left the Corporal to give such news as they had to the others and continued past the barn. As he walked round the corner of the forge, he saw that someone else was going in the same direction and he immediately recognised that the figure in front of him was Serjeant Granville. Aaron slowed down and tarried by the forge to watch the man in front. He walked up the steps to the house and without knocking, went straight in.

The action of the Serjeant shocked the watcher. Surely, he thought, if he was collecting his laundry, he would knock on the door.

Aaron stood by the forge waiting for Granville to come out. He waited for a long time but the man had not reappeared when the drummers called the time for the tea meal. He went into the forge, propped up his firelock and took off his knapsack. The hearth was still warm, though the workers had finished for the day. Aaron warmed himself as he waited in the cover of the forge, from whence he could see the house. By the time the door of the farmhouse opened, the hearth was stone cold and Aaron, who had had a long journey and no tea meal, was tired and hungry. He moved further into the forge to hide more securely while he watched the Serjeant leave. To his horror he saw Granville embrace Sarah, who was dressed in her white night shift. The noise in the Private's ear was almost intolerable; she had been unfaithful to him and with the man who had been the author of his damnation. Despite his shock he remained absolutely still as the Serjeant walked past the forge on his way to his billet.

As soon as the officer had walked far enough to be out of sight, Aaron left his knapsack and bounded towards the house. He banged on the door and waited for it to be opened. As soon as Sarah stood in front of him he shouted, "What was the Serjeant doing here?"

"Shh, Isaac is asleep," said the surprised widow.

Aaron made to go into the building, but she pushed him back.

"Why can't I come in?"

"It would not be respectable, for I am to marry Serjeant Granville when he returns from the campaign."

Aaron was stunned and paused a moment before he said lamely, "But he's an old man!"

"No, he isn't. It mattered not to you that you were with a woman ten years older than yourself. Well, he is just ten years older than me."

"But I love you. Don't you love me?"

"Granville can offer me much more than you can. He has money and good pay, and he brings me things like food and cloth for sewing."

"But I thought we had an understanding. Why did you change your mind about me?"

"You will understand one day and you will thank me when you find a girl your own age."

Aaron tried to force his way into the house again.

"If you don't go I will tell the Serjeant that you were violent to me. It would be the worse for you."

The Private began to realise the impossibility of his situation. He dare not risk being accused of assaulting a civilian and certainly not the future Mrs Granville. He took one step down backwards, his mind trying to comprehend what had happened. He recognised that he had the same feeling in the pit of his stomach as he had had in Salisbury the moment when he discovered that his neck pouch had been stolen. And just like then, he was completely helpless, unable to comprehend the disaster. For the second time in his life he had been betrayed. He was hurt, deeply hurt, but also angry. He was infatuated with a woman who now rejected him in favour of a man who could provide things which he could not – a man he despised. He took the second and last step down to the ground and stood with his hand pressed on his left ear looking at the now closed door, though in the dark he could only see its outline from the light of the candle within illuminating the cracks around the door frame. Then he saw through the window that the room was plunged into darkness and he knew that the candle inside the house had been blown out. He remained still, cherishing the memory of the hours he had spent inside. His hurt and anger changed gradually to sadness. He turned and went to the forge to collect his things before going to the barn to face his friends.

"Hello, Mewie," said Graham, "the Corporal tells us that you have returned without news of Rev's fate."

"Yes, after we had given our speech we were ordered to return to Saint Nicholas. The members were deliberating when we left."

"What was it like?" asked Bell.

"I was right nervous, there were nine officers and our Lieutenant as well."

"You don't sound too happy to be back."

"If truth be told, Clipper, I decided that I should forget about Widow Rasmussen and find a girl of my age."

There was a pause as his friends looked at each other. Brooks broke the silence.

"That's a good thing, Mewie, 'cause we seen Grabber makin' his way to the farm on several occasions while you've been away."

Aaron feigned surprise. "Well, I ain't going to compete with the likes of him."

The comfort of being with his friends brought Aaron some solace, but he felt very uneasy about not telling them the real truth of the matter. Their continued questioning about his experiences in Quebec and on the journey served to force him to put the issue of his relationship with Sarah to the back of his mind. However, after lights out his thoughts quickly returned to his rejection by the woman he loved and the part played by the man who was responsible for the torment of the noise in his head and for him being in the army at all. But then his reasoning went round in circles, for if Granville had not tricked him into uniform, he would never have met Sarah. Suddenly, he realised that he had forgotten about the plight of Rev and felt very guilty for doing so. He might have been shot by now and if so, it was mainly because of the evidence which he, as a witness, had given.

Two days later Lieutenant Stephens arrived back at the village. He went straight to the Captain's quarters and after a few social formalities he said, "Sir, I have the transcript of the court martial for you."

"Well, open it and read it to me then, if you please."

Captain Trowbridge broke the seal, unfolded the document and proceeded to read: "*At a General Court Martial held at La Citadelle Fortress in Quebec City the 2nd April 1777 under a warrant of His Excellency General Carleton dated at the Governor's Residence, Quebec City. Major George Grant, Adv. General presiding. Members: Capt. Richard Frith 9th Reg...*"

"Yes, yes, Lieutenant. Get to the point, skip the members."

"*The Court being duly sworn adjourned until twelve o'clock. The Court being met pursuant to adjournment proceeded to the Trial of Fabian Villiers Private soldier of the 62nd Regiment for desertion. The prisoner being asked if he is guilty or not guilty of the crime laid to his charge, answers he is not guilty.*"

The Lieutenant then started to summarise the court proceedings. "The first witness was Corporal James Reid – he stated that the prisoner joined the 62nd in 1765. When questioned about the prisoner's army record, he mentioned that Villiers had gone absent once before when the regiment was stationed on Dominica. The second witness was Private Mew – he told them the same story he told us. Finally, the prisoner was questioned."

"What did he have to say for himself?"

"I'll read what the transcript says: *Fabian Villiers, Private soldier in the 62nd Regiment being duly sworn deposes that he was overcome with zeal to save the Wendat savages from popery and paganism and to this end with the Blessing of the Almighty, he left the camp to preach to the savages.*

"*Q. Did you not realise that your first loyalty is to the Army?*

"*A. Like any Christian soldier one must deport oneself like Janus, looking in two directions – to our Heavenly Father and to our commanding officer – and serve both loyally. We were not in action and I had time on my hands to heed the call of my Maker.*

"*Q. Did you not consider that your absence would be punished?*

"*A. Any penalty decided by the court will be of no consequence to me, it will be my own Private Calvary. The Court having maturely considered the evidence brought in support of this charge, with what the prisoner has said in his defence, is of the opinion that he is guilty of desertion in breach of the first Section of the 6th Article of War. The Court does therefore sentence the prisoner Fabian Villiers to receive a Corporal Punishment of one thousand lashes, at such time and place as his Excellency the General Carleton shall appoint.*

"*George Grant. Major to 21st Regiment.*"

"Hell's teeth, Lieutenant, the man is his own worst enemy. His religious fervour is laudable, but he is not in the army to be a missionary."

"I am afraid that he came over as petulant at the trial, sir. It was almost as if he wanted to be punished as a martyr."

"Well, if that was the case, he got his wish then. Do you think that he will survive the cat?"

"Oh, I don't doubt that, sir. He is very tough, and if I may say so, a brave and resilient soldier."

"I suppose they will keep him in the regimental hospital until he is ready for duty again. Now, we are advised by the locals that the ice on the river will break up in two weeks or so. Before it does, we need more horses brought over while they can walk on the ice. It will be much more difficult later to transport them by boat. I know that the General has been trying to find hundreds more beasts to fulfil the predicted requirement to transport our ordinance and supplies once we start moving. Please get an estimate of how many we need."

"Yes, sir."

"Oh and Lieutenant, please let me know when Villiers returns to us."

"I will, sir."

But the recalcitrant soldier's return to Saint Nicholas was delayed, for although the surgeon had declared the cuts on his back sufficiently healed for him to resume service, he was unable to cross the river. On 12th April, the loud sounds of the cracking of the ice had been heard from the village. Before long there was open water in the middle of the river where the current was strengthened by the snow melt. Over the next few days the soldiers took every opportunity to watch the violence of nature as ice floes passed the village, colliding with each other in their haste to reach the Atlantic. And from that direction, *HBMS Apollo* was making her way westwards from England. On board was the newly promoted Burgoyne. The King had been impressed by a paper written by him proposing strategy for crushing the rebellion in New England, and had appointed him to take command of the army in Canada, thus usurping General Carleton.

Other ships arrived before the *Apollo* and with them they carried the news of the change of command and even details of the General's campaign strategy.

Eventually, at the end of April, Rev managed to cross the river to rejoin the regiment. As his friends gathered around to welcome him he picked Aaron out from the crowd and rushed over to him. He gave him an embrace and with his arm around Aaron's shoulder, turned round to the assembly and shouted, "This man, my friends, testified against me!"

There was silence in the crowd. "But he did so with integrity, and I want all to know that I bear no grudge. Beware, however, that if you intend to commit any felony, do not let honest Mewie witness you or you may hang."

There was a roar of laughter as Rev continued, "Gentlemen, I bear tidings of great import regarding our crusade against the perfidious rebels."

"Please explain it simply, Rev," said Bell.

"Well, the simple fact is, my friend, that we have a new commander. General Burgoyne will have sole command of the army and as you can guess, General Carleton, whose frugal hospitality I have recently enjoyed, is not best pleased."

"Why is this?" asked Corporal Cutler.

"Only His Majesty the King will know, but there are rumours that our blessed monarch was not impressed that we fought our way to the gates of Ticonderoga, but did not open them."

"So what is now intended for us?"

"That, dear Jamie, is what I am about to impart, and it is no secret, for every vagabond in Quebec City seems to have heard. General Burgoyne proposes to split the rebellious New England colony from the less fractious southern colonies by having all the forts from Canada to New York occupied by our forces."

"But why?" asked Bell.

"Ting, the simple fact is that the General has decided that if the rebels from different colonies are denied the possibility to unite, the troublesome New Englander rebels will be more easily crushed and the whole rebellion will wither on the vine."

"Are we to fight all the way to New York?"

"Such a plan would be too ambitious, Mewie. What the General has proposed is that we should repeat our progress of last year, crossing Lake Champlain to Crown Point and then take Ticonderoga before continuing to the town of Albany. However, a small part of our force, mainly Germans and savages, will go a different route down the St Lawrence to the Mohawk River, subduing the resistance of the rebels in that region, and meet up with us in Albany."

"And after Albany?" asked Bell.

"There we will link up with General Howe's army, currently occupying New York, which will have progressed up the Hudson River occupying all the forts on the way."

"And then the war will be over and we return home?"

"If only we could be sure of that, dear Mewie, but perhaps so."

On 8th May, the *Apollo* arrived at Quebec and shortly after the General gave the order for the whole army to be mobilised and to leave their various quarters for the campaign to begin. The General had 7300 men of which 3700 were British. The remainder were mainly German mercenaries from Brunswick, with a small corps of French Canadian militia. In addition there were two thousand women and several hundred children.

As they began their march, Aaron found himself looking round several times at the old farmhouse to see if he could catch a glimpse of Sarah. The weeks that had passed since that fateful evening had served to dampen his ardour, but time had not yet extinguished it. The infectious enthusiasm of his comrades about the campaign ahead of them served to subdue any sadness he felt.

Chapter 19

As more and more troops arrived at St Johns having marched from their winter quarters, many comrades who had not seen each other since the cold, wet days at Crown Point last autumn were reunited and enthusiastically related tales of their experiences of the winter in Quebec province. In the harbour a large fleet of many different types of craft had been gathered to transport the army south across the great Lake Champlain.

The 62nd Light Company was camped on the outskirts of the small village and the men were anxiously awaiting their orders. At last, the drum beat calling orderly non-commissioned officers was heard. The chain of command was long. When the General issued an order it was always in writing. First, the orders were copied by the Adjutant General and then dictated to the Brigade Majors, who wrote them out and distributed them to the brigade's Adjutants or Majors. They then read the orders to the Colonels and other officers before dictating them the duty Serjeants of the different companies for them to write out in their orderly books. Finally, the orders were passed to the men by the Serjeants. With the orders came the parole or password for the day and the reply or countersign. Most often at this time the parole was the name of a saint and the countersign a place name.

When Serjeant Ryan returned from the briefing with his orderly book, he assembled the other Serjeants and the Corporals to pass on the General's orders. Finally, the men got the news they had been waiting for.

"We strike camp as soon as the ships are loaded. You lucky bastards are going for a sail on the new ship, the *Royal George*," shouted Granville to the assembled men. The ship he referred to was a 32-gun schooner which had been built during the winter at St Johns.

The Serjeant continued, "We are to be carried in the van of the convoy sailing south to Crown Point."

It was three days before all the artillery and wagons had been loaded and the fleet were ready to sail. There had been numerous problems with the transporting of cannon and supplies. The army had far too few horses and many of the carts which had been built hastily during the winter using unseasoned wood were unreliable. This situation was made worse because of the overloading of ammunition carts, often by officers trying to transport personal baggage in them. Despite these difficulties and material shortcomings, it was a confident army which embarked in the middle of June. The long convoy of vessels of every description left the harbour and with a favourable wind headed south. The fleet was led by a large number of Indian canoes transporting the five hundred Native Americans; it was followed by the two largest ships, the *Royal George* and the *Inflexible*, and then a long line of other craft making the whole nautical assembly a spectacular sight and a formidable one to the enemy.

The ships stopped at various places on their way down the waterway disembarking various units.

At a strategically important farm near to Willsboro on 12th June, four companies of light infantry made an encampment to prevent the enemy using the road which led to Canada. They were joined on the 16th by the other six companies. Finally, on June 25th, most of the army had arrived at Crown Point. The advance had not been bloodless. There was much skirmishing between the two sides, in particular when scouting parties went out ahead of the main army; frequently the Indian scouts returned to the encampment with the scalps of American soldiers.

The most effective unit for gathering intelligence about the enemy was led by Captain Alexander Fraser. He was Superintendent of Indians and had a specialised knowledge and experience of fighting with irregular troops in hostile terrain. Many of his men were expert marksmen and were chosen for this and their physical abilities. On 22nd June, Captain Fraser took three hundred Indians, two companies of Canadians and twenty men of the light infantry on a week-long scout to gain intelligence about the Ticonderoga defences. The information he gleaned spurred on the advance and he and his marksmen led the skirmishing which took part of the army within cannon range of the great fort.

"See, the two big ships are now positioned in the waterway," said Aaron as he crept out of the tent at first light. He, like the rest of the company, had been awakened by the reveille drum.

"They must be just outside cannon shot from the fort," answered Bell.

The company had arrived just after dusk and were now encamped at an area called Three Mile Point.

"Jesse, just look at the fort, Mewie. How in God's name do we take that?" said Graham.

"The two rebel deserters who came in yesterday said there were three thousand troops up there commanded by General St Clare, just waiting for us," added Bell.

"The Serjeant said it was well defended, but it would be possible to take it from the land side."

"That's what the British said in the French and Indian War, Aaron, and look what happened," interjected Corporal Cutler.

"What happened?" asked Aaron.

"The French General Montcalm laid a terrible trap, an abbitas for our men in the narrow strip of land leading to the fort. It was like a slaughterhouse for our troops. Four thousand French beat off sixteen thousand British."

"We shall have to await the order to see how we are to go about it."

"I think that we will first try to take the fort on the opposite side of the waterway, Fort Independence. You can't see it from here, but it is smaller, although it too is on a hill. The Germans are moving towards it."

There was silence while they contemplated the Corporal's remarks. They were joined by more of their comrades, all looking at the massive Ticonderoga fortification which because of the dark, they had not seen last night. The fort was situated on a high promontory where the waterway narrowed and turned a bend before continuing south. The building was surrounded by thick woods which rose up on the steep slopes to the walls. Had they been able to see the fort from above they would have seen that the French builders had constructed it like a four-pointed star. Each of the points of the star was bristling with cannon and thus able to reach an attacker from any direction.

"What's that they are doing in front of the ships?" asked Bell.

"I think the sailors are laying out a boom to prevent the enemy sending fireships to attack the schooners," said the Corporal.

"Looking at the next challenge for us are you?" The familiar voice was of Serjeant Granville. "Well, we ain't goin' to take it by standing and talking are we? Get a bloody move on – we got to cut a road through these woods to get our artillery up."

While spending several hours felling trees the men could hear the sound of cannon and firelock fire from both sides of the waterway. When they returned to their encampment they found a number of wounded men of the 53rd Regiment on stretchers, who were waiting to be taken behind the lines to the hospital.

"We cleared the hill behind the fort – Mount Hope – and now General Fraser is pushing on up Sugar Loaf Hill," said one of the stretcher bearers.

"Where's that?" asked Corporal Cutler.

"It's a damned great mountain south of the fort. It is so impossibly steep that the enemy have not defended it – they never thought anyone could get up there. But Fraser is going to try to drag twelve-pounder cannon to the top of it."

"How's he going to do that?"

"The men are pushing and he's got cows pulling. The thing is, it is much higher than the fort. If he gets cannon up there, they will be able to shoot straight down on the enemy. And mark my words, the enemy will not be able to elevate their cannon high enough to shoot back."

He bent down and grabbed the stretcher as the man on the other end did the same at the other end.

"You'd better hurry to the hospital with that one," said Bell.

"He ain't got much of a chance. His leg is smashed, but we'll try anyway."

The men could not but find themselves surveying the bloody mess that had been the unconscious man's right leg and not many were yet so inured to seeing wounded soldiers that they were unaffected.

At noon of Friday, 4th July, the 53rd Regiment succeeded in

placing cannon on top of Sugar Loaf Hill. On the following day, the American commander, General St Clare, decided that because of this, his position was untenable. He ordered the wooden buildings in the fort to be burned and after dark hastily evacuated all his troops out of the fort and across the waterway past Fort Independence, to march south to Fort Anne. On the morning of the sixth, the British flag was raised on the ramparts of the fort.

It was well before dawn on that Sunday when Aaron, who was on sentry duty, heard someone coming towards him.

"Halt, who goes there?"

"Messenger for Captain Hawker."

"Advance messenger and give the parole."

"Falmouth."

"Pass on messenger, all is well."

"Can you direct me to the Captain's tent, Private?"

"Yes, sir, it is the second bell tent behind me."

The effect of the message was almost immediate. Within a short time the drummer was beating reveille and in the first faint light of dawn soldiers were scurrying around having been ordered to prepare to march as soon as possible.

"What's going on, Corporal?" asked Graham.

"We are to march to catch up with General Fraser. He has given chase to the retreating Americans who have crossed to the New Hampshire Grants."

"What about the tents?"

"We leave them for others to strike for us."

Within a short time the men were ready to march. They had not breakfasted and the only food they had was whatever was in their bread bags. The Americans had previously built a substantial floating bridge with twelve spans across the waterway from Ticonderoga to Fort Independence, over which they had made their escape. Before fleeing, they had made an attempt to burn the bridge, but though damaged, it was still intact. However, since this barred the way for the British ships to chase the American craft heading south with stores and baggage from Ticonderoga, seamen and engineers started to tear down one span as soon as the light infantry had tramped across it. By nine o'clock they had opened a passage for the *Royal George* and the *Inflexible* to chase the enemy's vessels.

When the company had assembled on the other side of the waterway, Captain Hawker took the chance to speak to the men.

"Brigadier-General Fraser has intelligence that the enemy rearguard is heading for Hubbardton. He has around six hundred men – that is four companies of grenadiers, and five companies of light infantry including us, as well as two companies of the 24th Regiment and about a hundred Loyalists and Indians. The Brunswick commander, Major General Baron Riedesel, will be joining the force as soon as possible with a strong force. We must make all speed to join General Fraser. Serjeant, take over."

"Company, with firelocks at the trail, march."

As the day began to heat up, the Serjeant ranged up and down the column cajoling and goading the soldiers he considered were not moving fast enough. Aaron had had a four-hour sentry duty during the night and having not breakfasted he was feeling weary. And the march was hard, for their route was uphill on the road which had been built to transport building materials when Fort Independence had been constructed, and the day became very hot. The pace only relented first when they came to a stream and they stopped to drink and later, when they stopped to eat such food as they had with them. Eventually, they caught sight of the rearguard of Fraser's force and soon after found the main force resting in a field. The soldiers had caught some cows and these were quickly slaughtered and prepared to provide food for the men. Before long they heard the tramp of many boots and from the dust being raised from the direction they had just travelled the men understood that the German force had caught up with them. Unbeknown to the men, the two generals disagreed about tactics. General Fraser wanted to press on to attack the Americans, but General Riedesel wanted to rest his troops and attack the next day. As the German was the senior general, it was decided that the force would camp and seek the Americans very early the next morning. The British moved on to within four miles of the Americans and set up camp; the Germans did the same some way behind. They had no tents so the men prepared to sleep in the open. Before they settled down, the Serjeants went round to brief the men.

"Listen up, our scouts tell us that there is a strong force of about a thousand Americans camped on top of a hill up ahead. They have built breastworks to defend their position. In our line we will take our usual position – what's that, Mew?"

"Er…left, Serjeant."

"Indeed it is. We will begin in line formation and then as the action requires it, fight as you have been trained in pairs and fours. Any questions?"

"How many are we, Serjeant?" asked Graham.

"About the same as the Americans."

"What about our artillery?"

"We have no time to wait for the artillery to arrive."

It was clear from his tone that he did not want questions. "Reveille is at three tomorrow morning. Check your flints and clean your firelocks."

The men found a patch of grass on which to spend the night. Fortuitously, the evening was mild and dry.

"This is it then, Mewie, our first battle this year," said Graham.

"Are you frightened, Clipper?"

"I have a bad feeling about this. Two equal forces with one of them comfortably entrenched on top of a hill."

"The General knows what he is doing. He is the best officer in the army," said Bell.

"Them German Chasseurs with their rifles will give a good account of themselves."

"Yeah, let's hope so, Ting. They may be more accurate than the firelocks, but they take so long to load," said Aaron.

At three in the morning the reveille drum started beating and men began to get ready for the march. The night was very dark and the advantage of an early departure to surprise the enemy was partly dissipated by the fact that it was difficult to find their way in the dark. This was even more so for the Germans who had camped further back than the British. Nevertheless, when the British force arrived at Hubbardton, they caught the 2nd New Hampshire Regiment off guard. A fierce battle broke out. The 11th Massachusetts Regiment, which had just been preparing to leave to march south, turned back to strengthen the American force. The Revolutionaries stubbornly refused to give ground and from behind cover, subjected the British to withering volleys of shot. General Fraser sent a detachment to try to get behind the left flank of the enemy, but in so doing he exposed his own left flank which came under heavy fire as some of the Americans left the breastworks to exploit the weakness.

"Jesse, Clipper, we are a bit thin on the ground on our side," hissed Aaron as he waited for his partner to reload.

"Where the hell is Redhazel and the Germans? We are well outnumbered just now."

"Fix bayonets, and advance!" yelled Granville as he moved forward of the pair of them. "Come on you asswipes."

The two of them ran after the Serjeant as he and others trotted up the slope. Through the smoke they could see soldiers, dressed in an assortment of uniforms with some of them in normal everyday clothes, advancing towards them. Despite the firing, Aaron heard a thud and a loud shout behind him. He looked round and saw his friend tumbling backwards down the slope. Aaron stopped and for a moment thought of going back to help the wounded man, but his training told him otherwise and he ran faster to catch up with the Serjeant.

"Graham has been hit, Serjeant," he shouted.

The officer turned and waited for Aaron to catch up.

"Pair up with me," he instructed as he fired at the oncoming soldiers.

Aaron waited for the Serjeant to reload, and as he did so he noticed three Americans, only one of them in uniform, coming at them. As they levelled their firelocks at the British pair, Aaron fired. One yelled and dropped as the shot struck him. With no time to reload the Private leapt forward to try to bayonet one of the others. He slipped and fell to the ground and one of the enemy swung his firelock to shoot him as he lay in front of him. There was a bang as Granville fired at the one aiming at Aaron. As the man dropped to the ground, the man in uniform fired at Granville.

Aaron scrambled to his feet and levelled his bayonet at the surviving American. The man bravely stood his ground, but before the duel between them could commence, there was another shot from nearby and the man fell first to his knees and then, face forward, tumbled down the slope.

Suddenly there was a crescendo of gunfire from further down the hill. General Riedesel had arrived and seeing the pressure on the left flank had sent his grenadiers to relieve the hard pressed 62nd

Company. As the Brunswickers streamed up the slope the British became aware of music playing and men singing. For those who had the temerity to pause and look down below them, the redcoats could see the main German contingent marching to their military band and singing hymns as they went into battle.

Even in the heat and confusion of the moment, Aaron had recognised that the Serjeant had saved him. If Granville had chosen to aim at the American who had just shot him, instead of the one who had attempted to shoot Aaron, then he would probably not have been hit by the American ball. The Private slithered down the slope to where the Serjeant was with difficulty, trying to sit up.

Blood was trickling from the officer's mouth as with much less venom than usual he snapped at Aaron, "Load, lad, before they come at you again."

As he was loading his firelock Aaron cast glances down at Granville. The red of his jacket was becoming much darker from bleeding on his chest. Aaron put down the firelock and sat down beside the Serjeant. The man was now too weak to protest about the Private's dereliction of duty.

"Mewie, Mewie, I gave you a rough time didn't I?"

"Er...no, Serjeant, no more than I deserved."

"You see, I never had a son and always wanted one. But in you I could see myself twenty years ago. I saw that you had the makings of a soldier."

"How do you mean, Serjeant?"

The officer was now coughing up blood and took a while before he could reply.

"I wanted you to be a good soldier," he gasped and his face winced with pain, "but I couldn't be seen to be favourin' you, so I done the opposite and picked on you, to mould you, to make you a man."

He spat out more blood and in a whisper continued, "You were wild when you signed up and had to be broken-in. I could make you like me."

Aaron thought for a moment. The situation was bewildering for him – what was it his officer was saying? Was all the humiliation and sarcasm part of a scheme to form him in Granville's image? Aaron tried to order his thoughts despite the cacophony of the raging battle. Roles were reversed. Now he was in control; he was the dominant one and the previously unapproachable tyrant was in a position of extreme weakness. Aaron took a chance and said, "Why did you take Sarah from me?"

The Serjeant's pained face changed briefly to a forced smile. "I couldn't let you waste your life with a woman ten years older and with a child to provide for. But here's the rub, I fell for her instead."

The Private reflected as he cradled the officer's shoulders. Gunfire was still booming all around where the two men sat. For a period, the only noise from the Serjeant was a gurgling as he tried to breathe. Then he slowly raised his right hand and laboriously whispered, "I ask you a favour, lad. Take my knapsack, in the bottom is my money. I trust you to make me a pledge."

"Of course, what pledge, Sergeant?"

"Look after Alice with it and give half to Sarah. Tell her sorry I…" He started coughing more blood and then toppled over and Aaron had to grab his jacket to stop the lifeless body from rolling down the hill. He dragged the man over against a sapling to prevent him from doing so. Then he picked up his firelock and rejoined the advance; now to chase the Americans who, although they were retreating, were fighting valiantly until they reached an open field. There, realising that they were surrounded on three sides, they raced to avoid the volleys of gunfire. Many fell including the commanding officer of the 11th Massachusetts Regiment, Colonel Francis.

The Battle of Hubbardton had indeed been a bloody affair. Roughly the same number of soldiers on each side were killed, but the British suffered more wounded casualties than the Americans. Even so it was a decisive victory, not least because 230 prisoners had been taken.

That night the exhausted and hungry redcoats reflected on the day's event.

"Corporal, have you seen Clipper?" asked Bell.

Aaron interjected, "He caught one when we were going up the hill, but I didn't see his body when we were burying the rest."

"He took a ball in the shoulder, passed right through under his armpit. He's with the wounded," said the Corporal.

"He'll be alright then?"

"Let's hope so. What happened to the Serjeant, Mewie?"

"I paired with him after Clipper got hit. We took on three rebels and one of them got him in the chest."

Aaron was not going to tell the whole tale, but he was anxious about the request that Granville had made.

"Jamie, as he was dying he asked me to take his knapsack. He said he had money in it he wanted his lass to have, or rather he wanted me to look after it for her. He wanted half of it to go to his espoused in Canada."

"Let's keep it between us, Mewie. If Mrs Saunders, who is caring for the girl, gets wind of money coming her way, it will all go on rum. Although I don't see as how you can pay money to Mrs Rasmussen. That is, unless we go back that way to Quebec."

"I really feel I must do it. It was the dying man's wish."

"Where is the knapsack?"

"Here, under my blanket."

"Let's have a look."

"He said it was at the bottom."

Corporal Cutler rummaged around in the bag and then withdrew an oilskin pouch.

"It's all in paper money, Mewie," said Bell.

"Well, you keep your thievin' fingers off it," said Aaron as he took the package from the Corporal.

Then he gave it back to the officer. "Here, you count it."

Jamie gingerly untied a string around the pouch and opened it. He pulled out the notes and flicked them as he counted.

"…One hundred and ninety, two hundred, two hundred and ten. That's twenty-one ten-pound notes, Mewie."

"Hell's teeth, that's a fortune," said Bell.

The Corporal started laughing.

"What is so funny, Corporal?" asked a bemused Aaron.

"I once told you there was good money in getting recruits, and do you realise that part of this money is the bounty Granville received for recruiting you two."

The men were not amused.

"Put it somewhere safe, Mewie. We can talk about it later. I am going to see if I can find where they have put Clipper. Are you going to tell Alice about her father when we get back?"

"Must I?"

"I think that it would be best, but remember, don't mention the money."

Aaron pulled out a pouch hanging on a leather thong around his neck, placed the notes in the oilskin cover, and tucked it into his safekeeping place. As he did so, he was reminded with some sadness of the last time he had put a large sum of cash into another similar pouch, one which his mother had made for him, and thought, what would she say if she could see me now?

It was their second night in the open and some of the men had tried to fashion simple huts from branches, but these proved to be poor protection against the heavy rain which started to fall. Nevertheless, most men slept. Although he was very tired, Aaron found sleep a distant friend. He anguished over the Serjeant's words and how the man he had despised so much, the one who had given him the anguish of the buzzing in his head, had saved his life. What had he meant when he asked the Private to "look after Alice"? After the battle, while many were plundering the corpses of the fallen Americans, amid a confusion of emotions he had made it his business to bury the man who had tormented him for two years. When he closed his eyes he could still see the bloodied stubble on the face of the corpse. He tried to think of other things and forced himself to consider the relief he felt, now that he was out of danger from the enemy. Gradually, the veil of sleep enveloped him.

But the danger was not over, for the next day General Riedesel decided to march his troops south, abandoning those who were left of General Fraser's six hundred men to fend for themselves against any new rebel attack. The British General had received intelligence that General St Clare with the main American force was but six miles away in Castletown. In addition to this concern, they had to guard 230 prisoners and to care for over 200 British and American wounded. They had very few supplies and no buildings apart from a tiny hut in which to house the casualties.

"The General has seen fit to entrust the prisoners to the 62nd Light. The thirty fit ones of us will march the Yankees to Ticonderoga."

Serjeant Ryan was now the senior Serjeant in the company and while he did not have the venomous tongue of Granville, he

239

brooked no challenge to his authority and no one was tempted to make a verbal observation. Nevertheless, there were some looks exchanged between the men as they considered being outnumbered by enemy prisoners by nearly eight to one on a long march with no provisions.

"General Fraser will march south with the other troops. Any questions?"

"What about the wounded, Sergeant?" asked Corporal Cutler.

"Serjeant Lamb and a small party including the woman who came with her husband will stay to care for them, though they have no medical supplies at this moment."

Ryan was referring to the wife of one soldier in the 24th Regiment who had insisted on accompanying her husband from Ticonderoga and stayed with him throughout the battle. What no one could have known at this time was that it would be seven days before medical help arrived for the wounded men, many of whom, friend and foe, simply bled to death in the meantime.

The next morning, Tuesday 8th July, at first light, the company assembled after partaking of the only refreshment available, water. The prisoners were paraded in two rows in a field and General Fraser attempted to get their commanding officer, Colonel Hale of the New Hampshires, and the prisoners to give their word that they would not try to escape on the march, but he also gave express orders that the British guard should shoot anyone who tried to do so.

After their twenty-five-mile march they reached Mount Independence. The Light Company were able to hand over the prisoners to the custody of the 62nd Regiment which had taken over garrisoning duties at the fort together with the German Prince Fredericks Regiment. The fort had been designated the general hospital for the care of the wounded. The company queued at the sutlers to get some bread, cheese and spruce beer before collapsing on the grass to have their first food for two days. Then Aaron went off in search of his friends.

"Welcome to Rattlesnake Hill, Mewie, the domain of the Springers."

"Springers, Rev?"

"It is a name bestowed on us by our worthy General himself, to denote our willingness and agility. I understand that your sojourn in New Hampshire has not been without incident."

"It was a tough fight, Rev. Granville was killed and Clipper lies wounded at Hubbardton."

"Oh, I am sorry to hear of the Serjeant's demise. I have known him for many years, a fine soldier. Though I assume that your grief is somewhat tempered by relief."

"I don't know what to feel, Rev. He asked me to take care of Alice."

"And how do you intend to do that, dear boy?"

Their conversation was interrupted by a shout from behind them.

"Here, Piercie, catch!" The voice was Barton's, the man who had supplied Aaron with his uniform two years before.

Rev and Aaron turned to watch as Barton threw a round grey object to the Salisbury merchant. He caught it and then screamed, "The bloody thing bit me," as he dropped it to the ground.

Behind Barton stood Private Goddard, carrying the headless body of a large snake. The two men strode forward to look at Pierce's outstretched hand.

"You bastards, the rattler bit me."

They stood looking with amazement at the fang marks in Pierce's palm. Aaron and Rev went over to look, after Goddard had kicked the snake's head into the long grass.

"But the bloody thing was dead," said Goddard.

"Private Barton, I hate to say it but you are the author of Pierce's damnation for I believe that it is a well-known fact that a freshly killed rattlesnake can still bite. It is what is known as a defensive reflex. This place is teeming with them. Be careful where you squat for many a place of easement is anything but that."

Pierce sat down on a bench in front of a tent holding his bitten right hand with his left.

"Dear God, this hurts," he said as more soldiers started to crowd around to look at the victim.

The crowd was joined by Corporal Reid, who said, "Get 'im to the hospital quick. Get a bier from over there." He pointed to some stretchers.

Pierce's hand had already started to swell as he was carried off to the fort. Barton stayed to watch as two army surgeons started to treat him. When he returned to the camp he was besieged by questioners.

"How's he doing?" asked Corporal Reid.

"Jesse, you should see his arm. They had to cut off his shirt. His whole arm and shoulder is swollen double and has gone orange colour, and he keeps throwing up."

"They haven't got medicine for snakebite?"

"Don't seem so, Corporal. They was just gettin' him to drink olive oil and rubbin' mercurial ointment into the bite. Am I going to be on a charge for this?"

"Nah, it was just an accident, but I'll warrant that questions will be asked if he dies."

Aaron waited until the crowd had dispersed and then asked, "Corporal, can you tell me where I can find Private Saunders' tent?"

"Yes, down the line over there," he said as he pointed at a row of tents beside the track to the waterway. "What do ye want with him?"

"I've got to tell Serjeant Granville's lass that her father was killed at Hubbardton."

"God's teeth, was he? How'd that happen?"

Aaron told the Corporal something of the event before he nervously set off down the hill.

"Mistress Saunders, good day to you. Um...is Alice here?"

"You heard what her pa said – you mustn't be bothering her."

"Um...You see I have a message for her."

"Just as I said, her father'll murder you."

"Well, well...the fact is, he is dead."

"Dead? What, killed?"

"At Hubbardton."

"Jesse, who is going to pay me now for looking after the girl. She don't earn her keep."

"Well...I suppose I could pay something for her keep."

"Ha, ha, you could, could ye? You are just like the rest of them. You drink what you got over after paying for your victuals."

"No, no, I don't. Well, not always. I'll give you a shilling a week."

"Let's see the colour of your money. A shilling, now."

Aaron was getting irritated with the woman and snapped back.

"In good time. I have to get it from my knapsack. Where is Alice?"

"She be down at the river washing laundry. Make sure you got the shillin' when you come back."

Aaron said no more but left the woman and walked off down the hill to where a row of women were on their knees on the stony shore, leaning over and dipping clothes into the water. It was not immediately obvious to the soldier which of them was Alice, but he made a noise on the shingle and several turned to see who was behind them. Alice looked even thinner than before as she shyly acknowledged him.

"Alice, I got a message for ye."

There was a chorus of laughter from the women and some ribald comments.

"Come 'ere, I got to talk to ye."

The women's comments got louder. Alice lifted her handful of laundry onto a rock, left it there and stood up. She turned and picked her way round the boulders to where Aaron stood. Several of the women had stopped and were turning their heads as if to try to hear whatever it was that the soldier had to say. He deliberately spoke softly to thwart the inquisitiveness of the washer women.

"Alice, I got a message for you about your father. He got shot yesterday."

Her already concerned face contorted. "No, no, it can't be. You sure?"

"I be so sorry, miss, but there ain't no doubt. I buried him."

Tears had welled up in her eyes and Aaron felt a strong urge to comfort her by putting his arms round her, but the dozens of eyes that were watching dampened his instinct to do so. The girl started to shake and wail, a sign that was quickly read by the very women who had taunted Aaron earlier. Several understood the purpose of the messenger and compassion took the place of ridicule as they stood up and took the girl in their arms. Aaron watched for a short while, then turned and retraced his steps up the hill.

243

Chapter 20

The Light Infantry Company stayed with the rest of the regiment at Mount Independence until 12th August. There was much to be done; transporting wounded, supervising prisoners as they were set to work, and ferrying goods and supplies down the waterway to the landing place, the 'portage', from where the army would cross into Lake George. At the portage, everything had to be transported overland a short distance, before being placed on boats to be ferried south.

Seven days after leaving Fort Independence, the Light Company had marched the length of Lake George and arrived at Fort Miller on the east bank of the Hudson River. Many of them had a memento of their stay of the last few weeks in the form of dried rattles from the tails of the snakes which had plagued them. The rattle skins were slid over to cover the leather frogs which held their bayonets.

The march was extremely hard; the weather was poor and much of the trail had been deliberately blocked by the retreating foe. It was bad enough for the soldiers, but even worse for the band of women camp followers, many with small children. Aaron had settled his financial transaction with Mistress Saunders, though he had still been unable to talk with Alice about her father's request as she was quite inconsolable. Nevertheless, the matter worried the soldier considerably.

"What's happening, Corporal?" Aaron asked as the men were setting up their tents at a place called Duar's House, near to Fort Miller. He had seen some wounded men being brought into the camp.

"A bloody disaster, that's what."

"How so?"

"You may not have heard, but General Howe, who is supposed to be taking his army to Albany to meet us, has changed his mind and gone to Philadelphia chasing another American army. He has sent just a small force up the Hudson to try to relieve us. We are on our own."

"Who are the wounded men?"

"You can't have failed to notice that we are getting very short of supplies – we have a very long supply line to Quebec and not enough horses and wagons. Well, as we need beef and horses, the German General proposed that we should send a strong force off to a place called Bennington where he had been told that the Americans had a large supply of horses and cattle which was guarded only by a small number of militia."

"What happened then?"

"Well, it was just over a week ago it seems that the German Colonel Baum took two hundred of the dragoons. They wanted the horses; after all, they are supposed to be mounted troops. There were savages, Loyalists and Captain Fraser's marksmen as well. Anyway, they didn't know that two thousand New Hampshire militiamen were gathering at Bennington. When he found out, he sent for reinforcements, but before they came the Americans attacked them and it was a slaughter. So anyway, when the reinforcements arrived, they were outnumbered too, and the Americans overwhelmed them."

"How many men did we lose?"

"About a thousand – over two hundred killed and seven hundred taken prisoner. And Captain Fraser's marksmen are almost wiped out, though he escaped and got back yesterday."

"Things had been going so well. We'll recover, you just see. We've taken Ticonderoga, Fort Edward, Fort Ann and Fort Miller. Albany is not too far now."

"Yes, but that is also a drain on our numbers. At each fort we have to leave a garrison to defend our supply line, depleting the number in our force. You understand what I mean? After Bennington, and the losses there, almost all the Indians have decided to go home too."

Aaron asked no more questions. He put his knapsack on the ground and got out his pipe; there was much to think about. It was true, his company had noticed that the supply of food was getting difficult and there was precious little forage to be had in the countryside where the Americans had already marched through and appropriated the harvest. Albany was on the west bank of the river and once the army crossed it, their supply line to Canada would be broken.

And more bad tidings were to come. On 28th August a messenger arrived with the news that General St Clare's expedition down the St Lawrence had failed after the Indian force decided to return home. No Indian reinforcements would be coming to the aid of General Burgoyne's army. The commander had to try to compensate for the loss of the Indians' special skills.

An order was issued and Serjeant Ryan assembled his company. "Listen up, men, I have a notice to read ye from the Adjutant General. As ye know, the enemy takes advantage of the fact that we no longer have the protection of the savages against skirmishing raids and the Americans are undeniably becoming bolder with such attacks – the General has decided to counter these. The order reads: *Camp at Duar's House, September 2nd 1777. General Order. Captain Fraser's Company of Marksmen is to be augmented with one non-commissioned officer, and sixteen privates from each British Regt. of the line, 53rd excepted. They are to be taken two from each company and chosen according to the order of last year – dated 6th September. Men of good character, sober, active, robust and healthy. They are to be provided with a very good firelock, and to be in every respect proper to form a Body of Marksmen. R Kingston. Deputy Adjutant General"*

"Corporal Cutler and Private Mew are to be transferred to Captain Fraser's Company forthwith."

There were some grins and murmured comments as eyes sought out where the two men were standing.

After some initial training the marksmen were soon in action. On Saturday 13th September, having built up their supplies as best they could, the entire British Army crossed the Hudson River on a bridge made up of boats and encamped. The following day a force of two hundred Americans appeared before the British position and Captain Fraser's men led an unsuccessful chase after them for several miles before returning with some captives.

"The prisoners we brought in told the Captain that the American army is gathering down river to block our path," said the Corporal as he wiped water from his face and replaced his water bottle on his hip.

"So there will be a battle then," said Aaron.

"As I see it the General has two choices – he can carry on the way we are and try to march past them alongside the river, or face them. If he tries to march alongside the river and they attack us, we will be easy meat for them as we move slowly along the low ground. The column is more than a mile long and can't move quickly – they've got to drag our cannon and supplies. So with the wide water on one side and the enemy on the heights above, that prospect ain't rosy."

"So, what will we do?"

"For now the marksmen have been put on the right, the inland side of the army column to protect against surprise attacks by the rebels."

"So, we've got to keep going up and down all the ravines that lead to the river, Corporal?"

"That's our orders, Mewie, at least until we see if the Americans make a stand. Which, since their army is three times the size of ours, they will certainly do."

The Corporal was about to move on down the slope when he leant forward to Aaron and whispered, "It seems to me that the best alternative would be a retreat."

"No, Gentleman Johnny Burgoyne would never agree to that."

At ten o'clock on Friday 19th September, on a morning with a sharp frost, General Burgoyne, having decided that his only way forward towards Albany was to confront the Americans, started to move his troops into position. The army was split into three columns. The Germans were ordered to go forward on the river path to protect the cannon and supplies and the left flank of the army. The column on the right under the command of General Fraser, which had the difficult job of traversing the hills and woods inland to try to get behind the Americans, comprised the Advanced Corps of Grenadiers and Light Infantry together with Indians, Canadians and Provincial Volunteers and Captain Fraser's Company. The rest of the army including the 62nd was in the centre column under the command of General Burgoyne.

At twelve o'clock all three columns formed in line of battle. In the Corps of Marksmen on high ground on the right, Aaron could see the other two columns forming into line in the same way as his column had. At midday they heard the sound of the signal guns and they began to advance. Their skirmishers soon came into contact with the American Colonel Daniel Morgan's corps of sharpshooters which had been deployed to deadly effect. They targeted every officer they could see in the British Advance Corps as well as the artillerymen. A strong detachment of Loyalists in the Advanced Corps ordered to counterattack ran past Aaron and his companions and forced the sharpshooters to scatter in the woods. By this time Burgoyne's column had reached a place which Aaron was later told was called Freeman's Farm, and set up its artillery. Although the Advanced Corps was meeting some opposition, they could see that the largest force of Americans was now attacking the centre column. A vicious battle was taking place there and it was clear the 62nd Regiment in the centre of the middle column was bearing the brunt of the fighting. There was a series of advances, retreats, attacks and counterattacks all along the line, but the British were outnumbered, and the situation was made worse since the Germans were as yet playing little part in the battle, still occupying the river trail as ordered. General Fraser decided that reinforcements were needed in the centre and he ordered some of his men to move there to help the hard pressed 62nd to regroup.

Aaron fought his way through the undergrowth towards the centre, as ordered. There he found his regiment temporarily retreating to reform. There was no panic, no rush, just an orchestrated movement of men back whence they had come. But the returning was as difficult as the advancing, for the briars grabbed and tripped the wearer of the boots trampling them, irrespective of the allegiance. Despite every effort of the few Serjeants who had survived, the varying mobility of the men dictated that the retreat was uneven. The line was broken and bent, not least by those limping or being assisted by comrades. They all avoided walking over the dead, but the cries of the wounded being left behind tore at the feelings of even the most brutal of those still unscathed. Not more than seventy paces away Aaron could see where the British soldiers had stopped and were forming a line to meet the advancing Revolutionaries. As he untangled a briar from his leggings to go to join them, he heard a voice from one of the fallen.

"Mewie, Mewie, is that you, dear boy?"

Aaron recognised Rev's voice but struggled to detect where it came from. He turned to his right and then to his left where, through the thick gun smoke, he saw three mangled bodies and a fourth propped up against them. Rev's gaunt face was unmistakable, but where his right arm should have been, white skin framed a bloody, leaking pit.

Aaron stopped and dodged two or three retreating soldiers from the 20th Regiment to move over to where his old mentor was sitting. He used his firelock for support as he bent over to speak to Rev.

"Come, Rev, I'll help you get back."

"No, 'tis of no importance. Hold me, Mewie."

Aaron knelt down, still holding his firelock and put his free arm round the man's back. From his new position he could see that Rev was holding his stomach with his one good hand. His entrails were slithering out from behind his hand.

Rev gasped and spoke very haltingly. The young soldier had to lean forward to hear what the older man was trying to say, the roar of the firelock volleys interrupting him several times.

"Aaron, what is hidden in the snow will be revealed by the thaw. You have been my north, my south, my east and west. While God is the fixed point in my firmament, it is you who he has sent to give me purpose. I have loved you since I first saw you in Sarum. You are my Adonis. You took the place of the love I once had, the shame for which forced me to join the army, and I am happy, I am redeemed in the eyes of God, for I have never touched you, nor told you of my love, for it is a love which is unspeakable. I will die ere we are overrun by the enemy. Pray give me one kiss, on the forehead, and then you should run. Run fast. Leave me."

Aaron was aghast – he was assaulted by bewilderment, affection, shock, pity and some revulsion. Of these feelings the revulsion was quickly subsumed by the recognition that the dying man had done so much for him and had never asked for anything in return. Aaron tried to grasp what torture Rev had gone through to hide his secret. Of the other feelings, it was pity and affection which were strongest, and it was these which caused him to lean forward and give the sweating brow a kiss. Rev exhaled and slumped sideways. As Aaron made to stand up a shadow fell across him, for the sun was just west of south. Looking up he saw three figures standing over him. One was dressed in a blue uniform jacket, but the others were in normal everyday clothes – each had a firelock. He instinctively started to raise his weapon, but before he could do so, the brass butt of an American weapon crashed on his head and he fell forward, united with his limp mentor.

When Aaron came to, he immediately realised that his hands were restricted by a cord binding them in front of him. He twisted round towards the direction where all the noise was coming from and saw the backs of the American troops as they fired at the British in front of them. But they were retreating and falling back towards him. He lay still, hoping that the blue jacketed soldiers would retreat past him and leave him to be recovered by the advancing British. It was not to be, for even before the Revolutionaries reached him in their retreat, he was yanked from the ground by two soldiers and dragged back towards the trees where he could see the American militia waiting to be called on. They were a motley crowd of men: some in odd uniforms, some in hunting smocks and others in their normal everyday clothes. As Aaron was dragged past them, there were many who shouted insults at him and others who jeered. But one was silent, for he had seen a redcoat prisoner whom he recognised.

The noise in Aaron's ear was as bad as it had ever been, but his main concern was the injury to his head, which was leaking blood. The red fluid was running over his forehead and blinding him in one eye. With the good eye he could see that he was being led towards a gap in the bushes where there were several other redcoat prisoners.

When they reached the group, several of whom were clearly badly wounded, a soldier with a green epaulette on his right shoulder said cheerily to him, "Welcome, Private, I am Corporal Strachan. You are a prisoner of the 1st New Hampshire Regiment. Stand there while I take off your ammunition pouch."

There was a whoosh and a thump as a cannon ball blasted a path through the group of prisoners. Two of them flew into the air as the ball struck them and a third spun round from an impact on his shoulder.

"As you see, your artillery has no great respect for where their ordinance lands," said a Private, splattered by the blood of others, who was guarding the prisoners.

"Come on you men, those of you still alive, follow me to the back of the lines," shouted the Corporal as he grabbed the tied hands of a British Serjeant from the 20th Regiment and pulled him through the bushes.

Aaron and four others who were able to walk followed them. He turned his head so that with his one good eye he could see the prisoners left behind; those unable to walk were looking piteously at the group being led away as they were left abandoned on the field of battle.

They walked through a clearing and then over a recently harvested field up a steep slope. After quite a difficult walk they reached a farm where cattle were being held in a small field fenced with tall sharpened poles. Aaron recognised the type of structure as one where farmers tried to keep wolves from their livestock.

"We have not yet had time to make arrangements for prisoners from the battle, so you lot will be locked in the stockade with the beef cows for the time being," said the Corporal as he pushed the Serjeant through a gate held open for him by a militiaman. The other prisoners lamely followed and the gate was closed behind them.

The ground around the cattle drinking trough was thick with manure, so the five men found a spot at the far end of the enclosure where they could sit on relatively untainted grass. Aaron tried brushing the now congealing blood from his forehead to retrieve the sight of his right eye, but he realised that he would have to get water from the trough to do so effectively. With his hands still bound in front of him he pushed the cows aside and squelching through the cow pats he dipped his head into the water trough and tried to clean the wound on his forehead. The water made the cut sting, and the pain was worsened as he tried to wipe the blood clear. He stood up with both hands grasping the trough, trying to steady himself in case he should pass out again. After a few minutes he returned to the group of prisoners and sat down beside them.

"The last I saw, the Springers and the 22nd were counter-attacking the rebels," said the Serjeant.

"I hope that they advance here soon so that we can get out of this dung heap," said a young voice.

For the first time, Aaron realised that one of their number was an ensign, a commissioned officer. He was but a boy, probably no more than sixteen years old. Aaron looked at him and wondered how such a young man could have a position of authority in the army.

"You should be thankful that the rebels didn't kill you. Ensigns live very dangerously carrying the standards. It is better for you to be in this field of shit than in a graveyard," said the Serjeant disdainfully to the boy, who was in fact his superior officer. Clearly the non-commissioned officer did not consider that rank was of any consequence in their present situation.

Thus the prisoners spent their first hours in captivity, though they were by no means exclusive to the cow pen, for from time to time more men and a few officers were bundled through the gate. Just like those already in the pen, the soldiers had blackened mouths from the gunpowder spilled from the cartridges they had been biting to open all afternoon. Several of the internees had provisions in their pouches; the contents of these and sips from the cow's trough were the only refreshments that the prisoners received before the booming of the cannon and the cracking of firelocks ceased at dusk. But these newcomers to the animal pen were the bearers of good news. Late in the afternoon the Germans had been ordered up from the river, leaving a guard with the supplies, and had turned the tide of battle in favour of the British. Burgoyne's men had prevailed and carried the field, while the Americans had retreated to their fortified lines. But it was a costly victory. The bearers of the good news also told that the 62nd had been almost wiped out in the action and that there were many hundreds killed and wounded on both sides.

As the light faded, the men made themselves as comfortable as they could for a night in the open. The temperature dropped and the prisoners, as well as the two armies, suffered a very cold night. The worst plight was that of the wounded still on the field of battle, for neither side dared to venture out of their lines to help them during the night for fear of renewed hostilities.

As he sat shivering from the cold, Aaron thought more about the circumstances of Rev's death, and what he had said. His shock about the revelation of Rev's feelings for him had disappeared and had been replaced by grief. He had now lost two good friends – Huhnie and Rev. Although there was death and destruction all around him, it did not diminish the impact of the loss he felt.

Suddenly he remembered the money he was carrying in his neck pouch. Would they rob me? he wondered. He fretted about this for some time and eventually, shielded from the view of others by darkness, and after some effort because of his bound hands, he managed to pull the pouch out from under his shirt. He opened it, unfolded the oilskin and took out one of the notes. He then refolded the oilskin and replaced it and the pouch. He then struggled to take off his left boot. He folded the note and put it inside his left boot and then put it back on.

The sounds of the American reveille drums were unnecessary; the prisoners were already awake, indeed some had not slept. Aaron's head was throbbing from the blow he had received yesterday but the bleeding had stopped. The sun rose, and the extent of the prisoners' muddy wretchedness became clear as they competed with the cows for the water. Soon after sunrise, voices were heard at the gate.

"Come and get this bread afore the cows do," called someone outside. The prisoners made for the gate and crowded round it.

"Here, with General Gates' compliments. He begs to remind you that he was once an officer in the British 20th Regiment himself and makes you a pledge that if you change sides, as he did not ten years ago, you will be well looked after."

The bearer of the bread passed loaves through the gate to the prisoners, who gratefully grabbed them.

"Ask him if we can have greatcoats, for we suffer badly from the cold," called one of the prisoners.

"We suffer from the same cold," called the American laughingly as he and his companions took their leave.

The time seemed to pass by very slowly. Occasionally they heard the sound of a firelock, but clearly neither side was in any major action. In fact, a truce had been called to enable both sides to collect their wounded and bury their dead. The British wounded had a mile's bumpy journey in wagons to their tented hospital below the Great Redoubt, a journey which killed many of them.

It was sometime after midday when Aaron was startled to hear his name being called.

"Mewie, Mewie, you there?"

Aaron stood up and walked over to the gate. He looked through the bars and saw a familiar face – it was O'Driscoll.

"Paddy, what in the name of hell are you doing here?"

"Shh, my comrades would doubt my credibility if they knew that I was talking to ye. Had a knock, did ye?"

Aaron was reminded and touched his temple to check that it was not bleeding.

"Why are you here, Paddy?"

"I'll tell you why I am here, Mewie. I got tired of the stupid way Carleton was running the campaign. And in any case I have more in common with a folk as is trying to get their freedom from the British than those who is trying to deny it. I joined the militia last winter."

"Were you fighting against your old friends?"

"I didn't have to, did I? The Americans had retreated before we were called on. My God, Mewie, that was a close thing, for it was the darkness that saved us. If the Lord had not set the sun when he did, we would have been utterly smashed. Smashed, I don't doubt it, by the British."

Aaron tried to prevent himself from commenting on the Irishman's treachery — he knew that this man could be useful, for he had decided that he would try to escape. He had to humour him by showing interest and without criticising him.

"Is it like being in the British Army?"

"No, no, this is a strange army, this militia, the Americans have, to be sure. The soldiers seem to have no inclination to be told what to do, but somehow the officers manage them. And that's another thing, it's very difficult to know which of them are officers, for many of them have no uniform, only a coloured sash across their chests. And the men just seem to come and go as they please. If it's time to kill the pig at home or dig the taties, they just take off and then come back when it pleases them.

"And they don't drill like the redcoats, but these are as worthy people who ever marched out of step. Make no mistake — they are hard workers and cunning fighters. Most have a trade and all of them seem to be able to turn their hands to any task, be it driving a yoke of oxen or mending a pair of shoes. These frontiersmen are good shots too. They have been handling guns since they could walk. There are some with rifles, they can hit a man at three hundred paces, that's why you are short of officers. So look out, Mewie, they can hit you even when you think you are safe."

Aaron paused for a moment and then said, "Paddy, can you help me to get out of here?"

"Did the knock on the head make you silly, Mewie? For the first, I believe in the cause I am now fighting for, and second, you were always a good friend. I would not want your blood on my hands. For how do you think you would fare wandering around the American camp wearing a redcoat? By Jesse, come and join us instead, for now the British have no chance of escaping General Grant."

"How do you mean?"

"Well, I saw men flooding in today to join us. America is like a giant ant's nest, like the ones we saw in the forest. Burgoyne has poked a stick in the nest, and the more he pokes the more ants come out. We had superior numbers yesterday. In a week we will have an army more than five times the size of Burgoyne's. And 'tis common knowledge that you boys are fighting on empty stomachs —that will get worse. We got all the victuals we need – you'll eat better here as a prisoner than in the British Army."

Aaron had heard enough and decided to change the subject. "Do you know how long we will have to live with the cows?"

"There is talk of moving the prisoners, for there are many more than you few here, before there is any more action, so I think it will be soon. Now, Mewie, consider what I have said. They would welcome a soldier from the British Light Bobs. I must go before they miss me."

With that, Aaron was left at the gate by himself.

Later in the day, some soldiers appeared. First, they cut the bindings on the prisoners' wrists and then herded the cows out of the pen.

"Are we goin'too?" asked the Serjeant.

"No, not yet. I think that the General is waiting to get some more like you to join the march," replied a militiaman in a brown jacket.

"What march would that be?"

"The prisoners are to be taken to Hartford, Connecticut, to the gaol there."

"Where is that?"

"Oh, I daresay about a hundred and fifty miles south east of here."

"Why so far?"

"I suppose so that you won't have any chance of escaping from there and rejoining your army, or what is left of it."

Beating one of the cows on the rump, he said, "Come on, the troops have need of these. We got hundreds more mouths to feed. More men are arriving all the time."

"Wait, wait, can you tell us what is happening outside?"

"There ain't too much to see – your women are out plundering the corpses. A few foraging parties have been shot at, and there are plenty of men busy with spades – 'tis grim work. Apart from the men killed yesterday, a whole number of the wounded died from the cold last night."

The man closed the gate and the timbers on the outside which secured it were slammed in place. The twelve officers and men in the pen competed to find a place to sit on the ground which benefitted from the late afternoon sun, to warm themselves before they spent their second night in the open.

The next day, 21st September, early in the afternoon, the hill reverberated with the roar of cannon. Those who counted reckoned that there were thirteen shots fired. The captives assumed that the battle had resumed, but after the last shot, silence prevailed. It was not until early evening, just prior to a heavy rain storm, that O'Driscoll made a reappearance. He was part of a detail that brought two tents and a large pot of porridge for the prisoners. He glanced at Aaron and pretended not to know him. The prisoner understood that their past comradeship was not something he wished his new allies to be aware of.

"What were the cannon firing at earlier?" asked the Serjeant.

"It was in celebration. The good news, from Ticonderoga."

"What news?"

"Our soldiers attacked the fort, but while they didn't take it, they managed to release over a hundred of our men who were imprisoned there and capture many of your 53rd Regiment who were at the portage at Lake George."

"I counted thirteen shots," said the ensign.

"One for each colony, of course."

After the detail had left and locked up the pen gate, the prisoners shared the porridge. While they were eating the rain started and they hastened to put up the two tents. The rain continued all night, turning the pen into a quagmire. Their miserable existence continued for three more nights during which time it rained incessantly. During that time O'Driscoll made another appearance on the outside of the gate alone and called to Aaron.

"Mewie, I'm hoping that you might have considered my suggestion that you throw in your lot with us. Have ye now?"

"No, Paddy, I can't. I've got to get back to the regiment. I made a promise I've got to keep."

"You would be risking your life, Mewie, for 'tis sure that the British are doomed."

"Can you help me?"

"Mewie, I already explained my situation. And in any case, tomorrow the prisoners are being marched off to Connecticut."

"I can pay you."

"It would take a lot of money to persuade me to take such a chance, even for a dear friend."

"If you can get me one of those hunting smocks some of the militia wear, a hat and a firelock, I will pay you ten pounds."

"Ten pounds, Mewie. Now where would a Private get ten pounds, and that honestly."

"I pledge to give you ten pounds if you can get these things for me."

"Show me."

"I can't do that, all the others are looking at us."

"How will you get out?"

"I can easily climb over the gate."

O'Driscoll thought for a while. Ten pounds was more than half a year's pay even if the Americans paid regularly, which they did not. There was a shortage of English coinage in the colonies and ten pounds would be more valuable than the face value. In a conspiratorial tone he whispered, "If I can steal a smock from a sleeping comrade, or a corpse, I will come late tonight to the gate. I am trustin' ye at your word, Mewie. You must have the money."

"I will."

Aaron turned and immediately noticed that all the others were looking at him.

"Who is he?" asked the Sergeant.

"He is a deserter from the 62nd, Sergeant. I was asking him about how long we must stay here."

"What did he say?"

"We leave for Hartford tomorrow."

There was a babble of comments from the prisoners as they lamented the fact that the long walk would take them so far from their regiments.

That night Aaron lay awake listening to the rain pattering on the tent roof. He waited until the other five in his tent were asleep and then stealthily crept out and stood by the gate. His redcoat was wringing wet as he took it off and turned it inside out. Though unseen because of the dark, he knew that the serge cloth lining would now make it appear that he was wearing a white jacket. For he had realised that even if he had a smock over his uniform, the soaking wet white cloth of the smock would reveal a red jacket underneath.

After what seemed an eternity he heard a noise outside – someone was splashing through the mud.

"Mewie, quick, before the sentinel does his round."

Aaron jumped up to try to reach the top horizontal timber on the gate. The mud made it difficult for him to jump, but at his second attempt he grabbed the wooden bar and hauled himself up to straddle the top. He then slithered down the outside and dropped feet first into the mud.

It was so dark that he could only just make out the shape of the man in front of him. The figure pushed a bundle into his chest.

"Here, here's what you're after. The firelock is against the gate. The money if you please."

"Wait, Paddy, I got it in me boot."

He leant against the gate and drew off his boot. He felt inside and pulled out the damp folded note. But it was obvious that the Irishman would not be able to inspect the note in the dark.

"Here, here you are, Paddy. Ten pounds. Trust me, it really is."

"I hope you haven't cheated me, Mewie, for if you have I shall surely arouse the guard to find you."

By the time Aaron had replaced his boot, he was aware that O'Driscoll was gone. He picked up the bundle from the ground and opened it. He felt the tricorn hat and put it between his knees while he pulled the smock over his head. It was a tight fit, but it would have to do as a disguise. He put the hat on and then groped around and found the flintlock. He was free!

Aaron had given considerably more thought as to how to get out of captivity in the pen than how to escape from the American lines. He had no idea of the disposition of the American troops, sentries and outposts, but he did realise that the river would lead him back to the British lines. And the river was on the other side of the great cannon battery on Bemis Heights. He decided to walk in the direction of this prominence. He stumbled and splashed his way over rough ground until at length he came to a trail which led in the direction he thought the river should be. It appeared to be unguarded as he was never challenged and eventually he slithered down a steep embankment onto some flat land which was the strip alongside the river. There he turned and started to follow the river trail north.

"Halt, who goes there?"

It was too dark for Aaron to see the voice's owner, but it was obvious that he was between him and the direction he wished to travel. The man must have heard his approach despite the noise of the wind and rain. Aaron did not know what to do. If he answered, he would give the sentry a good indication of his exact position, as surely the sentry could not see him.

"Halt, who goes there?" repeated the voice.

At the river's edge, Aaron could just make out the shape of a large boat and realised that it must be an American supply ship which the man was guarding. He turned and ran inland to hide where he sensed there were trees. He immediately tripped and fell into a ditch. As he scrambled up the other side he heard two voices shouting to each other.

Then one called, "Halt or I shoot."

There was a flash and a crack as the firelock discharged. Aaron heard the ball smash against a tree. Then there was a click and a curse. It seemed that the second guard had got his powder wet. He knew that the first man would be reloading, so he felt for a tree trunk and placed himself on the other side of it. Sure enough there was a second bang, but this time no sound to indicate where the shot had gone. Aaron stayed completely still, waiting to hear if the men tried to follow him.

"Probably one of the savages out scouting," said a voice.

"We're best off staying out of the woods then," answered the other.

Aaron felt his way through the trees until he decided that he was well clear of the sentries and then found his way back onto the trail. By this time the light of day was creeping over the eastern side of the river and it was not long before he was visible to anyone watching the track. His ear was buzzing loudly, but more worryingly, it was beginning to ache. While aware of this, he had no time to consider what might be wrong with it.

The daylight brought skirmishers out of the opposing camps and such was the likelihood of him being spotted that he decided to get off the trail and try to progress northwards through the woods. As he did so he became aware of the sound of movement on the river trail and he stopped to listen. Soon, through the trees he saw a large band of men coming from the direction of the American camp. As they got closer he crouched low behind a tree and waited for them to pass. They appeared to be militia; few had uniforms and several had the same type of smock which he was wearing. Not long after they had passed, they left the trail and fanned out into the woods – clearly they too needed cover and Aaron realised that this must be because they were near to the British lines. Excited by this, he decided to take a chance. He pulled his hat down over the injury to his forehead and hurried to catch up with the American skirmishers, hoping that the militiamen did not know each other well. He soon found himself parallel with two of them as they slowly crept half-bent through the undergrowth. One of them had a red epaulette on his right shoulder and it was clear that he was an officer as others were looking to him as he made hand signals pointing to the direction they should go.

Suddenly, there was the familiar sound of whooping and the crash of flintlocks being fired. The Americans ahead of him and the officer turned and came rushing back as fast as the tangle of briar undergrowth would allow them.

"Retreat to the trail and regroup," shouted the officer as he tried to make his way past Aaron.

"Come on, soldier, hurry up," he called as he passed.

But Aaron continued forward. As others stumbled past him they shouted for him to turn back before it was too late. Some of the few Indians left with the British had ambushed the skirmishing party.

He pushed a low branch aside and there, directly in front of him, were two Iroquois warriors, their faces painted a gaudy green with parallel red stripes. He threw his flintlock to the ground and raised his arms, desperately hoping that they would accept his surrender and that they had been given instructions to take prisoners for intelligence gathering. One of them held his flintlock hard against Aaron's stomach, while the other took out his knife. They shouted something at him and indicated that he should kneel. The Indian now transferred the end of the flintlock to his head. Meanwhile the other stepped sideways and bent down into the undergrowth. He pulled out the body of a wounded militiaman, grabbed him by the hair and accompanied by the man's screams he proceeded to remove his scalp.

Aaron was terrified. There was no point in him trying to escape – he would be shot before he even stood up. Just then, two more Indians pushed their way through the bushes in front him. One was wizened and clearly older than the other warriors. He shouted to the one holding the firelock against Aaron and beckoned for the soldier to stand up. Clearly he was giving the younger men some reprimand. One of them picked up the American firelock, aimed into the forest and pulled the trigger. The shockwave blasted near to Aaron's head, painfully reminding him of his earache. Later, the effect of this blast would become more evident. The warrior then gave the unloaded firelock to Aaron for him to carry as they shoved him in the direction from which they had come, towards the British defences. The rain was still falling heavily as they walked past the scene of the earlier battle. The deluge had washed the sandy soil away from many of the shallow graves, revealing decomposing bodies and releasing the pungent smell of corruption.

"Which regiment are you fighting in, Private?" asked the Major, as Aaron was pushed in under the wet tent flap and into the presence of two officers.

"The 62nd, sir."

The two officers looked at each other quizzically.

"What do you mean the 62nd? You are a rebel, aren't you?"

"No, sir. I have served in Lieutenant-Colonel Anstruthers' regiment since two years back."

"When did you desert?"

"I ain't, sir. I just escaped from their prisoner compound."

"What do you make of it, Lieutenant?"

"You stand there dressed as an American, having been captured with an American firelock. Do you seriously expect us to believe that you are not a deserter?"

"Yes, yes. I still got my King's uniform on under this. I am English. I come from Fordingbridge in Wessex."

They watched as Aaron struggled to take off the wet smock. His inside-out jacket was thus revealed.

"Turncoat – the Wessex turncoat. It's obvious, sir. The man is a deserter," he said sarcastically.

The Major scratched the stubble on his chin and reflected. He still had some doubt.

"If you are, as you say, an escaped prisoner of war, how did you get captured, and how did you get this disguise to escape?"

"Sir, I was fighting with Captain Fraser's marksmen on the right of the field of battle when I was ordered to reinforce General Hamilton's Battalion in the centre. There I was bludgeoned by an American and taken to where they kept prisoners."

"Which regiment captured you?"

"First New Hampshire Regiment, sir."

"And the disguise?"

Aaron continued to be questioned for some time before the Major said to him, "The Lieutenant and I will consider your story, but be prepared that it is likely that you will face a general court martial. We have just flogged one of the 62nd today – perhaps you know Patrick Skeen? He was sentenced to a thousand lashes for desertion. Go now and report to your regiment. You will find those who are left camped north of the Great Redoubt on the other side of the Great Ravine. They are being rested for a few days."

"Thank you, sir."

Towards midday, Aaron found the tents of the regiment and was directed to Corporal Reid's mess.

"Where the hell you been, Mew? We'd given you up for dead."

"Yeah, there are more of our regiment dead than alive," said a soldier who Aaron recognised as Private Snow.

"How many are left then, Corporal?"

"We've got about sixty men and five officers left fit to fight. That's out of nigh on four hundred and fifty who started out from St Johns."

"What about Corporal Cutler?"

"Dead. He was picked off by the sharpshooters."

Aaron was aghast; another of his good friends was gone. He

tried to take in the news of the death of Jamie, a man who had always been so kind to him from his first day in the army and with whom he had forged such a strong bond. He mourned two good men – victims of the battle. Two people he could always rely on were no more. He reflected that of the six men who had been in his tent in Salisbury, three were now dead.

"What about Clipper?"

"Yeah, he's still with us. He was listed as a convalescent at the time of the Freeman's Farm battle, but he is back on duty now. He's sharing with Snowy and me. We got room for you if you want to join us."

"What happened to Pierce and Goddard?"

"Pierce is still about but Goddard was wounded. He is down at the hospital below the Great Redoubt. So, what happened to you?"

"It's a long story, and it looks as if I may get court martialled for it. I'll tell you later. I'm not feeling so good, Corporal. Can I lie down for a while?"

"Yes, you do that. Jamie's knapsack is down there – you can take his things. Oh, by the way, Mistress Saunders has been looking for you. Her husband got hit by a twelve pounder. Wasn't much left of him."

Aaron's ear was now extremely painful and the buzzing was overwhelming him. He took off his wet jacket and unclipped the dead Corporal's greatcoat and blanket. He stretched out on the damp groundsheet and tried to sleep.

The soldier's next hours were lost in a haze of pain and feverish delirium as he suffered from an acute ear infection; the after-effect of a ruptured eardrum. Occasionally, he would vomit and sit up fighting for breath. It was later, much later, when the pain started to subside, that he became aware of someone bathing his forehead. He opened his eyes and tried to focus on the figure kneeling beside him. She was wearing a knitted shawl over a brown dress. On her head was a battered bonnet, protruding from the sides of which was wet, light brown, straggly hair. Her face was thin and her appearance, though not unpleasing, was very anxious.

"Alice, what are you doing here?" asked Aaron.

The girl withdrew her hand quickly and to avoid eye contact with the sick soldier, she looked at the ground. Aaron struggled to sit up.

The girl got up, straightened her dress, pulled her shawl tightly around her shoulders and took the wooden bowl from Graham, who was sitting silently watching Aaron from the other side of the tent.

"How did she get to be here?" asked Aaron.

"Mistress Saunders was here looking for you. She was after rum money, I think. When she saw the state you were in she brought the girl to nurse you. Said she wanted to keep you alive."

Aaron felt for the pouch under his shirt. It was still there.

"Did you give her money?"

"No, and today she came in leading the girl and said that the maid would have to live here 'cause she doesn't want her anymore on account of her, Mrs Saunders that is, getting married to Corporal Cole of the Light Company."

"But her husband only just died."

"There are a lot of widows about, Mewie, and if they don't remarry quick like, they ain't got no chance of making their way have they?"

"Why is she leaving Alice here?"

"Corporal Cole doesn't want anyone in their tent, and she said you ain't paid for a week anyway. Why are you paying her, Mewie?"

"Er…well, I made a promise to Granville when he was dying."

"That's a funny turn of events, I do declare."

"She can't stay here," said Aaron.

"Why not? There's a woman in most tents – it's good to have someone for the washing and cleaning."

The tent flap opened and the girl came in carrying the bowl.

"Ah, here you are, Mewie, porridge. You haven't eaten for two days."

Graham got a spoon for Aaron from Jamie's knapsack and gave it to the girl before he left the tent. She put the bowl down, and without making eye contact with him helped him to sit up, before she passed the porridge and the spoon to him. She sat back and waited in case her help was needed.

Aaron ate the porridge and passed the bowl back to her. As she made to take the bowl, he feebly grabbed at her hand, held it and said, "Alice, I thank you for your care. You ain't got reason to be afeared of me and Clipper. We know that you have had it rough since your ma died and the Serjeant never had much time for ye.

And I have a notion that Mrs Saunders near starved you."

The girl still had her eyes averted from him, but slowly she raised her head and through tear-filled eyes very quietly said, "I got nowhere's to go, Private Mew, and I can't go back to Mistress Saunders, or Mistress Cole as she now is."

Although Aaron felt pleased that he would have an opportunity to satisfy part of the pledge he had made to the dead Serjeant, he also felt overwhelmed with pity for the orphan girl and there was no denying too that he had some longing for female company.

"Aaron. Aaron is my name, you call me that. You can stay in our tent, if you can do the cleaning and mending chores for us. That alright?"

"But where can I sleep?"

"Don't worry. Clipper will get blankets for you."

"I'm afeared of the other men. They may take the advantage of me."

"Don't be afraid, they are good men and they feel sorry for you."

"Where should I put my things?"

"Put them besides my bed, you can sleep here. I'll protect you if you are frightened."

The girl nodded silently, took the bowl and left the tent.

Chapter 21

Seldom can two armies have faced each other for so many days without either taking major action against the other. It had been more than two weeks since the battle which had raged around the farm of John Freeman. The British had spent that time, with ever dwindling supplies, on improving the defences around their positions and foraging to find what food they could for themselves and their horses. Their army was much depleted after the costly victory and there was only a faint and diminishing chance of reinforcements, for the military expedition coming from New York was progressing with no haste. General Burgoyne's greatest hope was that the pressure exerted by the British force would make General Grant divert some of his troops southwards to meet the threat. The American army grew in size daily with the arrival of new soldiers and militia. With the increased numbers, the General's strategy was to gradually surround the stranded British and to starve them into surrender.

The weather helped neither side but it was a timely reminder to the British commander that winter was approaching and he could not stay where he was for much longer. Most of his senior officers including General Riedesel urged him to withdraw and to find a safer position further north, on the other side of the Hudson. Finally, on 6th October, General Burgoyne agreed with them with the caveat that the next day, with a limited force, he would test the defences of the great American vantage point of Bemis Heights. If he found it vulnerable, he would launch the whole army to attack it on 8th October. If it were decided that the heights were too well defended, then the army would retreat, as counselled by the officers. Generals Fraser and Riedesel agreed with this proposal.

"Welcome back to the Light Infantry Company, Mew," said Serjeant Ryan.

"Thank you, Serjeant," answered the young soldier, fresh from his convalescence.

"Gather round, you men, and hear up."

The company, now much reduced in size, stood informally as a group in front of the Serjeant.

"We are going to move on the enemy's left to probe their defences. We will attack the breastworks you see on the hill. Captain Fraser and his rangers have already left to try to get behind the enemy. We have a thousand men of the line with us as well as seven hundred of our Advance Corps. We have the grenadiers on our right. Brigadier-General Fraser himself is commanding the reconnaissance. Any questions?"

"What about artillery, Serjeant?"

"Corporal White asks about artillery. We have two twelve pounders and some six pounders and howitzers which we will place on the hill over there." He pointed at a grassy prominence in front of them, behind which was a wheat field. "Be easy now. Check your flints and wait for the bugle."

The men stood around anxiously awaiting the call to send them forward. The memory of the carnage of the last battle was still fresh in the minds of the waiting soldiers. Most men felt some fear, but all knew what they must do and no one questioned their orders or showed hesitation. Aaron suddenly realised that the buzzing in his ear which had plagued him for two years at times like this was no more, for in this current nervous state of anticipation, his ear would normally be tormenting him to an extreme. But there was nothing. Nothing apart from the sound of men's hushed voices, the occasional crack of a firelock and the boom of the cannon. The noise in his head had stopped; the source of his customary vexation which had caused him so much anguish had disappeared. He wondered how this could be and hoped that the respite would be permanent. And so, as he and the others gazed with anxiety up at the formidable American defences, willing the artillery to breach the breastworks before they received the command to advance, he had a sense of joy intermingled with dread.

The bugle sounded the advance and the American outposts were quickly overrun. But then, instead of staying behind the breastworks and waiting for the British advance, the Americans were ordered to attack and they did so in numbers far superior to the reconnaissance force. First to clash with the Light Company were Morgan's men. One of them shot and badly wounded Brigadier-General Fraser, before other American regiments advanced and caused heavy casualties. The bugle sounded for the British to retreat and they rallied around two of their hill forts or redoubts. One of them, known as Breyman's Redoubt, was taken by the Americans at great cost to the British. The 62nd Light Company found refuge on the other hill, Balcarres Redoubt, until darkness stopped the attacks.

"The devil take them all, Mewie. You alright?" whispered Clipper. He spoke quietly as there was no way of knowing how close the enemy were to their position.

"That General of theirs on the horse was completely mad, the dickens himself. They gave us Jesse."

"They say that he was General Arnold. Did you see how he whipped up his men?"

"And we lost our General."

"Is he dead, Mewie?"

"I saw he got a shot in the belly. He was alive when they carried him back."

"So what do we do now, Corporal?"

"A runner has just arrived. He's talking to the Serjeant. We most assuredly will get orders soon. Do you have shot left?"

The two men felt in their ammunition pouches.

"A few."

"And you, Mew?"

"None, Corporal."

"Here, take some of mine."

As the Corporal was fumbling with his cartridges a figure with the unmistakable voice of Sergeant Ryan joined them.

"We are all to move up to the heights nearer the river so that we have a better defensive position for when the enemy attacks tomorrow. We need to hide our withdrawal, so gather up all the wood you can find. We are going to light fires all around our position here, with the intention of persuading the enemy that they are our camp fires and that we are still occupying Balcarres."

The following day the enemy did not attack in any great force and preparations were made for the retreat. But Burgoyne's lack of enthusiasm for a withdrawal north was reflected in several delays and these, together with torrential rain and the consequent difficulties in moving the artillery and provisions, dictated that it was not until late on 10th October that the exhausted army arrived at their old September positions at Saratoga. There they found that the bridge over the Hudson had been burned and over the next three days the Americans blocked every avenue of escape north. With increasing casualties from constant enemy cannon fire and with mounting numbers of desertions, on 13th October, General Burgoyne had only four thousand men fit for action. He decided to consult all his officers, down to the rank of Captain, to agree on a course of action.

"Mewie, did you see the officer on horseback going out with the flag of truce?" exclaimed Clipper.

"Praise the Lord, has Burgoyne seen some sense at last?" interjected Corporal White.

"Yes, thanks be to God. We have been continually at arms for four days. I have two cartridges left and nothing in my bread bag."

"Same here, Mewie. The whole army is short of ammunition and we can't get to the provisions barges as they are constantly fired on," answered Clipper.

"Or captured."

"That's right, and they do say that the only way we can get water now is to send women to the river to get it. The rebels don't often shoot at them, although they did kill a few yesterday when they were foraging for potatoes."

"Why did he wait so long? We have no chance. Our numbers dwindle daily – they say that hundreds of the Germans have gone over to the enemy, and more and more of the men suffer from camp fever. It is no better for the wounded. I saw the hospital was hit yesterday, the poor bastards," said the Corporal.

"Do you think the rebels will give us terms to let us go home?" asked Aaron.

"We will have to wait and see, but at least the firing has stopped since the flag of truce went over."

It had stopped, but several times over the next days it started again when the negotiations between the two sides broke down and General Burgoyne threatened to resume the now hopeless conflict.

In the dusk, three days later, Sergeant Ryan gathered together the remaining men of the 62nd Light Company.

Beaming from ear to ear, he said, "The good news, boys, is that we are all going home!"

There were cheers from the tired men. They knew that some announcement about surrender would be made, for that morning the contents of the army money chest had been distributed amongst the officers and the troops.

"When, Serjeant?" called Corporal White.

"Yes, when?" chorused several voices.

"Wait, wait, let me give ye the details, though there is much verbiage here so I will tell the summary."

He referred to his orderly book and shouted, "Now listen up." He paused as he flicked through the pages.

"Right, in the Articles of the Convention signed in Saratoga, the 16th of October, 1777, by Lieutenant-General Burgoyne of His Majesty's Forces, and Major General Gates commanding the Army of the United States, the following was agreed as which affects us. Tomorrow, 14th October, the regiment will parade with full equipment and tents at ten o'clock. The special companies are herewith disbanded, including our Light Company, and you return to be part of the regiment. We will march out with the full honours of war, that is to say, with our flintlocks, our standards flying and the fifers and drummers playing. We will then ground our arms at the appointed place. Is that clear to all?" He flicked through his orderly book again. "Corporal, could ye be bringing that lantern over to help me see this?"

The soldiers waited patiently while this was done and then the Serjeant resumed.

"On condition that we all agree not to serve in North America in the future, a free passage is granted to the army to march to Boston to be transported back to England."

The Serjeant was interrupted by some cheering and expressions of general approval.

"Quiet now, 'cause you'll like this one. The troops are to be supplied by General Gates, on their march, and while in quarters awaiting transport, with provisions at the same rate of rations as his own army."

The atmosphere became even more lively as the soldiers exchanged comments of approval.

"Let me see. The officers, to retain their carriages, horses, their baggage not to be searched, they can wear their swords, and yes, the Canadians, sailors and Independent Companies to be allowed to return to Canada. It states that we are to march to Massachusetts Bay by the easiest, most expeditious and convenient route. Any questions?"

"Serjeant, what is to happen to the women?" asked a voice in the darkness, though several of those nearby recognised it as Aaron's.

"They will keep the same half rations as now and follow the troops on the march to Boston."

Already, the soldier from Wessex was beginning to anguish over how he was to fulfil his promise to Granville to look after Alice and to give Sarah half of the money.

Next morning, at ten o'clock, the British Army was paraded and then marched, following the drummers and with their bands playing, down the hill on the west bank of the Hudson. The column first had to ford the stream called Fish Kill and then proceed to the appointed place. The American troops lined both sides of the route to the site for the grounding of arms, which was observed by the commanders of both armies. The vanquished redcoats were watched by almost twenty thousand assembled Revolutionary soldiers and militia men. But they neither rejoiced, nor mocked the surrendering soldiers and the whole ceremony took place in a solemn and sad atmosphere. The only note of levity was that an American band played 'Yankee Doodle Dandy', but the significance of this was lost on the British, who knew it as a tune played in England called 'Lydia Fisher's Jig'.

The emotions of the defeated soldiers were a mixture of relief, anger and pride. Relief that they had survived the terrible onslaught of a numerically superior foe, anger at the humiliation brought on them by the failure of their mission and the paucity of the support from General Howe in New York, and pride that their gallantry was rewarded by them being allowed the full honours of war in their surrender. The anger that was felt was given vent to when, instead of laying down their flintlocks on the grass, many men took their weapons by the barrel and swung the stock hard on the ground so as to render the gun useless to the enemy.

"What happens now, Corporal?" asked Graham.

"We camp here tonight under guard, and tomorrow march down the river to Stillwater and there cross over to the east side."

"Thank God, one night here with the stench of the dead horses is enough for any man. How far is it to Stillwater?"

"I'll find out from the Serjeant."

"And ask him how far it is to Boston too."

As the men proceeded in a long column, they were followed by their women and children, numbering many hundreds. They made a pitiful sight. Most were undernourished and many of the women having had no opportunity to maintain their clothing were in rags and walked barefoot. They carried their chattels on their backs; the majority had baskets or bags supported by a carrying strap which passed over their foreheads. Some carried infants; others had to cajole their young children to walk and keep up with the pace of the army. Behind the British marched the Germans and at the end of their column followed a bizarre collection of animals which they had captured and tamed during the campaign. These included a black bear, deer, foxes and a racoon.

"The Serjeant said that we should stand to at first light to march out to Stillwater. It is a march of nine miles."

"And how far is it to Boston?"

"Just over two hundred miles."

Aaron considered this reply. Two hundred miles and marching in the oncoming winter weather! He cast his mind back to when a walk of ten miles from his home to Salisbury in fine weather had seemed a momentous journey. Later, as he lay trying to get some sleep, his thoughts were muddled when he considered the import of the situation he now found himself in. He could satisfy the dead Serjeant's request to take care of Alice, return with her to England and easily pay off the debt to the Squire and perhaps have enough money to start his own smithy. But would Alice survive the long walk? And if the future did follow this course, he would fail in his pledge to give half of the money to Sarah.

The next day began the epic march for officers, men and camp followers. While senior officers made the journey to Boston by carriage or wagon and many junior officers on horseback, the men, women and children walked the whole way in worsening weather, in stages of between five and twenty miles each day. On 6th November the British column arrived at Cambridge, eight miles from Boston, and set up camp at a place called Prospect Hill in the rough huts which had been built by the rebels two years earlier, when they had been besieging Boston. The huts were in a terrible state of repair. Most had no foundations and were just placed on bare boards on the ground. There were no windows, only uncovered openings and some huts lacked a roof. The severe shortage of timber meant that not only were there no building materials to repair the huts, but there was very little firewood to heat them. Twenty to forty persons, men, women and children, were placed in each hut. Here they awaited the ships which would take them back to England. The army had dwindled in size. Through exhaustion and disease the trail from Saratoga to Cambridge was punctuated by the graves of men, women and children who would never more see their home countries. In addition, a number of soldiers had deserted along the way. In particular, some German troops, who owed no loyalty to the English crown or the American flag, took the opportunity to find a new life in America.

Conditions in Cambridge were spartan and squalid for the men but also for the officers, as they too lived in the same conditions. Military discipline was, however, maintained. Each day there was a roll call, there were regular drills and there were general parades at twelve o'clock on Thursdays and Sundays, though with the soldiers in increasingly tattered and worn uniforms. However, to Aaron's relief, he heard no more about the threat of a court martial.

"You ain't still worried about the court martial are you?"

"I wonder if that Major who threatened to take me to one got killed in the battle, I've never heard anything more. No, Clipper, I have another worry."

With the death of Jamie, Aaron had no one he felt he could confide in. Bell knew about the money he was carrying, but he had not been seen since the Battle of Freeman's Farm and everyone agreed that his body had probably been so badly disfigured that he was never identified before being buried.

"You see, Clipper, when Granville died I promised to look after Alice."

"Well, you're doing that all right. You been keeping her warm in your bed this last month."

"No, I mean, he wanted me to somehow see that she was cared for."

"Why don't you marry her then, or do you still have a sweet spot for your Canadian widow?"

"Well, that's the cause of my discomfort. You see, Granville asked me to give her in Canada, some money."

"What money?"

"He gave me some for her."

"How much, Mewie?"

"That doesn't matter. Thing is, when we sail for England, I ain't going to have a chance to give it to her."

"Have you written to her to tell her that Granville is dead?"

They were interrupted by the sound of the drummer calling the men to the Sunday church parade. As they made their way out of their messes and trudged through the new snow to the square where the snow had been cleared, Aaron was considering what Graham had asked him. Perhaps it should be him who told Sarah of the Serjeant's death.

After the service, Serjeant Ryan detained the men of his company, lined up on the square.

"Company, be at ease. Everyone here, Corporals?"

The Corporals busied around checking that the men from each mess were present and then the senior Corporal reported.

"Twenty-nine men present, Serjeant, three in the hospital."

"Listen up men, some of you might have heard the rumours that have been spreading. I'm the bearer of bad tidings and to be sure it gives me no pleasure. On the 8th January, the Congress of the United States suspended the Convention of Saratoga. That is to say, the agreement between General Gates and our commander that we should be transported back to England. Do I make myself clear? Any questions?"

"What's their reason for breaking the agreement, Serjeant?" asked Corporal White.

"Ah, they have made up some story that we did not give up our cartridge boxes when we grounded our arms."

"But we had no ammunition anyway, Serjeant."

"I think that the Congress fears that if we return to Britain, on the pledge not to fight here again, we could just replace another regiment which could come here instead."

"So what does this mean for us, Serjeant?"

"It means, Corporal Reid, that you won't be seeing the spring flowers in England this year."

"We won't be leaving?"

"Exactly so. And as a consequence, instead of being free to return home, we are now prisoners of war, though they don't call us as such 'cause if they did, we could be exchanged for American prisoners held by General Howe in New York. The high ranking commissioned officers will try to get swapped for American officer prisoners held by General Howe, but that I'm afraid to say, won't happen for us."

The parade was dismissed and the disconsolate men returned to their duties. While many of them had work maintaining and improving the camp, a proportion of the fitter men went out each day and sometimes for longer periods to work on the local farms. They gave their parole, a promise to return to the camp each day or after a longer period for those working further away. Each of them was issued with a gate pass. This work provided the only source of income, for there had been no army pay since Saratoga. Aaron worked on a small estate assisting the blacksmith. The work gave him a great degree of freedom from the restrictions of army life in the camp and on more than one occasion he had considered deserting to find a permanent job, for there was a severe shortage of manpower in the country. But to go on the run in the middle of winter was too risky. In addition, his responsibility for Alice had quickly evolved into affection for her.

Nevertheless, he took the opportunity when it arose at his work to buy a used jacket from a farmhand, which he could wear should he ever have the chance to shed his redcoat and desert. Many of the men working on local farms stole clothes and food when they could, but Aaron had established a good relationship with his employer and he was careful to maintain it. On several occasions he was given discarded clothing for himself and Alice. There was a constant shortage of supplies in the camp and the surrounding area and most of the prisoners were still wearing the clothes they had surrendered in. A number of men had deserted, including the whole of the 62nd Regiment band. Most escapers tried to make their way to New York to join up with British forces there. For the latter reason, many of the officers encouraged men to try to escape and often helped them to do so by providing money and drawn maps. The officers, aware of the men's primitive living conditions and lack of food, also did all they could to alleviate the soldiers' discomfort. But the winter was harsh and there was no supply of winter clothing. In four months, seventeen men died of hunger and cold. In spite of this the men made their captors and the camp guards' lives as miserable and difficult as they could by being uncooperative and regularly insulting them.

The need to inform Sarah of Granville's death plagued Aaron through the winter. The only time he could write a letter was on a Sunday afternoon, for when he returned from work each day it was dark and they had no candles, only a small lantern in the mess hut. Eventually, he managed to write to her.

Cambridge nearby Boston
My Dear Sarah,
It is me, Aaron, who is writing to you. I hope that you are well and that this terrible winter is soon over. Please give my greetings to young Isaac.

I am very taken with sadness to have to give you the solemn tidings of the death of Serjeant Granville. He died bravely and I can say this as I witnessed his death at a place called Hubberton in New Hampshire. I buried his body myself and though there was often much animosity between us I have him to thank for saving my life.

It has troubled my mind greatly that I have taken so long to write to you but now I send you my deepest condolences as one who was your friend. He asked me to pass on some effects to you and this I will do one day God permitting, although presently I am a Convention prisoner. I do hope that this letter finds its way to you in these uncertain times. It is posted by my employer Jethro Page of Newtown Farm Cambridge Mass who regularly visits Boston.

Respectfully Yours,
Private Aaron Mew
62nd Regiment of Foot
February 1778

Chapter 22

It was in March, as winter began to loosen its grip and bring with it the prospect of spring, that there was a palpable sense of relief among the camp dwellers: they had survived the awful winter.

There was little privacy for anyone in the cramped conditions of the huts so groups and couples took the opportunity offered by the warmer weather to take a stroll around the camp perimeter after the parade on Sundays. Thus it was that Aaron and Alice found themselves taking the air, before returning to the crowded quarters.

Alice was wearing a dress which Aaron had been given for her at the farm. It was threadbare and patched and too big for her, but still made her one of the better dressed women out walking that afternoon. She had her old shawl around her shoulders, for the air was still quite chilly. Her auburn hair trailed over the top of the shawl. She walked with her arm through Aaron's.

"Aaron, how long do you think we will be living in this hut?"

"It could be a long while yet for the Serjeant tells that it will be first when we have won the war that we might be freed."

"But do you think it will be in a six month?"

"I really can't say. But it ain't too bad here now we got the roof fixed, and as long as I go working I can beg and buy extra things for us."

"Aaron, I really do hope that we can be just the two of us together soon, for it is fair crowded in the hut and soon there will be one more."

"How do you mean?"

"Because I will be having a baby before autumn."

Aaron was silent for a moment and then said, "How do you know?"

"I just do."

"You sure then?"

"I'm sure."

Aaron was shocked and there followed a period of silence while he considered the news. Alice stopped, turned to Aaron and said, "What had you expected to happen? We live like husband and wife."

"But, Alice, this ain't a proper place to have a baby."

"That's a consideration you should have had some time ago. You do like me, don't you?"

"Yes, of course I do." He hesitated for a moment and then said, "But you're only seventeen."

"How old are you, Aaron?"

"Twenty last Michaelmas."

"Well, that's plenty old enough to be a father."

"Would the babe have my name, Mew?"

"Of course, if we were married."

"I'd have to ask the Lieutenant's permission to do that."

"Wouldn't you like to have me as your wife?"

Once again there was a long silence and they started walking again.

"I can't deny that I have a strong fondness for you, Alice, but what kind of life would it be for you and a babe, living with a soldier."

Alice was silent for a minute. All her life she had been under the domination of others, a strict mother and a father who was preoccupied with the army and made no secret of the fact that he regretted that his daughter had not been a son. Aaron treated her with respect and affection; she was happier than she had ever been. She stopped, turned to face him and said, "Aaron Mew, I know no other life than that with soldiering, and despite the poor state of our present circumstances, I wouldn't be anywhere else than living with you."

After a while, Aaron said, "I'll ask for permission to speak to Lieutenant Stephens."

In mid-April, Alice became Mrs Mew. The money Aaron carried on behalf of Sergeant Granville was still untouched in his pouch and he now dreamed of the time he could use a portion of it to set up a home for his wife and child. But he was a prisoner, and as long as the Revolutionary war dragged on, he had little prospect of being set free by the Americans, and if it did happen he was still in the British Army.

At first, Alice's pregnancy gave Aaron cause for concern. She was worryingly frail, having suffered much from the lack of nourishment while in the care of the parsimonious Mrs Saunders and also the rigours of the long march to Cambridge. But the accidental timing of her current state was good, because with the spring upon them and summer beckoning, life in the camp became much more tolerable. Using the money he earned, Aaron was able to provide extra victuals to enhance their meagre prisoners' rations and buy clothes as Alice outgrew the dress and the rags she had worn when they arrived in Cambridge. By the end of May his thoughts of desertion had been overtaken by the anticipation of fatherhood and the need to stay in their simple but secure quarters. The uncertainty of the future became of less concern too as the prisoner community began to accept the fact that they would have to wait for the war to end before they would be shipped back to Britain. They had had some faint hope that they might be set free when a British fleet attempted to rescue the prisoners. It came to naught when the efficient American system of calling the militia by burning pitch-filled beacons on the hills brought together a strong force to oppose any British landing.

When Alice went into labour, Corporal Reid allowed a messenger to be sent to the farm where Aaron was working, to fetch him back to the camp. The other occupants of the hut had been turned out so that the women could attend to the birthing.

"You be waiting here, Private, while the womenfolk looks to the birthin'."

The woman pointed to a bench in front of the hut. Graham saw him sitting there and joined him.

"How long do this business take, Clipper?"

"It'll take the time it takes, Mewie. You got to have patience with these things."

Graham's statement was punctuated by a scream inside the hut, followed by another. Aaron jumped up, and began to tremble.

"Jesse, Mewie, I've seen you in battle and I have even seen you after a taste of the cat-o'-nine, but I never saw you so nervous."

"Well, the whole thing was my doing, Clipper, wasn't it?"

Graham laughed and said, "But 'twere a natural thing to happen, Mewie."

There were several more screams and then only the sound of the women exhorting Alice.

"I be going mad, Clipper. What's happening?"

"I should think that all is well. You'll hear soon enough."

They sat in silence. Aaron had his hat in his hands and kept slapping it on his thigh in exasperation. The door creaked open and the woman who had told him to sit on the bench looked down at him.

"You'd best come in, Mewie. You stay here, Clipper."

Aaron's heart was beating fast and furious as he first caught sight of the bloodstained rags on the table where Alice had been laid to give birth. He looked down at the straw mattress on the floor next to the table. Alice was lying under a coverlet with her head protruding, her face looking up at the ceiling, though her eyes were closed. The three women in the room quietly moved behind Aaron, so that he could approach the girl. Beside her was a smaller head, a much smaller one with wet dark hair, its sightless eyes turned towards the dead mother. The electrifying shock which he felt was like the one he had had when he realised that he had lost his neck pouch in Salisbury, but many, many times worse. He stood looking down at the pair, open jawed, then raised his arms and slapped his open palms against the sides of his head and kept them there while he contemplated the horrific scene and tried to understand it. He turned round to the women who were standing in a row behind him, waiting to see his reaction.

"Are they, are they dead?" he stuttered.

Two of the women were avoiding eye contact with him, looking at the ground, but the third, with a tear running down her cheek, nodded. He made to crouch down to embrace Alice, but the tearful woman leant down and grabbed him by the shoulders.

"Best leave them where they be, lad," she said softly.

He turned his head towards her and she saw tears in his eyes. Tears that no other pain, physical or emotional, had evoked since childhood.

Sobbing, he said, "What, I mean what, what was wrong with her? I mean, how could this happen?"

"The poor little lass just didn't have the strength to do it, Mewie. We done all we could, be assured."

The other women nodded with assent, murmured unintelligibly and started to tidy up and clean the hut.

"T'were a little girl, Mewie, but she hadn't been given enough life in the womb to survive."

Aaron turned back to look at the inanimate pair. He bent down, stretched out his left arm and gently caressed the cheek of the baby and then the mother.

"We'll leave you alone together for a few minutes so that you can say your farewells before we finish here and wash them for the mortuary," said the woman.

Without looking up, Aaron nodded. As he absentmindedly beat his fist on his chest trying to wake himself from the nightmare he was experiencing, he felt the pouch hanging under his shirt. It immediately evoked in him a feeling of profound regret. He had not done as the Sergeant had asked or as he had pledged, but worse, he had acted in such a way as to lead to the death of the person he should have helped. He stayed kneeling for several minutes, praying such as he knew how. Then he stood up and, gazing at his dead wife, found himself thinking about the first time he saw her, on the ship from England. She had suffered all the privations and dangers of the army on campaign as well as the loss of her mother, the negligence of her father and the cruelty of those she lodged with. Somehow her frail body had survived the long march from Saratoga and then the discomforts of their current circumstances. He could only take some small crumb of solace from the fact that she had found some happiness as their relationship had developed. But he also had the stark realisation that the relationship had ended – he had lost her, lost her before he could provide a normal life for her with the benefit of her father's legacy.

Over the next few days, Aaron wrestled with his conscience and finally, overcome with remorse, he made his decision. He would atone for his transgression by ensuring the fulfilment of the dying Sergeant's second bequest. He would deliver the money to the widow at St Nicholas, and that as soon as possible.

After the funeral, Aaron started to look for ways of evading his captors, but the task had now become doubly difficult. Now he had to escape from the increased surveillance of the American guards who were trying to stem the tide of desertions. He made some preparations by collecting items of clothing which he could use to disguise the fact that he was a runaway redcoat: a waistcoat, a shirt and woollen breeches. At kit inspections he hid his wardrobe under his mattress, a fact noticed by Graham with whom he had to confide. But others noticed too and before long Corporal Reid took him aside and said, "You got plans to leave us, Mewie?"

"How do you mean, Corporal?"

"Come on, lad, I ain't stupid. Everyone knows you got civilian clothes hidden under yer mattress."

Aaron hesitated for a moment and then said, "Well, what's going to happen to me?"

"Nothing, Mewie. But I will have to tell the Sergeant."

Aaron had several worrying days while he waited to see what reaction there would be to the Corporal informing the Sergeant. Four days later, he was summoned to see Major Harnage. The Major, who had been severely wounded at Saratoga, had recovered and now he and his wife shared a hut with several other officers. Aaron saluted an orderly outside and announced his errand. After several minutes the Major came out of the hut. Aaron stood to alert and saluted.

"Be easy, Private Mew. I understand that you are making preparations to escape."

Aaron had decided that there would be no purpose in lying and said, "I can't deny it, sir."

"Good man. General Howe could use men like you who have served in the Light Company. How do you propose to escape?"

"I ain't got a plan yet, sir. But I thought to go north to Canada, not to New York."

"How so?"

"Most of the enemy is south or west of us. I thought that my chances were better that way, sir."

"Umm…yes, there is something in what you say. You could join up with General Carleton's army. You know the route north of Saratoga, of course."

"Yes, sir."

"Do you have money? You need specie to bribe locals to help you. They don't like the paper dollars."

"No, sir."

"Let me know when you plan to escape and I will get you some gold or silver money."

"Thank you, sir."

"Good luck, Private."

The Major and Aaron saluted and the officer went back into the hut.

Aaron was greatly heartened by his conversation with the Major, but as autumn began to give way to winter 1778, he had still not found an opportunity to realise his plan. The possibility of escape was soon to become even more remote. Since mid-April, the Americans had been transferring the prisoners regiment by regiment to the village of Rutland, sixty miles to the west of Boston. There they occupied a far more secure place than the barracks in Cambridge. The huts were surrounded by a fence almost twenty feet high. At the beginning of October, the 62nd and the 24th Regiments were marched to Rutland.

It was in the first week of November, very early in the morning, that the Corporals went round the messes to tell the soldiers who were preparing to leave to do farm work that they were confined to barracks to attend a special parade later that day. The temperature was hovering around freezing point and there was a light dusting of snow on the ground when the company stood waiting for the Sergeant.

"Company, be alert!" shouted Corporal Reid as Ryan appeared carrying his orderly book.

"Company, be easy," he called as he strode out before the two ranks of men.

"Listen up, men, it can't have failed to have come to your attention that the standard and quantity of the victuals supplied to us is found to be wanting. The authorities here are finding it difficult to obtain supplies sufficient for the Convention prisoners. General Philips has been informed that all the Convention prisoners, that is British and German, are to be moved to Charlottesville, Virginia. There it is said the supply situation will improve. Any questions?"

"When will we leave, Sergeant?" asked Corporal Reid.

"In two days. Men who have been working on the farms will no longer be permitted to do so."

There were gasps from the men in the ranks.

"But the winter is upon us, Serjeant."

"That's as maybe, Corporal, but the information is that General Philips will lead the British Army, leaving on Friday 8th November. The Americans are to provide carts and wagons for the women and children, so it should be easier for them than the last march."

"How far is it, Serjeant?"

"Six hundred miles. That's all for now. Kit inspection tomorrow morning at ten."

"Company, be alert!" shouted Reid.

He saluted the Serjeant and then turned back to the assembled men, many of whom had started commenting on the news.

"Quiet men, be at ease." He waited a few moments and then said, "Company, dismiss."

The men gathered in small groups to bemoan what they considered the insanity of attempting such a long march in mid-winter.

"How far was it from Saratoga to Cambridge, Corporal?"

"About two hundred and twenty miles, Clipper."

"That was bad enough, but now we must march almost three times the distance."

"And in winter," said Aaron.

"I wonder which direction Virginia is?" said the Corporal.

"South, due south," said Aaron, for with his planned escape in mind, he had spent some time finding out as much as he could about the geography of America. And it was this knowledge which now made him desperate, for each day on the planned march would take him further from his intended destination.

Two days later, at first light, amid swirling white snowflakes, the men were paraded with their full kit. Most had left their blanket coats in Canada before the march south and only had their greatcoats to protect them from the cold. In place of the regulation headgear, many had woollen hats. A column of men had already passed them and at the given order, the 62nd joined the long procession heading south west. The Germans, who were still quartered in Cambridge as they were deemed to be less troublesome than the British, left for Charlottesville on the same day.

Each day's march varied in length according to the nature of the land, the steepness of the hills, the weather and the distance to a village of any size where the cooks could set up their field kitchens. For the first few days and in particular through the mountains it snowed incessantly. Occasionally, some of the women and children could find shelter for the night, but often they had to sleep in the carts in which they were travelling. The men had to sleep in the open, often on the snow with only a blanket for cover.

On 15th November, after walking ninety miles, the procession crossed the Connecticut River. The weather was wild and two men of the 9th Regiment drowned during the crossing. Two days later at Simsbury, they halted for a day to rest. Twelve days later they arrived at Fish Kills, near to the bank of the River Hudson. The stormy winds were driving sleet at them as they camped for the night near to the large American army base.

"Corporal, when I met Major Harnage he promised to help me to escape to go north to Canada."

"Why go that way, Mewie?"

"Now we have reached the Hudson, I can follow it up north to Fort Edward and then cross to Lake George. If I can steal a canoe I can follow the waterway all the way to St Johns."

"I'll ask the Serjeant to see if the Major will speak with you."

Later, Aaron repeated his plan to the Major.

"Mew, wait until we have reached the other side of the river. This side is teeming with American soldiers from the encampment. It is going to take some time to ferry the army across and there is certain to be confusion while large groups of soldiers are waiting on both sides. Over fifty men have managed to escape on this journey already."

"Yes, sir."

"I will get specie for you, see Serjeant Ryan about victuals. He is going to fill your bread bag. Remember to keep clear of the forts, especially Fort Edward. They are all occupied by the enemy. And Mew, you would do better to pay the savages for a canoe. They do not take kindly to theft and are bereft of a forgiving nature."

"Thank you, sir."

"By the way, in army records you will be noted as a deserter."

"Even if I join General Carleton's army?"

"Even so, though you might be paid a bounty. General Howe is paying a bounty to deserters from our army."

When Aaron joined his messmates he was in a high state of excitement. Tomorrow was the day. After three years of living with the companionship and support of others, always being told by his superiors what to do and when to do it, he now had the realisation that the next day he would be on his own, fending for himself in a hostile country. Inspired by the conversation he had just had, he gave in to the constant questioning about why the Major had asked to see him and told his closest friends of his impending plan.

Chapter 23

"Mewie, here is a package for you from the Major and a note," said Corporal Reid.

He handed a small heavy leather purse to the Private and a sealed note. They were standing in a long queue with no shelter from the driving sleet, as they waited to be allocated places in the small craft which were ferrying troops and camp followers across the wide river. Without opening the purse, Aaron swung his knapsack off his back, lifted the goat skin, unbuckled it and pushed the leather container to the bottom. Then he remembered something which had happened a long time ago and far away, and advice he had been given by a ruffian who had once helped him. He withdrew the purse, opened it and took out two coins, which he put in his pocket before replacing it in the bottom of his bag. Then, holding tightly to the note, he broke the seal and read the contents.

> *Private Mew, seek an opportunity to change into your disguise at the earliest opportunity after you have crossed and attempt your escape. Be expeditious, for we have intelligence that General Washington has sent five hundred extra troops to guard our army for the next part of the march and they will soon arrive.*
>
> *When you get near to St Johns look out for Roger's Rangers irregulars' patrols, they will help you to get from there to Quebec. They wear green jackets and waistcoats, with red facings. Take one of your 62nd Regiment uniform buttons with you, to identify yourself to them and the Army in Quebec.*
>
> *Please destroy this note.*
>
> *Good luck.*

The note was unsigned and Aaron understood why. He tore it into several pieces and let the wind take them. Then he ripped one of the buttons with the name of his regiment from his jacket, and put it in his pocket.

It was late in the afternoon before Aaron's company was gathered on the far shore. The weather had improved and there was a red veil of sunset behind light clouds as they prepared themselves to continue their march to their next overnight stop, a village which was called Little Britain. The 62nd formed into line ready for departure. As the men did so, Aaron made off to the northern side of the track, as if to seek a spot to relieve himself. This was a prearranged signal for his company to turn and, as one-man, charge off the track towards the forest on the other side. The guards desperately chased after to round them up and amid much shouting and protesting the British soldiers abandoned what had appeared to be a mass escape. Meanwhile, Aaron was well into the forest when he stopped to change into his disguise. Then, using the setting sun as a guide, he circled north around the track and towards the trail which followed the river towards Albany, seventy-five miles away. He was free and on his way to Canada to fulfil his promise to Serjeant Granville, before he crossed the St Lawrence to Quebec and reported for duty at General Carleton's Headquarters.

As darkness fell Aaron started making his way north on the trail. The track was rutted by the passage of wheeled vehicles and the ruts were full of water and mud. While there was enough light to guide his steps away from the deep wheel marks, he was able to make good speed, but as night came on, and with it snow showers, he was forced to walk slowly and with caution. After two hours, the trail was so deeply covered with snow that the fugitive was forced to consider stopping for the night and continuing in daylight. Aaron searched for a spot in the forest at the side of the road where he could shelter under bushes and try to get some sleep. Eventually, he found a hollow beneath a large tree and made himself as comfortable as he could, sitting on the snow-covered ground with his blanket over his head. He ate some of his provisions and then dozed fitfully, suffering increasingly from the cold and woken often by the howl of wolves.

The next day, at first light, he continued his walk. The first time he met someone on the road his instinct was to hide, but he quickly realised there was no point in doing so as although the forest afforded plenty of cover, his fresh footprints in the snow would easily give away his presence and awake suspicion. So when he passed others, he responded to their greetings, but avoided conversation. And so he continued, plodding in the ever deeper snow drifts and meeting fewer and fewer people. Very occasionally, he passed a habitation. The three or four shacks he had seen were near the road and he gazed with envy at the curls of smoke betraying the fact there was a warm fire within.

In summer, the walk to Albany should have taken four or five days, but at his rate of progress in the difficult conditions it was clear that his journey would take much, much longer. It was on his second day on the road that Aaron began to ration his food. It was very difficult, for he was constantly hungry. The cold and the effort of negotiating the deep snow were telling increasingly on his energy reserves. The lack of sleep and the discomfort of the chaffing from his wet clothes added to his woes.

By the fifth day, having been walking on an empty stomach for two days, combating the worsening weather with decreasing strength, he knew that he was in serious trouble and must find shelter and food. He had not passed any other travellers for two days, neither had he seen any houses. After staggering from snow drift to snow drift for several hours, probably in mid-afternoon, he could go no further. He was very cold and hungry, and had begun to have what seemed like nightmares, though he was wide awake. He was also feeling more and more remote from reality; everything seemed unreal and distant. He stopped and with difficulty, tried to brush the snow off a fallen tree trunk to sit down. The snow had stopped. He sat and gazed helplessly and hopelessly at the long white track ahead of him, which could only be identified because of the fact that it was a narrow channel between the forests on both sides. After a few minutes, he began to doze and so desensitized was he that he did not notice as he slipped from the log into the snow below.

Chapter 24

It was fortunate that the snow storm had abated, for otherwise the unconscious body lying by the roadside would have been covered by a freezing white blanket and not been discovered until the spring.

The traditional homeland of the Wampanoag Indians was in Massachusetts, but in winter, when the Hudson could easily be crossed on the ice, they occasionally overwintered and hunted further west. The tribe had little to thank the white men for. Two generations ago their numbers were decimated by European illnesses and many of the male survivors were sold into slavery in the West Indies, while the women were enslaved in New England.

When the hunting party emerged from the forest on the east side of the road, travelling easily on their snowshoes, curiosity dictated that they pause to look at the body of a white man lying in the snow. When one of the warriors made to lift the knapsack from the recumbent form, he was surprised when the arm that held it snatched it back. As the figure in the snow struggled to sit up, one of the Indians stooped down and helped him. Aaron sat surveying the men gathered around him, quickly realising that this scene was not part of the fantasy of his hallucinations.

They were all dressed in heavy coats, not dissimilar to a blanket coat, which were gathered in at the waist, and had deerskin leggings. Unlike the warriors who had been with the British Army, these men wore their hair long, tied in plaits on either side of their heads. Each of them had a short firelock strapped to their backs together with leather knapsacks. Long knives hung from their belts and Aaron wondered if he was about to be scalped, but found himself caring little. He looked up at them and raised his hand to his mouth to try to indicate that he was hungry. The men spoke to each other in their own tongue and then one of them, who appeared to be the leader, thrust his hand into a pouch on his belt and pulled out a piece of dried meat. He handed it to Aaron, who snatched it and pushed it into his mouth. Others also gave him food, some offering a kind of hard bread, others small pieces of dried meat. The effect of the food slowly started to revive him. They helped him to his feet and he swayed unsteadily. He put his hand into his pocket to get one of the coins to give to the leader as a thanks offering, but his fingers were too numb to grip anything. He tried several times while the men stood around him, wondering what he was doing. Eventually, he managed to pull out one of the small gold coins. He handed it to the man who had first given him food. There was hubbub among the warriors as they passed round the coin, each of them examining it.

"Where you go?" asked the leader.

"North, north to the land of the Haudenosaunee."

There was heated discussion between the Indians. Had Aaron but known it, the two tribes were enemies.

Clearly, some decision had been made. Two of the warriors dragged Aaron to his feet and each pulled one of his arms over their shoulders. They stood supporting him and then moved off north along the trail with Aaron walking between them as best he could, without the benefit of snowshoes.

The warriors travelled silently, with no words being spoken to him or between them. The curious procession continued until, just before darkness fell, Aaron became aware of an unmistakable smell of wood smoke.

As they left the trail and entered the snow-covered track to the little farmhouse, a dog started barking. When they got closer, perhaps just fifty paces from the ramshackle porch, the front door was thrown open and silhouetted against the oil lamp light behind her, an elderly woman levelled a flintlock at them. Beside her the barking dog was tied up on the porch. The fact that she was defending her property immediately suggested that she was alone in the house and Aaron at once realised that he had brought danger to her. There was a tense moment while he wondered what he could do to help, and then relief as it soon became clear that she knew the Indians. As she lowered the gun, she shouted first to the dog, "Hush, hush, Benjamin," and then to the warriors, "You here again. What do you want this time?"

Without commenting, the two braves who were supporting Aaron pushed him forward and released their grip on him. He immediately fell into the snow in front of the woman.

She motioned with her hand for the warriors to pick Aaron up again and shouted, "Get him inside, he ain't looking too good."

The leader understood enough to comprehend her instruction and he indicated to the others what was to be done. Once inside, she indicated a cot in the kitchen and ushered the men to place him there. Then the leader turned to her and said, "We sleep here."

"Yes, you can sleep in the barn, but leave my damned chicken alone this time."

The Indians left and she closed the door. Aaron was slumped, sitting on the edge of the cot, his knapsack still on his back.

"Oh my Lord, what have we here? Where did you spring from, son? It ain't exactly the time of year for a promenade."

Aaron was too weak and confused to consider subterfuge. "I ran away from the army."

"You did the right thing, son. If only my boy had done that, I wouldn't be here alone now."

Without thinking, he blurted out, "What happened to him?"

The woman took a deep breath and sighed. She looked directly into Aaron's eyes when she said, "The fact is, nothing need to have happened to him. Me and my man, God rest his soul, wanted no truck with the British or the rebels, we just wanted to get on with our lives. We've got good land here and we were prospering. But living by the main road like we do, my boy, Rolf that is, got all fired up when he saw the soldiers marching past. He joined the New Hampshire Regiment in the spring of seventy-seven and was killed by the damned redcoats near Saratoga.

"How old are you, son?"

"Twenty-one, ma'am."

"My boy, Rolf, would have been thirty this year. You did the right thing, lad, this country needs its young men. Too much blood has been spilled for God knows what cause."

Despite his state of mind, Aaron realised that when he had told the woman that he had run away from the army, she had assumed that it was the American army and that he was an American deserter. There was a long silence, the memory of her son having been evoked. Aaron felt he had to fill the period of quiet and said, "You are a widow then, ma'am, are you?"

"Nigh on two years."

"What happened to your husband?"

The woman's voice dropped as she quietly said, "He went to his maker the same year as Rolf. He was defending our animals from the thieving redcoats, you know, that butcher Clinton's men. They were trying to get north to Albany, but soon come running back. So living by the road, we got to suffer from their plundering twice, up and back."

"Did they shoot him?"

"Not before he shot one of them when they tried to drive our cows off to their camp. He were scared of nothing. Had it been an American soldier stealing, he would just as well have shot him."

There was a silence; the woman was obviously thinking about her loss. Then she turned to Aaron and said, "Now, lad, let's get your wet things off and dry them by the fire, then you shall have some soup. You'll soon get your strength back."

"Ma'am, I am truly grateful to you for taking me in."

"Schultz is the name, my late departed husband was German. And don't think that you'll have an easy life here, it's many a month since I had a man around the farm, there's much to be done. The road is going to get worse before it gets better, so you'll have time to give a good account of yourself. Where are you headed anyway?"

"Canada."

"Canada? Oh my word, that's a journey. What do you want to go there for? Those that aren't French are British. I don't know which is worse."

"I have to meet a woman."

Mrs Schultz laughed and said, "I should have guessed, only an affair of the heart would drive a man to walk nigh on three hundred miles. What's your name, son?"

"Aaron Mew."

"Come on then, Mr Mew. Off with your breeches and jacket. You can keep your shirt on to protect your modesty, but don't think that I shock easily."

Aaron lamely did as ordered.

And so began Aaron's five months on the farmstead. If Mrs

Schultz ever suspected the truth about him, she never said, but neither did she ask any questions about his regiment or indeed his family. That is not to say that she did not talk a great deal, for like any person starved of human contact for months at a time, she took every opportunity for conversation. It mattered not to her that Aaron contributed very little about himself in their discussions. She was happy to talk at length, and interestingly, about her girlhood, her family, the farm, her experiences in the great French and Indian War and occasionally about her mistrust of politicians and authority. Her brain was as clear as a bell and rivaled in sharpness only by her tongue when she expressed an opinion about something or someone she did not approve of. At an early stage in his stay, Aaron realised that although she had the appearance and movements of an elderly person, she was not much older than his own mother, but arthritis and the physical effects of the years of heavy work on the farm had aged her greatly.

The remoteness of the farmstead suited Aaron perfectly; he had learned from his near disastrous recent journey and reconciled himself to the fact that he must wait for the spring before he could continue north. The farm provided good security for him. The isolation of the settlement inflicted by the winter weather meant that the only people they ever saw were the occasional traveller on snowshoes and infrequently, the Wampanoag hunters when they asked to sleep in the barn. Neither did he have a bad conscience about the fact that he was having free board and lodging, for the farm had been badly neglected since the menfolk had gone and there was much for him to repair and improve.

As the weeks wore on and the results of his work were ever more obvious the widow seemed to be becoming more and more dependent on his efforts. At the same time, Aaron was getting increasingly concerned about how she would manage without him. This concern reflected the growing bond between the guest and the hostess, an attachment which was beginning to liken that of mother and son.

By April, the road was beginning to become much more populated, but the severe winter had rendered the treacherous road surface even worse and made travelling on it precarious for horse-drawn vehicles. Several damaged carts were stopped outside the farmstead while the owners made repairs and frequently Aaron's skills were called on.

Mrs Schultz knew that she was going to lose her young companion and rather than put him in the awkward position of telling her that he was leaving, she took the initiative.

"Aaron, like the geese, you'll be wanting to make your way north now that spring is here. Why don't you go to Canada and fetch that gal of yours and bring her back here? I got no relatives and the Lord ain't got much more use for me on this earth, what with me aching hands and wobbly legs. When I go, the farm is yours for the taking. This place needs kids around it."

He was astounded at her offer and stumbled to find words. "What, what, you mean that you would gift the farm to me?"

"Well, I ain't got no one else to leave it to and you have become as near to family as I have left."

This was too much for Aaron. His conscience had troubled him for months about the fact that he had inadvertently misrepresented himself as an American deserter.

"Look, missus, I've got to be truthful to you for I have lost many an hour's sleep worrying about my dishonesty. I never said I was an American deserter, though you thought so. Fact is, I am a redcoat, or was anyway."

The old woman laughed. "Son, I may be old but stupid I ain't – I worked that out long ago. 62nd Regiment, ain't you?"

"Well, that's the truth of it. How did you know?"

"Well, I can't read words, but I do know numbers. It ain't difficult to read the number on that button you keeps by your bed."

"Why didn't you throw me out then?"

"Lad, I don't care if you belonged to Beelzebub's army. These past months I've seen you for what you really are."

Aaron did not feel that he could tell her that he had no intention of bringing a fiancée back to the farm, but that he was simply going to visit her to pass on the legacy. Neither could he say that it had been his intention to report to the Army in Quebec. He simply said, "I'd be away a long time, ma'am."

"Well, you could make it quicker. Why don't you offer to travel with one of the carters, for you are a very handy man and I am sure that it would be reassurance for a driver to have company such as yours."

"What if they ask about me? There'll be a bounty on British deserters."

"Leave that to me."

As always Mrs Schultz enjoyed conversation and when carters stopped outside the farm she sometimes offered them a glass of her homemade wine. In so doing, she sought to find a suitable conveyance for Aaron, one with a driver who was honest and who had business as far north as possible. One day she called Aaron in from the barn.

"Aaron, this is Mr Brownlee. He is transporting furniture for a Loyalist family who have fled to St Johns."

"How do you do, sir," said Aaron.

Brownlee looked Aaron up and down and said, "Your ma has asked that you might join me travelling north. I'd be glad of the company, the road is rough and dangerous."

Aaron immediately grasped that Mrs Schultz had passed him off as her son to give him credibility.

"Well, sir, I'd appreciate that. I'd be no trouble and I am good with horses."

"I've got to warn you that we might have trouble at the border. The British don't exactly welcome Americans into Canada."

"Oh, don't concern yourself, sir. I've met a few British. I know how to deal with them."

The deal was agreed and the next day, with a good supply of victuals from the farm, Aaron joined Mr Brownlee and they set off.

The journey was long and uncomfortable, but when, three weeks later, they were stopped on the road by a patrol of men in green uniforms, Aaron remembered the Major's advice that he should look out for Roger's Rangers. He decided that it was now safe to reveal to Brownlee who he really was and with the evidence of his button, he was able to persuade the rangers that he was an escaped Convention prisoner. With his status thus enhanced by the admiration of the Loyalists, entry into Canada was permitted for him and the carter, and they were escorted by the patrol as far as St Johns. There, Aaron bade farewell to Mr Brownlee and set off to walk on a route he knew so well from his time in the shipyard – the road to Chambly. He found that the shipyard was no longer in use, but there were two British merchant vessels moored against the harbour wall. One of them, berthed facing upstream, appeared to be preparing to leave the dock. Aaron stopped to watch.

The master of the ship was pacing the poop deck, alternately peering up at men in the rigging and down at a man with a long pole who was attempting to lever the ship's bow off the harbour wall to turn her enough for the light headwind to wear her round for departure down river. Aaron put his knapsack down and walked over to help the man.

"Thanks, friend, this ain't easy."

"Why don't other crew help you?" asked Aaron.

"What other crew? We are so short-handed that we hardly have enough to raise a sail. Half of the men we do have are drunken redcoat deserters who know nothing of seamanship."

"What happened to the sailors?"

"Some jumped ship, others died of ship fever. Nigh on twenty men are gone."

"Where are you going?"

"Down to Quebec to take on cargo and passengers and then to England. Why, you looking for a berth?"

"If you need another hand."

The man called up to the master, "Captain, got another one here, do you want him?"

The officer walked forward on the ship until he was almost level with Aaron and the seaman and shouted, "We've got enough scoundrels on board already."

He looked Aaron up and down and noting that he was well built and seemingly fit, added, "You got a trade?"

"I'm a blacksmith, sir."

"Ever worked on a ship?"

"Yes, sir."

"You want to work your passage?"

"Yes please, sir."

Addressing the other man, he said, "Get him to jump for the rail when you do."

"Grab your bag, friend, and jump for the rail as she turns."

A few moments later, Aaron was on the deck of the ship adjusting to his new surroundings.

"What's your name, soldier?" asked the master.

"Mew, sir. Aaron Mew, but how did you know I was a soldier?"

"Obvious. Where else would a strapping lad like you suddenly turn up from in St Johns? There are thousands of British and German soldiers fighting here for the King and you aren't alone in deciding that soldiering is not for you."

Aaron did not protest, but asked, "Where should I mess, sir?"

"The bosun will give you a space below and a hammock. Take your bag down and then come back to report for duty."

As Aaron picked up his knapsack, the master added, "Don't leave what pay you have saved in your knapsack. I'll lock it up for you in my cabin. We've got company on this ship who wouldn't think twice about slitting your throat for a groat."

Later, when he had been allocated a hammock, Aaron slipped his hand into the bottom of his knapsack and found the five small gold coins he had not used in his escape. He put them into his pocket before placing the bag on his hammock and going on deck to report to the bosun.

"It's holystoning for you, lad. We've got to get these decks tight before we face the Atlantic. Join the other deserters over there." He pointed to four men who were working by the starboard rail.

As the ship made its way slowly down the Richelieu River towards the St Lawrence and Quebec City a hundred and fifty miles away, with a near following wind, the men hauled a large stone in a wooden frame back and forth on the deck. The action of the 'holystone' on the deck planks was to smooth them ready for the gaps between them to be caulked with oakham.

"Where'd you come from, soldier?" asked one of the gang, when Aaron knelt down to join them. He had previously noticed the man as he appeared to be wearing a stolen officer's jacket.

Aaron answered, "A long way away."

The man grabbed Aaron by his wrist and growled, "When I ask a question you answer it. You understand me?"

Aaron had not been bullied since the episode with Kemp and his first reaction was to retaliate. However, he quickly realised the futility of antagonizing one of the crew, someone who he might be sleeping beside for the whole voyage. He resolved that if action was needed, it would be in a manner and at a time of his choosing. He knew that the other men in the gang were all watching him, waiting to see how he reacted.

"Sorry, friend. I meant to say, Albany."

The man stabbed a knife hard into the deck plank very close to Aaron's right hand and said, "Just a warning, lad. Joe, that's me, expects some respect."

He replied lamely, "Yes, Joe."

"Then we understand each other, one soldier to another. What's your name?"

"Mewie."

The gang worked on in silence until a long section of the deck had been caulked and then a member of the crew appeared with a bottle of linseed oil and showed the new crew how to oil the planks.

Aaron had had time to survey the other members of the working party. He found it difficult to believe that his filthy, villainous-looking companions had once looked smart in a redcoat's uniform for now they looked like the dregs of society. When they were released from their work to have their tea meal, he sought the company of one of the original crew, the man he had helped on the quay. He learned that his companion was called John and hailed from Plymouth.

"Be careful of those four, they ain't to be trusted. But I'll hazard a guess that they will be as good as gold until we have left Quebec, for they wouldn't want to be put ashore there. Carleton would have them hung in no time. You too would be in danger I warrant."

"How long before we get there?"

"Well, if the wind holds, we should be in port the day after tomorrow. Then we've got the long haul to England, perhaps thirty days."

"So in a month and a half we would be in England?"

"Surely, for we should get westerlies in the Atlantic this time of year."

The soldier reflected. He could be in England in six weeks.

Later, Aaron stood at the rail of the ship watching the countryside passing. It was a route which he was now travelling for the fourth time, but before he had been tramping along a rough trail in an unwelcoming wilderness. Now, from his vantage point on the ship, he could see the untainted beauty of the forests which stretched as far as the eye could see. He reminisced about the companions he had had on the earlier marches to and from St Johns, who would march no more; he thought of Rev, Jamie and Grabber, and then there was poor Huhnie who never even got across the St Lawrence. He found himself wondering what they had all died for. And Alice too had marched up and down the trail, undernourished and ragged. When he closed his eyes he could still see the dreadful image of her and the baby. He mused that once he would close his eyes and visualize Peggy, but the impression of her face was long forgotten. Then he had a sudden thrill when he realised that he might see her again in not much more than six weeks, for the master of the ship was surely of the view that he would serve for the whole voyage. He had two hundred pounds in the pouch round his neck and gold in his pocket. He could repay the debt to the Squire and have plenty of money over to start his own smithy. The prospect excited him and he found himself consumed with enthusiasm as he went below to his hammock.

The scene which awaited him there shocked him out of his trance. The men he had worked with on deck were sitting in a circle on the floor, smoking under the hammocks with several rum bottles in front of them, and they had been joined by other 'temporary' crew members. Already two men had passed out and were lying in their own vomit. The circle of men looked wretched and depraved.

There was a chorus of, "Mewie, where've you been, come and join us." Aaron had no choice. When he sought his hammock in the dim candlelight to get his pipe, he found that his knapsack had been emptied and the contents strewn across the hammock. Silence fell among the revelers as they watched him. He knew that they were waiting to see how he would react; equally he was determined not to give them the entertainment of seeing him lose his temper. He bit his lower lip, turned to the men, pointed at the assortment of clothes lying on his bed and laughed, saying, "I'd better get this cleared up before the Serjeant comes for kit inspection."

There was a moment's silence, the crowd waiting to see how Joe reacted, and laughter when he said, "This bastard's funny. Had a tough Serjeant did you, Mewie?"

"I did indeed," he replied. He picked up his tin cup from among the clothes and joined the circle.

Later, much later, it was clear to Aaron that he would get no sleep until all the men had drunk themselves into a stupor. He stood up, pushed his belongings into his knapsack and unnoticed by those still able to sit, he went up the companionway onto the deck and made himself as comfortable as he could, to sleep under his greatcoat. But in spite of, or perhaps because of the rum, sleep did not come easily. He found himself thinking about Mrs Schultz and the promise she had made for him to take over the farm. He was also greatly concerned about how she would be managing now; there would be the calving, the hoeing and myriad other jobs to be done to ensure a good harvest to see her through the next winter. If he delivered the money to Sarah in the next few days, he could be back on the farm in three or four weeks to help out. Then he reminded himself that he was still a soldier, a redcoat – he could be in danger if he travelled back. A soldier, yes, it had been his intention to give Sarah her legacy and then to report to the army in Quebec. As he tried to order his confused thoughts, sleep overtook him and the resolution of a course of action was postponed.

The next day was also spent holystoning and Aaron continued to suffer the humiliation of humouring the detestable Joe and his acolytes. All the while, Aaron was aware that the hour was coming when he had to make a decision. The watershed was unavoidable.

Later, he again sat on a bench with John eating their tea meal. Aaron was surprised when he said, "Mewie, why are you doing this? When you arrive in England you will be just like those rogues." He pointed at Joe and his henchmen and continued, "You will be identified as a man with no honour, identified to be no better than those villains. How are you going to explain to your family and your friends how you come to be at home?"

"What do you think I should do then?"

"Join us, become a member of the crew. There's honour in being a sailor."

Aaron did not answer, but changed the subject. That night he once more tried to sleep on the deck, but John's words kept coming back to him. It was true, if he sailed off to England it would be without honour, and more so because the money he was carrying was not his. He would be a thief without honour. And yet, he was only six weeks from a homecoming – he would see his parents, Matthew and perhaps Peggy. He anguished through the night and as dawn broke, he still had not decided on which route to take at this crossroads of his life.

As the massive bulk of the redoubt of Quebec Fort revealed itself ahead, Aaron found himself looking in another direction. On the starboard side of the ship, easily visible, was the village of St Nicholas. He could make out the little church and soon the barn and the small farmhouse and the smithy. The more he looked, the stronger was his longing for the happy time he had spent there. What he did not know, was that on the cupboard in the room he knew so well, there was a letter waiting to be posted. It was a letter he might never see.

Widow Rasmussen had been anguishing about whether to post her reply to a letter she had recently received from the young Private she once knew. It had taken over a year to reach her, but it was a miracle that it had arrived at all during the current period of conflict. Though it contained bad tidings, she was glad to know that Aaron had survived the terrible battles she had heard about. She had written her reply, but with the state of war between the British and the Americans, it was very uncertain that a letter would reach its intended destination. To add to the unreliability of communication, many ships out of Quebec were plundered or captured by American privateers. She also had some doubt about how welcome the letter might be, and she was unsure about whether she was doing the right thing in sending it. After much thought, she had eventually decided to take the next opportunity to have the letter taken to Quebec to be posted.

To Mr Jethro Page, please pass to Mr Aaron Mew, Newton farm, Cambridge, Mass.

My dear Aaron,
I thank you for your letter which reached me two weeks ago. The news was painful but no more than I had expected for my fate has been badly dictated by the misfortunes of this war. If there is any good from this conflict it is that we have now lived in peace here for over a year, though I continue to be persecuted with much spite for my previous allegiance to the American cause. If I had the means I would happily leave this country and move south.

Isaac remembers you with great fondness and hopes for your safe return, as do I for now I have two more mouths to feed and times are very hard. My twins were born healthily, praise the Lord, just before Christmas in 1777 and they have the fair hair and blue eyes of their father as you surely are. I wish you Godspeed to St Nicholas.

With affection,
Sarah Rasmussen
Forge Farm
St Nicholas
18th April 1779

Once the ship was berthed there was much activity on deck. The cargo of timber and packs of furs was hoisted aboard together with chests of victuals for the journey. Often while they were working, the deserters in the crew cast anxious glances at the quayside, worried that the military authorities might search outbound ships to see if there were those on board who should be serving their King. Finally, the passengers came on board; there were about thirty men, women and children who walked up the gangplank carrying their effects.

In the evening, when the ship was fully loaded, the crew had some spare time. They were to cast off on the ebb tide early in the morning. Aaron sought to be alone, aware that his options for choice were all still open, but would not be for much longer. The gangplank was still down, but it would be brought onboard shortly to prevent unwelcome two-footed and four-legged visitors during the night.

He fingered the package hanging under his shirt; across the river he could see some dim lights, the oil lamps of the houses in Levis, a village just east of St Nicholas. With his other hand he pulled from his pocket something he had carried for the last six months, a button from the uniform of a private of the 62nd Regiment of Foot – his button. In the light of the lantern illuminating the gangway, he looked at the inscription on the button. He put it back into his pocket. With no further hesitation, he bent down, hoisted his knapsack onto his shoulder, quickly made his way down the gangplank and disappeared into the darkness of the quay.

Afterword

Many real historical figures are mentioned in this book, of these, apart from the King, General Burgoyne is perhaps the most famous or perhaps notorious. Though he was a brave and often outstanding general, his arrogance and refusal to listen to his fellow officers' advice, led directly to the British catastrophe at Saratoga. Unlike the men who had served him so courageously, he did not have to stay long in America after the defeat. He was permitted to return to England where though initially shunned by the King, he prospered and apart from being awarded civil and military appointments, he was a successful playwright.

The German General, Riedesel, survived the rigours of the campaign despite his age and he and his wife were permitted by the Americans to sail from Boston to Canada. Her story is most remarkable. She followed her husband throughout the North American campaign, sharing the discomforts and dangers with him. During the battle of Saratoga she sheltered in the cellar of a house adjacent to the battlefield together with her three children, one of whom had been born in America. Her diary gives an extraordinary account of the hardships not only suffered by her on the long journey from Canada, but also those endured by other women and the foot soldiers.

Lieutenant-Colonel John Anstruther, the commander of the 62nd Regiment, was wounded in the battle. He recovered and after some delay, he was exchanged for an American officer of the same rank, held prisoner by the British in New York. He sailed for England in May 1778, but the ship was captured by an American privateer and he, together with six other officers, was handed over to the Spanish in Coroña. He was quickly repatriated and oversaw the reforming of the new 62nd Regiment in England.

Edward Pellew, who nearly came to grief when the mast was

being raised on the *Inflexible*, took part in the battle at Saratoga gallantly defending the supply barges. He survived the action and became an outstanding sea captain. Using his swimming skills to good effect in 1796, he swam out to a grounded ship off Plymouth, U.K. He carried a lifeline to the stricken vessel and over five hundred passengers were saved. Eventually, Edward Pellew became a Vice-Admiral and 1st Viscount Exmouth.

Around six hundred officers and men of the 62nd Regiment embarked in Cork in 1776. It is estimated that no more than fifty ever made the crossing back over the Atlantic. It is most probable that these were the ones who managed to escape from Cambridge, or eluded their captors on the winter journey to Virginia and rejoined the British Army in New York. There is no record of what became of the 225 women and 500 children who started out with the soldiers on the long march from Saratoga to Cambridge, after the surrender in 1777.

Of those soldiers, women and children who survived and were released from captivity at the end of the American War of Independence in 1783, it is likely that most settled in America.

The Battle of Saratoga was not the conclusive battle of the War of Independence, but the defeat of the British gave France and Spain the confidence to join the war on the side of the Americans. Apart from providing much needed supplies to the Americans and causing threats to the British navy, the French help was largely ineffectual until 1783. In that year a French army, supported by a naval squadron, exploited the lack of determined British leadership in New York and performed a brilliant entrapment of a British army at Yorktown. The surrender of General Cornwallis to General Washington, ended any hopes King George III had of keeping his American colonies.

Endnotes

62nd Regiment of Foot - in 1781 it became known as the 'Wiltshire Regiment, 62nd Regiment of Foot'

Abbitas – a wall of sharpened poles pointing away from defenders, to hinder an enemy advance

Beating order – a recruitment party

Birds' Islands – now known as the Magdalen Islands

Brickett's Hospital – Brickett's Almshouse

Carriol – a fast horse-drawn sledge

Caulked – filled

Coining – debasing coinage by clipping or filing precious metal from coins

Commission – officers up to the rank of Lieutenant-Colonel bought their commissions to join the army as officers. In 1775 the price of an ensign commission (the lowest commissioned officer rank) was £400

Common time – marching at normal walking pace

D – a tattoo put on the arm, chest or head of army deserters

Dickens – devil

Double time march – quick march

Draghall Street – now called Exeter Street

Firelocks – 18th Century name for a musket

Fish Kill – one of several places in North America called Fish Kill, originally named by the Dutch 'vis kil', meaning 'fish creek'

Frog – sheath

Fugleman – an experienced soldier who demonstrates to others

General Arnold – Benedict Arnold, later to defect to the British side

G III R – George the Third Rex, (King)

Groat – a silver coin worth four 'old' pence

Halberd – a short spear carried by Serjeants

HBMS – His Britannic Majesty's Ship; the title HMS was adopted in 1789

Hostler – a person who takes care of horses, especially at an inn

Howitzer – a short-barrelled cannon designed to fire at a high angle to drop ball at a steep incline

Judge Advocate General – a military judge responsible for the court martial process

Kingstown – now called Dun Laoghaire (south of Dublin)

Leagues – unit of distance commonly used at this time, roughly equivalent to 3 miles or 4.8 kilometres

Loyalists – American citizens loyal to the King of England, who formed regiments to support the British

Nec aspira terrent – difficulties do not terrify

New Hampshire Grants – now Vermont

Oakham – tarred fibres from old ropes

Orderly – on duty for the week

Parole – password

Piss dales – tubes leading out through the hull to be used as urinals

Pot valiant – one who is abrasive and aggressive when under the influence of alcohol

Redhazel – the redcoats' nickname for the German Major General Riedesel

Roger's Rangers – a Loyalist Light Infantry group specialising in warfare and intelligence gathering in wilderness country.

Saratoga – now Schuylerville

Sawyer – men working in a saw pit with double-ended saws to make planks from logs

Seats of easement – wooden platforms on the hull of the ship with two holes used as a toilet

Second clothes – when the soldier's normal uniform was worn out, the cloth was used by the regimental tailor to make second clothes, often fatigues; these were used when a soldier was doing manual work such as digging or tree felling

Serjeant – 18th Century spelling of Sergeant

Small beer – weak beer

Specie – gold or silver

Stand of Arms – a firelock and the associated equipment

St Johns – now St Jean

Struth – God's truth

Sutler – a trader who was licenced to supply the army

Tories – civilian supporters of British rule

Tow rag – a cloth towed in the sea on a line outside of the hull, used in lieu of toilet paper

Tripod shear – the lashing of two poles to the mast; the legs of the shear are gradually spread to lower the mast. Conversely, a mast can be raised the same way

Bibliography

The Story of the Wiltshire Regiment (1756 – 1959) by Col. N.C.E. Kenrick D.S.O.

Redcoat by Richard Holmes. Published by HarperCollins, 2001.

For Want of a Horse by George Stanley. Published by Tribune Press Ltd, 1961.

The Men Who Lost America by Andrew O'Shaugnessy. Published by One World, 2013.

The Last of the Mohicans by J. Fenimore Cooper. Published 1826.

Chronicle of the Indian Wars by Alan Axelrod.

Endless Street by John Chandler. Published by Hobnob Press, 2010.

A Memoir of Alexander Fraser and his Company of British Marksmen 1776 – 1777 by Stephen G. Strach. Published by the Journal of the Society for Army Historical Research.

Escape In America by Richard Simpson. Published by Picton Publishing, 1995.

1776: America and Britain at War by David McCullough. Published 2006.

A Few Bloody Noses – The American War of Independence by Robert Harvey. Published by John Murray, 2001.

Primary Source Material

The Journal of Lieut. William Digby, 53rd Regiment of Foot, written 1776– 1777.

The British Invasion from the North by James Phinney Baxter. Published by Joel Munsell's Sons, 1887.

A Journey to Canada, 1779, by Cartwright.

The Letters and Diaries of Baroness von Riedesel, 1776-1777.

Travels Through Interior Parts of America, vols 1 & 2 by Thomas Anbury, 1777.

A Journal Kept in Canada and Upon Burgoyne's Campaign by Lieutenant James Haddon 1776–1778.

American War Service Memorial of 2nd Lieutenant John Dalgleish, 1777.

Printed in Great Britain
by Amazon

12782860R00181